# ROCK BOTTOM TENNESSEE

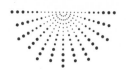

## KIMBERLY NIXON

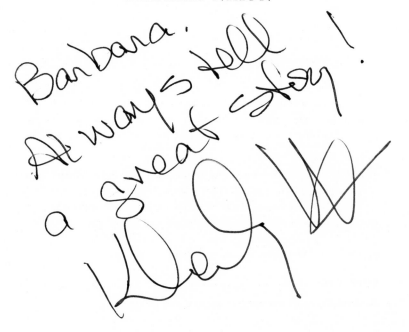

Barbara,
Always tell
a great story!

ROOTS AND WINGS PRESS, LLC

Cover design by Damonza.com

Published by Roots and Wings Press, LLC, Austin, Texas

ISBN: 978-1-957513-01-0

Library of Congress Control Number: 2022902180

*~For my mother, who told countless family tales while I sat at her feet.*
*Thanks for giving me the passion for the family story.*

# PROLOGUE

*September 1900*

*A*fter supper, Timothy and Belle sat on the front porch, looking over the blue-tinged mountainside while their two boys played on the weed-filled yard with their shepherd dog, Gus. The tulip and beech trees near the house in Poplar Cove had started to turn color but stalled due to this heat wave. The warm weather had given Timothy extra days to finish the harvest.

"Doc said the baby could come any time now. I hope so." Belle looked over at Timothy, who had already nodded off. She held her breath as her abdomen tightened. The baby could barely move in such a small, cramped space.

Belle had a name ready if it turned out to be a girl: Ruby Beatrice. Ruby Beatrice Sullivan. She'd had five years to imagine what it might be like to have a daughter. The boys—born only ten and a half months apart—were like lion cubs with each other, the way they tumbled around. A baby girl would be gentler and sweeter and someday would lend a hand with all of the household chores that had to be done. This baby girl would be the apple of her papa's eye. She hadn't given thought to it being a boy.

After six years of marriage, Belle still counted her lucky stars she had landed in this spot. Oh, she knew she would live in the hills of Tennessee—all of her family lived here and had for generations. In the distance were taller mountains behind theirs, providing a fence of sorts around their heritage. These hills, and all the people who filled its nooks and crannies, had become a part of her.

Since eighth grade, she'd known that Timothy would be the one who would sit on the porch with her every night until she grew old. The combination of his deep-set blue eyes and his red hair had attracted her attention. What she hadn't expected was that being with him would make her so content. Night after night, they sat together on the porch, taking in the sun as it disappeared over the mountains. Each blissful day ended with a celebration of painted sky, streaked orange and blue—combined with gentle conversation. These mountains had sealed her off from the rest of the world, and she enjoyed her cocoon of happiness.

Belle sipped sweet tea and marveled at tonight's troubled sky. It grew darker until the mountains blended into the heavens, both of them turning pea green. The ions in the air gave a first whiff of what was to come, and Belle's skin tingled in response to the wind picking up.

Lightning cracked the tree limb across the lawn the same instant Belle's pain intensified. She gasped and felt another, sharper pain, this one only a few minutes after the last. She paused and bent over a little to ease it, lifting one leg when it held on longer than the others.

"Timothy"—Belle crossed the porch to shake him—"Timothy, go get Doc. I'll finish getting the boys to bed. Go now, before the storm gets bad."

That short nap on the porch must have done him some

good. He moved with urgency, reaching for his raincoat and hat on the hook by the door. "It's hard to saddle up a bedded-down horse. Are you sure, Belle?"

"I am. This baby is coming tonight."

TIMOTHY SET out to trek the five miles down the mountain to Doc's place in Rock Bluff. He glanced over at the cornfield, grateful he had finished the harvest before this storm came through. He held a firm hand on the reins to negotiate the terrain, zigzagging through the mountain pass into the thunderstorm. The spruces, usually staid, swayed as the strong winds blew through the mountain gap. Lightning illuminated Timothy's way at times, and in between flashes of light, he prayed his way to Doc's, fighting to keep his skittish horse under control.

To calm himself, Timothy focused on the upcoming changes in his household. Belle would be busier now, attending to the new baby. He had enjoyed spending the evenings with her on the porch after the boys went to bed. Her opinions and humorous musings delighted him. This sweet communion before bedtime bore into his soul and made him better. His marriage blessed him, no doubt.

Belle was the family he needed, which was a good thing since he had been orphaned so young. His grandfather raised him after his parents died, doing the best he could. Left to his own devices, Timothy would slip into his grandfather's house at nightfall in time to help with evening chores and to eat a quick meal before sleep.

Belle had treated Timothy like her best friend in their school days, helping him with his homework and seeking him out to ask about his fishing line or muskrat trap. He knew early on that he would either marry her or, if she didn't agree to that, live next door to her so they could continue their friendship. Lucky for him, she chose to be his wife. It tickled him to see her pregnant again, her thin muscular body with a solid baby belly in front. She would be back at her chores within days of delivering the baby, despite his encouragement for her to take time to heal.

Looking ahead through the torrential rain, Timothy saw Doc's house appear beyond the oak trees in the valley below. His horse Gabe would deserve a reward tonight for maneuvering the wagon beneath the perilous fingers of lightning that jabbed the sky. He hoped Robert and Timmy were now sleeping, giving Belle a much-needed break, but the storm would almost certainly keep them awake. Timothy rapped on the door of Doc's house. Both he and Gabe jumped as lightning struck a tree up the hill from them. He waited until after the next strike and knocked again, louder and longer.

Doc Livingston cracked open the door and held it against the strong wind.

"I hate to ask you to come out on a night like this, but the baby's on the way." Timothy, sopping wet, shivered in the gusts of wind.

"What a night to have a baby, Timothy. I'll skip the wagon and ride horseback to your place. It'll be faster. I'll get dressed and be on my way."

BELLE PUSHED herself up on her elbows when the door opened. Doc took off his wet coat and hat and hung them on the post by the door. The drops from his drenched rain gear streamed over the pine floor, converging toward her room as if leading the way.

"You picked quite a night to have this baby, Miss Belle. How are you progressing?" Doc peered around the corner into the bedroom. Belle had made a pot of coffee, and he took the time to pour himself a cup before entering her room.

"I'm getting close, I think."

Doc rolled up his sleeves and lifted the sheet to examine her. "You're almost completely dilated. This baby'll be here in no time, maybe another thirty minutes."

Doc sipped more of his coffee before getting everything ready for the baby's birth. He walked to the front door and peeked out.

"Doc, is Timothy back yet?"

"I don't see him, but it's dark. There's too much rain to tell if he's putting Gabe and the wagon away."

She held on to the side of the bed and arched her back. Her lips widened into a grimace, and her eyes squinted shut. That contraction passed. She relaxed and eased her body fully back onto the bed.

"Let's check how you're doing here . . . I think it's time. Start pushing now on your next pain. This part should go pretty quickly. Ready? Come on . . . Push, you're almost there."

Belle strained, even though exhausted.

"A little more. Stay focused, Belle. I see mats of curly red hair."

Belle grunted and relaxed after that contraction.

"Okay, rest for a moment. One or two more pushes before we'll have another Sullivan child."

Belle panted and wiped her brow as the hail began to hit the bedroom window. Flooding would occur in the mountain creeks after this storm.

"Last time, Belle. Push hard."

A delicate long thin girl wailed her way into this world.

"What's her name, Miss Belle?"

"Ruby." Belle grimaced as the afterbirth slipped out. Whew, this birth was easier than the other two had been. Placing an ax under the bed cut the pain, just like the mountain folklore promised it would.

Belle smiled and raised her head to take in her little girl. Doc examined Ruby, placing the cold stethoscope on her chest. Ruby squirmed and belted out a rebellious cry, stretching her arms out as if to fight off this chilly invasion.

What about Timothy? Belle moved up the bed, straining to see beyond the bedroom door. A wave of anxiety overcame her, and she panted as she had during one of the contractions.

After the next thunderclap, Robert and Timmy appeared at the doorway of her bedroom in their nightgowns, rubbing their sleepy eyes.

"Hey, boys, look what we have here. Meet your baby sister, Ruby." Belle lifted her so the boys could see.

Belle moved Timmy's hand when he reached his finger out toward Ruby's eye. Belle whispered to Doc, "Where's Timothy? He should be back by now."

When Timothy Sullivan left Doc's house, he took shelter under a large oak to wait for the storm to let up before he started back up the mountain road. He should have brought his older mare on this trip; though she wasn't as quick as high-spirited Gabe, she was more sure-footed and steady.

The mountain storms were usually fast and furious and short-lived. It had taken Belle nearly fifteen hours to have baby Robert, so Timothy decided it would be better to wait for the skies to settle down than to risk the muddy mountain road with this wagon, as much as he wanted to be at her side. He should still be able to get home in time to help with the boys, although he was grateful Doc had gone ahead on horseback to check on Belle.

"Easy, Gabe. It's okay, just a storm. Settle down. Settle down, boy." Timothy pulled back on the reins firmly to persuade his horse to stay calm.

A sharp crack of lightning startled Gabe, who reared back in fright and took off running before Timothy knew what had happened.

Gabe started full speed down the path, in the wrong direction from Belle and on the most treacherous route, a newly rutted road. Gravity aided Gabe's getaway. The horse set off, gaining speed in reaction to the spider-like lights in the sky, even as the ruts slowed the wagon down on the mountain road. Timothy hung on for dear life.

The wagon wheel hit a large rock and tipped to one side. The force of the impact threw Timothy out of the seat and over the side. He sailed through the air and rolled to land some thirty feet below. The rain pelted Timothy as he lay motionless on the rugged mountainside.

BELLE LET the baby girl suckle off and on through the night. The boys next to her slept soundly as the newborn baby whimpered next to them. The lack of sleep and recent birth affected Belle's efforts to get out of bed, but truth be told, it was fear that kept her from putting her foot on the floor. Only a catastrophe would keep Timothy away from her on the night of the baby's birth.

Little Timmy and Robert stirred next to her—their cheeks flushed from the warm coziness of the bed. She watched them sleep and took a moment to smile at her three babies before tears rolled down her cheeks. Dear God, she missed Mama. Mama, gone only a few months now, had been a significant force in Belle's life.

She still couldn't get used to the idea that her pa had married only one month after Mama's death. Pa's new wife, Margaret, recently divorced, had lived on the farm down the road from Pa and Mama. Margaret, tired of her wretched husband beating her regularly when he drank too much moonshine, decided she'd had enough and used his shotgun to run him off. With time on her hands, Margaret offered to help take care of Mama in the last months, giving Belle a break to return home and manage her household. Margaret, twenty years younger than Pa and only ten years older than Belle, became a balm for his grief. It took a partnership to survive the rough mountain life. But Belle couldn't help but wonder if Pa and Margaret had arranged to marry while her mama lay dying.

"I had a baby girl, Mama," she whispered toward heaven. "She's pretty. She has a little pointy nose and red hair and reminds me of you."

Belle heard a loud commotion at the door and strained her neck, hopeful that Timothy would walk through the door at last.

Doc called out, "Belle, I'm back to check on you. I have Deacon Preston with me."

The boys beside her fully awakened and started fighting over the covers. Baby Ruby simultaneously woke up with a loud cry and wet the blanket. Belle studied the expression on the deacon's face and grasped that Timothy was in trouble.

"I found him near Grimsley Fork, Belle. I hate to deliver this news." Deacon Preston came over to the bed to hold her hand as he continued, "Timothy didn't respond when I called his name. There was a bloody gash on the back of his head caused by the rock he lay on. He had no pulse. I'm so sorry, Belle. Gabe was entangled in the wagon rigging up the hill from him, his leg broken. He was having a difficult time breathing. I had to shoot the horse to be merciful."

Agony rushed into Belle's soul as she joined the cry of her newborn. Belle's piercing wail traveled out the front door and seemed to combine with the clouds that always hung over their side of the mountain. Robert and Timmy held their ears at the sound coming from Belle but soon joined in the emotional outpouring the circumstances provoked. Their papa was dead.

Belle rolled over and laid her face in the soaked spot Baby Ruby had created minutes ago. Tears rolled down her cheeks, melding into the wet mark on the cornhusk mattress.

THAT AFTERNOON, Deacon Preston returned to the Sullivan house, bringing a pine box from the church's back lot. Three times a year, the men of the church came together to assemble caskets of many sizes—tiny for infants, various sizes for youths and small women, and one size that would accommodate all adults. The supply was depleted often because of the tragedies of mountain life. In 1900, the life expectancy in rural Tennessee was merely forty-eight years, but numerous illnesses and accidents took loved ones earlier. Death was not the opposite of life; it was a part of it.

Deacon Preston walked into the house and found Belle there, sitting in a rocker pulled close to the kitchen table. She rocked back and forth and, remarkably, looked at peace. He wondered if Belle's father and Margaret knew she was here.

"I couldn't leave him, Deacon. He doesn't deserve to be alone." Belle had pulled out Timothy's Sunday suit and pressed it. It lay on the table beside his body.

"Will you help me prepare him?"

"It's the least I can do for him," Belle spoke just above a whisper.

The deacon got a washbasin from under the indoor sink and filled it with water from the pump outside. He carried it inside, and Belle already had a washcloth and towel ready to clean her husband's body. She knew Timothy's spirit had already left, but his body had loved her for all of her adult years. Timothy Sullivan had been a good man. Whatever would she do without him?

Deacon Preston unbuttoned Timothy's shirt, ripped across

the sleeve, and moved the suspenders down off the shoulders. After taking off his shirt, he pulled Timothy's union suit down to his waist. Belle took the washcloth and first cleaned the gash on her husband's head. It oozed as she softened the crusted scabs that had formed around the wound. After several attempts with the lye soap, his hair was clean.

Belle washed his face and closed his eyelids. With the deacon's help in raising her husband's upper body off the table, she dressed Timothy in his best white shirt, buttoning it up and straightening his collar, much as she had done for him before they left to go to church together. His body stiffened as they worked, and Belle and Deacon Preston had to act in haste before the death stench set in. When they laid him back down, Belle placed a silver coin upon each eye to keep the lids closed. Belle set a cloth soaked in camphor on Timothy's face. That would preserve his color until the service tomorrow morning.

Belle had done this for her mama a few months ago. But this death was more brutal to absorb—she knew this man's body intimately, and his death had come before she'd finished mourning her mama. Sorrow had a way of compounding all previous losses, intertwining the new pain with the pain that still lingered, snowballing it into something much more significant. When Belle finished dressing Timothy, she wanted to put his boots on him but comprehended how wasteful that would be. Someone could use those work boots. He wouldn't need them anymore.

# PART I

# CHAPTER ONE

*September 1907*

*G*ood morning, Ruby. You're here early on the first day."
Alice MacCallum smiled at her and set down her bag
on the porch before she swung the wooden pin at the
top of the door to unlock it. "I guess you liked it so much last
year that you decided to come back."

The make-do lock kept animals out of the schoolroom, but it
wouldn't keep out a person if anybody wanted to get in. Miss
MacCallum's younger brother Joseph, taller than all of them,
brought in the teacher's bag as they all entered. He set off to the
back of the room to start the fire in the stove, tripping over his
untied shoelaces.

"Good morning, Miss MacCallum. I did get here before the
others. Robert and Timmy went into the woods on the way. I
didn't want to be late, so I came by myself." Ruby stood by the
desk, watching her teacher unpack her schoolbag. She didn't
have an assigned seat yet, so she stood there and waited close
to Miss MacCallum, trying to hide her beat-up old shoes
under the desk. She had to lift her heels out of them this

morning and walk on the backs of them so they didn't hurt. Granny said there wasn't any egg money for new school clothes this year.

"See the hole in my smile, Miss MacCallum? Two front teeth fell out this summer." Ruby smiled as big as she could to show off this marvel.

"I see that, Ruby. You're growing every day, aren't you? Are you all ready for your second year of school?"

All summer long, Ruby had played teacher, imagining a classroom in front of her. She'd counted the days until she could start back. This morning, she'd left earlier than she should have. Timing her departure by the sun, she forgot that the late summer days were shorter and couldn't figure out how much time to give herself. Granny—Pa called her "Margaret" but everyone else called her Granny—had told her once that the walk to the schoolhouse from their farm was three miles down the mountain. Easy enough to get there and hard to go home. Hard for many reasons, especially with Granny being so crabby lately.

Even though they all shared a room in Pa's shanty, Ruby woke up and got herself ready, careful not to wake her mama. Granny, busier than ever with chores, didn't pay much attention to her, not like she used to. Granny had more work to do, or so she complained, with Mama hardly around the house at all now. Ruby fixed her own breakfast and then tricked her brothers into leaving early. She told them Granny said it was time to go, but Granny never said that. Robert and Timmy would make her late for school if she let them.

As she'd done last year, Miss MacCallum let her pass out the slates and chalk to each of the two-student desks. Miss MacCallum made most of the children stay outside while she got the classroom ready for them. But Ruby did the necessary morning duties without bothering her teacher. She cleaned each slate to remove chalk dust, then placed them on each desk. She selected long chalk pieces and laid them next to the slates so every student could start the day fresh.

Joseph started the fire each morning, chopping and bringing in the firewood from the pile outside. He acted as if he taught the class sometimes, raising his hand to give more information about the lesson than Miss MacCallum did. The other students didn't seem to mind him, although they teased him about the three strands of hair that would never lie down across his forehead as they should. They stood there at attention, almost like Joseph himself.

Miss MacCallum prepared lessons by grade on the large chalkboard at the front of the room. Ruby could tell she loved her younger brother. They said "please" and "thank you" and seemed to care for each other. Not like her family.

"Ruby, will you hang up my coat at the back of the room and then ring the bell to get school started for the day?"

Ruby beamed at the honor and stepped outside, clambering onto two bricks to reach the school bell. It clanged as she rang it for several minutes, giving it all the effort she could muster.

The children lined up by grade outside the schoolhouse door. Ruby breathed a sigh of relief when Robert and Timmy stood in the lineup—no one would be in trouble at home today. If Miss Alice sent a note home from school, Pa would get mean and then blame Mama for being too lenient, and just like that, everyone would be mad at each other, buzzing around with angry talk all evening. It reminded Ruby of the hornet's nest Timmy had hit with a stick—the hornets buzzing around, all riled up.

As the children came in, Miss MacCallum assigned seats to them. They waited patiently at the side of the room to learn if they would sit with friends. Miss MacCallum pointed Ruby to a seat in the third row, next to Hattie, who teased her just for spite. Last year, she'd told all the schoolchildren Ruby smelled like pigs.

"Ruby, I want you with the third graders to start this year."

"But I'm in second grade," Ruby looked down as if Miss MacCallum was punishing her for something she'd done.

"You're already reading in the third primer, so let's move you to third grade."

Ruby couldn't wait to tell Granny this news. She would be proud of her for being promoted. A buzz of conversation started among the older girls in the room.

"Teacher's pet," Hattie sneered.

"Teacher feels sorry for her," whispered one of Hattie's friends behind her.

When it was her turn to recite from her reader, Ruby spoke just above a whisper out of shyness but didn't miss a word. She didn't want to call attention to herself.

When Miss MacCallum rang the dismissal bell, Ruby stayed behind; she was usually the last student out of the door. She collected the slates for her teacher. Ruby wanted to teach someday.

Her brothers didn't wait for her to begin their walk home, but it didn't matter because she knew the way. She carried the new third-grade primer in a leather strap over her shoulder and started up the dirt trail to home. She liked the way the road curved around beyond the grove of evenly spaced black gum trees. Perhaps someone had planted them a long time ago just for her, to show her the way home. She trudged uphill, stopping when she needed to catch her breath.

Ruby picked up people noises ahead of her in the woods, well beyond the loblolly pines and cedars. Maybe her brothers were up to no good—no telling what trouble they'd found. Granny rewarded her with a peppermint when she snitched on them.

She left the path to wander toward the source of the noise. This part of the woods didn't have footpaths; it was more over-grown than the cut-through. Ruby wiggled through the trees, walked about forty steps, and crouched in the woods behind a large blackjack oak. She sat on a dead log and peered around the tree, then placed the reader on the leaf pile next to where she sat, careful to make no sound.

Beyond the tree was some sort of round contraption that appeared to wear a tin hat, almost the same shape as the one Pa wore, but pointier. It looked funny to Ruby—she imagined the shiny structure with eyes and a mouth. Steam rose out of it, giving it life. Maybe it was on fire. Next to it sat a washtub connected to spindly pipes, coiled in a circle like a snake on the ground. The other end of the coil connected to old wooden barrels, like the ones Pa used near the garden to collect rainwater.

The small lean-to over it, with a funny opening for the hat part, had no walls. On a wooden table beyond was Mama, wearing her best gingham dress, and she kept tucking her hair behind her ears. Mama smiled—something that didn't often happen—and looked prettier than she ever did at home. Next to her, a man held a small enamel cup in his hand, like the one Ruby had at Pa's house, only larger. He offered it to her mama, who took it with both hands. Ruby almost called out but thought better of it; Pa would give her the switch for not going straight home after school. Somehow, she also understood Mama wouldn't like it one little bit if she knew Ruby was watching all this.

Her mama took a drink from the cup and then whooped as she swallowed it. The man laughed at her, throwing back his head and laughing to the sky.

"Would you like a little more?" he asked.

Mama shook her head, gave the cup back to the man, and then reached out to him. He set the mug on one of the barrels, took off his flat hat with the band around it, and placed it next to the cup. He moved closer to Mama, who lifted her face to his, and Ruby watched them as they wrapped their arms around each other. They didn't move for a while, except to kiss.

"Eddie, tell me. You aren't married, are you?" Mama said.

His name was Eddie. Ruby didn't know him. He didn't go to their church, and she hadn't seen him when she went into town with Pa. Mama laughed when the man led her over to some pallets by the stack of cut wood. He removed his jacket and mumbled something in her ear. Ruby stood up suddenly from the log and reached for her satchel. In her haste to grab it, it dropped back into the pile of leaves. Both Mama and Eddie stopped and looked her way. She stood still so they wouldn't spot her. After a minute, they again focused on each other.

Mama helped the man take his jacket off. She lifted the starched collar off his bright white shirt. Ruby had never seen a man wear that color. He unbuttoned his shirt and slid the suspenders off his shoulders, and they hung by his side. Mama squealed as he reached around behind her and unbuttoned the back of her skirt. It fell to the ground in a heap around her feet. She unbuttoned her lace blouse without taking her eyes off of the man in front of her. Right there in the middle of the woods, Mama stood there in her chemise and drawers. Was this how adults played with each other? Even though she and Mama shared a room and dressed together, Ruby had never seen those undergarments before today.

The man named Eddie stopped for a moment to drink again out of his cup before he offered another swig to Mama. One thing was certain: Ruby would be in big trouble if Mama caught her watching this playtime. She took in the scene before her. She considered sneaking away but didn't want to rustle the leaves to call attention to herself again.

Eddie put the enamel cup down and wrapped his arms around Mama one more time. He pushed Mama back while kissing her neck—not in anger but carefully, to lay her down. When he leaned over to kiss her chest, Mama threw back her head and made a strange sound, almost like the cows bellowing at night before bedtime but softer. He unbuttoned his pants, and they dropped onto the pallet. The man stood in his white drawers. He didn't wear a one-piece union suit like Pa's—the dull red one she had hung on the line to dry. Mama turned over, facing away from the man, and backed herself against him. She leaned over a bit, and he placed both hands on her chest as he made breathing sounds as if he had been running hard. Their movements, almost like dancing, didn't require music. Ruby's eyes opened wide to take it all in, but she couldn't fathom what made Mama act like this.

Ruby grabbed her books and made her way slowly back onto the path home. Mama and the man were creating enough noise that Ruby didn't worry about them paying attention to her. She decided she'd better not tell Granny. But at some point, if she got the nerve, she might ask Mama about her activity in the woods.

# CHAPTER TWO

*Fall 1908*

*B*elle hurried away that afternoon from the farm and onto the main path to town while Pa worked in the fields. Avoiding confrontation, she had delayed leaving until Pa went to the corner field. Belle understood that her pa knew about her job at the tavern after five years, but he didn't speak of it for whatever reasons of his own. Every time she left, she expected him to stop her in her tracks.

She wore her oldest dress, complete with an apron, and carried a bag that contained her entertainment attire. Belle continued to keep up the charade that she cleaned the church and school well into the night. She knew Pa liked the money she brought home, and maybe that's why he didn't challenge her about how she made it. Granny knew, and it had created a coldness between them. But Granny didn't say a word. Pa—fifty-seven on his last birthday—ran a strict house. She had heard Pa's father, a grandfather she'd never met, had used physical punishment with Pa as a boy. Maybe that was why he treated everyone as he did.

She made over eight dollars a week now, a fair amount of money considering the times. She gave two dollars to Granny to help with expenses at home, took a couple of dollars to buy decent dresses for work, and saved the rest, giving her a sizable nest egg. She considered looking for a house in town or nearby Crossville, but even that presented a dilemma. If she bought a house, her pa would have to acknowledge her illicit employment publicly, humiliating him. Everyone understood that cleaning the church and schoolhouse didn't bring in that amount of dough. The dance of pretense would be over.

On her walk into town, she tried to recall Timothy's face, the sweet way he had looked at her at the end of his day. She would give anything to have those days back. The day he died was the day her miserable life at Pa's began. The evenings when she'd sat on the porch with him, looking out over the valley, seemed like a lifetime ago. She would put Timothy out of her mind when she worked at Edna's place—her job at the bar would have disgusted him. Oh, how her life had changed.

When she arrived at the tavern, Sammy, the bartender, was standing behind the bar, washing glasses and opening jugs to get ready for his customers. Sammy and Edna had met as children. Her father had owned ten slaves—Sammy's father being one of them.

Belle slipped into the back room to change into her work attire. When she came out, Sammy and Edna were finishing their late afternoon shot of the local whiskey, a tradition they'd shared for as long as Belle worked there.

"Belle, have a seat over here, darling," said one of the regular patrons.

Belle reached down, grabbed the hem of her new red dress on each side of the split in its skirt, and tied it up in the front in a knot barely above her knee, exposing black cotton leggings. "Why should I sit with you, Carl? You haven't been in to see me in over a week."

The men laughed before turning their chairs to face Belle at the head of the table. She raised both arms, exaggerating the movement to fix the hairpin at the side of her head. When she laughed, the curls bounced with her, sometimes flinging hairpins in every direction. She had come a long way from when she'd first started working here. Back then, she would place the drinks at the table without looking at the customers. Over the five years she'd been working here, she'd come to know the men—who their families were and who could hold their liquor. Belle no longer simply carried drinks to the tables but took time to entertain the men, sometimes just talking to them. Other times she had to be more creative. Edna paid her a higher wage when the workers returned to the tavern several times a week. The flourishing business rewarded them both.

"Eddie, Tommy says he can beat you at arm wrestling. But my money's on you, sweet man. Are you willing to show me what you've got?" Belle sent an exaggerated wink in Eddie's direction.

Eddie and Tommy slowly rose from the table amid encouragement from their friends and rolled up their right sleeves. Eddie stopped to face Belle, but she pushed him away and guided him to one of two chairs at the small table in the center of the room.

"Gentlemen in the bar, you know how this works. You bring me a nickel; I give you a ticket. Write your name on the back of the ticket, along with the name of the man you think will win, and drop it in the jar. After the winner is declared, I'll draw a name from the winner's jar to see who gets a third of the jackpot. The champion gets a third, and well, I think the judge of this contest should get the rest, don't you, Eddie?"

On cue, he nodded in a silly, exaggerated fashion.

"And who will determine the winner?" Belle was walking around the room as she spoke. "That's right—me. Competitors, do you need to warm up or stretch? Oh, Eddie, I believe Tommy has bigger muscles than you do."

Holding these competitions several times an evening brought in enough money to help pay Belle's wages, and the men enjoyed it. They loved seeing their names on a placard as champion at the end of the night. Only occasionally would the competitions get out of hand; that was why Edna paid a guard to stand at the door. They also prevented revenuers from entering, should they come—or at least gave a fair warning before the government agents entered. The last time they'd made an unannounced visit, the guard talked loudly with them outside until the jugs were hidden and every glass dumped.

Belle finished selling the tickets for the jackpot and walked around the table to start the competition. She slowly removed her long white gloves and handed them to one of the men standing nearby. She took in every eye that focused on her. The power she held at work was a sharp contrast to her status at home. She was an actress on a stage.

"Eddie, are you ready?" She stopped to wink at him as he nodded. Before she continued, she pulled her shoulders together, which naturally raised her bosom to Tommy's eye level. "Tommy, do you need me to go over the rules? You must stay in your seat this time. Do you promise me? Promise me . . ."

Eddie and Tommy placed their elbows on each side of the painted line on the table and locked hands. Belle placed her hand over their clasped fists, held her other arm straight up in the air, and paused to look. Most of the patrons had returned from the week before to watch this grudge match.

"Ready, set . . ." Belle smiled, removed her hand, and shouted, "Go!" She took her gloves back and watched Eddie initially take the lead.

She leaned down to table level and whispered to him, "Come on, baby. Give it all you've got. My money's on you."

He smiled back at her, giving Tommy a chance to take

advantage of Eddie's moment of distraction. The men gathered closer and shouted out the name of their favorite wrestler. In a sudden burst of energy, Tommy slammed his opponent's arm on the table and stood up to celebrate his victory.

Belle grabbed Tommy's hand and held it high with hers. "Winner declared. Gentlemen in the house, here is your champion."

She divided the money and awarded Tommy his share. She stuffed her third into her stocking for show.

Belle reached into the jar to pull out the prizewinner's name. "And the lucky jackpot winner of this bout is . . . Frank. Come here for your prize, sweetie." He reached for her and she backed away. "Oh, no, silly. You get the money—you don't get me."

Eddie looked at Belle and winked. He understood he would get his kiss later for participating in the show. She broke into a smile, wishing she didn't have to wait to give him his reward. He was her ticket out of Pa's house, and she would do anything to leave that place.

Right before eight o'clock, Belle left the bar floor to change into tights and a dress she'd shortened to right below her knee. She kicked her shoes off and let her hair down, finger-combing it out around her shoulders. She took a moment to check her appearance in the looking glass. She almost didn't recognize herself—the black kohl eyeliner she had added to her stage makeup made her look like a vamp. She flipped her hair over her shoulder and became another person. All the years of fighting with Pa had hardened her—she was nothing like the woman she used to be before Timothy died. She wiped some of the smudge away and, for a moment, hung her head. Timothy would be ashamed and shocked at her appearance.

As the clock hand indicated the top of the hour, she walked back out to the bar. Belle put a ragtime song written by Scott Joplin on the Victrola. Sammy brought the lantern over to shine a light on Belle as she sashayed to the music. He held the barstool steady as Belle climbed it to sit on the bar before standing and positioning herself on the makeshift swing that hung from the ceiling.

"Gentlemen, tonight's entertainment brought to you by our Belle." Sammy stretched out his arm to present her.

Belle took her time getting the momentum going, lying back as the swing moved forward and pumping her legs as it swung back, in perfect time with the music. The short pieces of ribbon on the rope highlighted Belle's swinging, and her dress flew up with the breeze created by her movements. The crowd stopped their chatter, and every man raised his drink as he watched her fly back and forth through the air. The bar patrons shouted boisterously every time she got close to the bell. Near the end of the song, when she finally got high enough to hit the bell with her foot, every man downed his drink in her honor and cheered.

Word got around about the scantily clad lady who swung above the bar at Edna's tavern. Edna upped Belle's pay to three dollars and fifty cents a night, based solely on increased moonshine sales.

Funny, she thought. She was finally living up to her burgeoning reputation as a hussy. But at least now she was a rich one.

# CHAPTER THREE

*June 1909*

*J*oseph stood on the porch to catch the sun rising over the hollow. The blue haze over the mountain beyond, combined with the orange glow of the first morning light, dazzled him. He would graduate today, and he wanted to savor every minute of it.

He laughed, knowing that more of his family members would attend graduation than there would be graduates themselves—only twelve students would receive high school diplomas this year. He had been chosen to present his honor's essay, "How the Highlanders Settled Fentress County," though the idea of speaking in front of a crowd made him a little nervous.

Rufus, his brother, appeared over the ridge on the horizon with his wife, Suzanne, and his three young boys beside him on the cart. Before Rufus stopped, the boys scrambled to the ground.

Joseph started off to the barn to help Father. Rufus had arrived early today to mend a fence between his and Father's properties. Graduation day or not, there wouldn't be a break from chores. While Rufus unhitched the horses, Suzanne headed to the house to help Mother with breakfast.

Rufus's youngest son ran to Joseph as he approached the barn. "Uncle Joseph, can I ride on your back?"

"Sure, hop on. But only for a short while so your brothers can have a turn too."

Joseph would miss his family in the fall when he started at Knoxville Normal School. Though he'd be home on weekends to help Father with the farming, he would board at the school during the week to complete his teacher's certificate in one year.

The state of Tennessee had changed its requirements to become a teacher. Joseph had been flabbergasted to learn he needed to take college courses to obtain a teaching certificate. Alice, his sister, became a teacher right after high school when schoolteacher Mary Johnston left to get married. Her only qual-ification was being the best student in her graduating class and willing to teach those younger than her. School districts could now levy taxes, allowing an increase in teachers' pay. Student attendance was now mandatory unless the student helped at home with harvest or slaughter.

After giving his nephews piggyback rides, Joseph went into the barn and found his father halfway down the row of cows on a milking stool. "Father, I'll take over."

"Not today, Joseph. I'll finish this. Go into the house and visit with your sister. Graduating with honors makes this a big day for you—for all of us. But before you go . . ." Joseph's father paused the milking for a moment.

His father stood and cleared his throat. "Son, you bring honor to this family—you're a fine, respectable man, and I'm very proud of you. Every day, but especially today. Your char-acter and good name will take you further than any amount of gold or silver."

Joseph smiled with his mouth closed, but his eyes moistened and he felt lit with pride. "Thanks, Father. Those words mean quite a bit, coming from a man of your integrity."

"Now, go on. Get to the house before we both get emotional like your mother and sisters." Father swatted Joseph's back and sat back on the stool to finish his morning chores.

Joseph wiped his eyes before he returned to the house. To be seen as honorable in his father's eyes made for an exceptional graduation gift.

# CHAPTER FOUR

*Summer 1909*

*B*elle finished in her dressing room and cracked the door to find Eddie waiting outside. He was chatting with Edna at the bar as she wiped down the counters for the evening. Most of the bar patrons had cleared out for the night. Everyone at the tavern knew that Belle and Eddie were linked romantically, but it didn't seem to affect her popularity with the men. Eddie stayed in the background while she worked. But every night, he walked her home, taking the long way to her pa's farm, through the woods and up the mountain. Eddie, married and the father of two young boys, never hurried to get home— his family was accustomed to his absence at night.

Belle turned down the lantern in her dressing room and opened the door. She sauntered over to Eddie, and he kissed her cheek.

"Good night, Edna. See you tomorrow evening." Belle grabbed her bag and started to walk out with Eddie.

"Good night, you two. See you tomorrow. Belle, your act is making us famous. Men are coming in from neighboring towns to see you swing over the bar. Can you imagine?" Edna hugged Belle's side before she left.

Belle and Eddie joined hands when they got outside. He called her "My Swinging Girlfriend," and she laughed as he teased her. These walks home, an antidote to the somber mood at pa's house, eased the transition back to her real life. They entered the woods and fought through the thicket, signaling to Eddie's men with a birdcall whistle they were coming. They approached the still and waved to the men who were stoking the fire. The men retreated to their camp, for the time being, knowing full well that Eddie would mind the burning flame that distilled the moonshine.

About one hundred yards from the still, Belle and Eddie had cleared out a place to spend some time together under the moonlight. A picnic table served as a makeshift bed or seat, depending on their mood. Belle took the old quilt, stored in the shed, and placed it on the table.

"Eddie, come over here, darling, and lie beside me. Look at those stars through the clearing."

Eddie laughed and joined her on the table. "Aren't you tired after a whole night of swinging?"

She had been a little tired lately, but that didn't keep her from wanting to be with him. They both lay on their backs and observed the night sky. Stars clustered together above them, more than Belle had ever seen before. The symphony of night insects and Eddie's peaceful breathing surrounded her, offering her comfort. A falling star flew across the sky and disintegrated before their eyes, adding to the night's magic.

As if sparked by the star, Eddie raised himself on one elbow and unbuttoned the day dress she had changed into to return to Pa's house. He pushed it down over her shoulders and pulled it off her arms. Belle stood up to remove her drawers and climbed onto the bench next to the picnic table. She stepped onto the table and stood over him, then straddled him and sat. Eddie met her eyes as she hovered above him. She bunched the top and bottom of the dress around her waist and removed her camisole. He raised his hips off the table and with both hands, slid his pants down as he lay underneath her.

Smiling, Belle beheld his eyes as they joined together.

"You're no longer the shy girl I met a few years ago at the tavern, are you?" He laughed at her audacity.

Belle raised both arms above her head. She closed her eyes and faced upward, rolling her head in a figure-eight movement, as if dancing to internal music, moving at her own beat. Her pace quickened. Belle pulled the dress over her head and threw it on the wooden bench. She looked down to meet Eddie's eyes and leaned closer to examine his face in the flickering light and shadows of the nearby fire.

"You know, Belle, I could get used to this." Eddie arched his back, gasping as he spoke.

After, he reached up to pull Belle down on him and wrapped her in his arms. She rolled over to lie on his arm and gaze at the sky, still smiling. She grabbed his coat off the chair to cover herself as they lay there.

Belle relaxed in Eddie's arms. "I'm going to buy a new house in town. I have enough money. It's time the children and I moved."

She secretly hoped he might join her, even at the expense of a scandal in his family. He caressed her hair while she talked, pulling it over to the side and tucking the ends into his large hands. She waited for his words, but they didn't come. Belle yawned, suddenly spent from her long day. Eddie rose and dressed, then helped her with her clothing before continuing their walk to her pa's house.

She gazed at him. He walked at her side, his shadow in the moonlight looming out in front of her. His silence deafened the hopes she had for a life with him.

# CHAPTER FIVE

*B*elle woke with a start to find her room empty, the children already out of bed. The sun came in at an angle through the trees that made her think it was probably mid-morning. Somehow, the children had dressed for school without disturbing her; they'd probably left for school already. Belle pulled back the curtain next to her; Pa had harvested about half of the corn. No doubt he had been out there since the sun came up.

Granny made a commotion in the kitchen, and Belle couldn't believe she hadn't awakened her to help on laundry day. Belle stretched and kicked the covers off before rolling out of bed. She sat back down on the hard mattress to hold her queasy stomach. She yawned, wanting to sleep even longer.

Belle threw on her robe and opened the door to the hallway. "Granny, I'll get dressed and come help. Why didn't you wake me?"

Granny shrugged in reply. She knew that Belle came in from work around midnight most nights, and she would let her sleep. Belle walked into the kitchen and took a bit of a biscuit from the table to settle her stomach. Was she getting ill?

"Granny, you're quiet this morning. Is everything okay?" Belle took the washed clothes from Granny as she finished each one on the washboard and fed them into the hand-cranked wringer. When she had collected a basketful, she would take them out and pin them to the line.

"Belle, Pa knows. Deacon Preston went by the tavern last night to help one of his parishioners get home after a night of drink. He saw you there and stopped by on his way home to tell Pa. I thought you should be aware the charade is over. We all knew what you were doing, even Pa, but for a while, we could pretend we didn't have a clue. I think Pa has to preserve his reputation now. That doesn't bode well for you."

Belle knew this day was coming. Granny had known for some time she worked at Edna's tavern. She'd seen the dresses Belle washed and hung in her room to dry. Belle appreciated that she hadn't brought it up for discussion. But now that Deacon Preston had brought it to light, Pa would confront her with his shame. He had to bring out in the open what he'd likely known all along. He could no longer tolerate her working in a tavern. It mattered to him what people thought. True to form, a blowup was coming.

"I'm not going to quit, Granny. I saved fifteen dollars last month alone. I appreciate you and all you do for the children and me, but it's too hard to be around Pa with his temper. I'm going to look for a place of my own. Surely you understand—you tiptoe around like the rest of us." The words escaped Belle's mouth before she became aware of the harm they could cause her. But she was proud of the money she earned, even if everyone else would condemn her.

"Well, nice for you to have so much money saved. It would've helped us to have some of it, you know. You don't think of others very much, though, do you?"

Belle stopped wringing the laundry and picked up a large-enough load of it to take outside. "I have enough money to buy a house in town."

"If you move out on your own, who will watch the children while you work at night? Have you thought of that? Those boys would kill each other without supervision. And they certainly wouldn't take care of Ruby." Granny slapped the clothes on the washboard with a little more vigor. Belle rarely experienced her anger.

Granny wasn't finished. "And what about the help we need here? You're ungrateful, Belle."

Belle didn't have an answer. Ruby was almost nine now, and the boys fourteen and fifteen. Robert and Timmy got into trouble more often. She'd caught them taking a sip of moonshine behind the shed last week before she went off to work, and Belle knew there were days they didn't attend school. No telling what would happen if she left them at night.

"Pa wants to talk to you today at lunch while the children are gone. I confessed I already knew and didn't bring it up to him. I don't like being put in the middle."

"What do you think he's going to say to me, Granny?"

"We'll find out soon now, won't we? Could you take that basket out and hang the clothes on the line while I finish up this last load?"

Belle nibbled the other half of the biscuit before she went outside, hoping her stomach might settle down.

She expected an ultimatum from Pa: either quit the tavern or leave his house. He would ask for all of her money if she stayed, now that she'd let it slip to Granny about her savings. Maybe she could appease Pa for the time being.

But her job wasn't merely about money. In truth, she enjoyed being out with other people. Of course, not many women went to the tavern, but Cousin Edna was there daily and had become her best friend. The men who came to the bar night after night were grand to her. Most of them were married, but a few were not. All of them treated her as if she was something special.

Belle took her time hanging the laundry. She examined Ruby's school dress, too short for her now. It didn't have any hem left to let out, and her daughter would need new ones soon. Ruby would be the one most affected if they moved out. According to Granny, she was a remarkable child—at the top of her class and reading well above grade level. Miss Alice had proclaimed Ruby her star student. Granny said that every time they went to the market, people stopped them to remark on what a beautiful child she was, tall and spindly like her papa had been. Timothy would have been so proud of her. She had his long thin nose. And Belle's eyes. The boys had teased Ruby often enough to make her a spitfire, red hair and all.

Belle glanced into the field, and Pa's stern stare met her eyes where she stood at the clotheslines. He seemed to be gritting his teeth as he walked behind the plow. Maybe if she worked hard, he would be less harsh with her at lunch. She finished hanging the clothes and started back inside to get the second load from Granny. Nausea overcame her, and she leaned away from the basket to retch next to the garden. She wiped her face with the back of her arm, waiting to recover before going in.

Granny had put away the kettles and washboards and started frying potatoes with ham for lunch. She came outside to ring the bell to give Pa twenty minutes' notice for lunch.

"Granny, I'll get this other load hung up and then help with lunch. Will you help me with Pa? I'm not doing anything wrong."

"No, I will not. You and your pa need to have this discussion. I'm staying out of it."

Pa came in after washing outside in the spring. He rose from the ground, using the post to get up off his knees. He was hunched over after a morning of holding the plow in place. Belle filled the plates with warm food and placed them around the kitchen table. She sat down and waited for everyone to join her.

Her pa sat down next to her and bowed his head. "Lord, you know our sins. Please help us to examine our lives and be true to you. Bless this food to our bodies. Amen."

Granny stood up and took her plate outside near the garden.

Her pa took his first bite and chewed with his mouth open. Belle hated the grunting noise he made when he ate. She pushed the potatoes around on her plate, and the noise of her fork on the plate echoed. Her pa cut the ham before laying down his utensils. He pushed his chair back from the table, raised his head, and glared at Belle.

"Pa, Granny said you wanted to talk to me. What's going on?"

"You know good and well what's going on. What were you were thinking, sneaking out every night to be a floozy at that bar? I won't have a loose woman living under my roof. You're a bad example to your children."

Pa spat out his half-chewed food onto his plate and stood up. "Here's what I have to say to you: quit working there now or leave today. And the children aren't going with you if you decide to go. I'll fight you on this one, and I will win. Think about that while you're making your decision."

Belle opened her mouth to respond, but she knew there wouldn't be any further discussion. Pa's hard-and-fast commands were not negotiable. She would find out soon if her savings from the tavern were sufficient for her and her children to make it on their own. She put her fork down and took a sip of her coffee. Granny peeked in and gave her a sympathetic smile through the screen, but she sobered up when Pa turned to scowl at her.

"I'm moving out, Pa, and my children are coming with me. I've saved enough money to buy a house in town. I'll quit working at Edna's and find other employment. Don't you worry about that." Belle leveled her gaze at her pa, looking at him directly in the eye.

"I'll go this afternoon to tell Edna I'm leaving and to pick up my things. With your permission, I'll ride Dublin into town, and I'll be back by suppertime." Belle turned her face to hide her tears. She wouldn't give him the satisfaction of seeing her cry. "I wish you'd try to understand what it's been like for me. It's not been easy since Timothy died."

Pa sat down to continue eating his lunch.

Belle grabbed her stomach and ran outside. She fell to her knees in the flower garden and again vomited. While kneeling near the last of the coneflowers, she remembered the nausea during Ruby's pregnancy. Her queasy stomach made perfect sense to her now.

She proceeded to the barn, stopping at the well to get a drink. What was the Bible story about the woman at the well? She was an outcast too, if Belle remembered correctly. She saddled up Dublin and set off to Edna's tavern. Dublin seemed to sense her mood and slowed down on the journey to town. Belle took a right at the corner, taking the long route to Edna's. Maybe she wouldn't be back by suppertime after all.

# CHAPTER SIX

*E*dna was sitting at the bar, counting change into the register, when Belle walked in. Belle's unkempt hair hung down into her eyes, which she knew had dark circles under them. Edna closed the cash register and walked out from behind the bar.

"What's going on, sweetie?" She put her arm around Belle and held her for a minute.

Sammy walked into the bar, bringing in jugs of whiskey for the evening business.

Belle surrendered to the hug. "Pa knows for sure, Edna. He found out from Deacon Preston, who confirmed that I work here. He says I have to quit or leave his house. But even if I move out, he's threatened to take the kids away from me."

"Oh, darling." Edna took a minute to sit with Belle. They'd both known this day would come.

"And that's not all—I think I might be in the family way."

Belle could tell that Edna hadn't expected this news. Her eyes, wide open, matched her gaping mouth. Edna pushed Belle back a bit, keeping her at arm's length to look at her face.

"I'm not kidding, Edna. And there's no question who the baby's father is."

"When was the last time you had your monthly?"

"It's been a while. I've been exhausted recently, and I can't keep anything down." Belle wrung her hands, then shrugged. "What am I going to do?"

"Let's take this one step at a time. Come up to the house and sit with me. I'll make you some tea, and we'll talk." Edna kept her arm around Belle as they strolled out of the bar and across fifty yards of grass to the house.

Edna bellowed over her shoulder, "Sammy, finish the setup for tonight. I need to go inside for a bit."

Edna and Belle entered the house, and Belle started to cry. Because she received comfort so infrequently, she had forgotten how it felt to have a friend. Edna stirred the fireplace, filled the kettle from the well pump outside, and heated water for their tea. Belle sat by the fire, using the hem of her dress to wipe away the tears as they came.

"Edna, I have seventeen hundred dollars saved. Do you think the Riley house in town is still for sale? It has two rooms, one for Ruby and me and another for the boys. Oh, wait, a baby too."

"We're not sure you're going to have a baby. Let's not jump ahead."

"What will Eddie say? You know him better than I do. Do you think he would leave his family to join me?"

Before Edna could answer, Belle looked out the window and saw Sammy running toward the house as if his life depended on it.

He came in the back door without knocking. "Edna, the revenuers are at the tavern. About twenty of them came through the woods. They want to talk to you right away."

Edna stood up, clutching her hands to her head to take a moment to think. "Can you stall them? Was the whiskey out of sight? I can't believe they came before we opened the tavern for the night."

The federal agents had imposed a hefty tax on whiskey, and no one in the hills of Tennessee liked that. Those big distilleries in the big cities worked with the government to impose standards and additional fees to eliminate the small competitors—the moonshine runners in the mountain towns.

Mostly, the revenuers didn't patrol the woods; instead, they traveled well-developed roads and paths. Bootleggers had been in this area since the Scots-Irish had settled here after the Civil War. They used the same recipe as then, making their whiskey without aging it, the traditional Appalachian way. Homemade alcohol remained a vital source of income for many residents. A code of silence honored its production, as everyone knew the ramifications of being raided: destroyed stills that would shut businesses down, not to mention jail time for the makers and runners.

Belle ran out the front door as Edna hurried out the back with Sammy to stop the government men. Belle took a different path into the woods than usual, trying to get under the cover of the woods before the men at the tavern noticed her. She had to warn Eddie. Was he aware of the raid? If the federal agents came from the woods, they had probably already visited his still, but maybe not. Belle also wanted to avoid arrest if that was what the revenuers intended. She had a million thoughts as she ran through the brush, jumping over the bushes to get to where she and Eddie had lain together last night.

Belle stopped to catch her breath, leaning over, her head at her knees. She brushed away spiderwebs, caught in her hair from running through the trees. Loud voices echoed through the woods—one of them belonged to Eddie. After walking her hands up her legs to force herself upright, she ran harder than before, moving closer to the shouting. She stopped to peer through the trees, hoping no one could detect her fast breathing.

About forty yards in the distance, five men pointed shotguns at Eddie, who crouched behind a barrel near the still. Belle and Eddie's makeshift bed was behind him in the trees, with the quilt still spread out on the table. He had his pistol out.

The revenuers encircled Eddie. "You're surrounded. Put the gun down."

Four additional men arrived, carrying axes, and dismounted their horses. One of the men took a large dead tree limb from the ground behind the shed and lit it from the fire nearby. They headed to the still with the flame.

Belle couldn't tell where Eddie's other men were, but she knew if the fire was burning, they weren't far away. He fired a shot at one of the government men, and they all opened fire. Eddie ran away from the barrels toward their makeshift bed, crouching down as he ran.

The man holding the ignited limb lit one of the whiskey barrels closest to the shed. Other revenuers chopped up the barrels nearby, careful to stay far enough away to avoid gunfire. A whiskey barrel near the shed exploded, setting fire to others around it. Belle backed up, careful to tread quietly over the leaves, and circled to the other side of the camp. She tripped over the body of Walter Higgins, Eddie's right-hand man, his head bleeding from a blow with an ax. A man dressed in government attire lay nearby, shot in the abdomen.

The government men continued shooting at Eddie. He held his arm and ran into a grove of oaks, then crouched in the underbrush. As he stood to run, a shot hit him in the back. He fell, dropping forward. Additional pelting gunfire caused his body to arch and jerk, rising off the ground, only to fall again. Belle placed her hand over her mouth to stifle her scream. The shooters rose and walked toward Eddie, their rifles pointed as they moved. He didn't move on the ground where he lay. *Eddie!*

Belle stifled a cry, stunned at what she had observed. She ran back to the tavern, avoiding the worn path and taking her chances with the thicket. She had to tell Edna what had happened in the woods. Belle tripped over a downed limb, landed with a thud, and lay on the ground a moment to catch her breath. She let out a bewildered sob before she pushed herself back up and lifted her dress to wipe away the blood on her forehead. Finding her second wind, she ran.

Belle reached the wood's edge and stopped to observe a man loading Edna and Sammy handcuffed into a horse-drawn wagon, while another agent pointed a gun at them. About eight men scattered around the property, pulling whiskey jugs from the cellar and taking numerous photographs, their flashbulbs exploding with every picture.

Belle backed up and made a widespread circle back into the woods to avoid detection by the revenuers. Her forehead, still bleeding, throbbed until it became numb. She crossed her arms across her swollen breasts as she walked—they were tender from all the running. She came to a pond and sat down, then laid her head on her crossed arms atop her knees. She questioned, with hope, if Eddie could have survived those gunshots. Night fell, but Belle had no desire to move from this spot. The woods became quiet and empty, much like the inside of her soul. Hours later, she stood to go home.

# CHAPTER SEVEN

*B*elle wandered up to the house well after dark. As she walked up the lane under the full moon, Pa's shadow appeared larger than life behind the window shade as he peered out. If luck were on her side, he wouldn't remember she had taken Dublin to go into town this morning. To avoid the federal agents, she had left the horse tied to the rail near Edna's house. She opened the back door and tiptoed inside. A plate from supper sat on the counter; Granny must have left it for her. She popped a couple of potato slices into her mouth. She hadn't eaten since the morning and had thrown up that meal.

Everyone appeared to be in bed. Belle half expected her pa to come out of his room to make sure she had quit her job at the tavern. If he only knew what had happened. But he would find out soon enough.

She crept into her room, the moonlight illuminating her way, and soaked up the image of her children asleep in their beds. As tired as she was, she took the time to study them. Robert and Timmy didn't fit on the small feather mattress together—only a short while ago, they had plenty of room. Robert took over most of the bed with Timmy laying on the very edge. She looked at each face. Who were these young men, now fourteen and fifteen?

Belle took off her dress and crawled into bed with only her chemise and drawers on. Beside her, Ruby's braids pointed in two different directions upon her pillow. Belle touched Ruby's thin arms and drew the covers up over her long legs. Ruby, already tall for a nearly nine-year-old, would be elegant when she finished growing.

What would her children think of her? Without a doubt, her boys knew she worked at Edna's tavern. Worked—past tense, not any longer. Things were different now.

Belle's forehead still had a bump, bruised from where she landed on it earlier that day during her run through the woods. Her breasts ached as she lay on them on the bed. She turned over on her back and put her arms behind her head, reviewing the events of the day. Eddie had died, killed in the exact spot where she had last lain with him. Edna remained in a jail cell in town. The judge would probably grant her a bail bond and release her before trial, but only if someone came up with the cash for it. Should she use her house savings to help her friend? She would think about that tomorrow.

Pa snored through the walls from the next bedroom over. Tears trickled down her cheeks, and she sniffed as quietly as she could to keep from awakening her children. She didn't know how she would go on from here.

BELLE MUST HAVE SLEPT a few hours. She opened her eyes and covered herself with a sheet when the boys moved. Before school, they had chores to do before school and slipped out of the room to avoid waking Ruby and their mama. Her pa had bumped into the wooden chair in the kitchen, creating a screeching noise as the chair moved across the stone floor. Ruby rolled over and pulled the covers up around her shoulders.

Belle couldn't forget the image of Eddie's body jerking after each shot from the revenuers' guns. He could still be lying on the forest floor for all she knew. Her Eddie.

She needed a plan for the day. Pa would find out when he went to feed Dublin in a few minutes that his plow and wagon horse hadn't come back with her from town. That would be the first question. The second question would be if she'd quit her job. Afterward, his fury would start.

Preparing for Granny's market day, Pa would hitch up the wagon with the old mule after breakfast since Dublin wasn't around. He would drop the children off at school before taking Granny into town to pick up supplies. By mid-morning, he would know what had taken place at Edna's the day before. That didn't give her much time.

She prepared herself for Pa's questions. She wouldn't tell him she'd witnessed the raid, nor about her relationship with Eddie. For now, nothing good would come of his finding that out. She would tell him she'd quit her job and afterward stopped in town to inquire about housing for herself and the children.

Belle rose and used the chamber pot in their room to retch. This baby was taking hold for sure. The noise woke Ruby, who had been sleeping beside her. She rubbed her eyes before looking over at Belle. Without a word, Ruby rose to go outside to use the privy.

Belle would tell Granny she wanted to work in the garden this morning. That would excuse her from going into town with her and Pa. Instead, she would walk into town to check on Edna and retrieve Dublin, avoiding Pa and Granny as they went about their business.

The back door slammed.

"Belle, get out here right now!" Pa bellowed.

Now it was starting. Belle grabbed her robe and walked into the kitchen.

"Where's Dublin? And what time did you get home last night?"

Belle opened her mouth to speak but took a deep breath instead. She looked beyond Pa when Ruby opened the door to come back inside.

Pa turned to Ruby behind him. "Go feed the chickens and get those eggs before you get ready for school, girl."

Sensing his anger, the child turned to go back outside before even putting on her shoes.

Belle sighed and finally answered him. "Pa, after I told Edna I quit, I went into town with her in her wagon to check on a house I heard was for sale. She offered to help me look. I walked home from there and forgot about Dublin. I'll go get her this morning. Sorry."

"Well, start walking. I want her home by the time I get back from town. She's pulling the plow for me this afternoon." Pa stomped out of the kitchen and returned to the barn to finish his chores.

Belle was turning to go to her room as Granny appeared in the kitchen. Granny stopped to search Belle's eyes, wanting news about what had happened. To avoid any conversation, Belle closed the door behind her in haste.

She thanked God Pa had sent her out now. She wouldn't have been able to eat across the table from him this morning anyway. She dressed as fast as she could and was leaving by the back door as Ruby came in carrying eggs in the skirt of her nightgown. They passed each other without a word. How distant she'd become from her children—they had no need of her any longer.

Belle arrived at the spot in the woods where the raid had taken place. They should have taken away Eddie's body by now, and his wife would know he had died. Dead. Echoes of the sounds of the last time they'd made love haunted her under the trees.

She approached Edna's tavern, and it looked as if nothing had happened. Eerily quiet. She entered the barn to find Dublin inside, chewing a mouthful of hay. Someone had moved and fed her after the raid. She looked around for Sammy inside the tavern but didn't spot a soul. Belle walked up to the house and peered through the window to find Edna sitting in a chair, wearing yesterday's clothing and pulling at her hair. Edna looked in her direction but stared at the wall beyond her, oblivious to her surroundings. It looked as though she hadn't slept all night, her eyes bloodshot and wild. Belle knocked on the door and opened it, hesitating to interrupt her cousin.

After a few moments, Edna looked at Belle. "It's all gone."

Belle walked over behind her chair and hugged her from behind, holding her for a few minutes. Edna relaxed with the embrace and patted Belle's arm.

Several minutes went by before Edna spoke. "I'm leaving. I'm joining my sister in Topeka, Kansas. She has a public house, and I'm going there to start over. I'm not going to jail over this."

Belle stood up but stayed behind her cousin as the words sank in.

"Honey, this place is yours if you want it, for you and the kids and your new baby. That is, unless the federal agents take it. I'm out of here tomorrow morning at six-thirty."

Belle walked around in front of Edna and knelt before her. "Can I go with you?"

"Aw, Belle. That life isn't a good one for kids. And I don't think my sister Annie would like having them around. You have to stay here, honey."

"Eddie is dead. My kids are better off with Granny and Pa. I can't stay here—the baby will make me a town outcast. Pa will take the kids anyhow when he figures out how I was involved yesterday and that I'm having a baby. I have to go with you."

"Are you sure? You'll never see them again, honey."

Belle took a minute to answer. Staying in town meant she might never laugh again. And if she left, it would mean a fresh start, away from her pa's tyranny, and that's what she'd wanted all along. A fresh start with Eddie's baby, a tiny piece of her old life.

"I'll go to the bank to get my money before I go home. I'll meet you at the station tomorrow morning, Edna. You won't regret letting me come."

Belle went to the barn to saddle up Dublin. She mounted, then guided her horse into town, treasuring the time to collect her thoughts.

Belle stopped at the bank, careful to avoid Pa and Granny or anyone she knew. She asked the teller to place all of her savings in a drawstring bag, which she put in Dublin's saddlebag. As she rode out of town, two women dropped their heads to avoid meeting her eyes. They knew. She journeyed out of town with haste to beat Pa and Granny home.

On the way, she rode beyond Pa's house to the family cemetery to visit Timothy's grave. She dismounted, gathered wildflowers from the field, and walked over to his plot. She knelt by the stone marker, placing the flowers next to it. With her index finger, she traced his name, then put her hand over the stone, lingering as long as she could given her time constraints. She sat back on her feet and dropped her head to cry as she remembered her night on the porch with Timothy before Ruby's birth. So much had changed since that night nearly nine years ago. She looked over the valley below and said her goodbyes to it.

Belle rode Dublin back to Pa's house. Mercifully, he and Granny were still on the road. She unsaddled Dublin and led her to her stall before extracting her money from the saddlebag. Belle packed most of her clothes into an old bedsheet, keeping enough in the drawers to avoid suspicion. She placed her mama's hand mirror in the middle of the heap, careful to protect it. She took the only photograph of her children and stuck it in her Bible, next to Timothy's image. After tying the bedsheet together, she ran her makeshift suitcase out to the woods under the lean-to, beyond the pile of chopped firewood.

As soon as she came back into the house, Pa and Granny pulled up in the wagon. Pretending everything was normal, she walked out the back door to help them unload the goods before Pa took the mule to the barn. He examined her face and didn't say a word about the raid on Edna's tavern. She didn't glance in his direction. Instead, she helped Granny climb down from the wagon and gave her the box of goods. Belle threw a sack of flour over her shoulder and carried it into the house. Granny followed her in and put the wooden box of food on the table. She took her apron off the hook and tied it around her back.

Granny paced before she asked, "Belle, were you there when the federal agents came yesterday? No one in town said anything about you."

Belle kept herself busy by putting the food away and didn't answer.

Granny started to prepare their dinner. "I wonder what's going to happen to Edna."

Belle opened the door to carry the wooden box outside near the firewood. She hated to answer Granny with silence, but she had nothing to say about yesterday's events. She headed to the garden to weed a row of green beans. She needed to focus on the task at hand and not allow herself to think about tomorrow. To avoid Granny's questions, Belle spent as much time as possible outside until the children came home from school. She brushed her hair back with her arm and continued to pull weeds. This would be her last time in the garden.

Pa walked up from the barn, giving her a piercing scowl. "I guess you didn't have to quit yesterday, did you? The revenuers took care of that for you. See what happens, Belle, when you don't follow the rules? Four men dead. Edna arrested. You were lucky not to be involved."

Not waiting for any response, he headed into the house to shove his dinner into his mouth before he started the afternoon plowing. Belle continued in the garden, glad that he and Granny didn't call her into the house to eat. Her stomach growled, but she would eat when they'd finished. In another hour and a half, the children would arrive from school. She bent over from the waist to work in the garden rows and paused to lift her head. Looking out at the field where she grew up, she remembered playing under the sweetgum tree, having a picnic with her dolls, and Jack, their dog. Mama had brought out biscuits with jam for the picnic. That is something she had never done for Ruby. Maybe Granny would.

Belle straightened up and headed into the kitchen a few moments after Pa came out. He wiped his mouth on his sleeve as he went to the barn. Granny had filled her soup bowl, and she sat down to sip the vegetable soup with a bit of beef fat floating on top for taste. The cornbread had been reheated. She slathered it in butter before she took a bite. She hadn't eaten since yesterday about this time. Only twenty-four hours ago, she'd told Edna she had to quit, and she was expecting Eddie's baby.

Granny removed the plates from the table and heated the water to wash them. Belle finished eating and returned outside to pick a row of okra. Granny would coat the okra in cornmeal and fry it in lard for their supper tonight. It would be their last supper together.

Granny would raise her children. The boys were nearly men already—there wasn't much left to do for them. They might stick around to help with the farm duties after they finished their schooling, but she bet they would leave town as soon as they could since Pa yelled at them all day long too. They might try for one of the coveted jobs at the aluminum factory in Knoxville.

Ruby would soon turn nine. At the age she most needed a mother, Belle was preparing to leave.

But Granny had been Ruby's teacher all along, giving her quilt material on a hoop so she could practice her stitches. She'd taught her table manners and helped her with her lessons—not that she needed much help. When Ruby wanted recognition in the family for a good deed done, she ran to Granny. Belle wouldn't be around to participate in any of that, and Ruby would hardly notice that her mama had left.

The wind picked up. Dropped leaves danced in a whirlwind between the house and the garden. Belle bit the side of her lip to hold in the sadness. She would start over with Eddie's baby in Kansas.

After a while, Ruby came up the lane. She skipped past Belle in the garden and entered the house with her satchel of books. The screen door slammed behind her, and Belle listened to her talking to Granny.

Robert and Timmy came in from the barn and pushed each other before they sat down to dinner. She marveled at how much they could eat—as if she had never really seen them before. They giggled at a private joke, and Pa reprimanded them for misbehaving at the supper table. Robert looked like his papa did when she met him years ago. She turned away from him to distance herself from the memories of Timothy.

After dinner, Belle cleaned up the dishes for the last time. When everyone else had gone to bed, she made herself a cup of tea. She took the bill of goods from that day's shopping trip, turned it over, and wrote Granny a note.

DEAR GRANNY,
*When you read this, I'll be gone. I'm going with Edna to start over*

*in another state. I'm counting on you to use your wisdom and grace to finish raising my children. Please always tell them that I love them.*
  *Belle*


SHE TOOK off her apron and hung it on the hook. When the ink dried, she folded the note and stuck it in Granny's apron pocket. By the time Granny read it, Belle would be on the train heading west.

# CHAPTER EIGHT

*R*uby opened her eyes in the first hint of morning light to see the shadow of her mama leaning over her. Mama, after fumbling with the buttons on her dress, stopped to pull the covers over Ruby, pausing to kiss her forehead and then her cheek. Wet drops fell on Ruby, and Mama used the bottom of her nightgown to wipe them off. Was Mama crying?

"Bye, little one." Belle stood at the door, lingering before she stepped away.

Ruby rolled over and took up the warm space her mama had vacated. She snuggled into it, the only place she'd ever received warmth from her. Her mama tiptoed out of the room and into the kitchen. The back door closed before Ruby went back to sleep.

When she awoke the second time, her brothers were already out of their bed. After entering the kitchen, Ruby got up and hugged Granny around the waist. As Granny fixed breakfast, the smell of the salt pork awakened Ruby's taste buds.

"Hurry, Ruby. Get the eggs. I'll need them in ten or fifteen minutes. It's cold out—grab your wrap before you go. And wake up your mama, for heaven's sake. I don't want Pa yelling because she's still in bed."

Ruby turned to go back to her room and remembered that Mama had left. "Mama isn't here, Granny. She took off in the dark."

"Did she say where she was going?"

Ruby shrugged. "I dunno."

"Go on, gather eggs." Granny patted her on the backside and pushed her toward the back door. Ruby pulled the shawl off the door hook to wrap around her nightgown before going outside.

On the way to the barn, she saw a man walking up the lane with Pa. She ducked behind the shed to cover herself. What was going on? The man wore a suit, a fancy hat, and a prominent golden star with a circle around it pinned to his coat. Pa did not look pleased. Nothing was more important to him than the morning chores—this man was disturbing his routine.

Her brothers peered out from the barn, remaining in the background as well.

Pa approached the back door while the younger man stood close to the well. "Margaret, this man would like to see Belle. Could you get her up and make sure she's dressed so he can talk to her? We'll wait outside."

"Belle isn't here. Ruby said she left early this morning. Who is he?"

"A revenuer. They want to know about Belle working at the tavern. Where'd she go?"

"I don't know, Henry. I have no idea." Granny fidgeted with her apron strings.

Pa returned outside, with arms crossed, to tell the man Belle had left. Pa shook his head and stomped his foot, which always made Ruby cower. But this man didn't move. He had more power than Pa.

"Let me see if she's in there. I'm not leaving until I check."

The revenuer put his thumb under the badge he wore and pushed it closer to Pa's face.

Pa hesitated to let him in, then said, "See for yourself."

He led the revenuer inside the house, and Ruby followed them, staying near the fireplace as they proceeded to her bedroom. The man looked behind the door and knelt to peer under the beds. He opened the wardrobe to see what clothes might be inside. He seemed satisfied Mama wasn't in the house, though he glanced in Granny and Pa's room before leaving.

Granny continued to cook breakfast, turning the salt pork before it burned. She peered around the corner to observe the man before wiping her greasy hands on her apron. She twiddled the apron strings around her fingers, holding her breath while the man searched through the rooms. Granny, the mistress of the house, had no choice but to give control to the revenuer. Ruby watched her reaction to this invasion of her home. Granny didn't offer him an invitation to stay for breakfast, though it showed terrible manners not to. Reaching into her apron pocket, Granny pulled out a piece of paper, and Ruby caught her eye. Granny unfolded a corner of it, then shook her head at Ruby, signaling her to hush, before shoving the paper back in the pocket.

Ruby ran out to the barn. Her brothers were still at the entrance, trying to see what they could over the half door.

"Ruby, what does he want? Is Mama in trouble?" Robert stood on his toes to see better.

"He's looking for her. I don't know why. She left this morning before dawn. She kissed me goodbye. I think she's gone for a while." Ruby gathered the eggs and hurried to go back inside.

She laid the eggs in the bowl on the counter as the revenuer stood his ground in the kitchen. Ruby slid sideways past him to get to her room so she could get dressed, but she left the door cracked open, careful to stay out of sight. She didn't want to miss any conversation and was waiting to see if Pa would have a tantrum to get the man out of his house. Ruby opened the wardrobe, causing empty hangers to clang against each other; Mama had taken all of her clothes. Gone—Mama was gone for good.

Pa glared at the man, not saying a word to him. His hands on his hips further showed his defiance.

"I'll be back occasionally to see if she's here. If you know what's good for you, you'll cooperate with the investigation." The man stepped outside, mounted his horse, and left.

Granny cracked the eggs, fried them up, and served breakfast. Everyone sat around the table and ate, keeping their heads down. Ruby had many questions, but considering Pa's temper, silence was safer than asking.

Granny took the note from her pocket as she sat down, and over Granny's shoulder, Ruby read the words her mama had written the night before. She focused on the scribble at the bottom of the page: "finish raising my children."

Granny raised her head. "Henry, Belle's not coming back."

Everyone stopped eating except Pa, who reached over to take Ruby's untouched eggs off her plate. She searched every face at the table for answers, and there were none.

This changed everything. Or did it? Granny would still care for her, make breakfast, and ask about her day. But nobody had stood up to Pa like Mama did. That part worried her.

Ruby would be sleeping alone in the bed from now on. Did Mama's leaving make her an orphan? Could Pa just give her away if he wanted to? Mama was the one string that kept her connected to Pa—the cord that bound all of them together, whether being tethered to Pa was a good thing or not. Ruby would have to follow his rules from now on because she didn't belong here by love. Love was not her birthright. The dance between playing by the rules or skirting them was her inheritance instead.

# PART II

# CHAPTER NINE

*December 1913*

Joseph had attended this school for as long as he could remember, but nothing could have prepared him for what teaching thirty-eight students in a one-room schoolhouse required. Standing at the large desk at the front of the classroom opened his eyes. He would wake up earlier than the rest of his family to make lesson plans for each grade, drinking yesterday's warmed-up coffee to help him concentrate. He would evaluate his students' work at night, marking their scores in his ledger. Most nights, he turned off the household lanterns, the last one to go to bed. How did Alice ever do it all those years while he was sitting at a student desk? She'd made it look so effortless. He had been lucky. Right before he graduated with his teaching degree, Alice got married to the widowed preacher and became a mother to his two daughters. No one else had the credentials to teach, so he inherited the job right out of college.

He arrived at the schoolhouse just after sunrise to get the fire going. Many of his students didn't have coats to keep them warm during the cold mountain winters, and the chill in the schoolroom could keep them from focusing on learning. He studied his grade book from yesterday and made a note to retest the fourth graders on the long division lesson. And he'd better reassess the Sullivan boy. Robert couldn't read well, if at all. His brother, Timmy, covered for him, perhaps explaining why Robert had advanced in school this far.

Children gathered outside in the schoolyard, and the murmurs and squeals penetrated the thin schoolhouse walls. The older students typically arrived after they finished their morning chores at home—no doubt some would arrive late. He was grateful when they came at all. Farm work continued to be the priority for these mountain families.

Though a cold wind swept through the schoolyard and the children huddled together to stay warm, Joseph remained strict about when he opened the classroom doors. He needed the time without distraction to prepare for his long day. He pulled a chunk of cornbread out of his lunch pail, which his mother had packed for him, and made a note to visit Granny Turner after school to discuss his suspicion that Robert couldn't read. He rose to write the date on the chalkboard and the various grade levels' first assignments. At last, he opened the schoolhouse door and rang the bell for the children to enter.

Ruby Sullivan came in first, rubbing her bare arms up and down to warm herself—she wore only a short-sleeved dress. He couldn't remember if she owned a coat. The other girls at the school teased her when they could about her mama, who had left town after the tavern shut down over four years ago. Ruby had started hanging out with the boys at lunchtime, which also concerned him. Though thirteen, she had been promoted a grade ahead of her age level. A gifted student, she soaked up whatever material he could give her. But she didn't have the social wiles to hold her own with those boys. When he visited the Turners' household this afternoon, he would tell Granny about Ruby and her social interactions. He would talk to the girl's grandmother, not Henry Turner, to spare the children any punishment Henry might dole out. Joseph knew Henry well enough to know that nothing good would come from telling him.

"Robert Sullivan, I'd like you to sit in the front row today, right next to Leon. Don't worry. Your brother will do all right in the back row without you."

Robert picked up his slate and books, using one arm to carry everything; he held his left arm close to his body and used his left hand to balance the load. In one motion, he dropped everything on top of the desk and sat down. Joseph noted bruising around his neck on the left side. A horse could have kicked him, or maybe he'd jumped from the hayloft. But more likely, Henry Turner had used physical punishment on his grandson. Joseph had suspected that for some time but didn't have proof. Mr. Turner wouldn't take too kindly to him interfering with the boys' discipline.

Joseph worked with the children by grade on their assignments, and the day seemed to be over shortly after it started.

"Robert, Timmy, Ruby, stay after class for a minute." Joseph gathered his grade book, a third-grade reader, and an eleventh-grade history book to take with him.

At the closing bell, the children burst out of the classroom, much like a mine explosion on the mountain. They scattered immediately after school, leaving only the Sullivan children behind.

"I'll walk with you to your house this afternoon so I can talk to Granny and your pa about your schooling. I haven't visited them in a while." Leading his horse behind him, Joseph maintained the Sullivan children's pace on the way to the Turners' farm.

He knew that the Sullivan boys wanted to set off to check their traps in the woods. Because he was only five years older than them, he could relate to that anticipation of the day's catch. But Robert and Timmy remained at their teacher's side. Ruby trailed behind them.

"Timmy, what are your plans when you finish your schooling? Have you given it any thought? A little more than a year left until your graduation."

"I'm leaving Poplar Cove, that's for sure. I'll try to work at the plant in Knoxville—I hear they're paying two dollars a day for help. Or maybe the coal mines if that doesn't work out."

"And you, Robert?"

"I'm going to marry a local girl—maybe Helen if she'll have me—and follow Timmy. We're going to be together, just as we've always been."

"You certainly do like to be with your brother—I can tell that. And what about you, Ruby?"

"I want my own business, maybe a store or a bank."

Robert and Timmy laughed at her response, but Joseph had no misgivings about her ability to run a successful business. But like most young women in the area, she would most probably find someone to marry and have children.

As they arrived at the farm, Mr. Turner stepped out of the barn door and rested his pitchfork against his shoulder. Ruby, Robert, and Timmy entered the kitchen's screen door, but Joseph continued to the barn to greet Mr. Turner.

"Good afternoon, sir. I walked home with your grandchildren today because I'd like to talk to you and Mrs. Turner about how they're doing in school. Do you have a minute?"

"What did they do now?" Henry barked. "If they're causing trouble, let me know and I'll take care of it. I told those boys, it'll be the switch if I hear about misbehaving."

"No, it's nothing like that. The boys are pretty well-behaved at school and respond well to my discipline. I'd like to talk to you about their future, though." Joseph held his hand above his eyes to shield the afternoon sun shining brightly behind Mr. Turner.

"Well, talk to Margaret then. She'll handle whatever it is. I'll be in when I finish spreading hay."

Joseph knocked at the back door. Granny Turner appeared before he opened it, wiping her hands on her tattered apron.

"Good afternoon, Mrs. Turner. Do you have a minute to talk about the boys—Robert in particular? Mr. Turner said you'd be the one to talk to if I had a concern."

"I certainly do have a minute. Please come in. Would you like some tea or coffee?"

"A cup of coffee would be nice, if it's not too much trouble." The children sat in the next room, their ears perking up to listen to the conversation.

Granny poured him a cup of warmed morning coffee from the tin coffeepot on the stove.

"Robert, can you come here? I'd like you to read this story to your granny if you would. It's from the third-grade reader, but it's a funny one. Could you start right here?" Joseph pointed to the top of the second page under the first word.

Robert seemed surprised at the request but came into the kitchen and sat beside his teacher. "I don't want to read while Timmy's here—he'll make fun of me."

"Timmy, can you leave us alone for a bit? Go on outside and see if your pa needs help in the barn," Granny said.

Timmy left the house, taking a piece of ham off the plate on the counter with him. He seemed glad to be off the hook, even if it meant he had to start his chores earlier.

Robert held the reader before flipping several pages ahead of where Joseph had indicated. "It's a stupid story. I don't want to read it."

"Just start, and I'll ask Ruby to finish it for us. Would you do that for me?" Joseph asked.

"I think Mr. MacCallum has a reason for asking you to read

aloud. Do what he asks of you." Granny lowered the glasses on her nose to meet Robert's gaze.

"Pa will get mad if I don't do my chores. Have Ruby read it for us," Robert said.

Granny reached over and tapped on the page, insisting he get started.

"The h-h-h-ouse saw brown—" Robert stopped and glanced up at Joseph.

"Continue, Robert," Joseph coaxed.

"A l-l-l-little grill, I mean girl, lived here, and her n-n-n-name saw Sally."

After several minutes of hearing Robert stammer through the words, Joseph dismissed him to go to the barn for chores.

After the boy left, Joseph brought out the history book and called Ruby over to read Lincoln's speech at the end of the Civil War. She picked up the large textbook and stood to recite the Gettysburg address. With emphasis, she read the words, "this nation under God shall have a new birth of freedom, and that government of the people, by the people, for the people shall not perish from the earth." Ruby stopped her speech, one hand left in the air as if she had given the original address.

"That's enough for now, Ruby. Could you go outside while I talk to your granny?" Joseph smiled at her, and Ruby left the two of them inside.

"Mrs. Turner, I know it's been hard for your family in the last few years. I'm here to see if we can help Robert do better in school. He's been misbehaving a little during the lessons, and I think it's because he can't read well. Now, I don't want to get the boys in trouble with Mr. Turner, but I have to mention it. They used to sit next to each other in class, and I separated them this week because I think Timmy has been doing Robert's work for him."

"Misbehaving? How? I hope to high heaven Henry doesn't hear about this. He'll take the switch to him," Granny said.

"I'm not here about his behavior. I'm concerned about his reading. I'll work with Robert more in school, but do you think you can also read with him at home? He's doing well on his mathematics and ciphering, but to graduate next spring, he has to pass the comprehension section of the Common Exam. So I'll leave these books. Find one at his level and have him read aloud to you every day when Timmy isn't around."

"How are the other children doing? Is Timmy going to graduate? And Ruby?" Granny asked.

"Timmy is on target to graduate and should pass the test easily, and Ruby is my best student. At recess, though, other girls tease her. Hattie Winston has rallied the girls against her ever since Belle left. They call her 'Orphan Ruby.' Hattie had all the girls over for a social a couple of weeks ago and didn't invite her. In the schoolyard, Ruby hangs out with boys in her grade, who are a couple of years older than she is. She's quite good with a slingshot, I can tell you. I'm keeping an eye on her, but I just wanted to mention it."

"Thank you for coming by, Mr. MacCallum, and for helping Robert with his reading. We'll start reading here at home with him. I 'preciate the warning about Ruby. I do worry about her. We don't want her to turn out like her mother."

# CHAPTER TEN

*June 1914*

uby sat on her bed and handed Timmy a folded shirt to pack into his make-do travel bag. The lantern's dim light cast a somber mood over the room as he prepared to leave town the following day. Timmy stuffed the shirt into his gunnysack, unfolding it in the process. The gunnysack would be plenty big for his belongings—two clothing changes, not counting what he wore. Timmy set out his shaving kit and put it on top of the bag so he wouldn't forget it in the morning after he shaved.

Earlier that evening, Ruby had sat in the front row with Granny and Pa at Timmy's commencement ceremony. Pa had bathed in the middle of the week and wore his church clothes for the occasion. When Mr. MacCallum handed Timmy his diploma, Pa stood and clapped, acting as if he had supported Timmy's success. Pa did the same thing when Ruby sang the closing hymn, standing up and turning around to encourage the others behind him to stand as well. His pride had surprised her.

When they returned home, Granny served an apple stack

cake made in Timmy's honor. She announced she'd used all of her molasses reserves just for Timmy. Granny gushed over him, proud he had completed his schooling despite the farm work—something most of the students on the mountain didn't accomplish. He was the first one to graduate from high school in their family.

Pa and Granny didn't mention Robert, who had traveled to Knoxville the day before to apply for a job at the aluminum plant. With a new government contract, the factory couldn't find enough men to fill it. They hired Robert on the spot. He told them about Timmy, and they also gave him a job, sight unseen. Robert had come home to get everything he owned and returned to Knoxville by train that night, avoiding graduation. He smiled when he told Pa and Granny about the job, but he didn't take time to say anything to Ruby, not even goodbye.

"What about Pa's hand-me-down suit that he gave you for graduation, Timmy? Are you taking it?" Ruby asked as the lantern's flame sputtered on its last drops of oil. She blew it out until she could refill it. The two of them sat in the darkness.

"I don't go by 'Timmy' anymore. I prefer 'Timothy.' And yes, this suit will come in handy for going out on the town. City girls like a man who takes care of his appearance."

Ruby took his jacket off the hook and folded the padded shoulders together at the seams to minimize wrinkles. At graduation, the threadbare dark suit coat had emphasized Timmy's strong shoulders, making him look more like a man. "Aren't you coming home on weekends to help Pa with chores? I think he's counting on it."

"Not if I can help it. I have better things to do with my time now. And I've had enough of Pa. He never treated us right." Timmy set his church shoes on top of his clothing and put the sack beside his bed.

"Hey, squirt, you can visit us in Knoxville this summer. It's an easy two-hour train ride. Come up on a Friday and we'll show you the town over the weekend." Even in the darkened room, Timmy couldn't meet her eyes.

"Pa won't let me come visit you. You just said that so you won't feel so guilty about leaving me." Ruby kicked Timmy's bag that sat on the floor and folded her arms, turning away from him so he wouldn't see her tears.

"Probably so. I wouldn't want to be in your shoes, kid." Timmy patted her back but didn't offer her any further consolation, then plopped himself on his bed and turned to the wall.

"I'll be the only one of us left here now," Ruby said.

And to that, Timmy—now Timothy—had no reply.

Ruby wanted to scream. So now she—alone—remained to deal with Pa and his dreaded farm chores. His anger would only have one target. She would get blamed for all of her mama's and brothers' faults—every single damn one of them.

The farm tasks were endless: milking the cows, slopping the pigs, throwing chicken feed, and feeding hay to the horses and cows in the winter. Firewood had to be chopped and brought into the house for cooking and warmth. Granny needed help with the garden, canning food for the winter, laundry, cooking, and cleaning. She used to manage her farm for years before she married Pa. Ruby also knew that Granny had her aches and pains—she was getting up in years. So far, the two females were spared from plowing, butchering the hogs, and fence repairs.

Ruby looked over at Timmy, who slept soundly in the bed next to hers. He planned to travel on the ten o'clock train tomorrow, joining Robert to find a room to rent near the plant. They would start work on Monday, working twelve-hour days but with weekends off.

Ruby lay down but couldn't sleep. She stared at the wall next to her for what seemed like hours and listened to Timmy snore. This room would be too quiet tomorrow night.

PA BANGED on Ruby's bedroom door the next morning before the sun came up. "Ruby, wake up and get your arse out of bed. You've got a lot to learn about these farm chores."

She rolled over, disoriented after only a few hours' sleep. To her surprise, Timmy was still in the next bed. Until now, she'd only had to gather eggs and feed the chickens before school, requiring an hour. Usually, Robert and Timmy woke much earlier to get their chores done. Timmy rose, grabbed his travel clothes, and stepped out of the room to give Ruby some privacy so she could change into some work clothes. Ruby found an outgrown pair of Robert's work pants and a rough old undershirt he'd left behind in the trunk at the foot of his bed. She put them on, surprised they fit her as well as they did. Ruby had only two dresses and wasn't going to use one of them for the barn chores, no matter what Pa said. She tied up her wild red curly hair with twine from the market and, at the back door, slipped on Robert's old boots, several sizes too big for her tiny feet.

Timmy walked with her in silence to the barn, dragging out his departure. She trudged beside him with a tight feeling in her throat. She tried to take in the blue mountains surrounding the holler but couldn't appreciate their beauty. The sunrise warmed her face, but it only cast an orange pall around her. One by one, her family had deserted her, abandoning her to the mountains. Her brothers would be on a new adventure, and she would no longer be a part of their lives. Her heel slipped inside Robert's boots as she walked, rubbing a blister in no time. Her brothers had each other, as they always had. She would give anything to have someone to share this load with her.

But she had no one.

Timmy showed her how to use the pitchfork to loosen the straw before picking it up to add to the horse stalls and mix the grain with the decomposed garden scraps to make the pig slop. Soon he hugged her, said nothing to Pa, and ran to the house to get ready for his train. Ruby paused in her chores to watch him leave. Without skipping a beat, Pa handed her the chicken feed.

As Pa started the milking instruction, the sun rose higher above the horizon, and she worried about being late for school. Today, they were having a field day and picnic to celebrate the end of the school year.

"Now you try, Ruby. Grab the teats and pull down on the udder. Pat Buttercup on the flank occasionally so she knows you're the boss." Pa pulled himself up off the milking stool by using the corral post as an anchor. He grunted and almost fell back down.

At seventy years old, Pa was in no condition to keep the farm going. He couldn't work the plow in the fields anymore; he simply didn't have the strength.

Yesterday afternoon before graduation, Pa had talked to young Leon Pennington, who lived farther up the mountain, about coming to help with the plowing and other chores that required a healthy body. Though about a year older than Ruby, Leon was a year behind her in school. Pa said that the bank had taken the Penningtons' farm equipment and animals last year after drought hit the region. Leon's pa couldn't even get a job in the mines, where they accepted anyone physically able to work. Leon's five younger brothers attended school barefoot, even in the winter. Any paying job would help his family, even if only two days per week. What would it be like working side by side with Leon this summer? He hadn't said two words to her after all their years together in school.

Ruby sat on the stool, positioned the bucket, and squirted Pa with milk when Buttercup moved away from her as she squeezed the teat.

"Dang it, Ruby. Watch what you're doing."

A mouse ran across the barn floor toward the door, and Ruby wished she could scurry away too; this lesson was consuming too much time. She brushed her errant hair away from her face with her forearm and finally filled the milk bucket.

Pa relieved her so she could get ready for school. She gathered eggs for breakfast before she went in. If she hurried, she'd still have time to get to school before the morning exercises started. She washed up a bit with the spring water in the barrel outside, doing what Granny called a "spit bath." Ruby sighed. There would be more barn lessons and chores when she came home.

Granny took the eggs from her before Ruby retreated to her room to change. "Ruby, I have a biscuit and ham sandwich for you to eat along the road." Granny studied Ruby's face for a moment before chiding her. "If you don't pull your lower lip up some, you might trip on it on the way to school."

Ruby walked into the empty bedroom—no trace of her brothers left behind. It would be strange to sleep in here alone. She would move her clothes to the top bureau drawer and try both beds to find the most comfortable one. She would use all the pillows and sleep with the outdoor cat if she wanted to. She tried to think of every advantage of being alone in the house with Granny and Pa, but her heart remained heavy with loss. Empty. That was it. She was empty. To Pa, she would only be useful for doing the chores or being the target of his ire. Otherwise, she would be forgotten. She doubted that with the extra workload Granny would have time for her.

Ruby changed into her school clothes. She combed her unruly hair and grabbed her ragged blue sweater, two inches short in the arms. She collected the worn green *Rudiments of Mathematics* textbook before entering the kitchen. After grabbing the promised breakfast from Granny, Ruby hurried out the door. It took her forty-five minutes to walk the three miles into town. Usually, she observed the sweetgum tree buds or the birds flying overhead, treasuring the time alone. Today she didn't; too many things were bouncing around in her head for the walk to be peaceful. With all the turmoil at home, she imagined school would become her respite, even with the teasing she endured there.

Slipping in the back door of the schoolroom, Ruby sensed the high energy; the assembly for the end-of-year picnic had already started. All of the girls her age stood around Hattie's desk. They tried to copy Hattie's pigtails, tying twine around their hair while listening to Mr. MacCallum. Picnic baskets supplied by her classmates' mothers lined the far wall. Just once, Ruby wanted to be like everyone else. Just for one day. She had eaten her breakfast from Granny's table but hadn't even thought about lunch, let alone a picnic.

Mr. MacCallum stood at the front of the room, in mid-speech about the day's proceedings. "We have four activities for the morning, students. We'll bob for apples, thanks to Mrs. Beaty's delivery of a bushel from last year's crop. The younger children will pin the tail on the donkey, while the older students will end the day with a tug-of-war, grades eight and eleven against grades nine and ten. But first, we'll start with the sack relay. There should be four to a team. I'll arrange the younger teams based on age. The older students can choose their groups. Each team captain should write the team members' names on the chalkboard."

Ruby's ninth-grade class had only five girls in it, including her. She knew she would be the odd girl out.

Leon stood at her desk with his head down but a shy smile. "Ruby, since we're going to work together this summer, let's be on the same relay team. We only have three boys, and it don't look like the girls want you anyway."

Long-legged Leon might give them the advantage. Ruby rose from her desk and approached the blackboard at the front of the room. She grabbed the chalk and wrote her name, then Leon's and the other boys'. At the back of the room, the girls laughed at her placement on a boy's team. "She's exactly like her mama," they whispered.

After all the teams were determined, the schoolhouse doors opened and everyone went outside. Two ropes were laid about fifteen yards apart for the first graders. Mr. MacCallum, who often counted on Ruby to help the younger children, asked her to take half of the teams across the field to the other rope and arrange them in their proper place. He laid out the burlap sacks to get them started.

While watching Ruby help Mr. MacCallum with the children, Hattie yelled out, "Ruby, is your mother coming later to join us for the picnic?"

The high school girls huddled under the shade tree started laughing. The teasing never stopped.

"You're jealous Mr. MacCallum didn't ask you to help, Hattie. Leave me alone," Ruby said.

"Are you sure he just doesn't feel sorry for you?" Hattie shouted for the whole school to hear.

Mr. MacCallum overheard the sniggering and frowned. "Hattie, enough."

Ruby usually ignored the pestering. During the school day, her classmates were tame, sometimes even pretending to like her. But the minute the last bell rang and they were out of Mr. MacCallum's sight, the gloves came off. On the way home from school, they would run up to her and knock her down, scattering her books on the ground. They called her names, words their mothers would be ashamed to hear. They taunted her for sport.

Hattie, the ringleader, had a different dress for every day of the school week—clean dresses that fit her. She had different-colored ribbons for her hair. Ruby only had two dresses, one she had outgrown. Hattie loved to talk about how much more she had than Ruby.

Today it hit a nerve. Ruby didn't like that Mr. MacCallum was witnessing this. Around him, she could pretend she fit in, though they both knew that she most definitely did not. He respected her and complimented her on her schoolwork, and Ruby could even pretend to be superior because of how smart she was. At school, she was her best self. But Mr. MacCallum knew her situation at home—how Pa treated her and how poor they were. She could see in his eyes that he knew it when he offered her his coat in cold weather when she had nothing to keep herself warm. Or when he shared some of his lunch when she had nothing to eat. Now, he was observing how others treated her. He couldn't fix that. And it would bring the worst pity of all.

Ruby lined up the children in teams, moments before her teacher blew the whistle to start the relays. The first child crossed the line and took off the burlap sack to pass it to the first one in her team's queue.

"Put your feet in the sack and pull it up. Go! Jump! It helps to hold the sack up under your arms when you start to hop. And keep moving—don't stop." Ruby lost herself in the game, encouraging the younger ones as she stood behind them.

When it became time for her age group, she and Leon stayed on the far side while their teammates lined up opposite them on the other side of the field. Mr. MacCallum asked them to pick up the rope and move it back an additional seven paces. Hattie and Winnie lined up next to Ruby and Leon. What luck, to be stuck right next to her nemesis.

As her teammate approached from across the field, Ruby kicked off her ill-fitting shoes and pulled up her woolen socks, waiting for the sack to be delivered to her. She wanted to be as fast as she could be. The newspaper she used to cover the holes in her soles came loose and blew across the field. If Hattie saw that, there would be further taunts. After grabbing the sack from her teammate Tate, Ruby pulled the potato sack up to her armpits and hopped.

Leon shouted words of encouragement behind her. "Go, Ruby, we're way ahead."

Hattie waited for her teammate to get close so she could take off. Halfway across the field, Ruby landed on a rock in her stocking feet and tumbled forward. She landed face-first with a thud, stunned as Hattie jumped past her.

"Catch me if you can, Ruby."

Ruby kicked the sack off so she could stand to get restarted. As she stepped back into the bag, her foot tangled and she fell again. Her legs went up in the air, exposing her drawers made out of a feed sack. The imprinted words SOUTHERN FLOUR MILL COMPANY were there for everyone to see. The laughter echoed in Ruby's ears. She wanted to ditch the sack and run down the hill into the woods. Why should she even try?

Leon ran toward her, his face showing pity. She jumped back in the sack to finish the race. Hattie had already passed her sack to the next person in line. Ruby handed the bag to her team- mate, but he didn't bother putting it on.

# CHAPTER ELEVEN

*July 1914*

"Ruby, hurry up, girl. This wagon leaves for church in thirty minutes, and you have to put the cows in the far pasture after you finish milking." Pa spat his tobacco out before he walked inside to get ready for church. "Stack the wood on the porch so your granny can cook dinner when we get home. I can't do everything around here. And don't think you're missing church again this week. Finish up your chores, then go get ready."

Pa rode her as he usually had most days this summer. Even the horses got a break when the summer humidity kicked in, but Ruby didn't. She worked from sunup to sundown, with a bit of relief only on the days Leon showed up. When he came, Ruby would work in the garden, help with the wash, and occasionally take Granny to the market. Those days, she avoided Pa and his verbal tirades, though she still had to work every waking hour. Pa didn't fuss as much with Leon around. He and Pa spent the day together in the fields, plowing or mending fences. Pa growled about having to pay Leon, but he seemed to like having him by his side.

Robert and Timmy didn't come home often on the weekends. They both had girlfriends now. Timmy wrote Ruby at times, asking her to visit him in the city, but he didn't send train fare with the letter. But even if she could afford a ticket, she wouldn't be able to get away from Pa or the farm. Before long, Timmy would forget about her, just like Mama had.

Ruby placed the milk pail on the ledge and led the cows through the barn's back door to the pasture to graze. She grabbed the bucket and hurried to the house with it, milk sloshing out the side as it hit her leg. She left the milk in the kitchen for Granny to bottle up and place in the spring to stay cold. Ruby gathered wood from the woodpile out back and dropped it outside the kitchen door. She stopped to look at her hands—bright red and cracked at the fingertips. Dirt filled the dry crevices. Lately, she couldn't scrub it out, hard as she tried. Ruby sat down for a minute to eat the cold, fried eggs Granny had prepared for breakfast an hour before and grabbed the last slice of bacon.

Ruby returned to her room and removed her brother's pants and the denim shirt she wore for farm chores. She washed and dressed in her Sunday best, the washed-out gray dress she had already let the hem out of twice. She went out the back as Pa pulled the horses up to the house.

Ruby didn't mind church so much—it helped break up the otherwise long, unbearable summer. She sat with Pa and Granny in the sixth pew back on the left. However, the other girls at church moved to the balcony to be together; they didn't want her to sit with them. No matter—she didn't like them anyway. Leon sat with his family in the pew behind them, choosing to sit there instead of with his friends. She caught him watching her instead of praying. He had paid particular attention to her the last couple of Sundays.

On this July day, the stuffiness inside overwhelmed Ruby, and she fanned herself with the hymnal. She felt woozy during the sermon and rose to get a drink outside, then pushed the church door open. A cool breeze cleared her head at once. She found her classmates already there, sitting on the porch. Ruby walked past them over to the well and pumped the handle, then drank from the large tin cup that hung over the knob. The girls laughed at her, pointing with one hand and covering their mouths with the other. Hattie cupped her hand over her mouth and whispered to the girl next to her.

Ruby paused to take a breath between gulps of water and looked Hattie in the eye. "Leave me alone. I haven't done anything to you. Shouldn't you be inside listening to the sermon?"

"Ohhh, Ruby, you don't know it, but you need us out here. You started your monthly, and it's all over the back of your dress. Can you imagine if you went back inside? Just think of the embarrassment. I hope no one saw you in church, but I do believe Leon was sitting in the pew behind you, wasn't he?"

The girls exploded in laughter as Hattie wagged her finger and continued. "Go home and ask your mother about menstruation. Oh, I keep forgetting. She isn't around, is she?"

Hattie flipped her long ringlets as she got up to lead the girls back inside and up the stairs to the church's balcony.

Ruby had no clue what Hattie was talking about. What was a monthly? What was on the back of her dress? She twisted her skirt around and found the dark reddish-brown stain Hattie and her group had found comical. What was wrong with her?

Ruby sat on the bench under the tree and fretted, waiting for her family to come out. Most Sundays, she walked home after church, taking her time along the way. Sometimes she joined Leon to skip stones across the pond near the wagon lot while Pa visited the other farmers. She wouldn't be doing either of those things today.

When church was over, Granny came out before Pa and motioned for Ruby to untie the horses and bring the wagon up. Pa usually liked to stay for a while to talk to Deacon Preston after the service, but Granny was trying to leave as soon as possible so she could start their midday meal. Ruby stayed glued to her seat in the front of the wagon while everyone exited the church.

Hattie's mother approached Granny, who was waiting beyond the church door. Granny turned to look at Ruby—they were talking about her, no doubt. She pulled the wagon up and stopped the horses a few feet away from where Granny stood. Granny hooked her arm in Pa's, giving him no choice but to walk with her to the wagon.

"Ruby, why don't you stay where you are, with Pa? I'll sit in the back to catch as much breeze as I can." With much effort, Granny hoisted herself into the wagon and maneuvered into the jump seat.

When Granny and Pa were both on board, Ruby lifted the reins and centered them across Dublin's back. "Let's go, Dublin. Let's go home."

"GO FILL your basin and clean yourself up, Ruby. Use lye soap to get the stain out of your dress. Here are some rags sewn together to put in your drawers. We used these as a diaper when you were a baby—isn't that something? Pin them to your knickers with the safety pins. I'll get dinner started, and then we'll sit and have a talk while the roast is cooking. I have an explanation for you, young lady." Granny's burst of energy to hustle and get the meal started distanced them. Ruby could have used a hug from Granny first.

She did as Granny instructed and gasped at the amount of blood on her undergarments. Was she dying? Why had Hattie shamed her? To bleed privately and deal with it by yourself was one thing. It was another to be so vulnerable for all the world to see. Did her every flaw have to be so damn public? The bleeding would be more ammunition for Hattie and her group. She washed out her clothing and went outside to hang it on the line to dry.

When Ruby came back into the house, she found Pa napping in his favorite chair by the fire. Smells of seared roast beef filled the house. Ruby inhaled and wished the smell brought her comfort. She should be grateful to be fed, but she craved so much more. Was it too much to ask to have a soft place to land when everything was so complicated? She ached for a friend, someone to provide some relief from her relentlessly hard life. But the joke was on Ruby—she'd started bleeding when she already wore the despair of being different from everyone she knew. Her brothers had left her and her mama was a mere memory. Granny chose to cower behind Pa and her work—too far away to stretch out her hands, or her heart, to Ruby.

Ruby sighed, walked into the kitchen, and picked up the bowl of potatoes to peel. She sat down at the kitchen table while she gathered her thoughts. "Granny, what's a monthly?"

"It's as simple as this." Granny started the explanation as if she had practiced it in front of the mirror. She cleared her throat, and with her eyes on the roast, began her speech with a stutter. "E-every month, your body gets ready to have a baby. If you don't get the seed from a man, you'll lose the blood that would grow the baby. The bleeding will last about four or five days." She turned from the stove to look over her glasses at Ruby. "But when you're in the family way, your monthly stops until you have the baby. We can track on the wall calendar with a small $x$ the day you start each month. Then you'll be ready for it each time."

Granny stopped and turned the roast to brown it on both sides in the cast iron skillet. "One thing you should know is that women are vexed during their monthlies and sometimes have cramps."

"Why were those girls teasing me? They have monthlies, too, don't they? They're older than I am."

"Ruby, I don't know why they tease you so. Ignore them. Don't let it bother you. I think they're jealous because of how smart you are."

"Granny, why didn't you tell me before?"

"I should have. I guess I put off thinking that you were growing up."

Ruby finished cubing the potatoes and gave the bowl to Granny. She went outside and pulled ready carrots out of the ground for the roast. Ruby took her time—she had some things to think about.

# CHAPTER TWELVE

*August 1915*

"Granny, I don't feel so good. I think I'm coming down with something." Ruby stood at the back door and averted her eyes to hide her lying. She sniffed for good effect.

Granny lowered her glasses and studied her for a few moments. "All right, then. We'll go to church without you. But unless you're bleeding to death or have a fever hotter than Satan, I expect you to clean the henhouse while we're gone. You were supposed to do that yesterday."

Granny finished breakfast. Ruby's eyes followed her as she walked into her room. After the bedroom door closed, Ruby poured herself a coffee, grabbed a biscuit, and walked out beyond the garden. She sat on a large rock to take in the view. The leaves moved with the breeze, hypnotizing her. Summer meant working from the time she awakened until she went to sleep. After a year of doing the morning chores under Pa's surveillance, she relished the thought of some time in the house. *Alone!* Church would take three hours when you counted the wagon ride, the service, and Pa's socializing afterward. This respite would be her church.

A loud crash inside, followed by a strange mewing noise, startled her from her sanctuary. Ruby scrambled to her feet and ran inside, dropping her coffee cup along the way. Pa lay on the floor near his chair, and Granny knelt beside him, trying to roll him over. His head bled where it had hit the side table. Pa opened his eyes for a moment, and one side of his face drooped. His wire-rimmed glasses lay broken on the floor.

Granny shook him. "What happened, Henry?"

Pa started to talk, but his words were slurred. He looked bewildered and tried again to speak, but only a howl came out. His left arm hung backward as Granny attempted to help him sit up.

"Ruby, go get Doc. Tell him I think it's apoplexy. Hurry! Don't bother with the wagon. Just hop on Dublin and go."

Ruby ran to the barn and opened the horse stall. She placed a blanket on Dublin and took the saddle off the fence post to place over the mare's back. Ruby slid the bit through Dublin's mouth and over her ears, grabbed the reins, and jumped into the saddle, then raced through the barn doors and down the mountain to Doc's house.

Apoplexy. Ruby repeated it so she would remember what to tell Doc. Whatever it was, it didn't sound like a good thing. After that last look at Pa, she knew instinctively things would be different now, for all of them.

Doc Livingston came out of Pa's bedroom carrying his bag. The examination had taken an eternity. If Ruby had to guess Doc's age, she'd say he was a few years younger than Pa, but he didn't look nearly as ragged. Doc nodded to Granny, signaling her to meet him in the kitchen. She already had the kettle on to offer him some coffee. Ruby could tell that Granny was keeping herself busy to contain her worry. She attempted to read Doc's face. He showed no emotion or urgency, so Ruby figured Pa had survived the fall.

"Ruby, you might as well come in here too. You need to hear this." Doc pulled out the kitchen chair for her. She slid into it next to him, bracing herself for what he had to say.

"Henry has had a major stroke, I'm sorry to tell you. He'll need complete rest in bed and someone to care for him for at least the next few weeks until we can see how much he improves. During this time, he'll need soft foods and will require help using a chamber pot. His heart seems stable for now, though. He'll be confused for the next few days and very sleepy. His left side is partially paralyzed." Doc blew on his coffee and took a tentative sip, as if waiting for Granny and Ruby to say something.

They both sat in stunned silence.

Doc continued, "I won't lie to you—this is serious. Henry's going to need full-time care."

Granny rubbed the back of her neck and kept her head down, fighting to stay composed. Ruby started to imagine what Pa's decline in health would mean for her. Who would run the farm? Would she and Granny have to do it all? Would she have to quit school? Not that—please, not that.

Doc forged ahead, answering questions before they could ask them. "I hear the Pennington boy has been helping you out here. Is there any way he could come every day until you get this figured out?"

As if to verify what Doc had told her, Granny got up and opened the bedroom door. Pa was sleeping. She watched him for a while from the doorway and then walked back to the kitchen. Ruby followed her every move, afraid to ask about her thoughts. Granny poured Doc more coffee and then stood in front of the sink, snapping the green beans for dinner. Ruby walked outside with Doc after he finished his coffee.

"I'm sorry, Ruby. I know your life isn't easy. Your granny will count on you to keep things going around here. I'll drop by the Pennington house to ask Leon to come help you with the afternoon chores."

Ruby wandered over to the rock she had sat on before Pa's fall. She lay back and looked at the sky. A cloud took the shape of a big basket. For a moment, Ruby imagined everything she'd ever wanted falling from above and landing in her cornucopia. She knew what she wanted: someone to rescue her from the endless labor asked of her. Ruby wished for a girl her age to move to the mountain and be her best friend at school—someone who walked home with her and surrounded her with laughter and tomfoolery. She imagined herself in a different family, one with a mother and a father, two younger sisters (why not!), everyone smiling because they enjoyed being together. For an instant, these wishes and dreams kept her from dwelling on everything that troubled her soul.

Granny summoned her to the back door. "Ruby, come get this chamber pot. Take it out to the outhouse and dump it."

Ruby pulled herself up and took the pot from Granny, careful not to spill any of the contents on herself on the path to the privy. She cried at God's response to her fervent prayers.

SHORTLY AFTER PA'S STROKE, Granny encouraged Ruby to go to church on Sundays, not denying her a respite at the seat of God. Ruby initially refused to go, not wanting to deal with the girls from school who still taunted her whenever possible. Granny sweetened the deal when she strong-armed Pa to agree that Ruby should get Sundays off after morning chores, but only if she attended church. Even though bedridden, Pa still influenced her life. Granny arranged for Leon to come by on Sundays for afternoon animal feedings and haul wood and water. Granny covered dinner and cared for Pa's needs, which were still many. Ruby knew freedom for an entire day by the grace of Granny, who held a little more power in their household now that Pa was down. Ruby could ride into town for church and spend the remainder of her day however she wanted.

Ruby arrived that first Sunday at her Baptist church. As if seeing it for the first time, she was struck by how shabby it looked, with its peeling white paint and rotted boards near the cornerstone. She climbed the orange clay-colored stairs to enter and took a minute to figure out where to sit. Other than Widow Nell, who wanted to sit in the front row, everyone else had someone to sit with. Every family had their usual place, but Ruby knew she didn't want to be in the sixth row, where Pa always chose to sit in front of Leon's family. She sat on the left side about halfway back until Mrs. Holloway asked her to move so their whole family could fit in "their" pew. Ruby moved to the back row. She slid onto a bench, out of view of the regulars. God knew she was there and the deacon too, but she didn't care about anyone else or what they thought.

During the opening prayer, she silently thanked God that Granny took care of Pa so she didn't have to. He was never pleasant to be around, and the task of taking care of him proved difficult. Ruby considered it a blessing she didn't have to do it. He couldn't get out of bed except for short periods, so he wasn't at the dinner table for meals. Talking was arduous for him, so he didn't go into his tirades as he had before the stroke. Ruby shook her head as if to scatter her thoughts. Was it wrong to be glad about the misfortune of others? To be delighted to get relief from Pa's harassment because of his stroke?

Ruby scooted all the way over when the Darden family came late and wanted to sit to her right. Mr. Darden had lost a leg in the war and banged his crutch on the ground when he sat down.

She then moved back to the middle when Mr. and Mrs. Oliver, who she hadn't seen at church before, approached the pew on the left. Mrs. Oliver had a hat pulled low over her head to cover her balding spots. She kept fussing at it, trying to hide what was obvious. Ruby looked right and left and determined she belonged in the middle of the misfits.

Deacon Preston compassionately talked about Job during his sermon. Job certainly had to tolerate many troubles in his life, but Ruby thought he had nothing on her. He had the advantage of starting out with a comfortable life and had wealth to boot, neither of which she had ever experienced. She had a litany of her own hardships she could put up against anything Job went through. Before her fifteenth birthday, she could match him a trial for a trial, and a tribulation for a tribulation. And the deacon was feeling sorry for Job?

The more Ruby heard about faithfulness, the angrier she got. She stopped heeding Deacon Preston's words when a sound came from her mouth, a wail that traveled to the end of the pew and up to the altar, surrounding every person in that church. The lament intensified in volume, carrying every injustice she had ever been given: her papa dying the day of her birth, her mama leaving town in disgrace, Pa's meanness and his resentment that Ruby lived with him. The wail got louder, carrying her brothers' abandonment, her classmates' teasing, and the relentless chores placed on her shoulders. Every. Single. Day. She had no hope her life would ever be anything different.

The deacon came from behind the podium, proceeded down the altar steps to the back of the church, and put a hand on Ruby's shoulder. He led her from the back row to the front of the church as she continued to howl, using this opportunity for an altar call. He motioned for Hattie's mother to come forward to pray with Ruby. Instead of offering an embrace, she placed her hand on Ruby's head and, in her loudest voice, said, "God, take away the sins of our sister Ruby and the sins of her mother's that torment this girl. They have cursed her. Wipe her soul clean, sweet Jesus. Erase the black mark on her heart."

Ruby broke away from her and ran out the back of the church to the woods beyond. The goldenrods were knee-high in the field, and she ran through them into the comfort of all the poplar trees she knew. The sugar maples, beeches, and black gums welcomed Ruby. She ran farther into the yellow birches, the lindens, and the horse chestnuts, leaving shame behind. This is where she belonged, away from anyone who threw contempt and judgment her way. The woods would be her altar, so if Granny asked next week if she'd attended church, she wouldn't be lying when she said yes. She would spend it in the thicket of trees—her only peaceful place in the world.

# CHAPTER THIRTEEN

*O*ver the next few weeks, Granny and Ruby worked out a division of chores that allowed them to stay on top of things around the farm. Granny hired Leon four days a week —to repair equipment, mend the fences, and do the heavy care for the animals. Ruby and Leon together could finish the harvest before school started. They would pay him for the extra days by selling a pig—Granny made that decision quickly because she had no idea how long Pa would be down. Ruby did the daily farm work, most of the laundry, and tended the garden, rising before dawn and stopping at dusk. Granny did the cooking, the canning, and cared for Pa. When school started, Ruby would attend as much as she could, but she doubted she would make it there every day.

Ruby interrupted her chores to come inside to change out the bibbed overalls she had put on that morning. The pants, too short in the body, cut into her, even with the suspenders let all the way out. She had grown "faster than a weed," Granny had said. Her growing chest interfered with milking and plowing. She rummaged through her brothers' old clothes to find the next size up to try on.

After lunch, Ruby would take the wagon into town to pick up feed. And the lumber for the fence repair was ready at the mill. She'd take Leon along to help get it loaded. But first, she had to finish feeding the animals.

"Granny, what is there for lunch? Should we have cold biscuits with ham again?"

"Yeah, get out the biscuits and slice some ham for you and Leon. Can you put a log on the fire, though? I'll be out in a bit to warm up the ham and beans for Pa's lunch."

Granny washed their one set of dishes from breakfast to use for lunch. She had tended to Pa since sunrise. He had messed himself during the night and grumbled at her to boot. He hadn't made much progress since his stroke. She had resorted to feeding him so she wouldn't have to change the sheets.

Granny put the dishes down and slumped in the kitchen chair for a moment's rest.

"Graaaan!" Pa bellowed. Though he could barely speak, he had no problems communicating. Everyone understood when he wanted something and wanted it now.

Granny went back to the bedroom. Most likely, Pa needed to use the chamber pot again.

"Granny, Leon and I are leaving for town. Do you need anything else while we're there?"

Granny set the soiled linens outside their bedroom door. "One of us will have to wash these sheets this afternoon and get them on the line. I can't think of anything else we need. And you better be changing before you go into town, Miss Ruby. It's unladylike to go like that."

Ruby weighed the trouble she'd be in if she disobeyed. She didn't have time to wash up, and the grime would only return when she did her afternoon chores. To distract Granny, she said, "I'll wash the sheets when I get back. You don't have to worry about it."

Leon pulled the wagon up to the back porch and tied Dublin up to the post. Ruby observed him peeking through the door, deciding whether or not to come inside. Since Pa stayed in his bedroom all day, Leon had started eating lunch with Granny and Ruby. Granny insisted that he wash up and leave his shoes at the door.

"Ruby, are we eating here in the kitchen?" Leon asked through the screen door.

"Let's take these biscuits and ham with us in the wagon. We'll eat on the way. Will you load the wood crates while I'm getting our lunch ready?" Ruby asked.

Ruby enjoyed these days with Leon. Before, when Pa worked alongside him, she and Leon barely spoke to each other. Now, with Pa down, they spent most days doing the chores side by side. Ruby relaxed with Pa no longer in the barn. In the middle of an unpleasant task, Leon could find a way to make her laugh. Ruby returned the favor. One day, she tied the milk bucket to Daisy's tail as they watched the cow kick and try to move away from it. That morning, she placed two potatoes from the garden in her shirt pockets and strutted around, posing with her arms overhead like the movie stars in the magazines in town. She gave him unsolicited advice about wooing girls at school, telling him how much girls liked wildflowers tied together with twine.

After Leon loaded the wagon, Ruby slipped out of the back door in her barn clothes, carrying their lunch, which she put into a feed sack.

She climbed aboard the wagon and plopped down on the bench next to Leon. "Let's get out of here."

"Ruby, you'll be in trouble with Granny when she sees what you're wearing to town. In fact, I think I might go in and tell her you're not presentable. I believe I have a duty to make sure you're a proper lady."

"Leon, it's none of your damn business what I'm wearing

and whether or not I get into trouble, now, is it? Let's go, or you might not get to eat lunch."

Ruby couldn't figure out sometimes if Leon was pulling her leg. He told stories as they worked, and she struggled to know if he was telling the truth or giving her pure nonsense. She played along. Most days, he seemed like a brother to her. She knew he had hardships at home, although he never talked about them. He would devour his lunch at her house, as if he hadn't eaten since the last lunch with them. Other times, he would almost fall asleep standing up. She imagined he worked another shift into the night at his parents' place. She was sure of one thing: he made her days bearable.

Leon had recently started visiting Hattie after church service on Sundays, and Ruby wasn't happy about that. Hattie still teased her at school, and she couldn't understand what Leon valued about that girl—maybe her flirtatious laugh and blonde curls. He could flirt, too, she'd noticed. She guessed Leon was handsome, but she never considered him that way. He had dark brown eyes that danced as he told his stories. His dark, bushy eyebrows moved up and down as he talked, enhancing the telling. When Leon smiled, dimples indented both cheeks. Gangly in ways her brothers never were, he was most likely in the middle of a growth spurt. She believed what Hattie enjoyed most about being in his company was that she was taking him from Ruby. Otherwise, why would Hattie have much to do with a poor farm boy like Leon?

"Leon, do you ever imagine yourself living on the highest mountain? Maybe in a big house with a window on every side?" The sweat dripped down Ruby's back as she swatted a horsefly buzzing around her head.

"Whatever makes you ask a question like that?" Leon laid the reins over the wagon bench and placed his arms behind his head to stretch, trusting Dublin to know the familiar way into town.

"I don't know. I think about it sometimes. I want to live at the tippy top of the mountain, where I can see what will happen tomorrow or the next day. I want to watch everyone down below and understand why some people have it easy and some have it hard. I mean, why was Hattie born with money? Her family's nothing special."

"Tippy top, huh? Well, I hate to tell you, but we're more likely to end up at rock bottom. That's where people like you and me live. Nothing comes to us the easy way. But my mama always says, 'If you do what you've always done, you get what you always got.' Maybe we have to change how we do things."

"Change, huh? Well, then, change it is. Let's park the wagon by the spring creek under the sweetgum tree and eat our biscuits there. It'll be cooler."

Leon pulled the wagon close to tie up Dublin to the low branch. Ruby scrambled down off the wagon seat, carrying the feed sack with her. Leon set the brake on the wagon before turning to join her.

She ran down the hill to the bubbling spring before he had jumped from the wagon. By the time he reached the creek bed, Ruby had taken off her overalls and cotton shirt and stood there in her sackcloth drawers, nearly naked. As she looked over her shoulder at him, Leon's eyes widened to stare at her; he was speechless. The wagon could have caught on fire up the hill, but he wouldn't have noticed. Take this, Hattie! She turned around before bending over to slip off her drawers, then glanced over her shoulder to observe him staring.

"The last one in has to swim to the big rock and back." She dropped her clothes and ran to the creek's edge, careful to negotiate the large cypress roots. She jumped in beyond the large rocks and splashed with both arms before she went under the water.

Leon couldn't be thinking about Hattie now! He hesitated before removing his pants but peeled them off to be as bare-skinned as she was. Leon soon followed Ruby into the water.

She watched out of the corner of her eye as he catapulted himself off the rock. She'd grown up with brothers but took note of his physique as he flew through the air toward her.

Leon came up out of the water and shook his head to clear the water from his eyes. "Ruby, you are one batty girl. What's gotten into you?"

She swam to the other side of the spring and turned to swim in another direction, zigzagging across the water like a caddis fly on the stream's surface.

"Argh, this water is cold, Ruby. How many boys have you done this with anyway?" Leon couldn't keep up with her.

She watched him come up for air, looking for her when he surfaced. "You're my first. You said we had to change how we did things. Well, I'm changing 'em."

Leon opened his mouth in surprise, taking in a mouthful of water before having a coughing fit.

Ruby swam away from him and tipped up her backside, exposing it to Leon before taking a deep dive into the water where the beavers had dammed the river. Poor Leon. Ruby was secretly delighted Hattie would be upset by her actions—it served her right after all of the things Hattie had done to bully her.

Leon swam to the big rock, and when he turned around, Ruby had already climbed onto the shallow part of the riverbank. "Leon, don't you look while I'm getting dressed, you hear me? I'll tell Hattie if you do." It was one thing to tease him beneath the cover of water and another to have him stare while she was getting dressed.

Ruby pulled her clean shift and apron from the feed sack, the clothes Granny would approve of her wearing in town. She'd prepared to change along the way somewhere to keep Granny, with her social graces, happy. What a lark to get in a swim so she could cool off before dressing to go into town. Ruby used the sack to wring out her hair. She walked back and sat under the tree with her back turned while Leon got out of the water and dressed. Though tempted to glance over at him, she didn't. She had caused enough trouble for one day.

"Leon, lunch is ready. Let's hurry and eat so Granny won't think we're gone too long."

# CHAPTER FOURTEEN

*Fall 1915*

*A*fter harvesting that year's crop, Granny sold all the farm animals except for one milk cow and Dublin, who seemed more like a family member than a horse. They needed the horse to get into town, but her plowing days were over. They kept the chickens and traded extra eggs at the mercantile to buy supplies they still needed from the general store. Since Pa's condition hadn't improved much, they wouldn't plant field crops in the spring as they had done in the past. Ruby would turn the soil for a bigger garden next year and use the surplus to barter scrap meat from the neighboring farms. They had enough to get by for a while anyway. Leon only worked a couple of weekends a month now, helping with repairs and other heavy jobs. Keeping on top of it all meant Granny and Ruby were as busy as ever.

Three of the chickens had stopped laying eggs, so Ruby would miss school a second day in a row to butcher them and can the meat for the winter. She had hoped to get to class this afternoon to turn in her math chapter, which she'd finished last night by lantern. She hung the third chicken's neck over the nail to drain the carcass as Mr. MacCallum rode up the lane to the house. He waved at Ruby standing outside of the chicken coop. She was conscious of the blood all over her work clothes, imagining it looked as if she herself had been slaughtered.

Her teacher came by every time Ruby missed school more than three days in a row to either drop off more work or pick up her assignments; this was usually about once a week. Ruby didn't need instruction the way the other students did; she could get the school assignments done on her own. Mr. MacCallum seemed determined to help her progress, despite her numerous absences. She didn't understand why he was doing it, unless he felt sorry for her. But he also helped many students.

Ruby wiped her hands and walked over to the house to greet him. "Mr. MacCallum, I apologize for my appearance. You caught me in the middle of an execution, I'm afraid. Why don't you go on into the house and say hello to Granny while I finish up? I'll get my lessons for you then."

"Well, it looks like you have your hands full—no pun intended. My mother gave me some salt pork to bring over in exchange for a dozen eggs, so I'll go ahead and take it to Mrs. Turner."

Ruby appreciated this connection to something beyond the farm. With Mr. MacCallum's encouragement, she hoped to finish her schooling and find a good-paying job to help Granny. Please, no more menial labor. She loved mathematics but didn't know how to turn that into something that could make money. Men held most jobs like that, such as running a bank, bookkeeping, or operating a retail business. Still, her teacher encouraged her to study hard and pursue it. He suggested that she consider teaching, though that required two years at a teacher's college off the mountain, which made it beyond her reach. Mr. MacCallum respected her, giving her the idea that she deserved better treatment than she received. What he saw in her, she couldn't fathom, but he seemed convinced of her worth. Since he believed in her, she sometimes imagined life after school as something beyond her current situation. It didn't hurt to dream, and she had plenty of time to think as she did her chores.

Mr. MacCallum had to be the kindest man she had ever met. She knew that the MacCallums already had enough eggs from their own chickens. He brought the salt pork to help them out, knowing that Granny wouldn't accept charity. He wouldn't embarrass them by implying anything other than a trade. Ruby repaid his kindness the only way she could, by doing her best with her lessons. She persevered to finish all of her schoolwork, no matter how tired she felt at the end of the day.

Ruby brought the drained and washed chickens into the kitchen and laid them in a tub on the kitchen table. She still had to pour hot water over the skin so she could pluck them before roasting them in the fire.

She cleaned off her hands and went into her room to retrieve her lessons. Laughter came from Pa's bedroom, a sound foreign to her. Pa still couldn't talk, but he could laugh, all right, and he did when Mr. MacCallum visited. Ruby suspected that Pa didn't make her quit school because he enjoyed the teacher's weekly visits. She wasn't sure how Mr. MacCallum found the time to ride out to the Turners' farm every week. Pa's mood always lightened, making him forget he remained bound to his bed.

Ruby entered Pa's bedroom, holding her tablet containing last night's notations.

Mr. MacCallum rose from his chair and patted Pa's hand. "It was certainly great to see you again, Mr. Turner. I'll leave the salt pork in the kitchen and collect my eggs from Ruby on the way out. She's doing well with her lessons. She's a remarkable young lady—you should be very proud of her."

He walked out of the room with Ruby and stopped in the

parlor to hand her the graded homework he brought back to her. Bright red As were circled at the top of each page. She gave him a new supply to take with him to grade.

"Ruby, I don't know how you do it. All of your work has been stellar. The sentences you diagrammed are perfect. And the trigonometry is almost perfect—you only missed one, a silly math error."

Mr. MacCallum continued, "The mayor came and talked to the high school students about President McKinley's assassination and how President Roosevelt succeeded him. I would like you to interview your granny about the same subject, what she remembers about that time, and write a three-page report. That will satisfy your civics requirement. When are you coming to school next? Do you know?"

"I intend to be there tomorrow, but I guess I'll have to see what tomorrow brings. I hate to miss too many days in a row."

Mr. MacCallum walked out the door, and after he left, Ruby remembered that she'd neglected to give him a dozen eggs. She would try to remember the next time he came.

Later that night, as Granny finished supper, Ruby lit the lantern to start her studies.

"Ruby, your pa would like you to read to him from the Good Book this evening before he goes to sleep," Granny said.

"I won't have time. I need to start this report on the assassination of President McKinley. Can you tell me what you remember of it, Granny?"

"You will do as I ask, young lady. We all have to pull our weight around here, whether we want to or not. I'll tell you what I remember after you go read to Pa."

Ruby had barely entered Pa's room over the past two weeks except to say goodnight. It surprised her how pale he was. She sat down and he started one of his coughing jags, spitting up bloody mucus that dribbled down his chin. She ran back out to the parlor to grab a handkerchief and returned to wipe him off.

This was still better than when Pa worked in the barn. She could work in peace from sunup to sundown, his contempt and abuse now contained in this room. To her, he was just one more set of chores that had to be done before the sun set each day. She and Granny would be better off if Pa died. Though her thoughts horrified her, that would give her the only chance of escaping this life to pursue her dreams.

WHILE MR. MACCALLUM helped her stay connected with her dreams for the future, Leon linked her to the outside world.

The following day at school, Ruby slipped into the desk behind Leon, wrote a note on her slate, and passed it to him while Mr. MacCallum scribbled the day's lessons on the chalkboard. *Why isn't Hattie speaking to you?*

Leon took his chalk and wrote, *I tried to kiss her on the way home from church, and she slapped me. Any advice?*

Ruby wanted to laugh with relief that Hattie wasn't interested in Leon after all. But she hid her glee, relishing the chance to torment Hattie further. *I think she wants you to try harder. She'll give the proper number of slaps before she kisses you back.*

Ruby missed her daily interactions with Leon; rarely did they attend school on the same day. Leon's pa had finally found a job working as a clerk for the railroads in Knoxville. He would leave on the train Mondays and return to his farm late on Fridays. In his absence, Leon helped his mama out with household chores, growing their food and feeding the animals since she had recently delivered her eighth baby.

Mr. MacCallum didn't provide Leon with lessons as he did with Ruby. It was just as well—Leon would most likely quit high school. The last time he came to the farm to mend Granny's fence, he disclosed to Ruby he ran moonshine some nights and got paid quite a bit of cash for his escapades. He would hide a stash in Pa's barn when he worked there, planning to deliver a jug or two on his way home from the Turners' farm.

Ruby studied Leon at his desk in front of her. Both of them knew how to survive. Life kicked them at every turn, but they didn't accept their fate. Feistiness, not acceptance. Leon fought back by delivering moonshine. She looked at Mr. MacCallum at the front of the room; he seemed intent on helping her find her way. Ruby would take any help she could get.

# CHAPTER FIFTEEN

*August 1916*

a year after Pa's attack, he was no better and no worse—still bedridden, unable to walk, and as cantankerous as ever. Ruby and Granny trudged together through the day's chores, establishing what had to be done and who would do it. Unless Ruby questioned Pa's demands, little conflict existed between them. Strangely, Granny listened to Pa and honored his commands without question, even the outlandish ones. She made it clear that if Ruby disobeyed Pa or didn't hold up her end of the work, she would be asked to leave the house. Whenever Ruby tried to talk to Granny about an idea to simplify their life, Granny shushed her. She took direction from Pa only, as feeble as he was. The bond with Granny that Ruby had as a child was broken. She had become a stranger in her grandparents' house.

Last Christmas, Robert and Timmy came to visit. Ruby had found little in common with them. She existed as a remnant of their past. They rode in on the train for the day with fancy gifts for everyone, bringing Ruby a delicate amethyst necklace.

Her first thought was to sell it to get money for clothes or shoes she dearly needed. They both dressed like city boys now, and each wore a chain that connected their pocket watch to the belt loop on their pants. Her invisible chains enslaved her while the boys enjoyed the big city. Pa became angry at them about some little thing, and Timmy and Robert left before the end of the night. Ruby believed they'd stayed only long enough to satisfy their guilt for abandoning her. They quit asking her to visit them.

Ruby put the memory of her brothers' visit behind her and finished picking the beans from the garden before the heat of the August afternoon came. The dust rose on the horizon, and Ruby made out Mr. MacCallum in the distance, riding toward her house. Her senior year would start in another three weeks, but why was her teacher coming to visit today? He wouldn't have an assignment for her before school had even begun.

"Good morning, Ruby. Do you have a minute to talk? Do you think Mrs. Turner could join us?" He smiled at her with his kind eyes.

Though he seemed accustomed to her work attire, Ruby hated that she wore her brother's overalls and undershirt in front of him. She brushed her hair away with her arm, leaving a smudge across her face. While he tied up his horse on the rail, she sat the basket of beans on the porch and rushed inside to let Granny know he had come to visit.

Ruby found her in the kitchen. "Mr. MacCallum's here to talk to us. I'm going to get out of these old clothes and wash up. I'll be out in a minute. He didn't say why he's here."

Without hesitation, she disappeared into her room.

Granny opened the screen door wide to let in the teacher. "How are you, Mr. MacCallum? Is your family well?"

"Please, Mrs. Turner, call me Joseph. My family is fine— thank you for asking. My mother sends her best to you. Is this a good time to talk? It's about a job for Ruby."

"Really? I don't know, Joseph. I need her around here, with Mr. Turner being unable and all."

"I'll explain when she joins us."

Ruby returned to the kitchen wearing her new dress, which she'd made for school. Her unruly red curls matted to her face with sweat, but she tried to tuck them behind her ears. She folded her hands, still dirty under the nails from working in the garden, and placed them in her lap under the table after sitting down.

Mr. MacCallum cleared his throat as if anxious to disclose why he had come. "Ruby, I just found out they closed the school at Stockton because they couldn't find a teacher over there. Mr. Gimble quit when one of the older students threatened him with a gun at the end of last school year. So an additional twenty-five children will be coming down the mountain to attend our school—I'm assuming the older students who work in the mines will drop out. I talked to the county officials, and they've allotted enough money for an assistant to help me with the increased load."

He paused. "I'd like to offer you the job—you're the most qualified. What do you think?"

She tried to keep up with what he was saying. Was he offering her an escape route? The possibility of leaving the farm excited her. By instinct, she held in her reaction to help her navigate the hurdle of what would undoubtedly be Granny and Pa's resistance. But she also caught Mr. MacCallum's eye and couldn't hide her smile.

Ruby looked across at Granny, who lowered her forehead into her hands and slowly shook her head. If Granny agreed to this, she would be overwhelmed with all the chores.

Mr. MacCallum continued. "I'm proposing you continue your schooling for the first two hours a day, then help the younger students with their lessons, teaching them reading and math. You would stay one hour after school to grade papers and prepare lessons for the next day. The pay would be six dollars a week. You were the first person I thought of to take the position, Ruby."

Six dollars a week? For part-time work?

Granny raised her head, and her eyes pierced through her wire-rimmed glasses at Mr. MacCallum. "Mr. MacCallum, er, Joseph, how do you expect me to manage all this without Ruby? You've put me between a rock and a hard place with this proposal. I'll have to discuss it with Mr. Turner, and we'll give you a final answer in a few days."

Ruby could tell that Mr. MacCallum was surprised at Granny's reaction. She wished Granny could consider the merits of additional money for the household. They'd paid Leon only three dollars a week when he worked for them full time. With her extra income, they could buy food in town and hire someone to do the minor repairs. It would allow Ruby to finish her senior year without disruption. She knew to be quiet, or Granny might give the answer she didn't want to hear.

"Mrs. Turner, please pardon me. I should have talked to you first. I need to find someone soon to take this position, but you should discuss it with Mr. Turner and let me know what you decide is best for your family. If you have any questions at all or think I should talk with him myself, I'd be happy to come back and discuss it further." Mr. MacCallum grabbed his hat, tipped it before putting on his head, and walked outside.

He rode off. Ruby watched him through the back door and found herself smiling. If Granny agreed, this would be the greatest gift she had ever received.

# CHAPTER SIXTEEN

The following week, Ruby rode through town on her way to the MacCallums' farm, hoping she wasn't too late to accept her teacher's job offer. After a whole week of discussion, Pa and Granny decided to allow her to teach at the schoolhouse during her senior year. Hallelujah!

Though elated to have this opportunity, Ruby believed something had changed with Granny, but she couldn't put her finger on it. When she left the house this morning, Granny told her, "Don't get too big for your britches," as she walked out the door. Ruby pondered Granny's reaction during her five-mile ride down the mountain. Pa's care and the household chores would fall entirely on Granny's shoulders. Before, she had shared the load with Ruby. Ruby would have to remind her they could hire someone to help if need be.

Surprisingly, Pa rejoiced that she had landed such a job. He knew her paycheck would help them all, mainly since they no longer farmed and couldn't live off the land.

Ruby tied Dublin to the rail near the MacCallum house and gazed at it. The log-shingled house appeared to be about five times the size of Pa's cabin and had six windows across the front and another four windows across the second-story loft. The front door porch wrapped around the side of the house and had about ten chairs on it as if they sat out there and drank tea on summer days.

After dismounting, she pulled her dress down in the back, smoothing it before climbing the porch steps to knock on the front door. Susie, one of Mr. MacCallum's younger sisters, opened the door—she would be one of Ruby's students. She peered inside. Mr. MacCallum was sitting at a desk in the corner. Several children, arranged in a circle on the parlor floor, were playing jacks, laughing together as the household cat jumped to get the ball as it bounced. She couldn't remember ever hearing such laughter at Pa and Granny's.

Mr. MacCallum rose and greeted her at the door. Though a sloppy dresser, he rolled up his shirtsleeves and tucked in the bottom of his dress shirt. "Ruby, please come in."

She entered her teacher's home and stood in the foyer, in awe of her surroundings. The place felt more like a sacred dwelling instead of a house. Everyone knew the MacCallum family to be one of the more prosperous and highly regarded in the community. A solid pine banister framed the stairs, and patchwork quilts draped a rail across the second-floor landing. A painting of MacCallum Mountain framed in weathered pine hung over her teacher's desk.

Mr. MacCallum's mother came around the corner from the kitchen, followed by Miss Alice, Ruby's first teacher.

Miss Alice, obviously pregnant, wiped her hands on her apron and hugged Ruby, leaning way over to get around her rounded belly. "How are you, Ruby? Look at you! What a beautiful girl you've become."

Ruby blushed at the compliment. Mr. MacCallum guided her to the kitchen table, covered in an embroidered tablecloth, and asked the children to go outside to play. His mother delivered tea in porcelain teacups on a tray with cream and sugar.

Ruby sat down across from her teacher and, after watching him do it, used tongs to add a sugar cube to her tea. Alice and her mother returned to making dinner for the family, a family so big and scattered that Ruby couldn't count all the children coming and going. Miss Alice and her mother worked together with ease, Alice humming a hymn.

Ruby looked directly at Mr. MacCallum, only to turn away when he glanced back at her. "Mr. MacCallum, my grandparents have talked, and they agree that I can work as your assistant. I hope the delay isn't a problem for you."

"Oh, Ruby, I'm so delighted you've accepted the position. I planned to ride over this afternoon if I didn't hear from you. We're going to be terrific teaching partners. I'll notify the commissioner that we've filled the position and ask him to meet us at the school the first day to get you on the payroll. Do you have any specific questions for me?" Mr. MacCallum caught his mother's eye, and they smiled as if sharing a secret.

"Not now. Well, maybe. Could I get a copy of the readers and math books for the younger grades? I want to look at them before school starts."

"Certainly."

"Mr. MacCallum, you won't be sorry you chose me as your assistant. I'm very grateful, and I'll do my best to make you proud of me. "

"You've always made me proud, Ruby. I should start calling you Miss Sullivan now, so we get used to it before school starts. That's what the children will call you."

Ruby bit her lower lip to keep herself from breaking into a full-out smile. It had been a long time since she'd grinned about anything.

She thanked Mrs. MacCallum and Alice for their hospitality. Alice wiped her hands on her apron and left the kitchen to go to a back room. She met Ruby at the front door with a couple of skirts and shirtwaists folded in a pile, holding them out to her.

"I can't wear these any longer, and there's not much call for them around the house anyway. I think they'll fit you, maybe with a little alteration. It'll be years before Susie can wear them. Would you be so kind as to take them from me? You'd be doing me a favor, as I'd know they were getting some wear."

The culture of pride persevered in the mountains, so Ruby didn't think she should accept. But she couldn't find a polite way to refuse. Alice could wear the clothing again after her baby's birth, and they both knew it; she was using her pregnancy as an excuse to donate the clothing to Ruby. Ruby walked outside, and Mr. MacCallum followed with the readers. He loaded them in the saddlebags for her, and she placed the outfits atop them before cinching the strap to hold everything in.

"I'll see you on the first day of school, Miss Sullivan. Give my regards to your grandparents, will you?"

# CHAPTER SEVENTEEN

*L*eon woke when his pa stirred in the other room. The full moon lit up the partially clouded dark sky. Would he ever get used to these early Monday mornings? He climbed over his seven younger brothers to get out of the family bed, all the other boys sleeping head to toe. He put on his work pants and a chambray shirt, then pulled the suspenders up over his shoulders. He grabbed his boots and left the room, tiptoeing so he wouldn't wake up his sleeping bedmates.

In the kitchen, his ma packed lunches for two, wrapping the hardtack and salt pork in wax paper before placing it into the metal lunch pails. She put additional salt pork inside for them to eat throughout the week. Other men at the rail yard had fruit or sweet treats in their lunch pails, but not the Penningtons. If they couldn't grow it, they didn't have it.

Leon sat to eat the four fried eggs his ma had prepared. He soaked up the yolk with a slice of yesterday's bread and took a long drink from the cold jar of milk on the table. His ma must have already visited the spring this morning to retrieve the milk she'd left there from last night's milking. She would go out later to milk the cows again after getting his younger brothers off to school.

It had taken Leon no time at all to quit school when he found out about a freight handler position at Knoxville's new train yards. At seventeen, he had no further use for school and thought that the sooner he got out of there, the sooner he could get off this damned mountain. He'd told his ma he earned thirty dollars a month, but in truth, he brought home thirty-five. She had requested his whole paycheck, but what she didn't know wouldn't hurt her. By adding his take to his savings from his weekend bootleg deliveries, he would be able to buy his ticket out of this mountain town in only a couple of more years.

They had electricity and dance halls in Knoxville, not to mention taverns. He wanted to have enough money to live there on his own and not have to go home on weekends. He wished he could find a way to meet his goal without so much hard work. Shoot, with a little luck, he might catch a girl with family money.

Leon grabbed his lunch, his duffel bag packed with work clothes for the week, and followed his pa out to the barn to get the horses ready to ride to the train station. His younger brothers would pick up the horses from the livery after school. By the time he walked outside, Pa had saddled the horses. His pa seemed to have more energy of late. After years of being unemployed and losing the farm equipment to the bank, he appeared to have a new lease on life with this job at the rail yards. Leon tied his duffel to his horse, then jumped into the saddle to ride in the dark into town. People told him he looked like his pa, but he was a good six inches taller than his old man. He could get the girls to turn his way, something he couldn't imagine his pa doing. His father rode ahead of him, kicking up dust in his wake. At the livery, they checked the horses in before walking across the street to the station—all before the sun came up.

Leon stood on the platform and checked the time on the big

clock next to the track. The train's steam rose in the distance. Though mountain culture was lackadaisical, the trains always arrived right on time. He would catch up on his sleep on the hour-and-a-half ride to the Knoxville rail yard. The sun peered over the horizon as he jumped onto the train after his pa. He sat across the aisle from him and opened his lunch pail to eat the salt pork.

His pa shook his head. "You're going to be mighty hungry come lunchtime, Leon."

"I'll deal with that at lunchtime. I'm hungry now. Wake me up when it's time to get off in Knoxville." Leon pushed his cap over his eyes as he slouched in his seat.

He knew why the rail yard had hired him. Young and muscular from the farm work he had done over the past few years, he could do the heavy lifting. His pa had lucked out and was a clerk in charge of inventory at the warehouse. The job suited his father, who had his own office and desk. He said with pride that he had the ciphering skills needed for the job. Leon knew he missed his wife and sons during the week. His ma stepped up to tackle the jobs left to her and take care of his brothers.

Before Leon knew it, his pa was shaking his shoulder, and Leon's hat fell into the aisle. He retrieved it, grabbed his duffel, and fumbled after his pa to jump off the train just before the conductor shut the door. He bumped into a young woman as he turned north to go toward the warehouse. She carried a river-cane basket with loaves of bread. She stopped to give him plenty of room as he hurried to catch up with his pa. He tipped his hat, and she lowered her head, blushing. From the way she looked at him—or rather, pretended not to look—he could tell she had no idea he was merely seventeen.

He turned around and walked backward to observe her go into the café down the street. He might explore the town a little after work today. Maybe he'd meet the girl of his dreams in this town. Or he might find the back room where the locals played a high-stakes game of poker. His pa knew that if he tattled on Leon to Ma, Leon would report that Pa spent some coins on whiskey at the local tavern after work.

Leon put his jacket, duffel, and lunch pail in his work locker and reported to the back warehouse. They expected a shipment of cigarettes today. Maybe he could pilfer a few if one of the wooden crates "happened" to break while lifted from the boxcar. He would turn around and sell them to add to his escape fund.

# CHAPTER EIGHTEEN

*R*uby arrived at the school on her first day of work before the birds started their morning chirping. She sat on the wooden bench in the schoolyard to wait for Mr. MacCallum. Ruby had walked to school early to settle down before the county commissioners arrived to set her up for payroll. She placed the borrowed readers on the bench beside her and pulled her sweater around her arms to combat the autumn chill.

Before long, Mr. MacCallum rode up on his mare. Ruby could see his shadowy silhouette in the gray folds of the morning light. Riding as if he had all the time in the world appeared to make him noble. Her teacher tied up his horse on the rail before unloading his saddlebags. He hadn't noticed her yet. Mr. MacCallum removed his hat and put it on the post, then unbridled and unsaddled his horse and led him to the fenced area in the woods beside the schoolhouse. His hair was thinning on top. Only in his mid-twenties, he already had more forehead than most men his age. His wire-rimmed glasses rode down his nose, and he continually pushed them up. She had never noted his features before; he had always been more of a kind presence than a physical being to her. Being around him felt like a haven—nothing awful could happen if he was nearby. He lifted his bags, put on his hat, and started across the yard to the school's front door. Taller than she remembered, he lowered his head to clear the doorjamb. She would call him handsome, she supposed. But then she shook herself at the notion of even thinking of her teacher that way. She would give him some time before she joined him inside.

In a few minutes, Mr. MacCallum came back outside to get wood to start the fire in the schoolhouse and spotted her on the bench. "Good morning, Ruby. Wait, let me start over again. Good morning, Miss Sullivan. I am proud to be your colleague."

He said that in an obvious way—teasing her, she imagined. But she didn't mind. His teasing was different from what she had suffered from her classmates. His voice was always gentle with her. She didn't know how to take his compliment because she had rarely ever heard kind words about herself. Granny was stingy with her praise, and Pa didn't have a gracious word to say about anybody or anything.

"Good morning, Mr. MacCallum. I thought I'd give you a minute before I came in. I think I got here too early."

"Don't be silly. I'll get the wood, and then I'll be right in. Bring in your books. Then just like you used to do as a student, get the slates ready to pass out. They brought desks from the mountain school that closed, so we'll have to arrange the desks too—it's a mess inside."

Ruby bobbed her head to whatever he said and went inside. She placed her books and sweater in the corner, got the broom from the closet, and swept the front of the schoolroom— sneezing as the dust rose from the wooden floors. Spiderwebs filled the corners of the room, and mouse droppings had accumulated on the floor over the summer. She didn't know if Mr. MacCallum would have swept the room or not, but she couldn't move the desks into place without cleaning first. There wasn't much natural light in the schoolroom, only one window on the east side and two small windows at the front. She started pushing the double-seated desks forward, lining them up in rows of six. After setting up five rows, she added two additional desks in the front to make room for all sixty-five students. There weren't enough hooks, so some coats and sweaters would hang on desk chairs for now.

After Mr. MacCallum started the fire, he helped Ruby. He grabbed the broom and swept off his desk at the front of the room. A plume of dust arose against the sunlight coming through the window. He pushed another large table from the corner next to his. After he cleaned it, she pulled a chair behind it, taking her place at her desk.

"This is a big day, Miss Sullivan. After you sign your contract with the county commissioner, I want to shake your hand. Then we'll explain to the children your new role. It will be good for them to see what can come of hard work," Mr. MacCallum said.

As he wrote on the blackboard, he continued, "Today, we'll start you right off with the younger children. I want them to get to know you on the first day. But tomorrow, we'll make sure you get your lessons first before switching to teaching. Does that sound all right?"

"Sure, whatever you think." Ruby took a deep breath to take it all in.

"And after school, you and I will have a short planning session for the rest of the week. It's a lot to digest, but the children are arriving, and I wanted to cover what I could before class starts."

She looked outside, where the students were assembling in the schoolyard. Two distinct groups gathered—the ones who had attended here the year before and the new ones from up the mountain. Maybe the first activity should be to arrange seating to integrate the groups, allowing them to get to know each other. Maybe being a teacher wouldn't be so hard after all. She was already starting to feel like one.

A man with a small mustache scurried through the back door, and Mr. MacCallum stopped writing on the blackboard to welcome him. "Mr. Groves, this is Miss Sullivan. She's the exceptional senior student I told you about. I can think of no one better to assist me with the children. Her work ethic surpasses any student I've ever had."

Ruby nodded to greet him.

"Miss Sullivan, it's highly unusual to hire a student to teach others. Mr. MacCallum assures me that you're the best candidate for the job. He also assures me that you can handle this without it negatively affecting your lessons. Can you promise you'll finish your schooling and won't let teaching interfere with your studies?"

"I give you my word you'll not be disappointed in my work with the students or my studies."

"Then will you sign this contract for the county? It will allow me to put you on the payroll." Mr. Groves was all business.

Ruby found herself humming with excitement. Every bit of work she had done on the farm had always been for someone else. She'd been given a task, told how and when to do it, only to have Pa yell at her for doing it incorrectly. Pa had called her lazy before he dumped another job on her, adding to the endless list of things to do. But starting today, she could decide what to do with the students, giving them tasks as she saw fit to help them learn best. She barely concealed her delight at having a real job, an employer who wanted her opinion, and the opportunity to use her mind instead of her tired body to make a difference.

Mr. Groves laid out the paperwork, and Mr. MacCallum went to the supply desk to get a bottle of ink and a fountain pen. Her hand shook some, and Mr. Groves smiled and exchanged a glance with her teacher. Ruby signed the contract.

The county commissioner shook her hand, and Mr. MacCallum followed suit.

The noise swelled outside because of the number of children gathering near the door. Mr. Groves left, and Ruby and Mr. MacCallum finished straightening the desks. They were already a team. He set the time on the wall clock from his wristwatch while she walked outside to ring the bell to start the new school year.

# CHAPTER NINETEEN

*October 1916*

Every part of his body ached from the morning cold. Leon wore gloves as he lifted the twenty-pound bags of sugar from the pallet onto the ledge of the boxcar. Because he had cut off the tips of his gloves to give him more flexibility, his fingers were bright red from the frigid air. As the day wore on, the embedded chill shook him, but he warmed up some as he moved around. This early-morning October freeze meant the winter would likely be a hard one. He yawned, and his breath mixed with the steam from the train engine. Leon plopped the last box onto the ledge and stopped to lean over to rest his back, his hands on his knees. He rose and blew into his cupped palms to try to warm up.

During the week, Leon and his pa shared a small room at the back of the train depot with hardly enough space for two bedrolls. Two crates turned upside down served as chairs for them. The best part of their lodging was the cost: free as long as they kept an eye on things around the depot after dark. After work every day, they grabbed a bite to eat at the boardinghouse across the street, usually soup, beans, and ham for ten cents each. But after dinner, they separated. Leon's pa often went to the smoky whiskey bar with the other rail yard employees, while Leon looked for trouble away from the older men. Tonight he had no problem finding it.

Off the beaten path, he came across a tavern south of town that stayed open all night. He sat at the bar and bought a shot of hard liquor with coins from selling the cigarettes he'd stolen from the cargo. He asked the bartender about the card game, and a barmaid named Sally with bleached blonde curls escorted him to the back room. He almost walked into a door while observing her ample hips sway back and forth in front of him.

Sally pulled out a chair, and he joined the men already seated at the card table.

"Who's this young fellow, Sally? You're robbing the cradle with this young'un."

"Oh, he's not that young. He's just better looking than the usual crowd. And he's got a jingle in his pocket—he's old enough for that." Sally stood behind him and rubbed his shoulders as the man across the table from him dealt his cards.

Leon held his cards close to his chest, not wanting Sally to tip his hand to his opponents.

He won the first round with two pairs, and Sally, her red lips shining like a polished apple, kissed him full on the mouth to celebrate his winnings. When he won his second hand, she leaned over—displaying her pronounced cleavage—and helped him rake in the loot. He enjoyed the view down her low-cut peasant blouse, his reward for bluffing and playing his cards well. Before his turn to deal, Sally turned toward him, brashly placed her hands on either side of her bosom, and shook herself teasingly at him. Leon took the view she offered. He didn't know which part of this night he liked the most: the quality moonshine, getting rich off his bets, or the woman hired to entertain in the back room. In truth, he loved life in the big city.

He bought his competition a round of drinks and kept his eyes on Sally as she left the room to retrieve them.

"Sally isn't part of the prize package, mister."

"You're just jealous, all of you. Let Sally decide what she wants." Leon's reply drew hard stares from the other men at the table. But when Sally delivered the drinks, tempers simmered down. Raising the ire of a group of men from this part of town would be the last thing Leon needed.

He stayed out late until dawn and went home a few dollars richer and with red lipstick all over his face. He knew it would be difficult to get up in a few hours for work, but he only had to make it through one day before the weekend. He liked his paycheck, so he would scramble out of bed when his pa did, whether he had rested or not.

LEON and his pa took the train home after work and stepped back into their lives in Poplar Cove. Even in the bed with his brothers, Leon slept well and woke early to help his pa repair the fence. After, the family sat in the sun on the porch to get reacquainted after their week apart. When Ma went inside to start the family dinner, Pa took over the Saturday baths by the fire in the sitting room until all seven younger Pennington boys were clean.

Too old for the family bath, Leon went to the river to wash up before going into town. The weather was warmer on this side of the mountain, though it was still too cold to jump in. Leon waded in up to his knees and splashed water over his face and upper body to remove the week's odor, then returned to the house to dress in his new tailored suit—a pinstripe he'd bought in Knoxville with his extra money. He applied a bit of hog fat to plaster his hair down to the side. He smiled into the window reflection, hoping Ruby would find him dapper.

Ruby. It had been ages since he had talked with her. He understood she now taught with Mr. MacCallum up at the school. She'd finally got a break from the farm chores, and especially from Henry Turner. He hoped she would attend the harvest social taking place late afternoon at the church.

Leon rode into town on the family horse, surveying the crowd before dismounting. How different Rock Bluff was from Knoxville—the pace was slower, and people looked you in the eye with sincerity. He saw a few of his friends from school, noting they hadn't changed much. His gaze stopped at Ruby, who stood off to the side of the rest of the girls, holding a picnic basket. He stood by his horse and remembered the day they went swimming in the spring on the way into town. That was something he would never forget—but they were kids then. Ruby had matured since they worked together on the farm. A blue scarf, contrasting with her hazel eyes, kept her unruly red hair out of her face. She was poised, with a little more confidence than he remembered. Good for her.

He jingled the coins in his pocket, counting his change so he could bid on her basket. He would offer everything he had to let her know he'd like to get reacquainted. Ruby looked over and lit up when she saw him. She waved and smiled.

He approached her. "Ruuu-by, look at you! It seems that teaching agrees with you. You look radiant. Are you expecting to find a beau tonight?"

"And look at you, Mr. Railroad Man, with your hair slicked back. Are you expecting to bid on a basket this evening? I hear Hattie has a whole pie in hers. It's cherry, your favorite."

"It seems Hattie isn't as interested in me lately. That might have something to do with her pa forbidding her to see me. But that's all right by me—plenty of other ladies are just as charming." He shrugged before looking Ruby directly in the eye and winking at her.

After a short silence, she turned to leave. "Well, I'll be making my rounds and enjoying the warm afternoon." She marched her basket up to the tables in front before laying a blanket down on the lawn to get ready for the auction. Leon walked across the gently sloped churchyard to the circle of former classmates standing on the far side of the field. He offered them each a cigarette while they all waited for the auction to start.

Dressed in his best church suit, Deacon Preston served as the auctioneer. He invited the boys—the potential bidders—to pay attention as he lifted a large square basket, its handle decorated with fall leaves. He acted as if it was too heavy to lift and identified the owner as Winnie. She waved to the crowd. Winnie was sitting beside Hattie on her blanket.

The deacon raised his voice to announce, "The proceeds of these baskets will pay for the senior trip to Lookout Mountain in the spring. Don't be bashful in your bidding, young men. And remember, if you're the winner, you get to eat what's inside the basket with whoever put it together. That's the deal."

The bidding started at ten cents. After some fast bidding, the deacon's son won Winnie's basket for seventy cents. He waved across the yard at her, and she squealed at the high price. He picked up the basket and made his way to her spot on the lawn.

Ruby's basket was the next one up. When Deacon Preston said her name, she stood and waved to the crowd, emulating Winnie. Ruby had tied her scarf to the small handle at the last minute to distinguish her basket from the others. Leon reached into his pocket and pulled out all of his change. He waved to Ruby from across the lawn.

"Do I hear a starting bid on this beautiful basket? I smell a freshly baked cake in here. Twenty cents? Do I hear twenty cents?"

Leon moved toward the auction table; his hand raised to place the opening bid.

"I have twenty cents, but let's don't be shy. Thirty cents. Thirty cents."

A loud voice from behind the boys countered with, "One dollar."

The deacon slapped his gavel on the table and said, "Sold."

A collective whisper spread across the lawn—the crowd seemed stunned at the abrupt end to the bidding. A group of boys parted, and Mr. MacCallum came forward to pay for his winnings. Leon put the change back in his pocket and kicked the ground in front of him. Why did Mr. MacCallum bid on Ruby's basket? The auction was for students, not teachers. However, as soon as he thought this, he remembered that Ruby taught now.

Mr. MacCallum collected the basket, and Ruby came forward. Leon moved closer to hear them speak.

"Miss Sullivan, I thought I'd be bold and maybe save you some embarrassment. I let the deacon know I'd be buying your basket. I know it must be awkward to be both a teacher and a student. I bought your basket to contribute to the senior class trip fund. I'll leave it with you, and you can share it with whoever you'd like," Mr. MacCallum said.

Ruby composed herself. "But what will you eat this evening? You can join me. The cake is quite good, and besides . . . it cost you a whole dollar."

"Well, then, if you're sure you don't mind, I'll join you."

They walked back through the crowd to her blanket. Mr. MacCallum straightened the ground covering and sat at the outer edge while Ruby unpacked the fried chicken, deviled eggs, and the promised cake. After the auction was over, Deacon Preston and his wife sat next to them.

On Leon's way out, he observed Ruby smiling shyly at her older companions. Maybe he still had a chance with her. Leon caught her eye, and her cheeks reddened. Perhaps she was embarrassed that he was watching her, or maybe she was uncomfortable with Mr. MacCallum's attention. She held Leon's glance. Ruby seemed to have a foot in two different worlds.

# CHAPTER TWENTY

*December 1916*

Outside Ruby's bedroom window, a gust of wind dislodged the few autumn leaves left on the large oak outside. The low deep blue clouds outside reminded her to grab her shawl on the way out of the room. It would be a cold one today, colder than usual for mid-December. Granny was sitting at the table drinking coffee when she came into the kitchen, the same spot she was in when Ruby went to bed last night.

"Biscuits and ham are in the larder from yesterday, Ruby. Grab yourself some. I didn't get around to making more." Granny looked as if she hadn't slept all night. Pa dozed off and on all day and tossed and turned through the nights. When he woke, he bellowed for Granny to find a bedpan or made another request, followed by a litany of complaints. How long would he continue to suffer and have the energy to make sure Granny suffered with him? Ruby avoided getting anywhere near him—easy to do because he couldn't get out of bed now. Granny dealt with her misery by kicking a can down the road.

When tired, she became grumpy and fussed at Ruby more than ever.

"Are you coming home right after school today, Ruby? If you are, I'd like some help with laundry."

"I'll be home after our planning meeting. It should only last thirty minutes or so. We're pretty caught up, and the holiday break starts next week." Ruby finished her coffee, grabbed a biscuit, and headed out the door. Though sympathetic to Granny's plight, she couldn't wait to leave the house each day.

Granny let Ruby take Dublin to school now since she stayed home with Pa all day. On her way to school, Ruby considered how grateful she was. By choosing her to assist him in the classroom, Mr. MacCallum had saved her. She could see the difference she made in her students' education, making her feel good about herself. Her teacher often complimented her on her patience with the students and her creativity in helping them understand. How different from working with Pa, who found fault with most everything. Each morning, she woke up refreshed, not with lingering fatigue from doing the heavy work of farm chores.

When Ruby arrived at the school, smoke rose out of the chimney; the room would be toasty before noon today. Mr. MacCallum smiled at her as she entered the classroom. "Good morning, Miss Sullivan."

She hung her wrap and her scarf and unpacked her satchel. "Good morning, sir. It looks like we might get some snow this afternoon, even though it's early in the season."

"If it snows more than a flurry, we'll cancel afternoon classes so the kids who live on the mountain ridge near Stockton can get home."

Mr. MacCallum pulled a coffeepot from his desk drawer and some ground coffee. He stepped outside to fill the pot with water from the well pump and made coffee on the warming stove.

He filled his cup and one for Ruby too. He knew her preferences now: one lump of sugar. She laughed—they were just like two old married people.

She placed the last slate at the back of the room, returned to her desk, and accepted the coffee from the teacher. The steam curled upward, and she held on to the mug to warm her hands.

Mr. MacCallum sat and turned his chair toward her. "I have a question for you. It's only the middle of the school year, but I wondered if you're thinking of going to teachers college next year after you graduate."

There wasn't any money for college. Ruby hesitated, perplexed at his question. She didn't know how to respond to him.

"Of course, this position here will still be open for you if you want it, Ruby. But if you want to get certified to teach, I'd like to help you with your application." Mr. MacCallum cleared his throat and turned back to his lesson book when she didn't reply.

Was he having these discussions with all of his students, or was he talking to her as a colleague? He did say "Ruby," which usually meant he was addressing her as his student. She couldn't fathom a world where she could go to college—it wasn't in the realm of possibilities for her. It would be easier for her to fly in the sky like the giant ravens that circled the trees outside.

"I won't be able to afford to go away for training next year. We don't have the money—I won't even ask Granny about it." Ruby turned her chair back to the center and studied the lesson book for her first graders. Right on time, she rose to go outside and clang the bell for school to start.

Right after the children's morning break for outside play, the snow started falling just as Ruby had predicted. Lunch would be inside. Ruby looked outside at the pasture; Dublin already had about an inch of snow on her back, even though she was shaking most of the snow off as it fell.

"Mr. MacCallum, look outside."

"I already sent Zeke up the hill to get his father's help for the Stockton children so they can get up the ridge. We'll stop class-work after they get here. The local children won't have any issues getting home, though I do worry about Jacob and Grace since they don't own coats."

They finished the math lesson, but Zeke hadn't returned with his father. Mr. MacCallum dismissed class.

"Miss Sullivan, I'm taking the Stockton children over the pass. I'll be back in an hour or so. Send the local children who live close home, but have the older children accompany the younger ones, if you will."

Ruby wrapped Grace in her shawl and gave Jacob her knitted scarf, wrapping it several times around his small body. She sent them out with some older children who lived on the farm adjacent to them.

Ruby went outside and got another log to stoke the fire. She walked to the corral and harnessed Dublin. While leading the horse, she couldn't see her previous footsteps—it was snowing that hard. Ruby walked beside Dublin to block the wind and led her to the schoolhouse to tie her up. She would be warmer there.

Mr. MacCallum returned well beyond the hour he said he would be back, but he had gotten all the mountain children home safely. Ruby had closed up the classroom and prepared the blackboard for the next day. She had just started studying her civics lesson when Mr. MacCallum came in. He walked in, shivering, snowflakes attached to his eyelashes, making him look like Old Man Winter. Ruby stifled a laugh.

"Ruby, come to my home until the storm's over. I'm afraid for you heading home now up to Livingston Gap."

"I promised Granny I'd be home right after school. I think she'll be worried if I don't go home immediately." She knew that riding without her knitted wrap would be a cold ride. She looked outside and saw that the wind had picked up.

"With this weather, Granny'll just assume you stayed at school. It's only fifteen minutes through town to get to my parents' home. We'll have supper there and see how the weather progresses. I'll ride with you home if the snow stops. Gather your things. Where's your shawl?"

"I gave it to Grace to wrap up in before she started for home."

Mr. MacCallum took off his overcoat and put it around Ruby's shoulders. Behind her, he fixed the collar to block the wind. She had never been this close to him. She grabbed her schoolbag and headed outside to tie it to the saddle he had already placed on Dublin. She didn't protest when he helped her up on her horse. With only his muffler around his neck and his thin sweater protecting him from the cold, he mounted his horse and began leading her to his house.

"Mr. MacCallum, where are your gloves? You'll be frozen by the time we get to your house."

"They're probably under the snow somewhere, having fallen out of my coat pocket. I can't seem to keep up with them." He sat tall in his saddle, shaking from either the laughter or the brisk wind.

A curl, usually combed to lie near his eyebrows, lifted off his forehead and danced in the wind. Ruby kept her head low to duck the wind and followed her teacher.

When the trees blocked the wind, he slowed to ride beside Ruby. "Ruby, at my house, you can call me Joseph. If you say, 'Mr. MacCallum,' everyone will think you're talking to my father. It could be confusing, and there's enough chaos at home. This evening, let's forget I'm your teacher and just be friends."

"Sure, Mr. MacCallum—I mean Joseph. I can do that."

She stopped behind him at the front of his parents' home. The faces of his younger siblings appeared at the window— Maggie was jumping up and down. Albert came outside to help Ruby off her horse and then rode it to the barn. Joseph's youngest siblings wrapped their arms around her as she entered the large parlor. She was awed to see enough seating for everyone. Mrs. MacCallum placed Ruby's things near the corner desk and asked her if she minded setting the dinner table. Ruby took Joseph's coat from around her shoulders and hung it on the coat rack near the door.

Though glad for something to do, she panicked. She didn't know how to set a proper table. At her grandparents' home, each person had one mismatched place setting, washed and reused for every meal. And they didn't have all these utensils. Most days, she ate with a spoon, and there was a shared knife for the table. She looked at the array of silverware laid on the counter, and as she unfolded the tablecloth to put it on the large dinner table, she called to Maggie, Joseph's youngest sister, to help her with the table setting. Maggie followed Ruby around the table as she set the plates down.

Maggie had a collection of spoons and forks in her hand and muttered to herself in a singsong jingle, "'Spoon' has five letters, and 'right' has five letters. The spoon goes on the right. 'Fork' has four letters, and 'left' has four letters. The fork goes on the left. A knife is always right." From now on, Ruby would use this verse to remember where to place the utensils when setting the table.

Ruby relaxed having Maggie nearby to help her—it was always easier to interact with someone closer to her age. Ruby poured water into the water glasses from a jug as Mrs. MacCallum brought the hot food to the table. The meat platter had several pork chops on it, almost enough for everyone to have their own. At her home, one of these smaller pieces would be shared between three people.

"Ruby, I'm glad you're joining us. Joseph tells me he's very pleased with your help. My children certainly love having you as their teacher." Mrs. MacCallum looked over the table to see if anything else was needed.

"Thank you, Mrs. MacCallum. I appreciate your hospitality on such short notice."

"There's always room for more at our dinner table."

Ruby watched to see when Joseph would come in from the barn and remembered he was outside without his coat. Several inches of snow covered the ground.

The rest of the family members came into the dining room when Mrs. MacCallum rang the outside bell for dinner. Ruby hesitated to sit, knowing that such a large family probably had their usual seating arrangement. Joseph sat on the far side in the middle of the table. He motioned for Ruby to sit next to him. Everyone found a seat, with Mrs. MacCallum located closest to the kitchen.

The younger children settled down, and Joseph's father started with the prayer. "Lord, bless this food this evening and bless the good woman who prepared it for our nourishment. Bless also our guest this evening, Miss Sullivan, and calm her grandparents, so they don't worry about her during this storm. Amen."

The table became bustling with activity as bowls passed from right to left, like clockwork. The mashed potato bowl was too large to handle with one hand, so Joseph held it for her while she spooned some onto her plate. The green beans with pork bits curled steam and a wonderful aroma under her nose. With each plate filled, all eyes turned to the elder Mr. MacCallum at the head of the table.

"So tell me, Maggie, what was the best part of your day?"

Maggie giggled through her response. "Getting out of school early and having Miss Sullivan come to dinner."

Ruby blushed and observed this family tradition. Never in her life had she participated in a ritual in which someone asked her opinion about something. Joseph's father rounded the table, asking each family member the same question, and it was soon her teacher's turn to respond.

Joseph looked at Ruby, a tricky maneuver with her sitting next to him, and answered with a laugh, "I think my answer is the same as Maggie's. I'm also glad that Miss Sullivan is here for dinner."

Ruby looked down at her lap, not knowing how to take his answer. The potato bowl made the rounds, distracting everyone and giving her a few moments to prepare her response.

"I'm mighty grateful to be joining you all this evening. Everyone's so nice to me. I thank you." Ruby looked up to see her teacher and his mother lock eyes and smile at each other. Some message, unsaid, had passed between the two of them.

After dinner, Ruby looked outside and decided to spend the night at the MacCallum home. The winds caused drifting, and getting up the mountain would be treacherous. Her teacher's family read the Bible together after dinner, and before bedtime, Mrs. MacCallum handed her a starched white cotton night-gown, folded into a square, and a pillow.

"Would you be comfortable sharing a bed with Maggie?" she asked.

Ruby had never been more comfortable in her life than she was this evening.

WITH THOUGHTS of Joseph's family swirling around in her head, Ruby didn't sleep that night. Could she tolerate her home now that she knew how good family life could be? The visit had opened the door to a new world. When she went into the kitchen the next morning, Ruby found coffee made and a full breakfast already prepared for the family.

She sat down first and listened to Mrs. MacCallum sing as her children came into the kitchen for breakfast, stopping to hug their mother before they sat down. Mrs. MacCallum could crack an egg with one hand and hug a child with the other.

Ruby studied the scene with curiosity as she ate her eggs. The outward expressions of affection struck her.

Across from her, Ruby watched Joseph use a piece of biscuit to absorb the runny egg yolk on his plate. He looked up and caught her eye. She looked away, blushing. Last night on the way to bed, Maggie and Ruby had held hands and recited a schoolyard jingle as they went down the hall. Ruby stopped when Joseph stepped into the hallway. But he caught Maggie's hand and continued singing the rhyme with them before turning into the bedroom he shared with Albert across the hall.

Joseph's father came in from the barn and sat at the head of the table. Like clockwork, Mrs. MacCallum delivered his plate of eggs, biscuits, and gravy, followed by coffee. They exchanged a warm look before she returned to the hot stove. Were her Mama and Papa the same way before Papa died in the wagon accident?

Joseph pushed back from the table. "Ruby, I'll start off for the schoolhouse in a few minutes to get the fire going for the children. I'll get Dublin ready to go as well, if that gives you enough time to gather your things."

Ruby drank the last sip of her coffee. "It'll just take me a few minutes. I appreciate your help with Dublin."

Mrs. MacCallum took the plate from Ruby, laid it on the counter near the sink, and hugged her goodbye. It took Ruby by surprise. She hadn't been embraced by anyone for a couple of years, ever since her brothers took to live in the big city. She wanted to stay in the warmth of that kitchen for a while longer.

"Thank you for your kindness, Mrs. MacCallum."

Ruby went outside when Joseph appeared at the front of the house with the horses, ready to leave.

He got down to help her mount her horse. "After we get to the schoolhouse, we'll see how the roads are. If it's clear enough, you should ride on home to let your granny know you're all right. I'll cover the classes this morning. I think we'll have fewer students today anyway."

Ruby rode several paces behind Joseph on their way into town, absorbed in her thoughts.

He slowed his horse to ride beside her. "Ruby, I talked to Mother, and we'd like to invite you and your grandparents over for Christmas dinner. My brothers and I can come collect you in our wagon to ensure that your pa is transported carefully to our home. Talk to them about it and see what they think. It'd be our pleasure to host you. Your brothers are invited too if they come home this year."

Ruby rode in silence. Why was Joseph —Mr. MacCallum— extending an invitation to her? Was it pity? She dreaded the thought of Pa's condescending attitude and Granny's cold demeanor ruining Christmas dinner at the MacCallums'. Not to mention the embarrassment of their backwoods ways. With Granny and Pa there, Ruby would always be on guard, lest they find out her grandparents didn't want her. On the other hand, spending Christmas vacation in her grandparents' home for two weeks stretched the limits of her tolerance.

Ruby looked at Joseph. "I'll talk to them, but I know what their answer will be. You and your family are very gracious to me. I appreciate it more than you know."

They arrived at school and could see that the snow was already melting. With a sigh, Rub rode on, her shoulders slumped as she journeyed up the mountain path—to a place that was anything but home.

# CHAPTER TWENTY-ONE

*T*he last two weeks of school before Christmas break were a blur for Ruby. Joseph had asked her to be in charge of the Christmas pageant, telling her she would earn a bonus of ten dollars if she did it. She didn't know if that came from the school budget or out of his pocket, but she couldn't refuse the extra money in either case. He had reserved the Methodist church in town for the Monday evening before Christmas. Alice had volunteered to help Ruby organize the production and play the piano for it. Being in charge of something was all new to her, and she didn't know where to start. It was one thing to be in a pageant as a child and another to be grown up enough to put one on.

One sunny afternoon the week before the pageant, Ruby met Alice at the church after school to plan the performance. She wore a suit Alice had given her at the beginning of the school year. Alice had just arrived, her youngest baby in their wagon.

"Ruby, could you hold Olive while I get the costumes we used last year from the back of the wagon?"

Ruby tied up Dublin and took the baby from Alice. Olive

wrinkled up her nose, opened her mouth, and wailed—which promptly caused Alice to laugh.

"She's already singing for you, Ruby. Do you think she could be Baby Jesus with a voice like that?"

Ruby couldn't resist chuckling. They went into the plain church, simply outfitted with ample rows of wooden benches for the parents and a large altar with enough room for all the children to stand. It was the only church in the area large enough to hold them all. Ruby set Baby Olive on a blanket in a collection basket on the altar. Alice spread out the costumes on the front-row bench for them to look over. After many years of use, the robes and headscarves were threadbare, and the seams had unraveled.

"How do you want to do this, Ruby? Should the children sing songs, or do you want them to narrate the Christmas story?"

"I'm not sure, Miss Alice. What do you think?"

"Just call me Alice. Well, have you thought about what songs you might use?"

Outside of the classroom, where Joseph welcomed her opinion, no one asked her what she thought about things. She was touched that Alice deferred to her, but Ruby hadn't participated in the school pageants in years; she hadn't been allowed. Pa disapproved, citing all the work to be done at home. At home, Christmas was like any other day except for the bread pudding Granny made.

Ruby opened up. "I could use some help deciding things. This is all new to me. And besides, you've done it many times."

Baby Olive started crying again, and Ruby picked her up, instinctively bouncing her up and down to soothe her. Olive was the first baby Ruby had ever held.

Alice made herself at home around the piano. She pulled out the bench behind it on the altar and opened the music book on the music stand. Ruby remembered this was the MacCallum family church and Alice played piano for services here.

From the piano bench, Alice offered Ruby ideas on how to start. Perhaps she could bring up the children in groups by age to sing a few songs each. Then the entire group could sing "Away in a Manger" and "Silent Night" all together at the end, in full costume for the traditional manger scene. She offered that the high school students didn't usually want to participate, but one might be willing to read *'Twas the Night Before Christmas* if Ruby wanted them to.

"I was only joking about Olive being Baby Jesus, but she is a good sleeper and might do the part if you'd like." Alice laughed and looked at Ruby for a response to her proposal.

"I like what you suggest. That flows easily and doesn't make the program too long. I only have to assign parts for the singing." Ruby swayed back and forth with the baby as Olive nodded off to sleep.

Alice trusted her judgment. If only she could see herself as Alice did.

As they finished, Ruby remembered that Joseph had volunteered to go over and help Granny with a few chores in the barn since Ruby needed extra time for the pageant. She cringed to think what Pa might say to him, especially about her. She wanted to keep Pa and him apart.

THE NIGHT OF THE PAGEANT, Ruby greeted the parents who came to watch their children. When it was time to begin, she corralled the anxious children onto the stage. She understood their nervousness—she was tense too.

Joseph went up to the altar to start the program. "Welcome, everyone. You're in for a treat. We have many making their theater debut tonight, starting with Miss Sullivan, who's directing this program. She's an excellent teacher, and the children are in good hands under her care. And Miss Olive Winters is starring as Baby Jesus. Don't applaud for her, though—it might wake her up."

The crowd, most dressed in their Sunday best, warmed to Joseph. They laughed at his remarks and settled down by the time he finished speaking and left the stage. Ruby stepped up to the altar and bowed. She arranged the younger children and nodded at Alice to start the first song on her piano. She stood to the side as they sang so she could help them remember their words. The crowd laughed when Otis bellowed out "Go Tell It on the Mountain," dancing and flinging his arms as if he had spiders crawling up them. After each song, Ruby turned to acknowledge the applause. After the first group finished, Ruby escorted them to the side to allow the older children to take center stage. Leon Pennington sat in the back, next to his ma and another woman Ruby didn't know. Why was he here? Leon did have younger brothers at the school, but it was a Monday night, and he worked in Knoxville during the week. Leon beamed at her and waved before she began the next song.

At the end of the program, all the children sang together. The younger children dressed as angels yawned, their halos cocked over their small heads. One lay down halfway through the song, using his white angel gown as a blanket, and started sucking his thumb. Baby Olive did her part and slept through the last applause. Joseph went up to the altar to thank the parents for coming and gave Ruby a spontaneous hug after asking her to take another bow.

Ruby couldn't have removed the smile from her face if she wanted to. This event was the most significant thing she had ever done in her life, and she was proud of how well it had turned out.

As the crowd dispersed, she gathered the costumes, put them in burlap sacks, and walked Alice out to her wagon. "Ruby, I heard your pa and Granny aren't able to come for Christmas dinner, but I'm asking you one more time to consider joining us. Your granny said it would be all right with her."

"Thank you, Alice. Are you sure it's no trouble?"

"My family would love your company."

"Unless Granny has a need, I'll be there. I do appreciate the invitation, and I'll bring a sweet potato pie for dessert." As soon as she spoke, Ruby knew they didn't have molasses to sweeten a pie. Holiday or not, they didn't have such expensive ingredients at her house.

"Well, then, Joseph will pick you up in the wagon Christmas morning."

Joseph had saddled up Dublin. He was on his horse and waiting for her to come over. "Ruby, I'll ride home with you this evening to make sure you get there safely in the dark."

As Joseph held the reins, Leon and his woman friend approached from the shadows of the churchyard. "Ruby, look at you! A teacher and all. I'll be! I hardly remember you without your brother's overalls on." Leon put his arm around his lady friend, who wore lip color and seemed to know him pretty well. She leaned closer to snuggle into his shoulder. "This is Miss Sadie from Knoxville. Ruby and Mr. MacCallum, my teacher. Tell her what a good student I was, Mr. MacCallum." Leon slurred his words.

Joseph laughed politely but otherwise sat patiently on his horse as the conversation wound down. Ruby mounted Dublin and turned with her teacher to head up the mountain. She couldn't believe that Leon acted as he did around Joseph, making it seem he was so familiar with Ruby. Had he been drinking? Miss Sadie didn't seem to care what the others thought as she wrapped her arms around Leon in front of them.

"Ruby, I'd like to come by and visit with your pa and Granny while I'm home. Tell them I'll come by tomorrow afternoon. It'll be just like the old days." Leon slipped back into the shadows with Miss Sadie.

"I'll tell them. Have a good evening." She rode behind Joseph to the main path.

"Ruby, you be careful around Leon. He's up to no good—but I'm sure you know that. I worry about him." Joseph left it at that and started to hum the songs the children had sung for the program.

Ruby rode in silence behind him. Being with him seemed as natural as could be. He knew pretty much everything about her life: her mama's disappearance and how gruff Pa could be with her. Yet he still treated her with respect and kindness. The night was clear, the quarter moon barely lighting their way. The stars overhead shone brilliantly, giving credence to the Christmas story. Whether he knew it or not, his gift to Ruby was the way he acted around her—always proper and respectful—and the way he treated her with kindness, even when no one else did.

At her grandparents' home, he helped her unsaddle Dublin and gave the mare some hay for the night before he walked Ruby to the door.

"I'll come in the wagon around eleven Christmas morning. We'll make up a dinner package to send home to your granny and Pa. That way, you and Granny don't have to worry about preparing food."

As he rode off, she marveled at his goodness toward her. If only she deserved it.

# CHAPTER TWENTY-TWO

*R*uby woke up to something pinging at her bedroom window. Last night, she'd stayed up with Granny, who had a cough that wouldn't stop. As soon as Ruby treated her with mint leaf, Pa demanded the bedpan. She had hoped to sleep in this morning, her first day of Christmas break. But most likely, Ruby would have her hands full all day. She had so much to do before Christmas dinner with the MacCallums. Ruby sat up in bed and wrapped the quilt around her like a robe before she parted the curtains. Leon sat outside on his horse. He motioned for Ruby to come out. Talking to Leon was the last thing she wanted to do this morning, especially since he looked like he hadn't slept all night. However, if she didn't respond, he would pound on the door, as drunk as he looked. Where was his girlfriend?

Ruby wrapped the quilt around her and opened the back door, keeping the screen between them. "Leon Pennington, what are you doing here so early? It isn't a good time for you to visit Granny or Pa. Granny's sick, and Pa's in no shape to visit anyone. Go on home and get some sleep. Come back later—for a short visit—if you want to see them."

Leon appeared to be perplexed. "Aren't you glad I'm here? All I do is think of you." He leaned closer to the door, a broad smile on his face.

"Go home. Sleep it off so you don't embarrass yourself. Or go back to your girlfriend. Now, shoo." Ruby turned her head. disgusted at his behavior.

"Awww, Ruby, you know she isn't my girlfriend. I left her with my last delivery of moonshine last night. She's probably back at the train station, on her way home by now."

Leon opened the screen door and pushed his way into the parlor. "Mrs. Turner, Mr. Turner, it's Leon. I just came by to say hello."

Pa yelled from his bedroom, "Leee-on, I want to see you."

Ruby knocked lightly on the bedroom door, and Granny said she would come out shortly. Leon sat down on the rocking chair by the fire. He wore a sheepish grin as he stared at Ruby. As he rocked, his smile got wider. Ruby adjusted the quilt around her shoulders, making sure nothing was exposed.

"You aren't wearing bibbed overalls anymore, are you? I saw you around Mr. MacCallum, trying to act like a proper grown-up lady."

Ruby, uncomfortable without her stockings, wished he knew enough not to barge his way into their home this early in the morning.

Granny came out wearing her housedress, her hair still uncombed. "Leon, pardon my dress. We had no sleep last night, so we slept in this morning for a bit. But it's time to get up for chores now, anyhow. It's nice to see you, young man." She coughed into her cotton handkerchief. "Pa wants you to come into his room. Be prepared—he doesn't look the same."

Leon followed Granny into the bedroom, and Ruby stood at the doorway to observe him. He reached out his hand for Pa to shake, but Pa, too weak to grasp anything, waved instead. Leon, apparently shocked at the change, looked around, probably considering how to escape. Ruby caught a whiff of his fruity breath when he turned in her direction.

"It's good to see you, Mr. Turner, but I can't stay long. I'm in town for a week, and I'll come back later. Let me know if I can do anything for you."

Granny walked him to the kitchen. "There's very little to do now that we don't farm. Only feeding the milk cow and Dublin and gathering eggs. Ruby can do that. I appreciate the offer, though. Tell your parents hello from us, Leon."

Ruby walked him outside. "Leon, don't you do this again. We both know you've been out all night on the town, carousing. My grandparents don't need to see you this way. Go home to your family."

"Ruby, I have a present for you. It's a necklace so you won't forget about me."

Ruby took the small wooden box and lifted the hinged lid. In the middle of a black velvet lining sat an ivory cameo pendant with an angel carved into it. The gold chain, long enough to fit over her head, spilled out into her hand. She shoved it back into the box and clamped the lid shut before handing it back to Leon.

"Give this to your girlfriend. I don't want gifts from you. Please don't come here pretending you want to visit Granny and Pa just to pay me a visit. And don't ever come here again after you've been drinking."

Ruby wished he would forget about her. Their unfortunate childhood circumstances had made them workmates on Pa's farm, but that was all. Leon was trouble, and she had enough to deal with already. He should stay in Knoxville.

She watched him mount his horse and meander up the mountain. Before he rounded the hill, he turned to look at Ruby one last time. He took the jewelry box and pitched it off the mountainside, then picked up speed as he rode away.

# CHAPTER TWENTY-THREE

*R*uby tried on her new suit, a gift to herself for Christmas. She'd ordered it from the recent Sears, Roebuck, and Co. catalog at the general store with part of her school earnings. Ruby had to wait three weeks, but as the catalog promised, it arrived in the nick of time for Christmas. She liked the way it fit on her—the belt cinched in the slight bagginess around her waist. The reddish-brown color of the jacket went well with her red hair. The pin-striped skirt had no pleats, fitting snugly around her hips, and the hem fell right above her ankles. She pinned her hair up on the sides and left her curly bangs to fall around her eyes. This would have to do for today's visit. She slipped on her worn church shoes, wishing she had boots to complement the suit. After adjusting her belt one last time, she stood ready for Joseph to pick her up for Christmas dinner.

She had used a portion of the money Pa let her keep from her paycheck to buy her grandparents small presents. This was a first for her, buying gifts for Christmas. Usually, she wrote a short poem or made a bookmark for Pa's Bible. Because their old robes were in tatters, she'd bought them new ones. Pa would like the new down pillow Ruby made for him, and Granny would cherish the sack of taffy from the general store.

Ruby had picked out a pair of gloves for Joseph and hoped she wasn't too forward with such a personal gift. She had never seen a person lose gloves more than he did, usually dropping them in the woods on his way to or from school. She'd also picked out a bag of butterscotch candies for the MacCallum family.

Ruby found Granny sitting by herself in the rocker by the fire. "Oh, Ruby, you look so grown up. Sit down. I have something for you."

Granny's demeanor toward Ruby, calm and inviting this morning, surprised her. She remembered the days Granny delighted in whatever she did. But all that changed when Ruby's mama left town. She couldn't blame Granny, stuck with Pa and his ways all day. Granny patted the stool beside the rocker, indicating that Ruby should sit next to her. Granny handed her a large box at her side, a big brown bow tied at the top.

"I have gifts for you and Pa too. I thought I'd give them to you when I got back from the MacCallum house. Should I get them now?"

"Open this now. We'll open our gifts when you get back."

Ruby removed the lid to see a small-brimmed hat with a ribbon and buttons and a large feather attached to the side, like the high-fashion ones she had seen when she ordered her suit. It must have cost Granny a few dollars—a few dollars she didn't have to spare. Ruby placed it on her head and looked in the mirror to see how it set off her new outfit. She should have given it back to Granny, but she couldn't bear to part with it.

"I believe Mr. MacCallum is smitten with you, Ruby. Your pa and I want you to know that you have our blessing if you have feelings for him. He's a fine man and from an honored family. You could do much worse."

Ruby didn't know what to say. Had Joseph talked to her grandparents? She didn't think he was "smitten"—perhaps Granny imagined something that didn't exist. Though it was preposterous to conceive, it warmed her heart to think that he might be. He showed kindness to everyone, to all of his students. However, his conversations with her had become more personal lately. Did she have feelings for him? Considering a relationship with him opened the door to a life she hadn't imagined.

With tears in her eyes, Ruby reached over and hugged Granny. She couldn't remember the last time Christmas was more than an ordinary day or the last time she hugged this woman who'd raised her. Granny, stingy with her time and affection, would parcel out her warmth, basing it on her mood, all influenced by Pa.

"I'll be back with supper and gifts for you and Pa. Thank you, Granny, for this gift. It means more than you know."

RUBY WATCHED out the window as Joseph pulled his wagon into the lane. As he came into view, his rosy red cheeks matched his glowing smile in intensity. His breath rose above him in the cold. She had never met a person who seemed so content with life. She didn't give him a chance to come inside, but she hastily gathered the few presents she had and the crate with the sweet potato pie. She placed her new hat atop her head and draped herself in her winter wrap before she stepped outside, just as he pulled the wagon near the back door.

"Merry Christmas, Ruby. Here, let me help you with that."

He scrambled down from the wagon and placed her crate on the floorboard before helping her up onto the wagon seat. She kept his gift with her and tucked it under her legs, not sure when she would give it to him. Joseph walked around the horses and climbed into the wagon, presenting Ruby with a lap blanket to keep her warm on this chilly morning. He had a knowing smile on his face as if he had a secret.

"Ready to go, Ruby?"

"Joseph . . . I have a little gift for you. Open it before we go."

She handed him the slim box with a red ribbon on it.

"A gift for me? Why, you shouldn't have." He lifted the lid, and his head tilted back as he roared with laughter. "You know I'll probably lose these, right? But I'm happy you thought of me. I appreciate the gift."

He put the gloves on and pulled the lap blanket more securely around her again before they took off.

"You might lose them, but for today, you'll be warm on the wagon ride. Thank you for coming to get me this morning." Ruby smiled and sat back to enjoy the ride.

Joseph slapped the reins against his horse, and they started on their way. He started singing "Jingle Bells" poorly, and Ruby laughed and joined in the frivolity.

As they pulled in front of the MacCallum home, Joseph's younger sisters lined up at the window to watch them. Against the backdrop of pine boughs around the log cabin door and the snow-covered roof, their red hair and white Christmas dresses painted the picture of a perfect Christmas morning. The fireplace gave off a warm yellow glow behind the girls as she walked up to the porch. Joseph retrieved her pie from the crate and walked her inside. His younger sisters swarmed her at the door; clearly, the family had been eagerly waiting for her arrival.

Mrs. MacCallum received her hat and winter shawl and warmly hugged her. "Welcome, Ruby. I'm glad you could join us."

Ruby gave her the pie and the small bag of butterscotch candies for the family. It seemed insufficient, but Mrs.

MacCallum thanked her and walked her into the parlor, where the family was drinking hot cocoa around the fire. Ruby could smell a roast in the oven, and Joseph's older sisters took off their kitchen aprons to join the family in the parlor before the Christmas feast. Their Christmas tree had a pile of packages underneath. There appeared to be a gift for everyone in the family—the boxes all bound in different-colored ribbons, a sight Ruby had never seen before. One of Joseph's nieces toddled around the room with a ribbon around her neck, causing the rest of the family to laugh as she took it off and put it back on when someone came to retrieve it.

Joseph took off his gloves and placed them in his coat pocket before hanging his coat on the rack. He sat next to Ruby on the settee near the fireplace, exchanging glances with several of his siblings. He put his arm around her and gave her a little squeeze.

His father's booming voice started off the gift giving. "All right, then, let's begin the Christmas chaos. But first, let's bow our heads and give thanks for our family's blessings." He waited for the room to quiet. "Lord, we are not worthy but are grateful for the gift of your Son. Let us exchange these gifts with love and appreciation for all you have given us. Amen."

During the prayer, Ruby watched Joseph. His closed eyes made him appear at peace. He raised his face toward the ceiling and smiled. Joseph looked comfortable wherever he was. He must have sensed her observing him as he reached over and squeezed her hand at the "Amen." Ruby had never witnessed a man bow his head and pray like that. With joy! At church, Pa always stared straight ahead with his jaws clenched, as if he was as mad at God as he'd ever been at Ruby.

She snapped out of her thoughts, mesmerized as she watched Joseph with his family. His father distributed the gifts, and rising squeals of laughter filled the room. She accepted three boxes from the elder Mr. MacCallum. While others in the room opened their presents, Joseph encouraged her to unwrap hers. She untied the ribbon on the smallest one and found a handmade Christmas card from Maggie, who was busy across the room trying on a new hair ribbon. Joseph urged Ruby to keep unwrapping. The second gift was a tatted handkerchief from Mrs. MacCallum.

Ruby rose and walked to Mrs. MacCallum. "Thank you for the handkerchief. It's beautiful."

Mrs. MacCallum put her presents on the floor and stood to hug Ruby. "Merry Christmas, Ruby. You're very welcome. I intend to pass around your candy after we finish dinner."

Ruby returned to the settee when the commotion in the room stopped—the whole family became focused on her. Joseph handed her the unopened gift box before she sat down. He stood and got down on one knee in front of her. Giggling, his younger sisters all gathered around Joseph, and the rest of his family stood.

He took Ruby's hand in his and cleared his throat. "Ruby, I know this might be overwhelming to you and that it's unexpected as well. I want you to know I've come to care for you deeply. You're a wonderful person, giving to others around you with patience and grace. I enjoy being with you and would like you to consider becoming part of this family."

Ruby couldn't look Joseph in the eye. He was her teacher and almost ten years older than she was. But many girls her age married men much older, even widowers with children. It wasn't out of the question to consider him. He had rescued her from Pa's mistreatment when he hired her to help him in the classroom. He had seen her worst days when her classmates teased her, when she arrived at school in clothes that didn't fit, and when he came to the house to observe her doing chores in her brother's hand-me-downs. Joseph had a kind heart and a smile in response to everything that pleased him. Joseph—a decent, respected man from an honest, prosperous family—wanted her to be his wife. Could she base a marriage on that?

"Ruby Sullivan, will you marry me?" Joseph took the box from Ruby's lap and lifted the top to reveal a diamond ring, aged but polished.

Ruby moved her eyes from Joseph's sisters back to his face. His moist eyes creased at the corners because of that smile.

"That is my grandmother's ring, and she said she would be honored—and I would too—if you'd accept it with my proposal."

Ruby moved her hand from Joseph's and put it over her mouth, speechless. In the next few moments, she grasped that this man could be the answer to every question she'd ever had, and even those she hadn't asked yet. Her life would be comfortable with him.

And easy.

"Yes, Joseph MacCallum. Yes."

Joseph placed the ring on her finger. His sisters jumped up and clapped, and his young niece gave Ruby the ribbon from around her neck. Joseph helped Ruby to her feet.

He hugged her gently and whispered in her ear, "Do you mean it? You look surprised, and I understand that. I've talked to your granny and Pa, and they gave me their blessing. I can give you time to think about it if you want."

Joseph's mother moved him out of the way and gave Ruby another hug. Ruby couldn't help but count the number of hugs she had already received that morning—more than she had received in her entire childhood.

Alice threw her arm around Ruby's neck. "I always thought of you as a younger sister. I'm so happy about this."

Joseph's father shook her hand, then hugged her. "Welcome to the family, Ruby. Joseph is a good judge of character, and he thinks the world of you."

Shortly after, Mrs. MacCallum and Joseph's older sisters

retreated to the kitchen to prepare the Christmas meal. Ruby moved to join them, but Mrs. MacCallum told her to stay with Joseph. The younger children each hugged her and left to play with their new toys.

Ruby moved the ring around her finger and looked up at Joseph. "I wasn't expecting this, Joseph. I didn't realize you had that kind of feeling for me."

"It's complicated because you're my student. I don't want this to be improper. We'll wait until you graduate to get married —or, as far as that goes, even talk about a wedding. You have a kind heart, Ruby. I've seen it with your students. You work hard to do your best for them." Joseph patted her hand as he spoke. "When working with you as a teacher these last few months, it became clear to me that I wanted to be with you—if you'd have me. I know life has been difficult for you—you've had some real hardships. I want to take care of you as best as I can. This has to be quite a lot to take in. You may not love me now, but I care deeply for you, and I believe our love could grow if you'd give me a chance."

Ruby screwed up her face and considered his words. As hard as she tried, she couldn't contain the tears that ran down her face. "You surprised me, that's all. You've been so proper that I didn't even know how you felt. I never considered a personal relationship with you, let alone a marriage."

Joseph's famous smile faded slightly before he gave her a little side hug. "Think about this. If you decide you don't want to get married, just tell me, and I'll understand. But right now, let's go play with the children. I want to see if I can beat Albert at his new chess game."

"You go play. I want to help your sisters with dinner. They're so kind to me. I want to ask them a few questions about you, if you don't mind."

"I do mind, Ruby. I don't want them to scare you away." He winked at her, and the dimple on his right cheek appeared. He walked into the roomful of children and made himself at home with them.

Before joining the women in the kitchen, she examined the ring on her finger. How her life had changed from this morning. What in the world did Joseph see in her?

# CHAPTER TWENTY-FOUR

*March 1917*

On her ride to school, Ruby stopped by her favorite overlook to take in the scene before her: the contrast of the peaks of dark earth highlighted by residual snow, accented with pussy willow buds and the hint of green leaves sprouting. Winter, usually stopped in time, had flown by this year. She stopped and started Dublin along the way, taking in the mountain and taking control—instead of letting life take her for a ride. Graduating and getting married were significant milestones—much like the giant boulders that marked her ride to school. She only had to take the state's standard exams to graduate. It was time to move on with her life, one that included Joseph.

For the first time, Ruby had a relaxed routine: a few chores in the morning for Granny, a meditative ride to school, three hours of instruction with the children, and her own classwork in the afternoon. After school, Joseph rode home with her and helped Granny with barn chores or repairs. Ruby's relationship with Joseph hadn't changed much after their engagement; he still treated her like a colleague in the morning and a student in the afternoon. They only stepped out of their well-worn roles on Sunday visits with his family. Ruby couldn't believe how Joseph's family accepted her. Surely, they knew of her home life and poverty. They probably also knew all about her mama deserting her. But none of that seemed to matter to them; if they knew all her flaws, they loved her anyway.

At times, she caught Joseph watching her with a sidelong glance, a look of delight and contentment. Life with him would be more comfortable and secure than any other existence she could have imagined. It could be a happy life. True to his commitment to avoid impropriety, Joseph hadn't yet tried to kiss her. He did hug her freely on Sundays at his home. These were much like paternal hugs, and she welcomed them. However, his mother and sisters hugged her more often than he did. She had never seen a family so generous and warmhearted.

They didn't know—not any of them—that she didn't deserve their affection. She knew herself to be unlovable and feared the thought of days upon days of acting as if she belonged. Her tough exterior—her ability to hold in her real feelings—made life tolerable. Being vulnerable could only be used as a weapon against her. Her classmates teased her for being odd, indigent, motherless, and an outsider. They punished her for being herself, and the truth hurt. She learned to keep her guard up and pretend she didn't care, just to get by. Pa had told her every day of her life she wasn't worthy. Her only value came from the work she could produce for him. She would never let Joseph or the MacCallum family figure out that she didn't have a birthright that included love. Let them think that she did; she would be an impostor to protect herself.

Ruby coaxed her old mare, Dublin, to start again toward the schoolhouse. She had lessons to plan for her troubled students, the older ones who couldn't read at their expected level due to school absences. When she arrived, Joseph, as usual, had a toasty fire going.

"Good morning, Ruby. How are you this beautiful morning?"

"I'm well. It looks like spring is coming early. Did you see the buds on the trees? By the way, you left your scarf on the fence again. I hung it on the hook next to your coat."

His forgetfulness might be the only flaw he had. Besides the fact that he wanted to marry her, that is. Did he know the mistake he was making in committing his life to hers?

"I'm afraid I didn't notice. I must try to be a little more observant. I have good news. Alice's husband is organizing the men in our church to frame our new cabin. I'm almost finished planing the logs, so the framing will be in three weeks."

Having this discussion with him at school blurred the well-kept boundaries and roles they had set for themselves. Usually, he talked only of school-related things in the classroom, whether about the other students or her studies. Only on Sundays would they discuss their future.

He continued, "Do you want to look over the drawings for the house? I'd like your final approval of the room placement."

"Could it wait until Sunday, Joseph? I have to finish the exercises for the reading group this morning."

"Of course. I'm sorry. I'm just so happy to get our cabin started. But we can certainly wait until Sunday to discuss it."

He turned to his desk and sipped his coffee. He had already poured some for Ruby and placed it on her desk. She set to work for the thirty minutes she had left before she needed to ring the bell for the children to come in.

# CHAPTER TWENTY-FIVE

aking advantage of the warmer-than-usual spring weather, Joseph spent every Saturday clearing a place for a cabin down near the stream on his father's land. He felled trees and cleaned and planed the logs that would be the beams in their new house. After attending the Sunday-morning service with Joseph at his church, Ruby changed into her work dress to walk the property with him. For once, his sisters let them have time alone, and Joseph and Ruby meandered to the clearing.

"Ruby, this stake here will be the edge of the porch. I think we've set the house high enough on the banks to avoid floodwaters. See that line where the rocks are shelved into caves up there? That's the highest watermark during the last flood where the river turns east."

"I suppose it's good. Does it ever go higher, or was last year's storm one of the worst?"

"Father said the flood of '05 was pretty bad, but he believes the house to be high enough right here."

Ruby nodded. She considered this to be Joseph's home, and she didn't know a thing about floods. Joseph and his father had already decided. But she appreciated Joseph's efforts to include her. She stood there in silence with her finger across her lips, pretending to contemplate his questions.

"That large rock there is where I will place the stove. The kitchen will get the morning light through a window by the indoor sink. This tree will have to come out, I reckon," Joseph continued, not waiting for her reply.

Ruby walked through the knee-high weeds to stand in the center of the four cornerstones, trying to imagine living in this place. The sunlight and the view were the least of her considerations. How would it feel to live here with Joseph?

"Ruby, give it some thought and let me know if you have any ideas or opinions. I've had more time to consider it than you have, and I'm afraid I'm overwhelming you."

He moved farther away from the small creek and rattled on. "And here's where we'll sit on the porch and have our coffee in the morning and watch the moon at night. I think that big oak on the side will provide shade in the afternoon. I see us spending most of our free time here."

This was the part that troubled Ruby. She had hungered for a better place in life, and with Joseph at her side, the daily offerings would be sweet ones. He had it all figured out. But sweet or not, she couldn't imagine an entire lifetime sitting on that porch with Joseph.

THREE WEEKS PASSED, and the day of the framing had arrived. The night before, the men from Joseph's church had set up lunch tables made of sawhorses and planks and arranged the stage for the work area across the field. To be available early for the cabin raising, Ruby had agreed to do the shopping for Granny after school on Friday.

She rode up to the clearing, goosebumps on her arms from the morning chill. The dew on the grass caught the early rays of sunlight, making the field appear filled with broken glass. The hustle of the day's activity had already started. In the distance, a parade of wagons from town drove down the mountain path, sending dust high into the air behind them. The volunteers carried their spare shorter logs and wooden nails for the cabin.

Ruby rode over to where Joseph stood.

"Good morning, Ruby. This is our big day!"

He helped her dismount and stopped to kiss her on the cheek, the first time he had ever done this.

"I've started a fire for coffee already. Let me take care of Dublin before I take off to organize the men." Soon he ran across the field to greet the wagons.

The dewy grass soaked the bottom of her skirt, weighing it down as she walked to the fire to make coffee for the dozens of men and women expected to show up. The dampened hem clung to her ankles, tripping her up as she walked.

Deacon Preston's daughter Amanda crossed the field to the makeshift picnic table with her husband, Thomas. She hugged Ruby as if they had been best friends for years.

"I brought cinnamon buns and extra tin cups for coffee." She presented two baskets, both covered by linen tea towels.

Ruby placed them on the table. "Thanks, Amanda. Can I pour you some coffee?"

As Joseph's bride-to-be, Ruby knew she would inevitably encounter all of the townsfolk. Most of them didn't have much to do with her on shopping days in town, but she was a curiosity now. If they embraced her, it would be in deference to him.

She observed Thomas and Joseph placing logs around the four sides of the house, then poured the first cup for Amanda and herself. They might as well get to know each other.

Amanda pulled a kitchen chair from their wagon and sat while Ruby restlessly moved the buns from one spot to another for something to do. "Well, Ruby, what do your grandparents think about your betrothal to Joseph?"

Alice crossed the field before Ruby could answer, her daughter Olive in front of her with arms outstretched to greet Ruby.

"Bebe! Bebe!" Baby Olive yelled as she toddled toward Ruby. Ruby stooped to pick her up, thrilled that she had already picked out a pet name for her new aunt.

Alice poured herself coffee. "I hear about twenty men will be showing up today for the framing, so they should be able to knock it out in one day. We better be ready for hungry men."

Alice took over the conversation as she always did, sparing Ruby the anguish of answering Amanda's questions about her grandparents. Olive pulled on Ruby's hair ribbon, causing her hair to fall around her shoulders.

More men arrived, most of them without their wives. They approached Joseph and slapped him on the back before joining in to lay out the logs between the cornerstones. Ruby sat Olive down and gathered her hair up to repin it. She poured coffee into tin cups and placed them on a small plank of scrap wood so she could walk across the field to offer them to the men. Ruby kept her head down, trying to contain the drink from slopping out of the cups. The men stopped their activities as she approached.

"Gentlemen, this is my Ruby." Joseph helped her distribute the coffee to them.

"We didn't think this man would ever find anyone good enough to be his wife. You must be a special woman, Ruby." The man who ran the post office slapped Joseph's back.

Ruby lowered her head as the men laughed. She wasn't what they thought she was.

"Thank you for coming. Joseph and I appreciate your help today," she said.

When they finished their short break, Ruby took their empty

cups and they returned to the work at hand. Men, unlike women, took what came without much judgment.

When Ruby turned, a flash in the woods caught her eye. Through the clearing, she could see Leon standing, beckoning her to come over. Ruby shook her head at him. He showed up in the periphery all too often; she tucked away the thought that he followed her. Leon didn't belong here. He held up his jug of moonshine and pointed to it, indicating he would provide a sip if Ruby wanted it. She wrinkled her brow, vigorously shaking her head as a group of ladies with crates of food walked toward her. The women knew each other, and bleats of conversation followed them as they moved—much like a flock of sheep on the way to the barn. Most wore hats, more for adornment than for shade. She stopped at the edge of the woods to take in the entire scene. These people who had never been her friends had come to help build her future with Joseph. They'd shunned her before her engagement but had come in force today to show support. Leon, always acting like her buddy, hid in the fringes of the woods. Old pieces of her life intertwined with new ones, creating a tangled, snarled mess in her mind.

This dream home being built across the field didn't belong to her. The woods remained her sanctuary—not the clearing where the community was working together to establish her life with Joseph. Ruby looked over her shoulder as Leon sauntered farther into the dense forest. She considered running into the thicket to join him. Instead, she took a step toward the approaching women and the solid foundation of her future home.

# CHAPTER TWENTY-SIX

*May 1917*

*J*oseph built a porch on three sides of the cabin, the most prominent one on the front. He had placed two old rockers from his parent's house on the raised porch so they could sit and face the creek to talk when they visited. Ruby sat here and slowly rocked, in thought, and waited for him. Joseph had asked her to come to the cabin after school to give her opinion on a few things. He wanted to know how big to make the mantel and where to put the kitchen cabinets. He had tethered the logs for their bed frame and wanted to know which wall she preferred for the headboard. The framing and roofing were completed; Joseph only had to fill in the chinks between the logs now. All the details of home construction gave them something to talk about as they got to know each other—allowing them to avoid talking about their feelings as they wove their lives together.

Ruby had passed her state exams easily and applied to graduate in June. She now taught full-time to get the younger children ready for their exams. Her childhood memories of enduring Pa's abuse faded, and Ruby welcomed the new way her grandparents treated her. She became an extension of Joseph. He came and went at Granny and Pa's house now, stopping by to see Ruby or repair something at Granny's request. He brought order to their home. Pa didn't order Ruby around as before, and he spoke heartwarming words to Joseph about "his Ruby" when her fiancé sat in Pa's room for a visit. Granny treated her as she would a guest in her house. Ruby took it all in as a show—her grandparents putting on airs to look good. Perhaps after all this time, they recognized her as valuable, but only in Joseph's shadow. She didn't trust it; their next blow could be the one that knocked her flat. She kept her guard up.

She looked up to see Joseph riding down the path, awkwardly carrying several stone crocks on his lap. Joseph had stopped at his mother's kitchen on the way to pick up dinner leftovers. They could discuss the building's progress as they ate and listened to the babbling of the creek. Ruby stepped off the porch to take those from him before he dismounted.

"Let's eat first, Ruby. I'm hungry. But first, come watch me wash my hands at the inside pump I installed for the kitchen sink. You're going to love indoor plumbing, my dear." Joseph winked at Ruby.

"No more carrying water. And no more sloshing it all over myself. That sounds nice." Ruby carried the crocks that contained their dinner to the porch and pulled the rockers into the shade before sitting.

Joseph came outside and pointed to the corner of the side porch. "I've ordered an icebox to place over there. The crocks under the house will hold the pickled vegetables and meats under lard in the winter. But we'll have ice delivered in the summer to keep the milk, butter, and meat cool without having to store them in the spring." He sat and took an enormous bite of his ham sandwich.

The kitchen would be much more convenient than Granny's.

Ruby would no longer have to make daily runs to the spring. With running water and a drain to the outside for dirty water, it would be much easier to cook a meal. A wood rack on the back porch would provide easy access to the stove. She smiled at what a little prosperity could get her. The smokehouse and barn would be in the next building over, up the hill and downwind of the cabin. Joseph would start that next, as the house neared completion.

"Ruby, I've been thinking. Why don't we get married the week after you graduate?"

"That soon?"

"Well, our cabin will be mostly finished by then. We could start the summer off as husband and wife and have time to get settled before school starts again in the fall."

Ruby picked at her sandwich, tearing off pieces of ham to pop in her mouth.

"I've considered that the ceremony should be at your house so your pa can be there. And Granny too. I could ask Deacon Preston to meet us there on Wednesday afternoon, the week after graduation. What do you think?" Joseph finished his dinner and sat back in his chair, matching his rocking to hers.

"We could, I guess. But I don't even know what I would wear. I mean, I'd like to have time to make a special dress after school's out."

"I'll give you money to get a dress at the mercantile. Or you could ride the train to Livingston if you need a bigger store. I'd like my entire family to come to the wedding, if that's all right with you. And my mother would make a cake for us if I asked her to."

All of his words were swimming around in her head. After they were married, she would no longer be able to teach. The district had rules about married women teaching, and even if she were allowed to, they certainly wouldn't approve of a married couple being together in a classroom. So many ways her life would change! She would be spending a lot of time in this cabin as Mrs. MacCallum. Would she ever feel as if any of this belonged to her?

Joseph waited for her reply.

Ruby rocked in the chair and watched the river run swiftly. The waters, swollen from the melted snow, curled around, and water spilled up the sides of the bank. The water danced with a life of its own, going wide when it held too much and going deep to contain itself. If she entered the life laid out for her, all she had to do was jump in and keep her head above the water. For years, she'd swum against the current, fighting to survive. How easy it would be to glide for a change.

"Joseph, would you come with me tomorrow after school to talk to Granny and Pa about it? They'll be happy if they hear our plans from both of us. And especially happy if they can attend. Thank you—I'd like to be your wife sooner rather than later."

He jumped up and held out his hand to help her out of the rocker. Hand in hand, they crossed the threshold and discussed how large the hearth should be.

# CHAPTER TWENTY-SEVEN

*June 1917*

*A*ll of Joseph's family came to see her graduate, which made up for Pa and Granny not being there. Granny had said she couldn't leave Pa for that long, though she would join in the picnic afterward. Her brothers hadn't replied to her invitation.

Ruby took out the hairpins and removed the mortarboard from her head before leaving the graduation stage. She'd been asked to give the graduation speech and declined; she didn't have words of wisdom to impart to others. Ruby gave the welcome speech instead—short and to the point. She considered talking about what the class had been through together, but she could only be so truthful about that. Ruby wanted to thank the graduates' parents, but it only reminded her that her parents weren't there. In the end, she welcomed everyone and thanked Joseph for being their teacher. The MacCallum family beamed with pride, raising their chins so they could see over the people in front of them to watch her on stage.

Ruby received her diploma from the county trustee. Joseph

stood next to him and shook her hand. She wanted to hug her teacher. Her fiancé. He didn't contain his pride in her achievement. She glanced out into the audience to check if, by chance, her brothers had shown up, but they hadn't come. Did they know she was to get married in a few days? She had changed her definition of family in recent weeks. A family celebrated the good times with you and stood by you during the bad. Her brothers hadn't been in touch with her in years. She'd heard that Robert had married and lost his job in Knoxville. No doubt, he ran illegal whiskey now to keep his family fed. Would he ever return to the mountains?

Did her mama ever think about her?

The ceremony ended all she had ever known. Besides the woods, the classroom had been her comfortable place—she was equal to anyone there. She would see what the next stage of her life held. She didn't know if it would be as satisfying as book learning.

Joseph talked to his students' parents after the ceremony and to the trustees for a few minutes after that. Ruby wandered outside and joined Joseph's family for a picnic they had brought to celebrate the graduation, a tradition honored by the community for years. She was flattered the MacCallums were doing it on her account. Maggie patted the blanket next to her to show Ruby where to sit. Mrs. MacCallum passed the bucket of fried chicken to Ruby after she sat down. Alice took off her hat and placed it on her youngest daughter's head to keep her occupied while the family ate their dinner. Albert poured her a glass of tea and brought it to her. Despite her promise, Granny hadn't made it after all. In four days, Ruby would officially be a MacCallum and forever linked to this family.

~

RUBY DRESSED IN HER BEDROOM, with Maggie helping her get ready. Ruby had insisted on a simple dress, even after Joseph allotted money to buy something more elaborate. She glanced at herself in the mirror. The dress had lace around the neckline, and the lace extended to the three-quarter-length sleeves. The skirt was straight with a band around the waist. The only other adornment was the peach ribbon woven into the waistband and a matching ribbon to tie in her hair. Ruby had cut her own hair comparatively short, a radical change from how she usually wore it. Her curls swirled around her face, framing it and making her look more mature. Maggie brought her mother's beads, and Ruby happily obliged her request to wear them. Having Maggie here took some of the pressure off her. She had no idea what the MacCallums were talking about with Pa and Granny in the other room, but she had to let it go. This day was much bigger than she was, and whatever the conversation, it was out of her control.

Ruby cracked her bedroom door slightly and looked out to see Joseph talking with Deacon Preston. The deacon had been a constant in her life, beginning with the horrendous day of her birth; he had been the one to tell her mama about her papa's death that day. He preached at the church where her family used to go. Granny and Mrs. MacCallum sat and politely laughed about something. True to the hillbilly tradition of not liking someone until you had reason to warm to them, Granny remained guarded with Mrs. MacCallum. She held her hand over her mouth and looked nervously toward Pa's bedroom as if he might beckon her to assist him at any moment. Joseph stood in the doorway to the bedroom and laughed at something Pa said or did. She couldn't imagine what he and Pa discussed.

Her brothers didn't come. She'd held out hope that they might surprise her. But having them there only would have added to the mixed-up feelings she had this morning. She had already packed her clothes and moved them over to the cabin for her first night there. Whatever she'd forgotten, she could retrieve in the next few weeks. Mrs. MacCallum had delivered a hope chest made by her husband, filled with embroidered tea towels and a quilt made by her and Joseph's sisters. Why was it called a hope chest? Granny gave her some new sheets as a wedding gift, a set she'd ordered from Sears, Roebuck, and Co. Ruby appreciated what it had cost Granny, both in effort and treasured coins. Granny had made some shortbread cookies for the wedding and placed them on the table next to the cake Mrs. MacCallum had brought. Granny would brew coffee after the ceremony.

Ruby looked one last time at herself and smiled at Maggie, who kept reaching for her hands.

Alice knocked on her door. "Ruby, do you need anything?"

"Come in. How do I look?" Ruby, holding her breath, stepped back to let her in.

"Beautiful. I approve, and Joseph will too." Alice hugged her and fussed over her hair, arranging curls around Ruby's face.

Ruby opened the bedroom door. Everyone in the parlor stopped talking as she entered. Her new buckled shoes made the only sound in the room, a clickety sound on the wooden floor as she walked across it. It was time for Deacon Preston to conduct the ceremony. Joseph rose and stood on the deacon's left at the front of the room. Ruby came and stood in front of him after taking a moment to peek into Pa's bedroom to be sure he could see them in the parlor. Joseph smiled from ear to ear. She turned to look at him. The elder Mr. MacCallum rose to bring the Bible to Deacon Preston and returned to a seat next to his wife.

"We are gathered together, loved ones of Joseph Absalom and Ruby Beatrice, to celebrate the joining of families." As the deacon spoke, Ruby thought about the lack of family she brought to the table.

Joseph turned to her and took her hand.

"Joseph, do you take this woman to be your wife? To have and to hold from this day forward, as long as you both shall live?"

"I do." He smiled and then bit his lips to contain his joy.

"Ruby, do you take this man to be your husband? To have and to hold from this day forward, as long as you both shall live?"

Ruby stopped to ponder the words, "As long as you both shall live." That was forever, wasn't it? It seemed like a lofty promise to a man she barely knew. But she should consider herself lucky to be rescued by him.

"I do."

"I now pronounce you husband and wife."

Maggie jumped up and down and ran to hug Ruby. Joseph embraced his mother and father, and then they hugged Ruby too.

Granny rose to boil the water for coffee. They would have to take turns eating because Pa and Granny only had six place settings in their house. Ruby rose to help in the kitchen.

"Go fetch a bucket of water, Ruby." Granny moved faster than Ruby had seen her do for a few years.

Ruby lingered, but Granny didn't have anything else to say to her.

"Can you believe I'm a married woman, Granny?"

"Remember that you're not any better than anyone else. Just because you have money now, you ain't any better." Ruby had let her guard down, and Granny's comment stung.

Ruby got the pail of water, and when she returned, Mrs. MacCallum was helping Granny slice the cake.

"Go on into the parlor and visit. It's your wedding day, after all. I'll take care of this," Mrs. MacCallum said.

How often would these two families be together now that they had a marriage in common?

Pa bellowed something, and Joseph and Ruby scuttled into

his room. Joseph grabbed Pa's hand, their thumbs wrapped together, and they stayed that way for a bit. Pa had had some trepidation about the service not taking place in a church. But after a few words from Granny, he'd appreciated that Ruby was marrying into the right family—no matter where the ceremony occurred. Ruby felt assured that Joseph would help take care of the Turner family, for a while anyway.

Deacon Preston asked Joseph and Ruby to sign the wedding certificate to register it with the state of Tennessee. Ruby almost signed it "Ruby Sullivan" before realizing her name had changed.

Ruby MacCallum. She tried her name on for size but had difficulty believing it was hers. From this day forward, she had a new identity. Joseph kissed her on the cheek after they signed and hugged her side. Looking into her eyes, he said, "Hello there, Mrs. MacCallum."

"How do, Mr. MacCallum." For the first time, Ruby allowed herself some joy on this day. Mrs. MacCallum, indeed.

Maggie delivered a piece of cake each to Joseph and Ruby. They rejoined Pa in his room to eat it. Pa tried to smile at her, lifting the right side of his mouth before drool dribbled down his chin.

Shortly after, Ruby and Joseph loaded up into Joseph's wagon and headed to their new home. Rufus and Albert banged some pot lids from the back of a cart together as they rode away. Ruby waved to everyone gathered on the porch and said goodbye to her joyless years on this farm. They rode past her papa's grave and onto the road to her new cabin.

Joseph held both reins in one of his large hands and reached for her with the other. "I love you, Mrs. MacCallum. Let's go home."

# CHAPTER TWENTY-EIGHT

*R*uby woke up to find the bed next to her empty. She smelled bacon cooking and saw a cup of coffee on the nightstand, warm swirls of steam fighting their way through the cold mountain air. Joseph hummed in the next room, something he never did in the schoolhouse. She sat up and threw back the covers, not believing she had slept in so late. Her new nightgown was white and coarse, and her inner thighs felt sticky from the night before. She looked for her shawl so she could use the outdoor privy, then remembered the chamber pot in the water closet off the bedroom. She got up and did her business.

Joseph poked his head through the room as she opened the water closet door. He was carrying a tray with bacon, fried eggs, and a biscuit, adorned with a painted trillium he'd picked and tied with twine.

"Good morning, Ruby. I was hoping you'd be able to sleep in a bit. And I hope you're hungry. Breakfast in bed for the bride this morning."

Ruby stopped to take this in, crossing her arms over her

breasts, naked beneath the thin nightgown. In all her days, she had never received a gift like this one. He must have been up for hours to get the fire going, gather the eggs, mix the biscuits, and cook for her. This new husband baked biscuits, delivering them with flowers while humming.

Ruby climbed back into bed, and Joseph came over and laid the tray on her lap. He placed his pillow behind her back, careful not to spill anything.

"Joseph, this is so nice. I'm sorry I didn't get up to cook for you. Please don't think badly of me." She pulled the covers up to her neck to cover her nightgown. She didn't have the heart to follow her instinct to pull away from him.

"Truly my pleasure, sweet bride. We'll get a morning routine down soon enough." Joseph beamed from ear to ear and leaned over to kiss her cheek.

Ruby punctured the fried egg, and the yolk covered the bacon. Joseph had put pepper on the eggs, something Granny never took the time to do. She liked these little touches that required energy and consideration—they weren't available when you were trying to survive from one day to the next.

Joseph retrieved a chair from the kitchen and brought it to her bedside. He carried a plate of breakfast he'd made for himself and set his coffee on the table next to them. She studied her husband as he ate. He hadn't combed his hair, and behind his small bald spot, the longish hairs stood at attention. With his shirt unbuttoned at the top, his reddish chest hair stuck out. Egg yolk slid out of the corner of his mouth and ran down his chin. To wipe it up, Joseph grabbed a napkin his sister had embroidered as a wedding present for them. Her teacher had jumped off the pages of a schoolbook and now sat before her in their bedroom.

He had been tender last night. He'd carried her across the threshold of their new home. As they shyly undressed for bed, he gave her the option of waiting to consummate the marriage. She kissed him and told him she was ready. Ruby had thought she would be the inexperienced one, but she would bet it was Joseph's first time as well. She remembered watching her mama in the woods with that man when she was a child. Her first night with Joseph was nothing like that—no laughter, only practical maneuvers as they tried to get to know each other. He sought her eyes, and she avoided his gaze. She saw him naked after, and it wasn't what she'd expected. He turned away from her to dress, exposing soft, curly hair all down his backside. His ribs stuck out on his tall, lean body when he bent over to step into his undershorts. Truth be told, married life was like one of the plays they put on at school. There was a script to be followed and places for everyone to stand. The costumes were designated, and everyone acted in the role assigned to them. She'd played her part. Now all she had to do was insert her soul into this marriage.

Joseph gave her a broad smile, exposing his crooked front teeth filled with remnants of biscuit. "I thought we might take a ride this afternoon and explore the back pasture. My mother invited us to dinner, if you want to join the family. It's totally up to you."

Ruby had never been given the option of deciding her day. Was this what ordinary people did? She took a bite of bacon, then dunked the biscuit in the runny yolk. She relished the fact that her husband had cooked it for her. So far, it was the best meal of her life. Joseph got up and retrieved two more biscuits, bringing the jar of homemade grape jelly from his mother's pantry.

"Would you like more coffee, Ruby?"

She didn't know what she wanted.

"Yes, please . . . Could you add more cream this time?"

Joseph seemed to delight in her answer as he took her cup,

then returned to the kitchen to fill it. He came back to her, smiling as he served her.

"Joseph, when we finish our coffee, climb back into bed with me. Let's have a lazy morning, and then we'll figure the day out together. How does that sound to you?"

# CHAPTER TWENTY-NINE

*September 1917*

uby kissed Joseph before he headed out the door. After three months of being at home together, duty called her husband. The commissioners had decided to open another school in the western part of the county, so Joseph's student count would be lower, requiring only one teacher at the old one-room schoolhouse.

Ruby watched him through the window, riding down the path out to the mountain road. He stopped and turned around to look back at the house. She glanced over to see his lunch still on the table.

She grabbed it and walked outside to hand the satchel to him as he was riding back to retrieve it. "Have a good day, husband."

Ruby had learned his quirks. He was forever forgetting things. It was not unusual for him to turn around three or four times to retrieve something before he disappeared for the day down the mountain road.

Joseph had been right about the layout of the house; the

morning sun warmed the kitchen, and the trees in the back shaded the porch from the afternoon sun. The gurgling of the stream outside their opened bedroom windows put them to sleep at night. Joseph had made some furniture to fill their home, and she'd set about to further decorate it with braided rugs, curtains, and such. They'd turned the bedroom on the far side of the house into a reading room; Joseph placed a leather rocker beside a small bookshelf, and he built a secretary's desk and would use the space to plan his lessons at night. They would move it to the parlor when children came.

She finished cleaning up the kitchen from breakfast and went out to pull a few weeds from their garden. The nights had started to frost, but potatoes and carrots remained to harvest before they'd turn the ground for the winter. The smell from the chicken coop beyond the garden indicated that it needed to be cleaned again. She would do that tomorrow morning, even though Joseph didn't like it when she took on outside chores; he considered it his job. When she leaned over to pluck the sedge that had popped up in the row of carrots, she put her other arm under her breasts. They felt tender, but not like the first days of her monthly. She had eaten part of a cold biscuit to calm her stomach when she woke up this morning. She suspected she might be with child—she remembered Alice talking about those symptoms during her last pregnancy.

She would talk to Alice later today at the quilting circle. Alice had asked Ruby to come over early to help set up the small luncheon before the quilting. It was still a novel experience for Ruby to be part of the MacCallum family. She never had a sister, and being with Alice was a cross between having the mother hers wasn't and a friendship she had observed—but not experienced—with her classmates. In her mind, Alice remained her teacher, the one who interpreted family jokes and traditions for her. Alice had no expectations from her—she simply allowed

Ruby the space to assimilate into the large family. Ruby had become part of the kitchen crew for the family Sunday meals, donning her own apron and laughing with them as they worked together. She couldn't help but laugh at their antics, but it was like speaking a foreign language when she tried some of her own. Ruby even learned how to laugh at herself sometimes. Last week, she'd made gravy for the family meal, and despite her stirring and adding more cream, it turned out like a thick paste. They joked, "Don't let Ruby make the gravy next time," and she acted insulted, but she laughed louder than they did at the teasing.

Ruby finished dressing and gathered her sewing supplies to take with her. Joseph had already saddled her horse before he left that morning. On her short ride into town, she looked in awe at the maple leaves, which had turned yellow-orange on the mountainside beyond. Ruby never had such a view when she lived with Granny and Pa; they lived on the rocky side of the mountain, where it was much less picturesque. She stopped to consider how much she enjoyed being married to Joseph.

Ruby opened Alice's door and heard her daughters shriek, "Ruby's here!" They all ran to hug her.

"Ruby, can you corral the girls and get them to clean up their dolls? They might listen to you."

Alice stopped to hug Ruby and hurried off to the kitchen to stir the bean soup for the meal. Alice's three girls were still too young to go to school—the oldest had recently turned five—but her older stepdaughters attended regularly. Ruby helped move the chaos to the back bedroom the girls shared. She came out, and the girls followed her like ducklings after a mother duck. She put her hand on her hips, and the girls did the same in a row behind her. They adored their new aunt, who seemed like a playmate to them.

"What can I do, Alice? Set the table? I'll get the girls to help me."

"Yes, that would be great. Only soup bowls and small plates for cornbread are needed. There will be eight of us," Alice replied.

Ruby had invited Granny to join her the last time the group met. She felt obligated to ask her to her new house. But Granny wouldn't leave Pa, and Ruby secretly cheered that Granny had declined. She found it best to visit Granny and Pa with at least one other person present, usually Joseph. It kept them from telling her not to become "highfalutin" and preaching to her about the perils of pride. She and Joseph spent several Saturdays going over to help Granny. Granny always needed repairs on the house, and Ruby took them a cooked meal. She knew that Granny needed a break from Pa. But if Granny broke into criticizing her, Ruby stepped outside to get away from it. They reserved Sundays for gatherings at the MacCallum house—her reward after a day of punishment.

The girls settled down and went back to their room to play. Ruby filled water glasses from the indoor pump. "Alice, can you keep a secret? I think I'm going to have a baby. I haven't told Joseph yet."

Alice came over and hugged her, spilling the last glass Ruby had filled. "That's great news. I'm so happy for you two. Although, I would have offered you a couple of my kids if you wanted them. You just had to ask."

They both laughed.

"Ruby, I'm teasing. I'm pleased with your news. How are you feeling?"

Ruby backed away from her embrace. "I've noticed some changes. I felt sick this morning when I woke up. How am I ever going to be the kind of mother you are? I didn't have a good example myself, as you know."

"We have a few months to talk about this. I'll tell you all the mistakes I made, so you know what not to do." Alice laughed. "But you'll be a good mother. And I'm happy for Joseph—he's waited a long time to be a father. I think he'll be a good one, even at his old age."

Ruby dreaded telling Pa and Granny and would wait as long as possible to let them know. She didn't want to subject her baby to their cold harshness and criticism. And she certainly didn't want their advice on parenting.

But she did look forward to telling Joseph. He always had a jocular look in his eyes and started his sentences with a half chuckle. This news would make him break into an unrestrained smile. He would be a good father.

Ruby rode home after the quilting circle ended, her face hurting from all the laughter. She hoped to get a short nap before starting supper. She entered the barn to dismount and unsaddle her horse. Leon stood against the stall gate with a piece of field wheat hanging out of his mouth, his cap sideways on his head. She hadn't seen him since he lingered in the woods during the house framing six months ago. He wasn't a boy any longer. He smiled a slow smile, and his eyes followed her.

"Leon, you just keep appearing out of nowhere. What are you doing here? Shouldn't you be at work?"

He helped her off the horse, taking the saddle and placing it on the saddle bench. Ruby led the animal into the stall and threw some hay at her. Joseph would brush both horses when he got home from school.

"Ruby, I took the day off and took the train in this morning. Aren't you glad to see me?"

"You can't visit me anymore. You can't. It's not proper now."

"I was just delivering something in town and thought I'd drop by. Why can't I visit? We're old friends, aren't we?" He placed his hand on his hip and acted surly, something Ruby hadn't seen in him before. Maybe she'd treated him harshly.

"Besides, I need help with an accounting question. I figured you could help me out with the math," Leon said. "But if you're too good now—"

"This isn't a good time, and I'm not too good, so stop that. Is it a quick question? Or can you leave it with me and get my answer in the morning when Joseph's here? You *are* leaving on the train tomorrow to go back to work, right?"

"Sorry I bothered you. I don't understand you sometimes. You didn't use to worry about being proper." Leon kicked the horse stall for emphasis before he settled down. "I don't need your help after all. Forget it."

Ruby turned to go into the house. "Leon, it's not a good idea for us to be friends. I don't want to mess up. Do you understand? This is the first good thing I've ever been a part of, and I need you to leave me alone."

She hurried to the side porch and sat on the rocker outside, watching him ride away. He didn't look back at her.

Ruby snoozed through the afternoon winds and woke to find Joseph on the rocker next to her, barely moving so he didn't wake her. It was way past suppertime.

"Joseph, I didn't know you were home. You must be starving. I'm sorry."

She jumped up to go into the kitchen and sat back down when the wave of nausea hit her. "I think I'm going to be sick."

Joseph fetched a pail and returned in the nick of time. She wiped her mouth on her sleeve, took the bucket from Joseph's hands, and set it beside her. She stood, pulled him closer to her, and looked up to meet his eye.

"How do you feel about being a father?"

Ruby bent over and retched again, and Joseph knelt and pulled her hair back as she did so. He rubbed her back and waited to see if her stomach had settled.

"I'm going to be a father? Are you sure?"

Ruby nodded.

Joseph lit up from the news. He hugged her, and she backed up to fold her arms, protecting her sensitive breasts.

"Joseph, can you cook supper tonight? I'm afraid I just ran out of steam."

"You bet I will." He still hadn't stopped smiling. "I would do anything for you."

# CHAPTER THIRTY

*May 1918*

"Just one more push and I think we've got ourselves a baby, Ruby. Wait until I tell you, then give it all you've got." Doc Livingston wiped his brow with his handkerchief. He sat down gingerly in the rocker in the corner, looking every bit his sixty-some years.

Ruby relaxed her face after that last contraction. When the next pain came, she let out a shattering howl. Why had no one told her how much this would hurt? Alice had promised it wasn't much more severe than menstrual cramps. Alice had fibbed, causing Ruby to forgo the mountain tradition of putting the ax under her bed to cut the pain during birth.

"Okay, push. Push! Bear down—"

Ruby grunted, reaching back to grab the headboard behind her as she worked to expel the baby. As her body did its work, she focused her gaze on the spring storm developing outside her window. She felt a powerful release and took a deep breath. It was almost as if the clouds had carried a child with them. The baby wailed as Doc held it high in the air.

"Well, well, well. Look at this. You have a little boy, Ruby. With a head full of hair." Doc placed her son in her arms. "Here, hold him while I attend to things."

She wasn't sure she wanted to hold him close to her. He wore blood everywhere and stared at her in stillness, as though he expected her to know what to do next. He seemed wise for a newborn, searching her face for answers she didn't have.

Doc accepted the afterbirth and placed it in the oaken bucket Ruby had put at the end of the bed; Joseph would bury it later. Doc opened the door to let in her husband. "Come in and meet your son, my friend."

Joseph had been waiting right outside but exploded into their bedroom, hitting the half-opened door in his haste to meet his son. "Is he healthy, Doc?"

"Healthy as can be. I bet this boy probably weighs about six pounds. I'll check him over before I leave, but I counted ten toes. Here he is, Joseph. Come take a look."

Joseph came to the head of the bed and knelt to kiss Ruby first, then looked over his newborn son. "Hello, little one. You certainly are an observer. That's your mama. You have a beautiful mama, my son." He touched his son's cheek, hesitantly at first.

The little guy sucked on Joseph's finger, trying to eat. Ruby looked at her son with an exhausted smile, not knowing what to do.

"Should I feed him, Doc?" asked Ruby. She was sleepy; maybe feeding him could wait.

"He'll let you know what he wants and needs. See him turn to Joseph's finger? He probably would eat. Offer him your breast and see what he does."

She positioned the baby and opened her birthing gown. Joseph gave her another pillow to put under the baby for support.

"Turn to one side, Ruby, and I'll remove the birthing sheet. Later, you'll need to clean up a little better." Doc dropped the sheet in a wooden crate outside the room.

The baby latched onto her nipple and she started crying, unable to contain her tears. Confused about her reaction, she stared out the window instead of at the baby in her arms. Joseph stroked her arm that held the baby.

When Doc finished cleaning and packing his things, he interrupted mother and baby, handing Ruby his handkerchief for her tears. "Let me take a look at this little one. It'll just take a minute."

Doc breathed on the stethoscope to warm it up before putting it on the baby's chest. But the little boy spread his arms and legs in all directions when he encountered the cold metal on his body.

"You have a beautiful, healthy son. Congratulations to you both." Doc picked up his packed bag to leave. "Joseph, can I see you in the other room before I go?"

He spoke to her husband in the living room, probably not realizing how far his deep voice would carry into Ruby's room. "I remember the night Ruby was born. What a night that was! After coming to get me, her father lost control of his wagon in the storm on the way back to his house. He died that night when the wagon overturned. I can't help but think how different Ruby's life would have been if she'd known her father. He was a good man like you, Joseph. Belle, her mother, was never the same after he died. And now Ruby's a mother. She's had it rough, and she'll need your help. She hasn't seen herself what a good mother is, so it might not come naturally to her."

The baby boy turned back to her breast, and he latched onto her nipple, pulling with a force Ruby wasn't expecting. The milk flow had its own energy, so she didn't have to participate except to support the baby's head. She watched him, and again tears fell down her cheeks. Is this love? Is this how joy felt? She held her boy in her arms, and in a way, he also held her. He watched her in stillness, not taking his eyes from hers, and seemed content to be close to her. How had her mama felt when Ruby was born? She hadn't heard from her mama since she left in the middle of the night nearly nine years ago, leaving her with Granny—as if Ruby meant nothing to her. That loss had seared into her soul and left an invisible scar.

Joseph returned to the room, holding some handwritten instructions. Ruby wished someone would give her a manual on what to do and how to feel.

"Ruby, what do you want to name him?"

"How about Timothy, for my pa and yours? And Joseph after you. Timothy Joseph. Timmy, for short."

"I think that's a grand name. So, what do you make of this boy?"

Ruby didn't know how to answer that. She couldn't find honest words and had little energy to try. So, she shrugged and gave her best effort, stretching her lips into a smile to please him.

He filled the silence. "After you finish feeding him, let me help you up so you can wash. I'll get a clean nightgown for you and put fresh sheets on our bed. Doc said he'd stop by your granny's on his way back to town to let them know. I imagine they'll be over later this afternoon to see our son."

After Ruby and Timmy napped that morning, Joseph prepared lunch for her. She had no sooner finished eating when a wagon with three people in it came up the long path. A man in the back of the wagon held Pa up while Granny guided the horses in front.

"Ruby, we're getting visitors already. I do believe that's your brother Robert in the back with Pa. I didn't know he was in town."

Ruby sat up. "Help me up. I want to sit in the chair in the parlor. Can you take Timmy for a moment?"

She grabbed her housecoat and a blanket to stuff around her legs. Joseph placed a pillow next to her in the chair and handed Timmy back to her. Right after Ruby got settled, Granny opened the door without knocking.

Granny came over to the chair and took the baby from Ruby's arms. "Why, look at this! Doc says we have ourselves a little boy."

Before Ruby could respond, Robert came in carrying Pa and placed him on the sofa with his back against one of the sofa arms. He lifted Pa's legs and put them over a goose-down pillow, then turned his head away from Pa as he sat him down. Joseph brought the matching pillow from their bed to place behind Pa's back to make him comfortable.

Ruby hadn't seen her brother in about four years. She observed him while Granny fussed over baby Timmy. Robert had filled out quite a bit, and his arm muscles had flexed as he leaned over to put Pa down. Given how formidable Pa used to be, it must have shocked Robert to be able to lift him so easily. Her brother had a full beard now, and his hair was receding a little bit at his temples. He was missing a front tooth on the bottom as if he had been in a fight or something.

Granny inspected her grandson after pulling back the yellow baby blanket Ruby had crocheted. Joseph brought over two kitchen chairs so they could all sit in the parlor together. Robert sat in the chair farthest from Ruby. He bit his lower lip and sucked that part of his mouth into the space where the tooth had been. He looked rough and worn.

"Well, what's his name, Joseph?" Granny asked.

"We named him Timothy Joseph. After Ruby's father and mine too. We'll call him Timmy."

Timmy started to whimper, and to soothe him, Granny got

up and did a bouncy dance step across the room. Pa drooled when he smiled as Granny leaned over to show Timmy to him.

"How does it feel to have a grandchild, Granny?" Robert asked.

"Pretty good, all right. See that Turner chin on him? You can't miss the resemblance."

The loud cries from Ruby's son and the chatter of her immediate family filled the room. Pa tried to talk, but it came out as a howl. Not one of them asked about her. She had just given birth a few hours ago, but she was fine—thanks for asking. They spoke as if she wasn't there. Joseph came over and stood behind her chair, placing his hand on her shoulder and rubbing it gently. She wanted Granny to give Timmy back to her. "Damn it —that's my baby!" she almost screamed.

"Tell me, Robert, when did you get into town?" Joseph asked.

"Oh, I stopped for a short visit on my way back to Knoxville. I just went to see my ma in Kansas. Did you know that's where she is, Ruby? Our brother lives there too. She owns a tavern and lives in a big house in Salina," Robert said.

"I've forgotten my manners. Forgive me. Would anyone like any coffee?" Not waiting for a reply, Joseph went into the kitchen to heat water, leaving Ruby to deal with private family matters on her own.

"I didn't even know if she was alive or dead, Robert. How would I know if she had a big house?" Ruby said.

"Ma's made it. She's rich. I'm thinking of quitting my job and joining her. What do you think about that? And she has a son too. He's six."

"A son, huh? Well, I suppose you can do what you want," Ruby replied.

Ruby tried to imagine her mama being here and, as hard as she tried, couldn't place her in the room. Getting news about her was like reading a book about her—she knew the character on paper, but not in her heart. The man across the room—her brother—had also deserted her in her childhood. When he talked, memories she had pushed down as best she could erupted.

"Well, you don't have to be that way, Ruby. We don't all get to move in with someone who has lots of money, just like that. You don't know how easy you have it, do you?" His temper flared as he spoke.

Ruby took a deep breath and studied Robert. Did he know he had horse manure on his boot? Joseph would clean the rug when they all left. Her husband observed them all from the next room. He continued his kitchen tasks, but his head had turned toward the parlor as he took in every word.

"I might as well say it since nobody else does. You aren't treating Granny and Pa right. They raised you, and you barely give them the time of day now that you live in a fancy house. You aren't any better than we are, Ruby. There. It needed to be said." Robert raised his chin high. His eyes protruded as he glared at her.

Ruby considered the words hurled at her. Robert hadn't contributed anything since he left, not coming for Christmas or when Pa got sick. Her brother had left the mess to her. He wrote home at first, but then not at all. She had invited him to her wedding, but she didn't hear a thing from him. She shook her head and squared her shoulders, refusing to accept the words he threw her way.

"And I'll also say this, Ruby. Your baby's going to turn out as you did—worth nothing at all. But uppity, just 'cause of where he was born. Let's not all go on pretending this is something better than it is." Robert looked at Granny and Pa for support. He then stared at Ruby, daring her to respond.

Granny nodded. She continued to hold Ruby's son as if he were a hostage.

Had Granny talked to Robert about her? Ruby stopped breathing, and heat flushed her worn-out body. She exhaled loudly, at last, looking across the room at her son in Granny's arms, then at Joseph, who had entered the parlor. The accusations imploded inside her, wiping out the last bit of energy she had.

"That's it. Out. All of you. I will not have my wife treated this way by anyone. This day is supposed to be the happiest day of our lives. We won't tolerate anything like this from family or anyone else. Out! And don't come back until you can respect Ruby and this family." Joseph loosened his collar, pointed to the front door, then opened it, almost yanking it off its hinges. He made a sweeping motion with his arms to usher them out.

Ruby's mouth fell open—she had never heard a harsh word from Joseph. She was as shocked that he'd stood up for her as she was that her brother had spewed his hatred. Joseph held the door, allowing Robert time to gather Pa from the sofa and carry him out of their house. Robert hesitated a moment and glared at Joseph as if he might continue his tirade. Pa growled to show his support. But Joseph, a full four inches taller than Robert, stared them both down, daring them to speak.

Granny handed the baby back to Ruby. "He's right about some of the things he said, Ruby. After you got married, you dropped us. Robert's words were harsh, but there's truth to them. After all of the things we did for you, you could come by and help us out more than you do." Granny followed Robert out the door, and Joseph slammed it behind them.

The words echoed in Ruby's ears as she adjusted the blanket around her new baby. Damn them! Damn them all to hell. Joseph paced the room, the vein in his neck pulsing; gradually, it slowed as he walked back and forth before her. Baby Timmy fussed, and she fumbled to unbutton her chemise, her fingers shaking still. Ruby took several deep breaths, relaxing enough to let Baby Timmy nurse.

Joseph ran his fingers through his hair and pulled his chair closer to hers. "Ruby, I need to say this. Your family has treated you like a hired hand for many years. I've worried about the neglect you've endured. Your years of toil for your granny and Pa have been heroic, and you should be proud of what you've done for them. There is no excuse for how your brother talked to you, considering the way he left you. He shows up out of nowhere to spew hate, but I don't think it has a thing to do with you. And Granny sure didn't hesitate to add to it. They're trying to control you, just like they have all these years. It's manipulation. None of it is true. Surely you know that."

Joseph scooted his chair over to sit directly in front of Ruby. He placed his hand on her left arm, opposite the baby's head. "A family is made of people you can count on, people who respect and support you, especially now that you've had a baby. Let's redefine your notion of family, Ruby. Let me show you how worthy you are."

Ruby stared at her son without seeing him. She searched Joseph's face, then tried to take in the presence of her son. Ruby nodded at Joseph, a numb smile on her face, and pulled the baby closer. The skies had darkened, and she could see her reflection in the parlor window. There sat an image of someone who looked like her, nodding as she tried to allow love into her heart.

"I heard in town that your mother opened a brothel in Salina a few years back, but I didn't know if it was true, so I didn't say anything. If Robert joins her, we won't be seeing him again. Ever. I can assure you of that. We'll do what's right for your granny and Pa, but I won't tolerate them treating you like you aren't the beautiful woman I married. That'll be their choice to make. I wish you could see yourself the way I do. That's my prayer for you—it always has been." Joseph rubbed Ruby's arm as he spoke.

She relived her brother's and her husband's words from the last hour as they still echoed in the room. She didn't know who she believed. If Ruby had to lay claim to either one's words, she would have chosen Robert's—they fit her best. She wore them like an ugly handmade shawl knitted from the bitter threads left by her mama. Knitted because her mama left and didn't come back. Knitted because of her miserable life with Granny and Pa. Knitted because Ruby wasn't worthy of love. On the other hand, Joseph's words felt store-bought—she simply didn't believe them, not even his prayer for her.

# CHAPTER THIRTY-ONE

*April 1919*

Little Timmy toddled after his new puppy as Ruby tended the kitchen fire. Alice had brought over the runt of her barn dog's litter last week, and Timmy had latched onto him. The fire became almost warm enough to bake the tea cakes. Alice and Maggie, Joseph's youngest sister and Ruby's shadow, would arrive with Alice's five girls later this morning. They'd planned a picnic on a quilt under the large sweetgum tree out by the river. Ruby would be glad for help chasing after Timmy; Maggie would corral him for her. He wiggled out of her arms and crawled faster than she could walk. Ruby rubbed her growing tummy as she stirred the tea and sugar, hoping it had time to cool in the icebox before her guests arrived. She placed Timmy in the corner and hooked the hinged gate to the wall so she could finish her preparations. Joseph had made the gate to contain their son when she had to retrieve something from outside or get the wagon ready for a trip into town. Timmy would be climbing over it soon.

Their second baby would be due a few months after

Timmy's first birthday. She hadn't told anyone yet. But last week at church, she caught a couple of people looking down at her belly—her tummy jutted out enough to be noticeable. Having a second child would make it hard to keep up with Timmy.

Ruby had been surprised how much she loved being a mother. After all those years of hard work, it taught her to play. She observed Joseph's mother repeating whatever sound Timmy made, turning it into a game in which they both ended up in fits of laughter. Playing didn't come naturally to her. For instance, she didn't think to sing to Timmy, something Joseph did when he put him to bed at night. She watched her husband repeat nursery rhymes, and it was like hearing a foreign language. Timmy would bounce on Joseph's lap and laugh. Her son started singing to her when she rocked him. He touched her cheeks with both of his hands and made his baby noises as his head moved back and forth. He was trying to be silly. She had no option but to laugh and repeat what he did. She loved his baby chuckles.

Joseph stayed in town more now. He had started a little general store last summer in an abandoned building next to the schoolhouse. He opened it for two hours after school and a few hours on Saturday mornings, with expanded hours in the summer so the farmers could get supplies without going all the way into town. Ruby and Joseph didn't need the money, but Joseph said it would be good for the community. Pearl Owens opened a small post office inside so the mountain folks could get their mail more than once a week. It made life easier for Ruby when Joseph brought home household supplies such as sacks of cornmeal or lantern oil. They gardened less and ate the fresh produce on its last days from the store. Every day he worked there, Joseph brought home a few pieces of hard candy —usually butterscotch or root beer barrels—for Ruby, offering them as a gift. He also delivered tidbits of gossip he'd overheard from the farmers and their wives.

Alice, her clan of children, and Maggie arrived as Ruby took the tea cakes out of the oven. She placed the hot cakes in the basket beside the napkin-wrapped punch cups. Ruby retrieved the cooled jar of tea from the icebox and threw a quilt over her arm. She grabbed Timmy and joined them outside, precariously balancing everything with her wiggly child.

"Ruby, hop in our wagon, and we'll drive down there. That's the best way to get all these moppets there quickly, and we can tie up the horses there in the shade. Can you hand up your basket?" asked Alice, placing it next to hers on the bench.

Ruby also passed Timmy up to her, then pulled herself into the back of the wagon, careful to arrange herself between the children.

After they unloaded the wagon and spread out the quilt, Maggie led the young ones to the meadow for a game of chase. Ruby and Alice sat on the back end of the wagon to talk while they played.

"You're having another baby, aren't you?" Alice said. "I can tell just by looking at you."

"I can't keep anything from you, can I?" Ruby laughed. "Alice, tell me. How do you love a second child as much as the first one? It makes me sad to think Timmy won't have as much time in my lap because another baby'll take it. I ache to think about it."

"Becoming a mother makes you the mother of all children, Ruby. You don't have to divide your love—it just multiplies, I promise. Love for a child is the greatest mathematical dilemma. Oh, listen to me—the teacher in me is popping out. But you'll see what I mean when the new baby comes. It throws open the door where pure joy lives."

Ruby opened her mouth to reply when Maggie screamed

down by the water. "Ruby! Ru-beeeee! Come quick. Timmy's in the water."

She turned to see her son bobbing in the river beyond the shallow bank. The current had picked him up where the sandy bank dropped off, his blond hair visible in the middle of the swirling river, the swirls much like the doodles she used to draw on her school slate. The water ran swiftly from the mountain winter snows that drained into it in the spring.

Ruby jumped off the back of the wagon and sprinted to the water to find Timmy floating facedown, headed to where some brush had coagulated in the stream. She pulled at the buttons on her shirtwaist, and they popped off as she tore her dress open. Ruby drew it over her head and threw it to the ground before jumping in. Her heavy, broadcloth dress would only pull her down. She gasped at the shock of the frigid water. She had to get to him quickly and swam in a diagonal path to where the current carried Timmy.

She reached him and lifted his face out of the water. He had turned bluish, and his facial features seemed frozen—she wasn't sure he could breathe. She turned him over and swam back to shore with all her might, using one arm to hold him up and plunging the other deep into the water. She would not let the river steal her child from her. Fierce in her efforts, she grunted as she fought to return to land.

She navigated around brush near shore until her undergarment caught on an underwater limb. Ruby pulled with her free arm, and the cotton ripped, setting her free. She sank beneath the surface but held on to Timmy. With one more kick, she reached the bank, and Alice helped her out of the water, ready with a quilt to warm her son. But first, he had to start breathing. Ruby turned Timmy over and slapped his back, trying to expel the water that kept him from her. She laid him across one arm and positioned his head lower than his body, but nothing worked. She laid him on his back, turned his head to the side, and pushed on his stomach, then his chest, working her way up his body in a rhythm that might bring him back to her. Push. Listen. Pray. Push. Listen. Pray. Dear God, help him!

He didn't respond. Ruby held him in the air over her head, her palms on his ribs, crying her prayer. She shook him in the air.

"Breathe, Timmy! You have to breathe. Mama wants you to breathe!"

Timmy let go of all the water that held his lungs captive, expelling it on her down below. He opened his eyes and wailed, shivering as Alice wrapped him and Ruby in the quilt. Ruby held him close and sobbed. Timmy held her as well, grabbing her wet hair between his chubby fists.

Alice drove them up to the house, leaving Maggie with her girls until she could return to pick them up. Ruby felt lost in a world of her own on the wagon bench, rocking Timmy back and forth and crying what seemed like twenty years' worth of pent-up tears. She wrapped her fingers around Timmy's wet curls and smelled that precious, sweet, little-boy breath. Ruby would have given her life to save his. No more doubting her motherly love—that feeling so raw and powerful and rugged. At the same time, it scared her more than anything else she had ever known.

Ruby looked up from her nap in the rocker, happy that Joseph had come home early from school that day. At least she knew what it took for him to interrupt his schedule in town; Alice had probably gone by the schoolhouse on her way home and told him what had happened.

Ruby's and Timmy's clothes were still damp from the spring when Joseph arrived. She had been too exhausted to change clothes and chose to hold Timmy instead. Without a word,

Joseph heated some water, placing Timmy close to the steam to ease his breathing. Joseph bathed him. dressed him in dry clothes, and laid him down. He then did the same for Ruby, undressing her and being careful not to put any pressure on her engorged breasts, so full of mother's milk. He washed her and wiped her tears. Ruby had never wept in front of him but didn't have the energy to try to stop it. She gazed at the baby next to her, sleeping with labored breaths, awaking at times with coughing fits but returning to sleep. Joseph dried her, dressed her in nightclothes, and placed her and Timmy in the big bed he and Ruby shared. He said he would sleep on a pallet on the floor tonight to watch over them. She should have felt comforted by that but remained too spent to feel anything at all.

Ruby breastfed Timmy whenever he wanted that night, willing to give him comfort whenever he asked. Her breasts ached, but it was no match for the ache in her heart. A sad pain held the place where her feelings for this child came alive, a powerful life force. She used baby talk and sang and stroked her son, feeling his body warm against her breast. He couldn't suckle properly for the congestion in his chest, but he kept trying between coughs. Her son, usually very active, lay languid in her arms. Ruby unconsciously rubbed Timmy's back with one hand and her growing tummy with the other.

Ruby didn't sleep much that night. She knelt beside her bed and bargained with God, the God she didn't know to be kind or willing to be bargained with. Ruby offered Him a simple deal: let Timmy recover, and she would follow all the rules and devote herself to her family. She would be as generous as Joseph was noble. Ruby would be kind and patient, like Alice. Mimicking Joseph's mother, she would open her arms to her family. Ruby would reject the only mothering she had known—the kind that had left a cold footprint on her soul. She would strive to be a perfect wife and mother. Even as she vowed to do this,

Ruby knew in her heart she would fall short. But if God did His part, she would give it every effort she had.

The sun was shining through the window the next morning when Joseph brought Ruby a mug of coffee. He pulled her long hair over to the side and leaned over to kiss her cheek. Timmy still slept but was breathing more comfortably.

"Joseph, we almost lost him," Ruby whispered. "I'm sorry for not keeping a better eye on him. Will you forgive me?"

"Honey, it wasn't your fault. Alice told me everything. It would have been a terrible accident, but I don't blame *you*. I'm grateful that you saved him." Joseph took her hand and held it to his cheek.

"I'm worried about not being a good mother—I don't think I can do it all by myself. Will you help me? You're the best person I know."

Joseph took a minute to answer. Most of their conversations lately were about household management or details of the coming day, not about fears or feelings.

"I'll help you. But you're a better mother than you think. Timmy loves you, and I see how you care for him. Give yourself a little credit for our beautiful boy."

Later the next day, Timmy's congestion was gone, and he returned to his squirmy self. Ruby couldn't take her eyes off him. God let him live! Now she had some work to do to honor her promise to Him.

# CHAPTER THIRTY-TWO

*Fall 1919*

The barn dogs barked when Joseph drove the wagon up the drive to his house, and Timmy's squeals greeted him from the front porch. Ruby placed Wilson in the cradle and came out to take Joseph's bag before he took the horse to the barn for the night.

"How was your day?" Ruby smiled up at him.

"It was nice. But coming home is always the best part."

"Don't dally in the barn—dinner will be ready in a few minutes. We're having our Friday-night special, a skillet of potato beef hash with extra onions, just as you like it."

Joseph had never imagined his life could be this good. Whatever he hungered for, he received in abundance. Ruby immersed herself in the boys from sunup to sundown, but seemingly with joy—a change since Timmy's near-drowning. Joseph looked over at the porch where his boys were. According to a tintype at his mother's house, Timmy was the spitting image of him as a baby: curly blond hair, the same broad forehead, and a dimple on the right cheek when he smiled. Timmy tried to climb down the steps to get to his mother, but his legs got caught up in his long frock. He rolled head over heels off the porch but quickly stood up and continued his journey.

Timmy wasn't too pleased with his new brother, Wilson. He covered his ears to get away from the pervasive screaming that came from the cradle. Wilson bellowed with colic most days about this time, preferring the afternoons to make his complaints known.

Timmy pointed to the field and said, "Baby out!"

"Ruby, Timmy just said his first sentence." Joseph laughed, slapping his leg. He agreed with Timmy: Wilson was a handful for sure. Joseph continued to the barn.

With each new baby, Ruby seemed to have more to give. From his observations, she spent less time in the weighty introspection that had enveloped her in the first year of marriage. Oh, how he'd worried about her! Lately, when he came home from town—even if he arrived late—she welcomed him and recounted her day with the boys. She seemed to have gained confidence as a mother. Ruby gave Wilson fennel for his colic but wasn't afraid to let him cry. She used belly bands to apply pressure on his tummy at night so they could all get some sleep. Whatever concerns Joseph had about Ruby when they were first married had disappeared; they were full partners in life now. He managed the life outside the house, and she tended to what went on inside it. The best part was knowing he had saved her. Her childhood had been filled with loneliness. But with patience and tender care, he had helped her leave her brutal past behind.

Joseph had recently been elected a justice of the peace. A while back, some county leaders had asked him if he'd consider running for the position. He agreed to file and garnered two-thirds of the vote without campaigning—because the community respected him, he supposed. His days in town were even longer than they were before. He opened the store every day after school but Tuesdays, and it was also closed Sundays. On Tuesdays, he held court. He ruled on the petty squabbles between neighbors and discerned the fine or other punishment if he found someone's behavior to be outside the law. He handled one divorce between Cy and Helen Walsh. He hated to play a part in separating a family, but he had to uphold the law. He did feel better knowing that Cy couldn't beat Helen or their children anymore. Joseph performed weddings, and that delighted him. Ruby became a witness if he needed one for the ceremony. He usually winked at her after the couple recited their vows as if the two of them shared a secret. It was almost like a vow renewal for them.

He walked into the cabin, and Timmy ran up to take his hat. Timmy put it on every day when Joseph came home from town, walking around with his shoulders back, imitating how Joseph moved, he supposed. Joseph picked up Wilson and held him across his body so that his tummy pressed onto Joseph's forearm. The infant stopped crying almost immediately.

Joseph leaned over to kiss Ruby on her cheek. "How was your day with these rascals?"

"If I'd known that was the trick to shush Wilson, I would have used it for the last two hours. You don't mind if I borrow that hold, do you?" Ruby winked at him as she said it. "I did get the boys to sleep at the same time this afternoon, and I fell asleep too. It was heaven. Come on, let's eat. Supper's all dished out and ready to go."

Following his nightly routine at the dinner table, Timmy picked up each chunk of beef and ate it before devouring all of the cubed potatoes. Wilson slept in Joseph's right arm as Joseph ate voraciously with his left.

"Mabel asked me to join her at the new movie theater in town tomorrow night. Mary Pickford's new film is showing. Do you mind if I go with her?" Ruby asked. "If I feed Wilson before we go, he shouldn't be hungry until I get back. Mabel said she would pick me up on her way to town."

Joseph had suggested that Ruby go out occasionally with her friends in the evenings or on weekend nights. She didn't get that opportunity as a girl because of how hard she worked for her granny and Pa. And now she worked long hours with the boys and the household chores. She deserved a break.

Ruby had reacquainted herself with some of her former classmates, even those who had bullied her in high school. Joseph had observed how they'd taunted her at school, over the fact that her mother had left her. Ruby seemed to have forgotten —or forgiven—their adolescent misdeeds. They looked up to her now, in a way they wouldn't have a few years back. Ruby even helped organize an ice cream social for the church, and some of her single friends got involved on the various committees.

The last time Ruby went out with her friends, she'd come home after Timmy went to bed. From the rocker on the porch, Joseph had watched the antics of Ruby and her friend. Mabel wore a fedora and mockingly bowed when she helped Ruby off the wagon, as a gentleman might do for his lady. Ruby had never played, and watching this warmed his heart. He suspected she probably required some freedom from motherhood that other women didn't necessarily need. His biggest desire was for her to become whole and happy.

"Ruby, let's go hear my brother play at the livery in town instead of going to the movie. He plays the washtub bass behind two banjo players—good ole mountain music. It'll be fun. I'd like to support them." Mabel put her hands up as if mimicking a pet dog begging for a bone.

"I don't know. I told Joseph we were going to a movie." Ruby hesitated. She wasn't sure what he would think of her changing her plans.

"We won't stay long, I promise. I'll take you home after an hour or so. Joseph won't mind."

At the livery, Ruby seated herself near the door and surveyed the crowd. The band played, and many young people took to the barn floor to dance. She saw some of her former students drinking from a jug of whiskey, and a few older men dressed in suits stood together and smoked cigarettes on the far side of the improvised stage. Across the barn from her, a buzz of energy emanated from a circle of girls. Ruby looked closer and recognized a familiar face.

So, the rumors were true—Leon was back to town. The work in the railroad yards had given him solid shoulders and bulky arms, and he towered over all the girls around him. With his confident smile, she could understand why they were attracted to him. He stood there as if on stage, surrounded by his female audience, maybe ten or twelve in number and varying in age from thirty down to about sixteen. If he raised his arms over his head, they looked up. If he pointed across the room, their eyes followed. He told some kind of story, and they listened as if entranced by his performance. Where did he get that double-breasted silk suit? They didn't sell anything like that around here. He wore a green silk scarf around his neck—a pretty unusual fashion for the hills.

Leon looked up from the crowd and caught Ruby's look, and with a smile, abruptly ended his storytelling. He strode across the barn floor, and her face reddened. She had been watching him for too long, and he seemed to know it.

He bowed before her. "Well, hello, Mrs. MacCallum."

The electricity between them ignited another tug-of-war conversation, like the last time they had talked. Leon would approach crossing the line with his words, and she would pull the conversation back to safer ground.

"Mr. Pennington. You have quite a following, I see."

With that glazed look in his eyes, she could tell he'd been drinking. Across the room, Mabel stood there watching her, her mouth wide open. Leon had his way with women—most women, anyway. Mabel probably didn't remember him since he left school after eighth grade to help his family. He had changed entirely since then.

"Ruby, remember that time—"

"Leon, be quiet. We'll not talk about that time or any time right now." Just like that, she avoided discussing that infamous swim they took one afternoon when they were children. She was back on safe ground until he tugged the conversation the other way again.

Mabel practically ran across the room to join them. "Mabel, this is Leon. Leon, Mabel."

Leon bowed graciously but stumbled when he swept his arm back up from the downswing. He moved closer to Mabel, and she reacted to his charm, giggling. Ruby regretted her decision to come here with her friend. She suspected that illegal alcohol was served in the backroom, and Mabel acted as if she'd already found some.

Leon looked over Mabel's shoulder at Ruby while he talked with her. Ruby hadn't seen him since before she had children, that afternoon when she sent him away from her barn.

He had been shy back in school, not fully grown. Ruby had been timid herself back then, and she had changed physically as well—no longer a schoolgirl but a mother of two. Ruby never considered him as anything but a friend when he worked on Pa's farm, someone to pal around with. Now, every bit of her sensed danger merely by being around him. Seductively, he kindled a fire in her. His magnetism pulled her closer than she knew she should be. She backed up several steps, afraid to respond to him. Mabel, however, had no restraint—she was captivated. Ruby would warn her about Leon later.

"Ruby, I didn't think I'd see you at a barn dance. Where are all of your children? And your fancy husband? I'm surprised he let you out."

She didn't dignify his comments with a response. How did he know about her children? Ruby didn't want Mabel to overhear this talk.

"Leon, you have some ladies waiting for you over at that other table. They're still watching you. Perhaps you should return to them before the music starts up again. Mabel and I will sit here near the stage to hear her brother play. He's chaperoning us tonight so that our excellent reputations are not tarnished in any way." Ruby sounded like Alice talking in her teacher's voice—not like herself at all.

The music resumed, and Ruby sipped her tea while Leon danced in circles with every single lady he could find. But as he moved, he kept his eyes on Ruby. He ended the evening by asking Mabel to dance to the last ballad with him.

When the music stopped, he delivered Mabel back to their table and disappeared into the back room. Her friend's brother loaded up the band instruments, and Mabel and Ruby waited in the wagon for him to finish.

"Mabel, do you see what I see? Look over there."

Leon was loading empty jugs into the back of his wagon, whistling while he worked. For every step forward, he took one step to the side to get his balance.

"I should have known that he'd supplied the backroom alcohol. That's why he's back in town."

Mesmerized, Mabel appeared not to have heard a word.

RUBY WALKED into their bedroom and undressed in the dark. Joseph was snoring, his breath whistling through his crooked front teeth. Careful not to awaken him or the boys, who lay on a pallet next to their bed, Ruby crawled under the covers, taking her place beside her husband. Despite her best efforts, she couldn't get Leon out of her mind.

What would her life be like with Leon in it? She straightened out her nightgown from between her legs and turned over to attempt to sleep. Although she hadn't seen him in a couple of years, Leon knew her better than anyone else did—they were cut from the same back-mountain cloth. He had witnessed her most difficult years. She pulled the covers over her shoulders, watching Joseph peacefully sleep. With thoughts of Leon churning through her mind, she tossed and turned, unsettled.

# CHAPTER THIRTY-THREE

*Summer 1921*

he little one inside her tummy stretched and fit a small foot under one of her ribs. Ruby should be delivering any time now if she'd done the figuring right. Goodness, this one was larger than the other two, but she hoped this birth would be as quick as the others had been.

Joseph dropped them all off at his mother's house most mornings, so Ruby could have help with the boys when he worked the long days in town. This arrangement made the days more manageable for her—her mother-in-law tended to her every need with a gracious heart. Ruby rubbed her side until the foot retracted; the baby relaxed and curled back up inside her.

Joseph's mother left her alone most of the day, taking the boys outside to help in her garden or showing them the newest litter of kittens. Ruby enjoyed having lunch provided by Mrs. MacCallum, and she napped when the boys did. Joseph's younger sisters helped out when they got home from school. The boys loved getting attention from their aunts and uncles.

Joseph had told her that he would be making a run to

Granny's after school. Granny had sent word that her roof needed a minor repair after the windstorm the night before. Ruby appreciated being spared from going over there with him. Just walking into her old home upset her. Granny seemed to use their time apart to become more resentful. Ruby understood that Granny wasn't young, and her hands were full with Pa. The house held a smell now that would spill out to the front porch when she sat on the rocker there during their infrequent visits. Urine, she thought. Or could a relationship smell? It couldn't be easy for her grandmother, but Ruby didn't have the energy to resurrect the relationship. Granny had plunged into bitterness, and even if she wanted to, Ruby couldn't pull her out.

Now that Joseph's family had enfolded her, it struck her that her grandparents blamed her existence for their hard lives. But didn't she deserve to be loved in the way the MacCallums loved her? Granny and Pa didn't want help; they desired only to complain and wallow in their misery. Granny had been pleasant to Ruby when she was a child, but she had it in her bonnet that Ruby owed her something now. Sometimes Granny's words hurt more than the cruel treatment Pa had given her as a child. A deep place in her soul had been bruised and had never healed.

Timmy, just turned three, became her little helper. Wilson, a runner, would take off when he saw something he wanted to investigate. Timmy had the gumption to fence him in to keep him out of danger. Still, Wilson would try climbing any obstacle in his way. And when he got agitated with his older brother, he would chase him, regardless of his smaller size. What a sight to see! As if running, Wilson would swing his arms and scream at the top of his voice. Timmy would take off, fearing for his safety.

"It's all right, it's all right," Timmy would repeat, trying to tame his baby brother's vim and vigor. Ruby stayed out of it unless real danger loomed. When she chuckled at their antics, she turned her head so they couldn't see her.

Joseph arrived at his mother's house as Mrs. MacCallum put supper on the table. The boys ran to him, chanting their alleluia chorus as they did every day when he returned from town. Joseph caught Ruby's eye and shook his head slightly from side to side to indicate that the afternoon repair at Granny and Pa's had taken a personal toll. He wouldn't talk about Ruby's family in front of his own, however—she knew that. He would tell her all about it on the way home.

Wilson hung onto Joseph's back, his arms around his papa's neck. Joseph swung him around and plucked him off his back, then placed him at the children's dinner table. Timmy took the opportunity to help Ruby out of the parlor chair. She put one hand behind her, arching her back as she got up.

Timmy pulled her with all of his might. "Come on, Mama. It's chicken and noodles tonight."

Later, after Joseph laid both boys on blankets in the back of the wagon, he practically lifted Ruby onto the front bench. He tucked a blanket around her legs before they headed out.

"A penny for your thoughts, Ruby," Joseph said quietly, lest they wake the boys.

"I'm thinking of the next few weeks, that's all." Ruby gazed at the full moon hanging over the mountain.

She couldn't muster the courage to reveal her truth. In a couple of weeks, she would have another little one to take care of. With Joseph's teaching career, the store, and his being the justice of the peace, she knew she would be alone often. Even with his family providing relief whenever she arrived at her wit's end, she was parenting by herself. Joseph left before the boys woke up most days and returned after dark most nights. Ruby had to admit that it was nice not having to think about money all the time—her consolation prize.

Something was troubling about Joseph. He needed others to think well of him, and she knew that serving his community fed that. His payment was the satisfaction of helping others, but it came at a cost to her.

Where was he when she needed him? She knew she pushed him away at times; when Ruby became overwhelmed, she needed to sort things out on her own. But being alone for days on end took her to a dangerous place, where her persistent sense of unworthiness lived. Past demons sat with her. She wanted to banish them, but they oozed into her and filtered her interpretation of his absence. He'd abandoned her.

"It will be interesting, won't it? Having another baby in our house," Joseph said.

In the quiet night, several minutes went by with no response from Ruby.

"Ruby, I have a big hearing coming up next week. I can't tell you much, but I should tell you it'll run at least two days, most probably three or four. That's what I've been spending so much time on. And I should also tell you that it involves your friend, Leon."

Ruby turned toward Joseph.

He continued. "Because it's a secret, it hasn't been part of the local gossip. Leon has been charged with hiring a man to provide an abortion for a lady friend of his. He paid a man who claimed to be a doctor from Knoxville a small sum for the procedure. He didn't know that this man worked for the state and reported all dealings against the law. It's complicated because the federal agents contacted the county about investigating Leon's moonshine running as well. I just wanted you to know because I'm fairly involved. And I know he's your childhood friend. But remember, it's a secret. You can't tell a soul."

Ruby's breathing quickened to hear about Leon's predicament. She switched hands to rub her protruding stomach. "What if the baby comes when you're gone? Can you postpone the hearing until after I deliver?"

"I can't move it because of the federal case. But I do think we should move you and the boys to my parents' house next week. Or to your granny's place, if you think that's better."

"Let's ask your mother. The boys will be happier there. How were Granny and Pa this afternoon?"

"The same as usual. I agree Granny wouldn't be much help to you. She's too tied up with Pa."

They rode the rest of the way in silence. The gigantic moon showed an idyllic image of a family nestled in a wagon, riding peacefully to their home. But the moon's shadows pierced and troubled Ruby's soul. Leon—she hadn't seen him since the dance. She remembered the way he had looked at her that night. Her friend—who knew childhood misery as much as she did— was in deep trouble. She knew what she had to do. She rubbed her stomach counterclockwise to calm the baby until they reached their cabin.

# CHAPTER THIRTY-FOUR

*L*eon needed some time to think. He sat in the jail cell, waiting to be escorted to his trial across the street. The sheriff sat across the room at his desk, pushing papers around and occasionally glancing at his watch. He'd allowed Leon to wear his own clothes today. Leon adjusted his suit jacket and pulled the sides together; it was looser since he'd last worn it. He picked some lint off of the sleeve. He finished his hard biscuit and cup of coffee the sheriff had brought him this morning. Tasteless.

Who could have known that finding someone to solve a little pregnancy problem would land him here? Oh, they set him up, all right; he didn't doubt that. Although the baby might have been his, they had no proof he was the culprit. He had just helped out a friend—well, a girlfriend, to be truthful. He had arranged to end pregnancies before; plenty of men were willing to do the deed for just a little money. He should have suspected funny business when this last connection involved a man he didn't know from the next county over.

His head hurt from the restless sleep. He rubbed his temples to try to alleviate the dull thudding. The jailhouse mattress needed to be restuffed with straw—maybe he should bring that up today, or perhaps he better not. If only he could get a swig of the whiskey he delivered, he'd feel better. He sat down on the bed and tried to focus on how to handle himself in the courtroom today. Would he get jail time if found guilty? Or merely a fine? He could deal with a fine, but he couldn't afford to be locked up—he had a business to run. His customers expected their moonshine, and he had already missed a week. He didn't want them doing business with the other boys on the far side of the hill.

The sheriff had left the keys in the cell lock. He could make a run for it, but he would have to take his moonshine business further underground if he did. Not to mention his recent expansion into selling boxes of cigarettes and other items he stole from the railroad warehouses. He hadn't established that business yet. Recent events had squeezed his entrepreneurial efforts right when the good times were rolling.

He still didn't know how he would plead to this misdemeanor charge. If he declared himself guilty, he might be more likely to get just a fine. No one liked to talk openly about abortion, so there would be only whispers about him, and the case would go away. Leon could handle the whispers. If he pleaded not guilty, they would bring up all kinds of information about him and details about his line of work. Who knows who they would call as witnesses?

Joseph MacCallum, his former teacher, would be the judge in charge. He knew Mr. MacCallum well enough to realize that he'd prefer not to go through a trial. Ruby's husband could be the man to condemn him. How ironic! Leon finished his coffee and wondered what his old friend knew. He would never forget the day they swam naked in the river. They'd helped each other get through some difficult times back then. She wouldn't have much to do with him lately, though. He imagined standing before Mr. MacCallum and saying that his wife looked mighty beautiful naked. And did she still have that tiny birthmark on her right hip? He shook his head; he needed to be sharp today. This was a minor charge, and he could still do business with a conviction. Life would go on.

A constable opened the front door. "I have a letter for Mr. Pennington from his mother. His younger brother brought it. Is he allowed to receive mail, Sheriff?"

"Let me see it." The sheriff skimmed the note. "It's from Leon's mother, all right. She's disappointed in him, but she still needs the revenue he sends her every week. She instructs him to plead guilty if he did it and start living a better life. That's good advice. Many of the words are underlined for emphasis. I don't see that it'd do any harm to let Pennington read the letter. Maybe it'll knock some sense into him."

Leon knew instantly that his ma hadn't written it when handed the letter. She had quit school in the fourth grade and was ashamed of her writing skills; she would never write to him. He recognized Ruby's handwriting from her lists when they went shopping in town. She looped the letter *l* so that it was as round as it was tall. Leon read through the note, saw the underlined words, and pieced the message together. It read, *The revenuers have you. Plead guilty.*

He knew what he had to do. Without a trial, they couldn't bring up the other evidence or additional charges. He would hope for no jail time and leave town for a while to let things simmer down. In the meantime, he would work in the background to ramp up his stolen goods business and lie low on the moonshine deliveries. Ruby was saving him this time. Maybe things weren't as rosy at the MacCallum house as he thought. Leon tucked away the letter with its valuable tidbit of information. Soon he would investigate why she had helped him.

# CHAPTER THIRTY-FIVE

*A*s close as she felt to Alice and Mrs. MacCallum, Ruby wasn't prepared for the intimacy of delivering a baby at the MacCallum house. It wasn't that they would see her naked; that was the physical part of giving birth, and after two children, she was over that. But every single time Ruby visited with Joseph's family, she carefully watched her every word and action so that they wouldn't know her for the fraud she was. She was an abandoned backwoods child from the wrong side of the mountain, and she kept that covered up, not speaking without carefully reviewing what she said. But it was too hard to pretend when she was in labor.

Ruby wore Alice's birthing gown with the tie at the neck. It had lace on it, for heaven's sake. Standing at her head, Alice wiped Ruby's face in the final stages of labor. The lukewarm water ran over her forehead and calmed her. While pushing, Ruby wanted to scream, but she muffled it. She went into labor, thinking this baby would just slip out; all third babies do. But after three hours of pushing, she was ready to give up. Prolonged labor had killed many of the women on the mountain. Maybe death wasn't the worst thing that could happen to her.

"I am pushing, damn it," she yelled when Doc told her to push with all her might. "Can't you pull it out?" Doc and Alice exchanged glances, and that reminded her to control herself. They were judging her in her worst state.

"The position of the baby is hindering things here. On the next contraction, don't push. I'll press on the baby's shoulder and try to reposition," Doc said.

Ruby could see his look of concern. She wondered if Joseph was in the other room with the boys or if the trial had kept him from being here. By all rights, he should be here with his family.

"Okay, Ruby, hold your breath. Hold it. Hold it." Doc's forearm felt as if it was inside her. "Now push. Push!"

Ruby felt instant relief as the baby slid out and into Doc's arms. Every bit of her remaining energy left with the baby.

"It's a girl. She's a little bigger than your others. She looks pink and healthy. I think she'll give your boys a run for their money."

"I don't want a girl. You keep her." Ruby winced one last time as he applied iodine to the small tears from childbirth.

"Are you sure? She has red hair." Doc chuckled.

"Okay, I'll keep her, then." Ruby exhaled and closed her eyes.

He placed the baby on the bed beside her. Alice covered Ruby with a clean cover, then left the room as Doc finished his work. After a short while, she returned with the boys to meet their sister. "What's her name, Ruby?"

"Mary. I'm going to call her Mary."

Alice lifted Timmy so he could see the newborn baby. Wilson climbed the rails at the foot of the bed. Just as she thought, Joseph hadn't made it back in time to meet his daughter. What could be more important than being with his wife when she gave birth? Baby Mary suckled and fell asleep. Ruby covered herself with all the extra blankets on the bed, seeking comfort for her raw soul.

# CHAPTER THIRTY-SIX

*November 1921*

ost days, Ruby worked as much as she had in her childhood at the farm with Granny and Pa. In many ways, her childhood after her mama left and motherhood itself had much in common. One should be the opposite of the other: mother-less and mother-full. But both entailed working nonstop from sunup to sundown. She wished she could say she had never worked harder in her life, but she had. This time, she received a few reprieves in her day, such as playing with Timmy. Mostly, though, whatever she did, she had three young children hanging on to her as she did it. Through her efforts, however, she broke a family pattern. *Her* children were allowed to play and enjoy their childhood.

But yet again, she had been abandoned. Alone. Hollow. Forgotten. Joseph stayed in town all day, returning home after dark, usually after the children were in bed. He would eat his supper late and then tell her about the town gossip and the schoolchildren's shenanigans. He didn't ask about her day much, nor did she volunteer information.

He spent all day Saturday at the store. Sunday was the only day he stayed with them. Sundays entailed getting the children and herself ready for church, then dinner at the MacCallum house afterward. Ruby was an essential part of the MacCallum kitchen crew and took breaks to nurse the baby while Joseph visited with his brothers and father in the barn. He did keep an eye on the boys to give her some respite.

In his musings to her on the porch late last night, Joseph had worn that half-smile he always had and told her that he had never been more joyful. His words exactly: "I can't believe that God has blessed me so."

But was it about God blessing a person or a family? Shouldn't everyone be blessed, or was God selective? Did he bless only men? Did she have to deserve a blessing? Why didn't he bless Ruby and her family when she was young? Why did her papa die the night she was born? She had been told he was a gentle, funny man. What would her life be like if he had lived? Where was that blessing? She went to church like everyone else. Why did her mama leave town when Ruby was nine? And why was the MacCallum family so wealthy while hers had been so poor? Did you have to wish really hard, like on a wish fairy? Because even though she had wished with all her might as a child, Ruby had never received a blessing. Never. Her life became better as Joseph's wife, but lately, she was left alone all day and most of the night to do the chores. The only difference between her childhood and now was she wore better clothes to do the work. She waited for Joseph to discard her, but he would keep her for the tasks that needed to be done.

From her quietness, Joseph seemed to assume she was content. He didn't press her much to talk to him. When she remained silent in the evenings, he'd only say, "A penny for your thoughts." But it was best to keep her thoughts to herself. Some days she suffered more than others, the patches on her soul threadbare and the deep wounds exposed. When she became exhausted, and one baby or another kept crying, she would escape to snippets of memories of the fun times she'd had as a child with Leon. The stolen trip to the swimming hole or the laughter when Leon imitated her grandfather. She enjoyed the taste of these little memories. They got her through the day.

She did have two joys during her week. Even though Mary was only five months old, Joseph insisted that Ruby take a break, encouraging her to go out with Mabel on Saturday night. Since she didn't get to play as a schoolgirl, he insisted that she find some recreation now. He brought evaporated milk home from the store and mixed it with cow's milk so Mary could take a bottle in Ruby's absence. After dinner, he bathed the children, getting them to bed with a Bible story and rocking them if they needed it. On top of that, Joseph saddled their mare so Ruby could ride into town. When she returned at night, she found him sleeping soundly, even if a baby squalled right beside him.

Oh, she laughed so much when she and her friend watched Mabel's brother and his band at the dance hall. She danced with Mabel, and it made her feel so free. At times, a fellow would join them for a ragtime number, claiming Ruby as a partner. There was no harm in it, as the dance brought partners together in the middle briefly before they took off in opposite directions again. Sometimes she jumped up on stage and grabbed the tambourine to keep time to the beat, shaking it at the end of a chorus. Mabel always filled her dance card. But Ruby, imagining gossip getting back to Joseph, would take a stool for the slow songs and sip her tea. From her observations, slow dances weren't as much fun anyway.

The other highlight of her week was being alone with Timmy without distraction from the babies. He delighted her with a three-year-old's wisdom. She put the young ones in their cradle and crib to nap and spent their naptime playing with Timmy near the creek outside their porch.

When Timmy played, she could anticipate his next move,

almost as if his thoughts flowed into hers. She watched him and saw herself—the life she could have had. He played with his favorite balls, the big red and blue ones, in the yard, and before he even moved, Ruby knew he would go after the red one. Similarly, if she deemed that Timmy played too close to the running water, he would say before she reacted, "Don't worry, Mama. I won't fall in." If she hid his toy behind her back during their game-playing, he always knew which of her hands held it. It was uncanny.

Maybe all mothers held this sort of special connection with their firstborn. This closeness to Timmy was a relationship unlike any she had known. That was why when he started coughing one morning, the hairs at the back of her neck stood at attention. Something terrible was behind it. Dread consumed her.

Timmy had stayed in his bed yesterday morning after waking. Had he said out loud that his neck hurt? Or had Ruby just heard his thoughts? He complained that his "froat hurt" shortly after. She made him a broth from one of their chickens, adding salt and a little more chicken fat to help it go down smoother. He ate some of it and pushed away the rest. He didn't even want the honey biscuit she put on the plate.

He slept on and off that afternoon. When Ruby went into his room after Mary's suppertime feeding, his head burned with fever.

"Mama, I'm scared."

"It's okay, baby. Mama's here." He calmed down as she rocked him.

"I've been thinking about clouds, Mama. Puffy clouds."

She was sure he said that.

"You'll be better in the morning, Timmy," Ruby replied.

But he seemed to know what she was thinking: he may not be better.

God wouldn't take her baby, would he? She'd made a deal

with Him when Timmy almost drowned. She'd vowed she would do everything to be the best mother, and in return, God would protect her children. They shook on it, and Ruby had kept up her end of the bargain. She took extraordinary care of her children, even though she hadn't experienced that same care herself. She rocked them when they needed soothing, she fed their hunger with tasty food, and she cleaned them every night to remove the day's dust. They wanted for nothing.

Ruby rocked Timmy—listless in her arms—until he returned to sleep. She looked out the window and up at the sky, holding him tighter and tighter when she felt him leaving her.

When Joseph came home that night, he took Timmy from Ruby and laid him on his bed, covering him for the night. He fell asleep, and Joseph led her into their room and encouraged her to rest.

Before the children woke up, Joseph prepared to leave early for school.

"I'm worried, Joseph. Can you send Doc over to check on Timmy?"

"He's a healthy boy. Don't worry. All children get sick sometimes."

"Can you come home early, with Doc?"

Joseph pouted as he considered her words. "He'll be fine, Ruby. But I'll ride into town at lunch to ask Doc to come to take a look at him." He hesitated at the door before grabbing his hat to leave.

To stay at Timmy's side, Ruby put Wilson behind his gate and let Mary cry in her cradle. He woke up, thrashing in his bed, his breathing labored. Ruby took a deep breath but couldn't inhale enough air for both of them. She picked up Timmy and observed him; he could deliver only shallow, quick breaths.

"Come on, Timmy. Breathe in. Breathe out . . ."

Let me help you, she thought.

She sat on his bed, and a cold, snake-like wisp entered the

room and surrounded him. The thief of life. Ruby raised his chin to open his throat. She moaned as she looked deep into his mouth; a thick gray mesh covered the back of his tongue, coating his tonsils. Ruby found a washcloth and tried to rub the foreign membrane out of his airway, clearing a passage for more air. He choked as she worked on him. Diphtheria. She knew the symptoms. Everyone did.

Where was Doc?

"Mama, something bad's in there and won't leave my froat. Can you get it out?" She hardly recognized Timmy's raspy voice.

His face almost sizzled at her touch. Ruby held him and breathed in shallow breaths with him until an hour later, when there were no breaths at all. She found herself alone in her thoughts—the communication between her and her firstborn son had stopped for all time. She wrapped her arms around Timmy and herself and sobbed.

Joseph came with Doc after school, and they could hear Baby Mary's screams on the ride up to the house. Joseph opened the door to see Wilson sitting on the kitchen counter—Ruby was nowhere to be seen. Wilson had knocked over the flour bin and drawn pictures through the flour on the floor with his finger. Joseph picked up Mary from her cradle. Her diaper was sopping wet; droplets of urine hit the floor as he held her up. Her eyes were red and swollen, apparently from hours of crying.

Joseph followed Doc into Timmy's room, and Ruby sat on the floor with both arms around the child in her lap, cradling him like an infant she prepared to feed. Timmy did not move.

Ruby stared out the window, shaking her head back and forth, repeating the same phrase over and over. "God, we had a deal."

~

THE WHOLE TOWN gathered at Joseph's family cemetery at the base of MacCallum Mountain. The sun shone behind them, but Ruby took little notice. A blanket of sorrow, much like an early-morning fog, covered her shoulders. Someone guided her to the seat under the shade tree next to Timmy's casket, the little pine box where her soul lay—her reason for living. Though numb, she obeyed and let Joseph fuss over her. She accepted the mountain people's condolences as they came. But make no mistake, this day wasn't for her—it was for all of them. She would play their game for now. She hadn't exhaled since the day before yesterday. She took in a breath and held it, not sure what would happen if she let it go.

Joseph stuck to her side; she could tell he worried about her. He put his arm around her, supporting her on the promenade up the hill. But where was his worry when it had counted most —when Timmy got sick? Joseph cried, dabbing at his eyes with his handkerchief, already soaked. Ruby remained stone-faced.

Joseph's entire family came. Alice held Baby Mary, giving her a bottle when she needed it. Mrs. MacCallum tried to keep Wilson close to her, pointing out the birds that flew overhead, a distraction she hoped would keep him entertained during the service so he would stay in her arms. Ruby looked over the crowd. She recognized the townspeople, those she had known her entire life, most of whom had shunned her. They were there for the MacCallums, no doubt. For all she knew, they were laughing at her again, taking delight in her failings. They always had. It was as if they were saying, "Look at Ruby—she couldn't even keep her son alive." Only Timmy had seen her differently.

Her brothers didn't come. She didn't know if they got word in time or if they simply didn't care. Shouldn't they drop everything to be at her side? Granny and Pa were over by their wagon on the path to the cemetery. Pa couldn't walk to where the rest of them stood. She hadn't seen them in quite some time. They both held their heads low.

Deacon Preston held the Bible, reciting scripture to begin the service. Ruby hardened. Who invited God to this service? She stifled a mighty scream and looked at the simple box, only four feet long, lying bare on the dirt mound before her. On unsteady ground, it tilted slightly away from the hole that was dug.

If Timmy were here, he would have asked her, "Why do you put people in the box?"

She listened for his question, but it didn't come. It would never come—the lid had been nailed shut. The deacon still preached and gave glory to God. She didn't buy what he was selling.

She surveyed the crowd and noticed Leon standing at the back of it. Their eyes met, and he tipped his hat solemnly. She knew he would be here. His eyes never left hers. With sudden clarity, Ruby realized she had found her soft landing—the place she would go when she couldn't hold up any longer. Unlike all the other people who stood around that tiny box, Leon knew everything about her and still showed up. He would hold her broken heart, not letting fear keep him away from what he would find there.

# CHAPTER THIRTY-SEVEN

*E*veryone who dropped by with food for the family days
after the funeral whispered and walked tentatively
through the house, as if shattered glass covered the floors.
Joseph didn't know what to do with Ruby. He had seen others
grieve over the years, but he had never lived with it. Ruby, who
recently didn't say much to him in any circumstance, remained
painfully quiet. She detached herself from him and suffered her
pain in silence as a warrior would. She wouldn't look him in the
eyes as he tried to console her. Nothing he tried gave her
comfort. She turned her rocking chair to the window and
looked out where she and Timmy had played by the spring.

"Ruby, Baby Mary is hungry. Are you ready to feed her?"
Joseph asked.

She didn't answer, so he placed his little girl in her arms, and
she absently held Mary to her breast. She lifted her camisole and
put the nipple in the infant's mouth. The milk flowed passively
from mother to daughter. Ruby continued to stare outside, not
even glancing at the baby she held. Baby Mary patted Ruby's
breast as she suckled, oblivious to the fact that her mother was
an empty shell. Joseph took Mary, holding her on his shoulder

and patting her back to help the air bubbles escape. Ruby didn't cover herself when he moved the baby, as if she just didn't care.

He turned Mary after she burped and placed her near Ruby's other breast. "I called off school for this next week. I'll be around except for Wednesday afternoon and Saturday morning when I'll keep the store open. I'll try to be here until this gets better for you. Just let me know what I can do."

"Where were you when our son was deathly ill, Joseph?" She followed that with a silent stare.

He didn't have an answer for her.

Joseph stood there, watching her heartache. Ruby remained stoic, like a dam wall that withstood any force. The suppression of her grief created more pain for him than any tears she could have shed. This was his fault. If only he had taken Ruby seriously and taken a day off work. His family deteriorated before his eyes, and he couldn't stop it—it was more fractured than he could fix.

Wilson peeked around the door to see where his mother was. He seemed to sense the gravity of her mood and didn't make a ruckus. He appeared to be looking for his older brother in all their good hiding places, but Timmy couldn't be found. Joseph stood in front of Ruby as Wilson toddled out the door and climbed down the front porch steps. Joseph watched his son's surprised look when his foot met air, and he tumbled into the dirt below. Had he been there, Timmy would have caught Wilson. Things had changed for all of them.

"What can I do for you, Ruby?" Joseph asked.

"Send word to Mabel that I want to go out Saturday night. Have her come pick me up in her wagon," Ruby replied.

"Are you sure? It's not been a week." Joseph tried to hide his shock.

It didn't seem right to want to go out on the town so soon after burying a son. But Joseph had said he would do anything for Ruby, and she was asking for this—it was her one request. He was beyond worrying about what others thought and would send word to Mabel to pick up Ruby tomorrow after suppertime.

Saturday evening, when Mabel arrived, Ruby rose to go outside, not saying a word to Joseph. He followed her out and exchanged glances with Mabel behind his wife's back. He tried to give Mabel a warning glance so she would understand how fragile Ruby was. Mabel hugged Ruby's side, and Ruby climbed up on the wagon bench and sat there as straight as a board. She returned Mabel's hug with about as much feeling as the wood she sat on.

When they drove off, Joseph feared he had lost her. Unless she could find a way to forgive him, things might never be the same between them.

~

"Ruby, we can just go to the café to talk if you don't feel like music tonight," Mabel said.

"Music might carry me through another day. I had to get out of that house, Mabel. I can't keep looking at where Timmy used to be—that's all. Joseph's tiptoeing around, not knowing what to do."

What Ruby didn't confess was her need to see Leon—it scared her that much. Whatever it meant for her marriage, her pain cleared the way to him, as if it had felled trees to open a secret pathway in the woods. She knew it in the way her body continued to breathe when Timmy's didn't. Whatever consequences followed from seeking Leon didn't matter to her.

That was her naked truth, but truth is rarely pure and never simple. Leon had flaws that made him dangerous. He rewrote his own rules of right and wrong to fit his purposes. But following the rules hadn't worked for her. Her son had still died. She needed to renegotiate the way she lived.

Mabel set Ruby up at the side table close to the stage where they usually sat. Everyone knew that the friends of the band would sit there. But Ruby asked to go over to a table by the door in the back corner. Mabel obliged, most likely assuming she didn't want others gawking at her so soon after her oldest son's funeral.

Mabel's regular dance partners found her and asked her to dance. She and George, her favorite partner, tried out an older dance called the turkey trot, and as Mabel learned it, her hat bounced on top of her head as if she was learning to ride a horse. Perhaps not knowing what to say or because of the shock of seeing Ruby out the night after the funeral, everyone left her alone. Three songs into the set, Leon came in and sat with Ruby in the darkened room. She knew he would be there, that he would come looking for her. He slipped some liquid from his flask into her glass of soda, knowing it would take the sting out of her misery. Nothing had ever tasted better.

And when the band played their first slow song, Ruby danced with Leon. At first, he held her up as they moved around the floor, supporting her lower back with one hand and holding her hand in his. He ran his thumb along the sensitive skin underneath her wrist as he held her. She didn't need to look at him, only to feel his presence. She let him be as close to her as he could. Putting her head on his shoulder, she started to cry in the darkness of the dance floor.

He dropped her hand and started twirling the ends of her hair with his fingers, then used his thumb to wipe away her tears. The music and his touch soothed her in her loss. They danced in a circle. There was no place they had to be and no direction they had to go in. Because of Leon, this moment wasn't all pain. Here she was, living with an injured heart but truly living— being held up by someone who really knew her but loved her anyhow. Round and round, she danced with him. She put both arms around his neck and kissed his cheek. She didn't care what others thought. Now that she was breaking her first commandment, they would all topple, one by one. Nothing would ever be the same for her again.

# CHAPTER THIRTY-EIGHT

*A*t first, Ruby just occasionally ran into Leon. If she was on her way home from the MacCallum house on her weekly Friday visit there, he might be on horseback, hanging out at the edge of the woods. Ruby would stop the wagon, and he would ask about her day. She knew the meeting wasn't coincidental. After a few words, he would retreat through the woods while she headed home. It mattered that he cared.

Then Leon started coming to the dance hall every Saturday night, an hour or so after the music began. He would wait until it became dark outside so that most people were already inside dancing. Knowing his timing, Ruby would get up to use the privy out back, excusing herself from Mabel's table. They would sit on the picnic table in the alley and hold hands—she was happy merely being next to him. Sometimes they talked nonstop until the music ended, interrupting the conversation only to go inside to check that Mabel wasn't alarmed by Ruby's absence.

Leon told her he'd quit his job with the railroad and started a new business related to his pa's employment. It required him to be in Knoxville from Tuesday to Friday most weeks, but he could see Ruby on long weekends.

Soon Leon was coming to her home on Mondays when Joseph taught at the schoolhouse. He would arrive when Wilson and Mary were napping in the afternoon and make sure to leave well before Joseph returned. If Ruby had worked hard enough in the morning, she could take a couple of hours to sit on the porch with Leon while the babies slept. Ruby sipped tea, and he added some kick to his cup from his flask. After a few years of not talking with Joseph, of holding in her innermost thoughts, she enjoyed talking with Leon.

He explained his new business, procuring surplus from the railroads and selling it to customers in several states. Ruby didn't know if he had the head for launching a venture like this; he hadn't done well in school, especially in math. Before long, without Leon asking for it, she offered to help him with the books. The next time he came, he brought over scraps of paper that passed for customer records and dumped them in her lap. She told him to bring a blank ledger from Knoxville, and she would set up procedures for payments and tracking customers. Leon laughed and said he was the idea man, and Ruby would be his bookkeeper.

Ruby kept track of the time during the visits so that Leon always left before Joseph might be home. Leon stoked the fire before leaving so that Ruby didn't have to do it to cook supper for Joseph. Their relationship might be improper, but it only involved talking—and laughing. And oh, how he made her laugh! Sometimes, they had to shush themselves if one of the children stirred in the other room.

Soon Ruby wrote to him every day he wasn't in town. Every morning, right after breakfast, she would pen a note to him, sometimes while breastfeeding little Mary. She became obsessive to tell him all the details of her day—the funny things

Wilson had said or a summary of mundane chores. She would remind him of the fun times on her pa's farm when they were growing up. Ruby mailed the batch weekly to his boarding-house in Knoxville, hoping he received them before leaving town again. She wanted him to know she was always thinking of him. He couldn't mail a letter to her for fear of Joseph finding out, but he brought some with him when he visited. Exchanging these notes mingled their souls and cemented their relationship. She never said anything inappropriate in writing. If anyone intercepted the letters, they would appear benign, as if she was corresponding with a male relative. By writing so often to him of the daily details in her life, she connected her thoughts to him. And maybe it meant something to Leon. She wanted him to know everything about her.

The closer she felt to Leon, the greater the distance between her and Joseph. Ruby didn't know how to approach the abyss Timmy's death had caused. Joseph still treated her tenderly and tried to comfort her, but he spent more and more time in town, which was apparently easier for him than coming home to face her. She couldn't forgive him. They wandered around the house in silence, with only the occasional echoes of what they once had.

When Leon came, he brought scraps of paper from his business and left them with Ruby to sort out and enter into the ledger books when she had time. It astonished her that he procured as many crates of cigarettes as he did to sell in other states. His wholesale price to his customers would be hard to beat; she could see why his business had picked up. His next foray was surplus clothing for men, women, and children. She asked for his expenses and his sources for inventory, but he put off bringing them to her. Leon pocketed a couple of hundred dollars a week from his connections, about twice what Joseph made with his three jobs combined. Leon started to pay her for helping with the books. He also asked his younger brother to join him in the business.

Before long, when Leon left her, he hugged her and gave her a little kiss. At first, she resisted, saying she didn't want this relationship to cost her a marriage. But soon, their relationship progressed well beyond the realm of friends. He visited one Monday during the children's naptime, and instead of going over the books and drinking coffee, Ruby made him a proposition.

"Lie with me." She walked onto the porch and turned back the covers on the daybed she used for the children when the weather became too warm to sleep inside. The cool air excited her skin, creating goosebumps when she took off her clothes and laid them on the side table. Her nakedness in front of Leon made her feel more alive than she had in years.

"Are you sure?" Leon's eyes didn't leave hers as she slid under the covers and pulled the quilt at the end of the bed over herself.

"I've never been more certain of anything in my life. Come here."

While he undressed, she remembered their day swimming naked in the river. They both had changed since childhood. But still, she knew him—in ways she had never known anyone before. He joined her in the bed.

Afterward, he held her as she cried.

Leon broke the silence. "I can't promise you anything, Ruby."

"I know that."

Promises. Joseph had promised her everything, but what good was a promise when it didn't hold any meaning? She willed herself to accept whatever helped her through the next days.

With no expectations about what the future held, she lay in Leon's arms for a long while as he soothed her.

~

JOSEPH WAS WELL into his lesson on the War of 1812 with the sixth graders when Pearl Owens, the postmistress who worked at his store, came into his classroom. She walked up the aisle from the back door and approached his desk, then leaned over to whisper into his ear so his students couldn't hear.

"Joseph, you should go home right now. I'll watch your classroom for the afternoon, and then I'll open the store for you if needed. Your children are fine but go home. There's a matter that needs your attention."

He didn't think to ask what the issue what might be or how she knew of it. He simply announced to the children that he had to leave, and Mrs. Owens would take over the afternoon studies. They were to listen to her, and if he heard of any misbehavior, they'd answer to him later.

Joseph left his coat and rushed out the door into the crisp late-fall air to saddle his horse for the ride home. For the life of him, he couldn't figure out what was going on. Pearl would have told him if Ruby had done something to hurt herself. He allowed himself to imagine all the possibilities, but nothing could have prepared him for what he found when he arrived. Joseph rode up to the back door and hitched up his horse to the rail in the event he returned to school to finish the day. He peered through the back porch screen to see Ruby in bed with Leon, the scene so shocking, he couldn't absorb it. Under the covers, lying side by side, facing each other, with only Ruby's bare shoulder exposed. Ruby laughed—*laughed*—at something Leon said and raised herself on her elbow to hover over him. Joseph froze, then shook his head to remove the image from his mind. So this was where Ruby took her grief.

Joseph got off his horse and charged to the back door. Ruby had the decency to cover herself when he walked in.

"Let me explain, Joseph." Ruby held the covers tightly around herself.

Leon rose, grabbed his pants and boots, scooted around Joseph, and ran out the back door into the woods.

Joseph slid down the logged wall and landed abruptly on the floor with his back to the wall. He sat there silently with his head in his hands.

"It won't happen again." Ruby sat up to start putting on her clothes. She had no tears.

Joseph couldn't look at her and searched for answers in the rafters of the cabin instead. He breathed heavily, in and out, trying to pump himself up off the floor, willing himself to move.

Minutes passed before he could find any words. "There's no explanation needed. I have a full understanding of what's going on. I'll take the children over to my mother's house, and I'll stay there until tomorrow evening. I want you to move out by the time I come home."

"Joseph, I'll stop seeing him. Don't do this. It's been hard on me. I've not been myself. Please, I'm asking for another chance." Ruby folded her hands together as in prayer.

"I can't give that to you. I'll go get the wagon hooked up for the children to ride in," he said.

"But Christmas is in four weeks. Let me stay until then. It'll be best for the children."

"A woman who lies in bed with another man isn't thinking of what's best for the children. Don't talk to me about that."

Ruby cowered at his words.

"You can stay until Christmas, but I'll take the children to my parents' house until then. Don't think about going over there and pestering my family. I'll tell them what they need to know. I'll let you know about visits when I settle down."

"Joseph, I think I should keep Mary with me. I'm still breast-feeding her. After Christmas, I'll go to my brother's place in Knoxville with her. Please. Let's not make decisions in anger."

Joseph took several minutes to respond. "The same brother who said you were worthless the day of Timmy's birth?"

Ruby simply hung her head.

"It's against my better judgment, but I'll let you keep Mary. I'll come to get her on Sundays for visits with my family until you leave."

On cue, Baby Mary woke up and cried for some attention.

"And don't let Leon back in this house, do you understand? That wouldn't be a good idea." Joseph spoke in a tone he had never used with her before. In fact, he couldn't remember using that tone with anyone—not even in his capacity of justice of the peace.

He didn't deserve this.

"Aren't you going to get Mary? Or are you going to just let her cry?" Joseph left to hitch the wagon to his horse and came back in briefly to get Wilson from his crib, bundling him up with some of his clothes and toys. He stepped out the back door without looking back.

RUBY CLIMBED BACK into the daybed and covered herself up to her neck. At the age of twenty-one, she would be starting over—with a baby in tow. Practically speaking, Ruby had been left to her own resources before and would be able to manage it again. She could do this. She could probably work for Leon until she got situated in Knoxville.

Ruby hated to think of leaving Wilson behind. Little Wilson, who'd always stood in Timmy's shadow. She would miss Joseph for the comforts he provided—a good home with nice things and his encouragement to sort out her difficult past. She had never known anyone so kind. She had tried to be a good wife to him, but her heart was never his—nor would it ever be.

There was nothing left for her here. Mary's cries escalated

from the next room, demanding her attention. Ruby rose, finished dressing, and retrieved her crying infant. At least Joseph was leaving her one child. She could still call herself a mother—if nothing else.

As she fed Mary, she watched out the window for Leon, but he didn't return.

# CHAPTER THIRTY-NINE

*December 1921*

*R*uby hadn't visited Granny and Pa in over three months. She knew they had probably heard about Joseph living at his parents' house by now, but she didn't know if they knew why. Ruby dreaded explaining the situation to them and saying goodbye. She would be contrite but ready to leave if they dug into her.

Ruby carefully dismounted so Mary wouldn't wake up. She had used yards of linen to bind the baby to her for the horse ride, a solution that worked since Joseph had taken the wagon. She leaned over and held Mary's back as she took one leg over the stirrup, balancing the added weight at the front. It wasn't too different from being pregnant. Ruby peeked down inside her winter shawl; little Mary slept, oblivious to the goings-on in her world. Her baby looked comfortable enough to sleep for a while, even in the bitter cold. Granny usually cracked open the back door when someone rode up, making it easier for them to get inside. But Ruby had to push the weathered door to open it.

A rug had been crammed at the bottom to stop the cold draft from coming inside. She moved it aside and entered.

Ruby didn't hear anyone. "Yoo-hoo, Granny."

She couldn't imagine where Granny had gone with Pa.

She took off her shawl and sat at the kitchen table to take off her boots. The fire had been stoked. After she unwrapped Mary, she peeked around the corner to find Granny in the front room by the fire, quietly rocking back and forth. To see this was eerily out of character. She couldn't remember the last time Granny had sat.

Maybe she had already heard the news about her and Leon. That would explain her stoic face. She could take Granny yelling at her, but the silence alarmed her. She walked into the front room with Mary. Granny usually lit up when she saw one of Ruby's children.

"How did you know?" Granny looked up and kept rocking.

"How did I know what?" Ruby looked around the room for a clue.

In her confusion, she wandered over to the doorway of the front bedroom, where Pa slept. She peered in to see his arms folded over his chest and his eyes shut. For the first time she could remember, he appeared to be at peace. She listened for his reproach, but none came. There was nothing—Pa was gone.

Ruby let out a big sigh, relieved she wouldn't hear a nasty word from him today—or ever again. But for good or bad, this man had been the only man in her life for many years. She tried to have a sad thought but couldn't muster one.

Ruby walked back into the front room and leaned down to hug Granny, who didn't reciprocate. She ended up patting her grandmother on the arm.

"You didn't help him much lately, Ruby. You'll have to live with that now," Granny said.

Ruby bound Mary again in her linen and put her shawl and

boots back on. "I'll go tell Doc and Joseph and telegraph my brothers. Are you okay for now?"

"I'll be fine, I reckon. But tell me, I have to know. Why did you come? Was it to visit your pa?"

"I'll tell you later. But for now, we need to let others know."

THE SERVICE for Pa took place on the hill midweek, as soon as the snow cleared enough for them to dig the hole. Robert came for the funeral and took over care of Granny. Her brother Timothy didn't acknowledge the telegram—either that or he didn't receive it at his last-known Kansas address.

Granny had aged many years in the last few months taking care of Pa. She had nothing to say when Ruby arrived for the service—she was grieving, most likely. Or maybe resting after years of nonstop care for her husband. Pa's lack of appreciation for Granny had made it even more tiring for her, Ruby supposed. Granny sat under the lean-to with a blanket around her legs, Robert at her side. Only a few townspeople came, evidence that Henry Turner had not been a loved man. The MacCallums offered to watch Mary, and Alice came by to pick up the child and offer condolences, but she didn't mention Ruby's separation and didn't stay to talk.

Joseph came to the services, paying his respects to Granny by taking her hand as he greeted her. Due to the extreme cold, Deacon Preston read the scripture and conducted a speedy ceremony. Joseph stood stoically during the service, never glancing at Ruby as he held his hat in his hand. He left shortly after the burial. As far as she knew, Leon didn't yet know that Pa had died. Since the day Joseph caught them, she hadn't talked to him. But Leon would have come if he knew. Wouldn't he? He had been closer to Pa than anyone except Granny. Pa had always warmed to him.

Ruby knew that Granny figured something had gone haywire with Joseph and Ruby but never asked about it. She didn't know that Ruby was preparing to leave. But Granny would be all right. Being from mountain stock, she would be resilient. She'd survive on her own.

After the graveside service, Ruby returned to Granny's house to cook a noon meal for Granny and Robert. Christmas was one week away, and she didn't have much time to tell them.

"Granny, Robert, there's something you should know. I'm moving to Knoxville."

"What do you mean, you're moving to Knoxville? That's absurd. Joseph wouldn't move away from his mother and father." Her grandmother stirred her mashed potatoes around on the plate.

Ruby's silence answered Granny's question. She would be going alone.

Robert pushed back his chair and laughed. "So Ruby isn't so high and mighty anymore. Did he finally figure out you weren't good enough?"

Robert's words hurt—they always did. Telling them about Leon would be too difficult.

"So, where are you going to live, Ruby? With two kids?" Granny asked.

"Well, I'm hoping to live with you, Robert, for a short while until I get settled. And just so you know, Wilson is staying with Joseph. The MacCallums will help him. I'm taking Mary."

Maybe because of the death fog surrounding her, Granny didn't ask another question. She had no fight left in her. Granny pushed herself back from the table, her plate still full, and took a sudden interest in Mary in the next room. She picked the baby up off the sofa where she lay sleeping and held her tightly before sitting in the rocker with her. Ruby caught her breath, taking in the enormity of the scene before her. She was leaving all she had ever known behind.

Robert tilted back his chair onto two legs and picked the ham out of his teeth. "Ruby, what did you do now? This doesn't have anything to do with Leon, does it?"

She didn't say a word. Robert had heard the gossip.

"You can stay with me for a couple of weeks, but that's it. I'm betting you won't even stop at my cabin, though, and you'll head straight for Leon's shack. You don't understand how good you had it with Joseph MacCallum. You're in for a rude awakening, I tell you. You've cooked your own goose, little sister."

And with that, Ruby put on her boots before retrieving Mary from Granny's lap. She wrapped the linen and shawl around them and left through the back door.

# CHAPTER FORTY

*J*oseph let her know how the last visit with Wilson would proceed. On Christmas morning, he would bring their son over after breakfast to the home Ruby and Joseph had once shared. Wilson would open his gifts from Ruby and see his little sister. Joseph and Wilson would leave in time to have Christmas lunch at the MacCallum house.

Ruby liked that he had arranged every detail; she merely had to follow his script—nothing else required on her part. Taking care of only one child made her life much simpler; taking care of three had consumed her whole day. But with the extra time, she mourned the loss of her family.

Leaving Wilson wouldn't be easy. He would be cared for, surrounded by cousins and all the female contact he wanted. She didn't know what they would tell him about her—that she'd died, maybe. She didn't know if she would be allowed to see him ever again. The thought of losing him compounded Timmy's death. Joseph would also miss his baby girl. The possibility of working out visits with the children gave her some hope and a little comfort.

Ruby prepared to leave a little part of herself behind. She

had hiked up the hill to Timmy's gravesite last Sunday when Joseph took Mary for the Sunday MacCallum visit. Ruby didn't have flowers but left Timmy's favorite wooden toy wagon on top of his tombstone. She sat on the wet ground for a while, visualizing his frolic. He would always be her cherished son. To her, he would always be three years old.

Christmas morning, Ruby got up and dressed, eager to stoke the fire for warmth before Joseph and Wilson arrived. She remembered last year—decorating the front door with mountain greenery and making sugar biscuits the day before to go with their Christmas breakfast. Timmy and Wilson had charged into their room before dawn, pulling on her hand to get her out of bed quickly to open presents. Timmy's infectious giggle had echoed in the rafters. There would be none of that this year.

She moved around the bedroom, aware of every part of it: the crispness of the sheets, starched from the last laundry, and the warm quilt on the bed made by Joseph's mother. Ruby had embroidered the pillowcases with ivy vines for his last birthday, like those that grew outside their bedroom window. Ruby memorized it all, absorbing every detail so she could take this mental souvenir with her.

Out the window, the snow had drifted in the field where she had played with Timmy. She stepped outside onto the porch and retrieved a couple of pieces of firewood Joseph had chopped in the fall so they would have enough to keep them warm for the winter. Her movements slowed as she thought, "This is my last day in this house."

Joseph and Wilson would move back here after she left. Joseph said he intended to start divorce proceedings. He would still have his teaching, his store, the court work, as well as his close-knit family. He remained highly regarded in the community—he would always have that, even with the scandal of her leaving. Joseph would suffer no disgrace.

He and Wilson pulled up as she finished making the coffee.

Mary made cat-like noises from the other room—her hungry signal. While she watched them out the window, Ruby fed Mary. Wilson was wearing his Sunday clothes and holding a wrapped present for her atop outstretched arms. The parchment and the red ribbon contrasted with the white snow. He toddled back and forth, carefully balancing the gift so it wouldn't fall. His hat fell over his eyes, but he didn't have a free hand to move it back up. He ran a few steps, then returned to walk with his father.

Ruby regretted not wrapping Wilson's gift; this would have given her a purposeful task in a day that promised to be difficult for them all. She had prepared for him the only photo she had of herself, a letter for him to read when he got older, and some Christmas cookies as well.

Joseph rapped on the door before he opened it and came inside. "Good morning, Ruby. Let me warm up my hands at the stove so I can take Mary off your hands."

She poured Joseph some coffee into his favorite mug. She added some cream to it, just the right amount he liked. Her familiar motions almost made it seem like a typical morning, not the goodbye it was. Joseph talked gently to Mary and soothed her. He stroked the reddish curls on top of her head tenderly, twirling them with his fingers, not taking his eyes off his daughter. He transferred her to one arm so he could wipe away the tears running down his cheek.

Ruby took the package from Wilson and placed it on the table before picking him up. She took his hat off, unbuttoned his coat, and then pulled each arm out from his woolen jacket. Wilson turned his shoulder away from her, turning to look at Joseph with Mary, and squirmed for Ruby to put him down. She couldn't tell if he wanted his father or to see his baby sister. He climbed upon Joseph's knee, peering alternately between his sister and his father. Joseph and Wilson belonged together.

"Well, Wilson, let's open our gifts, shall we?" Joseph said. "Give your mother the present you brought."

Ruby wanted to give Wilson his present first, but she let Joseph decide how the morning would go.

She untied the ribbon and leaned over. "Why don't you come closer, Wilson, so that you can see better?"

He inched closer to her, then scrambled back to his father's lap.

She opened the box to see an antique hand mirror, beautiful in design, the handle inset with rubies. Perhaps Joseph had purchased it long before he caught her with Leon.

"Thank you, Wilson." Ruby leaned across her chair to hug him in Joseph's lap. Joseph backed away. "Thank you as well, Joseph."

"Ruby, I can't help myself. You're a capable woman—beautiful and intensely smart. If only you'd believed it. Even after what you've done to our marriage, I hope you'll take a look at yourself occasionally and come to recognize the woman I loved."

She choked at his words. He could have asked that she look in the mirror and reconcile who she saw there with her latest actions. But he didn't. She inhaled quickly to stifle a sob and kept her head down. "Thank you. I'm very sorry, Joseph. I didn't mean to hurt you."

Ruby stepped into the bedroom to retrieve Wilson's present but hesitated—giving a young boy a picture of his mother wasn't the best present; she needed something more. She reached into her closet and grabbed a sock doll—one she had made for Timmy. She sat down across from Joseph and laid everything on the floor in front of her feet. Wilson slipped off his father's lap to pick up the photo and the letter before turning to give them to his father. He ran back to her to grab the sock doll with one hand and the cookies with the other.

Joseph reached into his leather satchel and held up a porcelain baby doll for Mary—one bigger than she was. Wilson came around the corner and pulled on the doll's dress as he took a look, then dropped the doll on the floor, cracking the porcelain face. Ruby stopped herself from scolding him. Mary's last memento from her father would be forever damaged.

"We better be going, Ruby. Mother will have Christmas lunch soon." Joseph paused. "I guess this is it. Let me know your address when you settle. I'm sorry I couldn't make you happy. Wilson, tell your mother goodbye."

Wilson hugged Joseph's leg and said nothing to her. She reached down to him for one last goodbye, but he wanted his father.

Joseph rose, picked up Wilson and his gifts, and left with tears in his eyes. Ruby stood there until their wagon disappeared over the mountain pass. With an empty hole inside her, she looked around the cabin. This place had never been hers, only a dream that had always belonged to Joseph. As hard as he had tried, he couldn't make her a part of it. If only she had loved him.

While Mary took her second nap, Ruby packed the trunk with all of the items she had selected to take with her the next day: her clothes, a photo of Timmy, and Mary's blankets and dresses. She would take the cradle if Robert had room in his wagon. The price of this would be listening to her brother's sarcastic comments, but she had too many things to travel by train with the baby.

Before she went to sleep that night, Ruby speculated about Leon's Christmas. She'd checked, and he didn't come back to visit his family this year. She would find out soon enough how Leon spent his days.

# PART III

# CHAPTER FORTY-ONE

*January 1922*

*R*uby stood between two railway maintenance buildings and watched Leon on the other side of the tracks. He held a clipboard and gave orders to his brother Ralph and another man Ruby didn't know. She hadn't seen him in work clothes in some time—not since the days they worked together on Pa's farm. Leon pushed his hat farther down on his head, his wavy dark hair spilling out beneath it; he needed a haircut. The men loaded a customer's unmarked vehicle with cases of what looked like cigarettes from the warehouse onto a truck. Leon commanded his employees by throwing his clipboard and waving his hands at them. She had hoped to find him in a calmer state before surprising him with her visit.

When the truck left, Ruby stepped across the tracks, soothing Mary by letting her suck on her finger. She didn't want Leon's first impression of them to be a noisy one.

Ruby had arranged to visit Leon sooner than she imagined because living with Robert had become unbearable in a few short weeks. Mary's cries annoyed him, and he raved about how stupid she had been to get into this predicament. Robert took his wagon and horses with him every day when he left for work, not caring about any needs she and the baby might have. Most nights, he didn't come back until bedtime. They were brother and sister in bloodline only.

"Leon? Leee-on . . ." Ruby adjusted the baby's binding to be more comfortable.

He looked up and over each shoulder, trying to find the source of the call. When he didn't see her, he turned back to the papers on the clipboard.

Ruby moved a few feet closer to him. "Leon."

He turned all the way around. His mouth dropped open before he finally took his hat off to scratch his head. It had been six weeks since they had been together on the porch. Leon couldn't have known what had come of Joseph's surprise trip home during the school day; her letters to him had stopped. For all he knew, Joseph had forgiven her and they now lived a happily married life. After a few moments, he walked over and gently hugged her. Baby Mary peeked out of the top of the bunting, staring directly at Leon. The baby bulk prevented them from fully embracing.

"I had nowhere to go, Leon. Joseph told me I had to leave after Christmas. No second chance. So, I've come to help you with your business. Like I was doing before, but I can help in other ways too."

She didn't want to beg but would do anything to be with Leon. No matter the cost. What other choice did she have?

Leon scuffed the dirt with his boot, avoiding Ruby's eyes.

When he didn't say anything, she continued, "I'm staying at Robert's room in the boardinghouse for the time being until I find another place to live."

"So what does this mean then?" He still hadn't smiled at her.

She didn't know how to answer him.

"I mean, I like you all right. We had a good time, Ruby. But a baby too? I'm not sure I'm ready for that. The baby isn't even mine."

The baby? "Her name is Mary," she wanted to scream but remembered that Leon had arranged an abortion for his last girlfriend.

"Let me finish up a couple of things. Then we can have an early supper at the diner in town. We'll be able to talk there. Go on over and get us a table. I won't be long."

He seemed cautious, stopping short of embracing her arrival. Maybe Leon didn't want her there. She might have to rethink her next steps.

RUBY TAPPED her fingers on the table and twirled her napkin, then juggled a sleeping Mary from one arm to the other. As she sat there, she digested Leon's initial response to her. He had been shocked to see her. It was painful, and she would bury his reaction for the time being. The only thing she could offer for now was her ability to help him with his business as she had done before. Over time, he would see they belonged together. She knew poverty and wouldn't go back to that for herself and Mary, even if she had to live in the shadows to get something better.

An hour passed before Leon, changed from his work coveralls, joined her. He wore a suit jacket, threadbare at the elbows, that she hadn't seen before. They looked at the short menu, and both ordered the daily plate. Leon asked for coffee and stirred it when it arrived, studying it for several minutes instead of looking at her.

"Ruby, I didn't think I'd see you again. Mr. MacCallum told you to leave, huh?"

"Joseph wouldn't forgive me. I broke every covenant I ever made with him, and I don't think he'll ever get over that."

He looked around the room while he drinking his coffee, still avoiding her gaze.

"I don't think it's a good idea for you to be here for the long term."

Ruby pounded the table, causing Mary to stir in her arms. "Where would you have me go, Leon? I can't bring myself to go back to live with Granny. I was kicked out of town by Joseph." She bit her lip to keep herself from crying. "You should know that Pa died right before I left. You were close to him, closer than his own grandsons."

"Closer? Hell, he was unbearable. Move in with your granny, then. It would be easier to stay there now without your pa around. Joseph can't force you to leave town. You shouldn't have come here."

"I thought I could help you with your business. You had me do your books before. I can continue that. Maybe help you with customers too, if you want. Fill orders. Do correspondence. I can find someone to watch Mary while I work. You said your business was growing faster than you could handle it."

Ruby heard herself begging, and it sounded pathetic.

The waitress delivered their food, and Leon shoveled it in, perhaps buying time before responding. Ruby pushed food around her plate as she watched him.

"You should know that I've moved on. I'm courting other women here in town. I didn't hear from you, you know. I don't know what you expect from me."

It hadn't been long since Joseph caught them. Didn't she mean anything to Leon? Had he been playing a game with her when he came to her house? She had taken all the risk, and to what purpose? She didn't try to stop the tears that dropped on Mary's head. Leon wiped his mouth, laid the napkin on the plate, and stood.

Ruby took his elbow to keep him there. "I can't go back to Poplar Cove. And I can't stay with Robert. I need a place to live

—now. I have very little money and no one to watch Mary. I thought you would help me."

On cue, Baby Mary started to cry.

Leon sat back down and stared at her for a moment as if coming to a decision. "Ruby, I'll help you, but only as a friend. I'm going to carry on with my personal life just as I was before you arrived. If you agree with that and don't whine about it, I'll hire you to take care of my books three mornings a week. Twenty cents an hour. There's a back room in the warehouse that I made into an office—you can stay there for a while for free until you find something else. It has a bed and a small stove for heat."

"Thanks, Leon." Ruby pulled her wrap over herself to feed squirmy Mary discreetly and protect herself against Leon's coldness.

"I'll send a wagon over to Robert's for your things tomorrow morning. Here's a couple of dollars to help you with expenses until you get situated. But remember, you are my friend. Nothing more."

He left coins on the table for dinner, turned his back, and walked out the door.

The job and warehouse room Leon offered would have to do for now; Ruby swallowed the terms he'd laid out. Leon had become calloused; not like he was when he had danced with her and played in her bed. She wrapped Mary around her and gathered her belongings to start the long walk to Robert's boardinghouse.

# CHAPTER FORTY-TWO

*April 1922*

*R*uby walked the half-mile to the second warehouse to talk to Leon and found him opening a wooden crate of linens. He extracted six sets of sheets before nailing the lid back on.

"Hey, Leon, we need to track the inventory so our customers know what's available. Use this form so I can enter it into my ledger. I don't have time to take inventory every weekend."

"Ruby, I don't work for you. I'm not going to fill out any damn form." He kicked the container for emphasis.

"It saves time. Fill it out and drop it in this box—it just takes a few seconds. We have to have these procedures since we're a larger operation now."

Ruby entered the newly acquired inventory into her ledger, not wanting to force the issue, and began to address what else she had come to discuss with him. "You could charge your customers about twenty-five percent more than you do, and they'd pay it. Your prices are set too low."

"Why don't you set the prices? I'll gladly hand that off to you too. That way, you won't be bossing me around every chance you get."

"Thank you. I'll give you the new pricing sheet when I finish it."

Whew! Leon was in a mood. Ruby walked back to the office, steering clear of him and whatever issue was bothering him.

She was just about over Leon, though she spent her evenings after Mary went to sleep thinking about a life with him. He knew her. And she thought she knew him. Why was he resisting her so? She imagined a clear path to her next life, with him in it. Perhaps over time, he would come to see that Mary wasn't a hindrance to a relationship.

It didn't take her long to figure out how Leon made so much money. He hadn't given her the cost-of-goods paperwork she'd asked for because it didn't exist. After hours, he gained access to the warehouse and pilfered items he could quickly sell on the black market. He then doctored the railroad paperwork to cover his theft—all right underneath his pa's nose. Taking a case or two of cigarettes or a box of leather goods before the shipment moved along the rails didn't seem to cause an issue.

When she realized how Leon made his money, she had written to Joseph to ask for another chance with him and Wilson, begging forgiveness for her indiscretion. Joseph still hadn't written her back, even though she had given details of Mary's latest trick of buzzing her lips together to produce bubbles and had asked about Wilson. Ruby again considered leaving to go live with Granny but couldn't make herself return to the poverty and blame that existed there. She was between the hard rocks of mountain poverty, bad decisions, and a fall from grace.

She had always been scrappy and made a way for herself. But starting a life of crime could be like tumbling down a mountain path, ending up in a spot unable to climb out. And if she did manage to get out, she would only get back to where she'd started in the first place. She was used to living in the shadows but needed some money to start over somewhere else. Though it gnawed at her before she went to bed at night, what choice did she have?

Leon had taken over an abandoned barn for his second warehouse, right along the tracks about a half-mile from the station, to store the stolen goods until he could resell them, keeping them away from his pa's eyes. Local customers sent their wagons there to pick up purchases and handed over cash as requested.

When word got out on the underground network, their enterprise couldn't keep up with the demand. Customers across the nation wanted in on the prices Leon offered. They heard from a friend who told another friend. The boys from Chicago arrived one day and asked Leon for exclusive rights to the inventory—especially cigarettes. He refused them, saying they would try to control him and set prices to their liking instead of his. He beefed up the customer demand by expanding the variety of items available; one-hundred-pound bags of sugar sold almost as quickly as cigarettes to his market. He began to divert whole railroad cars of goods. His buddy Edgar, an engineer who worked for the railroad, would stop the train at the barn and wait nearby until the boys emptied a few railcars—all for a handful of bills. It bothered Ruby that so many people around the country knew what they were doing; the law could be watching their operation. She carried on business as usual while looking over her shoulder for strangers.

Except for the few new employees Leon had hired, including his brother and Ruby, he had no costs and paid no taxes. Ruby couldn't help but wonder when the jig would be up.

Leon said his pa had once asked about the reduced inventory of goods in the railroad warehouse, and Leon told him he figured business had slowed down for the railroad. He showed his pa the doctored books, and he asked no further questions.

Ruby started answering the newly installed phone in the office when Leon was out and developed the keenness to discern who could be trusted and who could not. She spoke cryptically, just in case the telephone operator was listening. Ruby took orders from local customers and made arrangements for them to pick up what they requested. She arranged train shipments to customers around the country, giving discounts if they placed a recurring order. Her three mornings a week turned into five full days, with only lunch breaks to breastfeed Mary at her caretaker's house a few blocks away.

After everyone left for the day, Ruby would retrieve Mary and retreat to the back part of the office, in the room next to where she worked. Leon would disappear right after work, keeping his word about dating others. He saw whoever he wanted and spent little time outside of work with Ruby. He seemed pleased she had taken over many of the operation's details, so he didn't have to keep track of them.

One night after Mary went to sleep, Ruby carried water from the spring for her washbasin and heard Leon and a girl carrying on between railcars. His lady friend was whooping it up, and Ruby couldn't resist turning to look. His date almost tripped over the tracks on the way to an empty railcar. Leon lifted her into the boxcar and scampered up to embrace her. Ruby watched as they went inside and out of sight. The woman's laughter followed her back into her room. Ruby paused, then turned to shout something tart to Leon before stopping herself. She had to make a living, so she never let on to him that it mattered. Ruby had already made one mistake with Leon. She wasn't about to make another one.

# CHAPTER FORTY-THREE

*July 1922*

*R*uby woke up to a soft knock on the office door. She covered herself with a cotton robe and peeked through the curtain. Leon stood there belting out the latest ragtime song. He tipped his hat to her and smiled that charming smile she'd fallen for back in another life. She put her finger to her lips, hoping he would quiet down and not wake up Mary, a little more than a year old. If she woke up, she wouldn't quickly go back to sleep.

Ruby stepped outside, and Leon grabbed her and gave her a big hug—something he hadn't done since she'd arrived six months ago. She retreated from his foul breath and backed into the doorway.

"Go home, Leon. I'll tar and feather you if you wake up my Mary. Go sleep it off." She wanted a few more hours of sleep. From his looks, she would be handling more than the books tomorrow.

"Ru-beee, I'm always thinking about you. You know that,

right? I did you wrong. I did you wrong. Wrong. Wrong. Wrong." Leon's tongue twirled around his words. He removed his hat and put it by his heart, pounding his chest with emphasis as he spoke.

"We can talk about it another time. Now go on home." Holding her robe closed, Ruby pushed his chest with her free hand. "Go sleep it off."

He turned to go and started speaking in a whiny voice. "You're the best thing, Ruby."

She pushed him away from her door and turned to go back into her room, closing the door behind her. She doubted that Leon would remember any of it tomorrow.

THE NEXT DAY, Ruby put together a report of all the earnings since she'd joined Leon in his business, comparing it to what they were like when she started working for him. She intended to ask him for a raise in pay. The company's sales had nearly doubled in six months because she had raised prices and cemented relationships with their regulars, who were happy to get their orders on time now. Ruby used prearranged codes when customers called in to order—just in case someone was listening to the calls. Leon paid no mind to what she did with the books. Had Ruby been skimming money off the top, he would have never guessed it. But she honored the relationship between them while receiving the same salary he'd given her when she started.

Leon sheepishly came into her office that afternoon. "Sorry to bother you last night. Did I kiss you? I think I might've."

"You did not." Leon relaxed when she dismissed his visit the night before. "But I'd like to talk to you if you have a minute. I have a report showing growth in the six months I've been here."

He pulled a chair up to her desk, and she placed the ledger between them. She sat beside him, closer to him than she had been in months. He twiddled his fingers on the desk as she talked.

"This chart shows how you were doing before I came to work for you. From what I can gather, you weren't filling orders that you promised to your first customers—I think you lost track. Partly because of my records, we've grown and are making double what you were back then. Here are the numbers from January through June. Your customers get regular deliveries now—they trust and count on me. I've been depositing the money in several bank accounts in the state, so no one suspects your windfall isn't legitimate. However, you're still paying me the same hourly rate you did when I helped you back in Rock Bluff. I want a cut of the profit, Leon. I think I deserve that. I believe twenty-five percent is fair."

She knew her request could make him angry. He could fire her, and that wouldn't be good. But she also knew he couldn't operate without her. It wasn't as if he could hire an accountant from town—not for the business of selling stolen goods.

Leon rubbed his temples and passed his hand over his puffy, bloodshot eyes. His clothes, deeply wrinkled, had the sickly-sweet smell of last night's moonshine. He slid his finger down the ledger as he studied it before leaning back in his chair.

"Awww, come on, Ruby. I'm giving my brother Ralph a percentage, but he's family. You already know that since you keep the books. You seriously think you deserve the same percentage I'm giving him?"

"I'm taking some personal risk here. That alone justifies a pay raise. Look at these increased profits since I arrived, Leon. I want a cut."

Leon pulled his long hair on top of his head. "I'll tell you what. You agree to take over the customers entirely and keep up with the books, and I'll agree to it. Plain and simple. I never liked keeping track of numbers or who needs what. I'm the idea man." Leon squirmed, hopping from one foot to the next. "But funny thing, Ruby . . . I came in here to talk to you about something else. Why don't you pick up Mary after work and meet me at the diner? We can talk there." He picked up his hat and left.

Ruby smiled, pleased with herself. He didn't bat an eye at paying her more; she should have asked for a cut sooner. But what was he up to? His demeanor had changed over the weekend. Until now, he'd snubbed her at work. She was merely his employee, a fixture in his company, much like the desk where she worked. But the fact that he remembered she had to pick up Mary impressed her. He usually acted as if the baby didn't exist when he asked her to work late, and he would hardly ever say Mary's name. What caused his change in demeanor?

Perhaps he knew of another property for her to live. The room attached to the office had worked for a while, but it would be nice to find a place with an indoor toilet and running water, farther away from the railroad.

RUBY PICKED up Mary and fed her some soda crackers while waiting for Leon to walk into the diner. Mary banged a spoon on the table, babbling as she did so.

Leon appeared out of nowhere. "That baby has your eyes, Ruby. She's a beauty like you."

Mary's eyes did catch attention—wide-open, hazel, and deep-set. They were the most prominent feature on her small face.

Leon leaned down to talk to her little girl, saying, "Bang, bang, bang," in time to Mary's rhythm. He made her laugh.

What does he want? It wasn't like him to coo over babies.

Leon sat down and ordered for all of them, requesting mashed potatoes for Baby Mary.

"Ruby, my pa is going to quit his railroad job and move home—he has cancer, Doc says. He's going to go back to Rock Bluff. So, I'll be going home with him this weekend. Is there anything you want me to do for you while I'm there? Or anything you want me to get for you?"

"It wouldn't bode well for you to ask Joseph for anything, Leon." One corner of Ruby's mouth rose, and she shook her head at Leon.

Their food arrived. Leon took a bite of his pork chop before continuing. "I'm going to try to get my pa's job at the railroad so we can keep our little business going. Another manager might find us out, and that wouldn't be good. If I get his job, it'd be up to you to run the business by yourself. I'd be able to take more product, I think. And we'd have to hire more help with shipping."

While eating, Leon paused to glance at Ruby. Why hadn't he mentioned all this when she spoke to him in the office? Why talk about this at dinner? He took his napkin and wiped Mary's chin after her spoon missed the mark.

"Ruby, how're things with us?" Leon half-smiled at her then looked off to the side.

"Leon, I don't think I heard you right. Could you repeat what you said a little louder?"

"I mean, do you think I could have another chance with you? I know I haven't treated you right. I wouldn't have been so sure that I'd stuck around if I were you." Leon reached over and gave Mary a pinch of his dinner roll.

"You were clear when I got here—you'd moved on. That was your choice, and you had other interests. You hurt me. Deeply. I gave up everything for you—my marriage, my son. And now you say you want another chance? I don't know what to do with that."

Leon squirmed in his seat. Ruby let him experience the full force of her words.

"Aww, Ruby. I've always had my eye on you—you know that. I've known you since you were eleven years old. We only had each other there for a while, during your rough days with Pa and all. Those other girls were just for fun. When I didn't want to be tied down." He paused, chewing his words before he spat them out. "But I can't get you out of my mind."

"I still have Mary, you know. She's part of whatever I do. I know you aren't fond of children."

"Geez, I know she's part of the deal. I'm warming to her. So, I can knock on your door, and you'll let me in next time?"

"Let's start with a picnic Sunday when you get back. And no relationship at work, you understand? I have to work like the dickens when I'm there. One more thing. I won't put up with any heavy drinking. You've been out of control lately. I don't want to be around you when you're that drunk. Let's just get it all out on the table."

Leon winked at her, and a grin spread across his face. "I'm just sampling my product, Ruby."

Ruby responded with raised eyebrows while shaking her head.

Leon faced her and his demeanor became solemn. "You're right about my drinking. I'll rein it in."

They finished supper, and Leon picked up Mary and offered to drive her and Ruby in his wagon back to their room. He whistled while he guided the horse and bounced Mary on his knee. Ruby took the time to settle her thoughts. Since she would make more money, she would look for a place in town and hire a horse to ride daily to the warehouse for work; she might as well spend the increase in pay on some items to make her life more comfortable. Leon pulled up outside her door and helped her climb down from the wagon.

"I'll be thinking of you while I'm gone, Ruby. Thanks for giving me another chance." He tipped his hat before he drove away.

That night when putting Mary to bed, Ruby relived their conversation. He wanted her again. She hoped it would go better this time around. But she wouldn't tolerate any of his shenanigans. If Leon didn't treat her right, she wasn't interested. She hoped she'd made that clear.

# CHAPTER FORTY-FOUR

*December 1922*

uby didn't get to sleep until after 3:00 a.m. Mary had woken up when Leon left at midnight and then cried half the night while rubbing her ear. This day would be a long one. As Ruby dressed, she looked around her new apartment and sighed. In her new surroundings, complete with indoor plumbing and a bed big enough to romp in with Leon, Ruby felt relaxed for the first time in months. She'd never felt this way in Joseph's home. The morning sun rose high enough to create an orange cast in her bedroom. Ruby shielded her eyes and pulled the shade down to allow a gradual start to her day. Mary slept in a closet off the kitchen that had a half door, perfect for containing her at night. Unlike her room in Leon's warehouse, this home separated work from not-work. None of her neighbors here knew about her past, and she could live without pretense. When the lady across the way asked, Ruby said she that had been widowed right after the baby's birth. The neighbor brought Ruby a loaf of homemade zucchini bread but otherwise left her alone.

Mary rustled in her bed and let out a high-pitched squeal. If only Ruby could be a better mother. She hardly thought of her second-born, Wilson, during the day, but memories of playing with Timmy filled her mind first thing in the morning and the last thing at night. Her Timmy—he'd be about four and a half now. Little Mary got her physical needs met, but she suffered for attention between Ruby's work and Leon's visits. Ruby supposed she ought to get Mary a little present for Christmas, but she still had a couple of weeks to think about that.

Leon spent most evenings at her apartment, sneaking in the back door so the landlady, old Mrs. Smythe, didn't catch him. Ruby would feed Mary, put her to sleep, and have dinner ready for Leon and herself, keeping it warm until he slipped through the door around 8:00 p.m. Over dinner, in hushed tones, so not to wake Mary, he listened to Ruby's suggestions, such as adding to their sales inventory with clothing: women's, children's, and men's woolen suits, in addition to household and grocery items like bedspreads and sacks of cornmeal. Ruby told him she'd found a new way for him to doctor the railroad waybills, erasing evidence that the stolen items had ever existed. Leon had changed, proving his commitment to her. He might drink on the weekends, but he refrained from consuming moonshine during the week.

As expected, he was handed his pa's job at the railroad. His pa had nominated him before he left for Rock Bluff, telling his boss that Leon had helped him and knew the ropes. Leon could now rig the books to steal even more inventory. With Ralph's help, they diverted full train cars to their warehouse before they reached the station, then emptied the product and refilled the railcar with shipments to their own customers. As Leon said, it was as easy as taking candy from a baby.

Ruby and Leon acted as if they were an old married couple— except for the lovemaking. Ruby learned to play with a man for the first time in her life, not counting swimming nude with

Leon as a young teen. Just last night, Leon had looked into her eyes one minute and teased her the next until they both rolled off the bed laughing. Leon's tricks excited her beyond measure. Naked and surrounded by candles, he taught her dance steps he had learned in the big city—all while trying to keep the noise down so Mary would sleep. He left the apartment after midnight, allowing both of them a few hours of sleep before the next day and well before Mrs. Smythe woke up.

Ruby finished dressing, entered the kitchen, and poured a bottle of milk before leaning down to pick Mary up from her pallet. "Are you as tired as I am, Little Miss?"

Mary rubbed her ear and laid her head on Ruby's shoulder. The baby felt warm to the touch; maybe that explained her incessant crying last night. Her baby molars could be popping through—Ruby refused to think about it being anything more than that. Nonetheless, she would keep her daughter home from the caretaker today. Mary would sleep most of the day anyway, allowing Ruby to finish her accounting work from home while she kept an eye on her.

AFTER WAITING for Leon and Ralph Pennington to drive away from the warehouse, Deputy Agent Marconi slipped inside Mrs. MacCallum's office and locked the door behind him. He knew she usually arrived at work by 8:00 a.m., but Agent Miller had reported she hadn't left her house this morning with the baby. Agent Marconi closed the curtains over the desk to begin his search. He pulled out drawers and rummaged through boxes, careful to replace everything where he'd found it. He discovered little of use to him in the cabinets; the accounting books must have been locked up, hidden, or transported home by Mrs. MacCallum. One scratchpad contained the words, *15 crates cigarettes per month, New Orleans REG.* Marconi took a photo of it and left it in its place. Even if he couldn't collect much evidence here, he would set up the wire today to record telephone conversations.

He scraped the insulation off the phone wire outside Mrs. MacCallum's office and tied an extension wire to it before trailing it across the street, hiding the wire in the grass, bushes, and rocks along the way. He attached a receiver to the other end of the exposed wire with metal clips and hung it on the wall of a nearby dilapidated, abandoned shed where an agent hid while collecting evidence. A few weeks of recording Mrs. MacCallum's phone conversations with the Penningtons or customers would clarify what federal agents suspected. The agents had tried to set up the wire the past several nights, but the somewhat erratic comings and goings of Leon Pennington made it too risky; Leon spent most—though not all—of his evenings in Mrs. MacCallum's apartment.

Earlier this year, the federal government made robbery from the railroad a federal crime and a violation of interstate commerce. There were only six hundred federal investigative agents in the country, and five of them were working full time on this case. The railroad had complaints going back as far as three years regarding the theft of goods, but until it became a federal crime, the perpetrators got away with it, as the states were unwilling to prosecute it. The Cincinnati, New Orleans, and Texas Pacific Railway brought two crates of evidence showing that shipments had disappeared over the three years, never getting to their destination. Three months after Marconi became the lead detective, he discovered that every missing shipment went through Tennessee. He set up a field office and traced fake waybills and shipments to narrow the thefts down to Knoxville. Careful gathering and documentation of evidence resulting in a conviction would boost Marconi's Bureau of Investigation career. They had allotted two years to bring indictments, so he could take his time to be meticulous in combing through the information he found.

When Marconi finished with the wire, he moved onto the warehouse recently vacated by the Pennington boys. With a man stationed outside the door as a lookout, Agent Marconi inventoried the loot, secretly marking some of the boxes so he could verify if they were the same ones to be delivered to an illicit customer down the road. They contained one-hundred-pound bags of sugar, several thousand cartons of cigarettes, children's clothing, men's woolen goods, and even children's toys.

The waybills attached to each container indicated *L & R Enterprises*, along with the recipient's address. He photographed these for evidence. They would help him figure out who received the stolen goods—the other part of the case. To his surprise, Leon Pennington hadn't even repackaged the cartons or removed the original customer's information; he'd merely covered it up with his own label. Sloppy work, in Marconi's opinion. It would be his pleasure to lock up these boys. Correction—Mrs. MacCallum and the boys.

# CHAPTER FORTY-FIVE

The next morning, Ruby rose from her bed, only to lie back down as fatigue overcame her. Her head and body ached. Ugh, she had caught whatever Baby Mary had. She felt her own forehead, but didn't think she had a fever. Baby Mary cried from the next room, asking to be fed, but Ruby felt drained. She would be slow-going this morning.

Nevertheless, she dressed quickly before Mary's cries escalated. Ruby didn't have time to be sick. She had to catch up on work she hadn't done after being home yesterday with her daughter.

After breakfast, Ruby dressed Mary. She pulled a smocked dress over Mary's head and directed her arms into the sleeves. Mary stood and banged her head against Ruby, who flinched at the pain. Ruby walked her daughter and her stack of clean diapers across the street to the babysitter's and returned to pack her lunch before going to the livery for her hired horse. The extra money in her paycheck allowed for such an extravagance.

She arrived at work before anyone else, unlocked the door, and threw down her bag on the wooden chair. She moved the curtain, bunched at one end, to let in more light. That was unusual; Ruby constantly adjusted the folds to look identical—she was particular that way. Perhaps Leon had been there yesterday. She took the books out of her satchel and quickly made a list of all the calls she would make that morning. Several issues needed immediate attention, the first being a mistaken delivery of baby clothes to a speakeasy.

Fortunately for her, Ralph picked up on the first ring. He ran the warehouse out of Wartburg to satisfy the customers west of them. The warehouse, more rural and hidden, had access to better roads and the western train route.

"Ralph, it's Ruby."

"Mornin', Ruby. Are you making that no-good brother of mine behave himself?"

As much as Ruby wanted to keep her work duties and her relationship with Leon separate, Ralph bundled the two together in every conversation. Would she ever attain a working relationship with him independent of her relationship with Leon?

"Well, this call isn't about Leon, Ralph. You had a big mix-up last week. The speakeasy in Chattanooga received a carton of baby clothing, and Martin's general store ended up with cigarettes. They don't sell cigarettes at Martin's. What happened?"

"Well, maybe they'll start. Ha! Don't worry. I'll fix it."

"No, this can't happen. We have to keep our customers happy. I've outlined the new procedure for repackaging goods for our customers several times. You can't just slap any label on a box and ship it. It needs to be checked and rechecked. You need to take the original waybill off the carton and attach the new one. We can't be careless. There's too much at stake."

"Don't get your petticoat all twisted up. Our prices beat everyone else's, so they'll tolerate a few mistakes. Besides, there are more customers where these came from."

"Our operations are getting bigger, Ralph. We're shipping to Texas, California, Ohio, Georgia, and North Carolina. It's not an easy fix when things go wrong. Let's just be careful. We don't want anyone snitching on us if they get mad. I'll send a checklist that you need to follow every single time a package is shipped. Do you understand me?"

"Don't be getting too big for your britches, Ruby. I don't like having a woman tell me what to do."

"I know you'll be careful from now on. But please nail the checklist up by the loading dock so everyone can see it. You have too much to do already to be packing up every box yourself. We have to train our employees, you know. Let's make it easy to do the right thing."

"I hear you, but Leon and I were doing just fine before you came along——"

Ruby hung up before he could finish. There was no need to discuss it further. She would remind him later how much more money he made now that she was running the office.

The phone rang before she began entering the week's invoices and payments in her ledgers. She pushed her chair back from the desk, fearing she wouldn't be able to attack the mound of paperwork anytime soon. She nibbled at her biscuit a little to settle her queasy stomach. She half expected it to be Ralph continuing his tirade when she answered.

"Hello."

"Hello, this is Mr. Herbert. I hear you're selling bootleg cigarettes."

Ruby hung up without speaking.

This call worried her. Ruby solicited all of the business; no one should have this phone number unless trusted contacts referred them. All customers from their network were told to start a phone conversation by saying, "The trains are running thirty minutes late from Knoxville," or whatever city they called from. She would then know that someone in their small network had vetted the customer. The local telephone operator may have overheard part of that call, and it was never good to talk about anything bootleg.

Only for an instant, Ruby thought about how wrong this could go for her. Little slips—like getting orders wrong or angering a customer—might lead to someone tipping off the authorities. They could be taken down quickly. She took a risk working with Leon, of course, but she had more money and felt the happiest she had ever been in her life. The calculated risk involved in their business had got her where she wanted to be. They had to be careful not to ruin things, that's all.

# CHAPTER FORTY-SIX

*July 1923*

*A*gent Marconi took off his wire-rimmed glasses to rub his eyes. The last few months of transcribing, cataloging, and analyzing these tapped phone conversations had aged him. A morning look in the mirror confirmed that his hairline was receding by the day. His wife begged him to come home every night when he called her. This case hinged on recording the information precisely and matching it with supporting evidence. He took a big bite out of his ham sandwich, and mustard dribbled onto his case notebook. He wiped it, creating a yellow splotch more significant than he had originally. Marconi had most of the customers figured out. They would initiate the calls using code and ask for the same items, with slight variation. Though slow-going, his work yielded significant results; he'd found almost twenty customers in twelve states. His boss had upped the number of agents from five to eight, and he used the additional manpower to determine where the orders were received. If this progress continued, he could wrap up this investigation with a fistful of federal indictments in another few weeks.

Customers—as far away as California and Ohio—purchased what Marconi knew to be stolen goods. In Oliver Springs, Texas, a pastor made a plea for some good ole Tennessee hooch to go along with his large order of name-brand cigarettes. He wished he could make this arrest himself—if only to see how the church fronted the illegal activity. In Asheville, a shoe store owner, probably trying to keep his costs down, just wanted leather pieces. Marconi waited for these customers to let it slip in recordings that they knowingly obtained their goods illegally. The Volstead Act, which had outlawed the sale of alcohol, helped that part of Leon Pennington's business grow. He and his brother could barely keep up with requests. A warehouse in Atlanta took every bit of moonshine the local scoundrels would send them, redistributing it to their customers farther along the line.

Mrs. MacCallum made about ten calls per day to take orders and check on shipments. She was a shrewd one and the brains behind the operation, as far as he could tell. She negotiated prices, making the Pennington brothers and herself quite a bit of money, considering they didn't pay for one iota for what they sold. He scratched out the numbers in the margins of his notebook and wished he made that kind of dough. But at least with this job and lousy salary, he didn't have to worry about ending up in prison.

Not all of the conversations incriminated individuals, but he recorded them as evidence. Marconi had to admit, Mrs. MacCallum fascinated him. He learned she had recently divorced her husband, a man of apparent good character from across the state in the mountains. Mr. MacCallum, a justice of the peace in his county, had to notify his ex-wife about an upcoming court hearing regarding their child. Her brother called her to report that Mr. MacCallum had sent him a note since he couldn't find her, saying he sought sole custody of their son. Agent Marconi had never heard of a woman losing guardianship of her children.

On the tapped call, Mrs. MacCallum's brother asked about her baby girl. Marconi made a special note at the front of his notebook to remember to arrange a child placement when he apprehended her. Furthermore, she revealed she was expecting another baby late in the fall—this one would be Leon Pennington's child. Marconi noted that a pregnant prisoner would require special handling.

Ralph Pennington, slurring his words as if he'd had too much to drink, called Mrs. MacCallum early one morning to say the three partners should share in all aspects of their relationship. Mrs. MacCallum slammed the receiver down, cursing him. Agent Marconi jotted down a note that he might use these relationship dynamics to get the hoodlums to inform on each other after their arrests.

Marconi listened to one call between Mrs. MacCallum and Leon Pennington several times. While he was out of town setting up a new delivery, she asked him if he had spent time with other girls. She whined that Leon hadn't touched her since she told him about her pregnancy. Agent Marconi tucked Mrs. MacCallum's jealousy in his side pocket; he could use this nugget later.

All in all, he couldn't believe his luck that he was assigned to this case—his first after joining the bureau. In his opinion, these backwoods boys didn't have enough sophistication to keep their noses clean. Some of the deliveries were made by teens, for heaven's sake. It wasn't wise to use underage kids to transport goods. Not only could a youngster mess up a delivery but involving a minor would bring additional charges in a federal case. He did have respect for Mrs. MacCallum—she might be a tough one to crack at trial. But Marconi didn't worry because solid evidence of conspiracy existed at all levels of their operation.

He poured himself a shot of pilfered booze and called his wife. "Honey, I believe this investigation will soon be over. I can't wait to come home."

BEFORE THE COORDINATED raid and arrests tomorrow, Agent Marconi had one more task to complete. After hearing a recorded conversation that Ralph Pennington would be in Knoxville the next day, Marconi planned to travel to the Wartburg warehouse. Marconi had waited weeks to do a scouting expedition there before a planned raid. He didn't feel confident sending an agent without casing the place first. Nervous about this undercover encounter in a remote location, Marconi bought some bibbed overalls at the mercantile and washed them in a tub with lye to fade them. He would pass himself off as a farmer who wanted to buy property for his wife and three children, and if anyone asked, he had photos of children to display. Everyone knew everyone else's business on this side of the mountain, and the mountain people—descendants of Scottish clans—remained wary of strangers. The less time he spent there, the better.

He parked his automobile on the side of the road seven miles from the warehouse and began his walk uphill, following the railroad tracks. When people came out of their shacks to size him up, he tilted his hat to cover more of his face, knowing they wouldn't be friendly until they had a reason to. At last, Agent Marconi approached the Penningtons' abandoned barn along the tracks and took out his handkerchief to wipe sweat from his face, then replaced the glasses that had slid down his nose. He waited beside a large oak tree to observe and, when he didn't see any activity, walked into the unlocked warehouse. His agents would drive here tomorrow, using the speed of their vehicles to give an element of surprise.

Beyond rows of crates, he saw clothes scattered in an area near a bed and determined Ralph must live as well as work here. Photos of nude women hung on a barn wall, attached with pieces of chewed gum, above a small unmade cot. Agent Marconi searched through a small table near the bed and clapped his hands with glee—he had hit pay dirt. He found what he had searched months for—a notebook containing all the customers' phone numbers, complete with dates when they sent product from this site. He couldn't wait to get back to his office to verify that this information matched what he had reconstructed in the investigation. Because the raid would take place tomorrow, Agent Marconi took the notebook, careful to place it in a gauze case to preserve any fingerprints. Ralph would be arrested tomorrow before he realized it had been taken.

Sixteen agents in seven states were in position to raid, collect evidence, and make arrests the next day at 1:30 p.m. Marconi would work out of Knoxville and coordinate the agents' efforts to shut down the Pennington operation. One agent could handle Wartburg. Agents in Atlanta and Los Angeles and small towns in Texas, Ohio, North Carolina, and Michigan would accost the customers receiving stolen goods.

Marconi walked back to his car and relished the easier downhill ride, going over the details in his mind. He still hadn't arranged a placement for Mrs. MacCallum's baby after her arrest. Without tipping anyone off, Marconi would call the home for unwanted children in the morning to ensure that they would take the baby that day. He would pass himself off as a gruff grandfather checking to see if they had room for another orphaned infant. He didn't want a baby on his hands tomorrow.

# CHAPTER FORTY-SEVEN

*R*uby pushed her chair back from the desk and got up to get the last little bit of coffee from the morning's pot. She turned her head one way, pushing her shoulders back to stretch them out after hours of desk work. Turning her head the other way, she felt her shoulder muscle pulling. Ruby had worked through lunch but had only made a dent in the pile of work she had. She needed to relax more while she worked. Maybe her muscles were tight from carrying Baby Mary around. In a rare moment while at work, she thought about little Mary. Ruby loved the way she chatted up a storm at night. Finding a good babysitter for her daughter had helped them both. Mrs. Anderson had four children of her own, and they accepted Mary as one of their clan during the day. Mary's favorite word was "mine"—most certainly one she often used with the other children.

Ruby took a big swig of coffee before a loud knock on her office door startled her back to reality. Leon could be playing a joke on her—he never knocked before entering her office. She pulled back the curtains to see three unknown men outside the door. The one in front held his arms behind his back.

"Who is it?" Ruby turned to her desk to place the accounting books in the top desk drawer.

"Agent Marconi. Bureau of Investigation. Open up."

Before she had a chance to lock the drawer, he pushed the door, and the loose latch gave way. All three men entered. The first held a gun to her face while the other two took the books from her.

"Put your arms behind your back." The man with the gun handcuffed her. Her heart raced while she figured out what to say. Just as if she was talking to a customer, she had to be quick-witted and hide her panic.

"Are you robbing me?" Ruby crossed her legs tightly together but couldn't hold it in. Fear took over. The pee ran down her stockings and puddled on the floor. The men backed up to avoid stepping in it.

The man in charge showed her his badge. "We'll talk later about who's doing the robbing. We're federal agents, and you're under arrest for larceny and possession of interstate freight—a felony, in case you didn't know. There might even be some conspiracy charges before this is over."

"I don't know anything, Mr., Mr. . . . . I just work here doing office work. I don't know what you're talking about."

"My name is Marconi. You don't know a Mr. Leon Pennington?"

"No, I mean, I know him, but I don't know anything about a larceny. You can let me go. I have a baby to take care of, you know. I'm picking her up from Mrs. Anderson's house at five. She's the preacher's wife. She'll vouch for me."

"It will be a while before you see your baby, Mrs. MacCallum. She's on her way to the state Home for Friendless Babies. She'll be safe there while we take care of this business of theft."

They took Mary to a children's home? She might not be able to talk her way out of this one. The men allowed her to sit at her desk—in her wet dress—while they ransacked the closet and desk and placed every item in cloth bags after they'd photographed it.

They didn't arrest women, did they? She wondered if they had also detained Leon. She needed to get word to him—he'd be furious if she didn't make an effort. The phone rang while they gathered items. She rose to answer it, forgetting that her hands had been bound behind her back. Ruby looked out the window; several agents stood outside the warehouse across the street. She couldn't see Leon.

The agent walked around the puddle on the floor and spoke before picking up the phone. "I'm going to put the receiver to your mouth, and I want you to answer as you normally would, Mrs. MacCallum. If you give anything away, it'll only mean more trouble for you. Do you understand?"

"Hel . . . Hel . . . hello, this is Ruby. How can I help you?"

The call disconnected before anyone replied. Marconi hung up and continued his work. Ruby glanced toward the warehouse again, and another car pulled up in front of it. Beyond the car, Leon stood handcuffed, kicking the dirt. His lips pressed tightly together, and he shook his head toward her, exaggerating his movements to indicate she shouldn't talk.

Refusing to cooperate, Leon swung his shoulders as an agent attempted to push him into the car. He bumped his head on the door before he fell into the back seat. The agent got in to sit beside Leon while another drove the vehicle away. Ruby wondered where they would take him. They led other employees, also handcuffed, out of the warehouse, loading them into the second and third cars.

Maybe they would let her go after Leon's arrest. Then, with clarity, she knew what she would do. No man wanted to deal with the complexities of a pregnant woman.

"Mr. Marconi, I'm in the family way. And I'm queasy. Could you take me outside so I can relieve my stomach?"

"Mrs. MacCallum, are you saying that you're pregnant?"

"I am. Can you free my hands? I don't want to retch all over your men or any of these bags you're collecting."

She pulled her stomach in and leaned over a bit while puffing out her cheeks. She didn't know if they would believe her, but it might speed up their decision to turn her loose. Mr. Marconi shook his head as if calling her bluff.

"We'll go outside when your ride gets here. If you have to vomit before then, please aim away from my boys and me, if you will."

They hauled the bags out the door, leaving little behind. How had they found out about the operation? As soon as she asked herself that question, she remembered the mysterious call she'd received a few months back from someone inquiring about bootleg cigarettes. She had hung up, but it worried her.

A black car with a gold star on the side pulled up to the office door. Two agents led her outside and into the transport without undoing her handcuffs. They helped her into the back seat, guiding her head below the roof of the car. Agent Marconi, smiling, entered the vehicle on the other side and sat beside her. He sighed as the driver pulled away. She stared straight ahead, pondering where they would take her and if they would keep her long. She held her breath, and bile rose in her throat. The smell of urine permeated the car, and Marconi covered his nose with his handkerchief as the driver continued into town. There wouldn't be a quick fix for this.

They drove past her lodging house, slowing down at the corner by the sitter's home. A police vehicle, with all doors open, sat outside. A nurse in uniform came out the front door with Mary bundled in a blanket, squirming to get down. Mary stretched her body as she tried to slip away. The nurse caught her arm and pulled her roughly toward the car. Mrs. Anderson stood on the porch, stomping her foot and gesturing at the officer before her. Her children held on to her legs. As she would greet anyone in town, she lifted her hand to wave to

Ruby as they drove by, then hesitated and lowered it. She gathered her children and went back inside but stood at the screen door with her hands on her hips, watching the nurse place Mary in the car.

Mary hadn't seen her. Her little girl would be with strangers tonight.

Ruby hung her head, hoping this would be over soon. It had to be.

# CHAPTER FORTY-EIGHT

*R*uby spent the night in jail, not sleeping a wink. At first, she remained stoic while thinking of a logical plan. It was best to get in touch with Ralph since Leon had also been arrested. She needed to hire an attorney for herself, given what she knew about cases Joseph had dealt with as a justice of the peace. Ruby had asked for a telephone call a few hours after her arrest, and they gave her one, but Ralph hadn't answered. All day, she had paced back and forth across her tiny cell all day but didn't know any more than she did when they took her into custody. Where had they locked up Leon?

At 4:00 a.m., she stopped thinking on her feet and started crying, feeling clueless—and powerless—about how to proceed. She slid down the wall and sat on the cold, hard brick floor, holding her head in her hands. Her dress, stiffened where she had wet herself, reeked, even to her. Ruby had run out of ideas.

She threw her head back against the wall in frustration and took a deep breath. When she exhaled, another option bounced into her head. If they let her, she would call her brother—he would come to assist her. Robert acted as if he didn't care and rarely talked to her, but he would help her out. He was family, after all, and her only option left.

At the first hint of dawn, Ruby's stomach growled, and her head hurt from lack of food; she hadn't eaten since breakfast the morning before. But she couldn't eat, as her stomach felt queasy.

"Deputy, can I visit the ladies' room? I'm not feeling well." Ruby threw up in the corner of her cell before the sleeping deputy could respond.

"For crying out loud, here's a towel. Wipe up your mess." Within minutes, he returned to his slumber.

As the sun rose, Ruby listened to the deputy snoring in his chair. A longing traveled from the base of her stomach to the top of her heart. Where had they taken Mary? Mary usually woke up at sunrise to eat. Then it occurred to her that mentioning her baby might help her get free.

The deputy woke up again when a café owner brought a basket of breakfast for both the prisoner and the deputy.

"Could you please give me a biscuit? I didn't get supper last night." To speak up for herself, Ruby stood. He might never feed her otherwise.

The deputy tossed her a biscuit, which she caught between the cell bars before it hit the ground. He devoured all the other items, exaggerating the noises of satisfaction as if to tease her. The aroma from the slice of ham made her salivate, but Ruby didn't say a word. Taking food that he thought belonged to him wouldn't get her any favors.

When he finished eating, she asked him, "Did your mama cook ham for you for breakfast when you were a boy? I used to warm up ham and cook eggs for my two-year-old daughter. I don't know where she is, and I'm worried about her."

He answered her questions with a loud burp.

She tried again. "Sir, could I have some of that coffee? I

noticed there are two cups on your desk. I didn't sleep last night and could use some."

Before he could answer, a colored woman came into the jailhouse, outfitted in a bright yellow housedress that buttoned in front to conceal a chest twice as large as her waistline. The deputy cast his eyes on her bosom—the buttons on her dress looked as if they might pop at any moment. The woman held her chin high and carried a piece of paper that must have held some critical information. She carefully laid it on the desk before the deputy with both hands. He took a minute to switch his gaze from her bosom to the paper presented to him.

"Mrs. MacCallum, this is your lucky day. I'm to release you to Mrs. Washington's care. It seems there isn't a place in the whole state that will incarcerate a woman who's expecting a baby. Now, let me be clear. You're not to leave her house, do you understand? If you do, then you'll be charged with escape from custody, another felony."

"Where's my baby girl? Mrs. Washington, do you know where my baby is?"

"She was taken to the Knoxville Home for Friendless Babies, Mrs. MacCallum. They won't release her to your custody until after your trial—that is, if you're found not guilty. She'll be with other babies there and be well taken care of, I'm told. I tried to get her released to me and wasn't able to do that." Mrs. Washington looked at Ruby with warm, caring eyes.

This woman had a no-nonsense approach to difficult situations, but Ruby hoped she would sympathize with her soon. Ruby walked behind her savior after the deputy opened her cell and sneered at him on her way out. She ached to hold Mary. She rubbed her stomach, remembering Leon's baby inside her. With God as her judge, she would not leave this one behind.

# CHAPTER FORTY-NINE

*August 1923*

uby waited until Mrs. Washington had placed the side dishes on the dinner table before unfolding her gingham napkin. Her host insisted that Ruby sit while she served dinner. Everything about Mrs. Washington appeared proper, except the unwed pregnant women housed in her modest but comfortable home. Ruby peered beyond the centerpiece of fresh wildflowers to study the other woman living in this house, a younger woman from Nashville who would deliver her own baby soon. Margie had pushed back her chair to allow her bulging stomach room at the table and fanned herself with her folded napkin. She sat in silence with her head down, as if in shame, or maybe she was ready to succumb to the late-summer heat. Ruby thought her to be about seventeen, about six years younger than she was. Margie's reddish complexion exaggerated the blemishes on her face. Holding her hands on her hips, Mrs. Washington scanned the table to confirm that everything needed was there and retrieved the pitcher of fresh iced tea from the sideboard before joining her guests.

"Dear Lord, bless these women and their unborn children. Nourish their bodies and nourish their souls, sweet master. In your name, Amen." Mrs. Washington picked up the platter and gave Ruby two slices of honey-baked ham.

"You should eat more red meat, Mrs. MacCallum. It'll help your baby's brain develop," Mrs. Washington didn't talk to her in a superior way as Granny did. She acted as if she cared, even though both women knew their roles. Ruby would have bristled if Granny had said the same thing to her. Granny's words would have tried to induce shame in Ruby or poke criticism at her mothering abilities.

"Mrs. Washington, you know a fair amount about mothering. Do you have children?"

"I do. I gave birth to fourteen children of my own. Three died as infants, but the others are grown and now have families of their own."

Ruby fantasized about growing up in a home like this one, with a mother who cared. Margie rubbed her belly while eating. Ruby knew how uncomfortable the last months of pregnancy were.

The girl lifted her downcast eyes and meekly smiled. "Mrs. Washington, will you be with me when I deliver? The idea of having a baby frightens me."

"I'll be there unless I have to be at court with Ruby. But don't worry, you'll do all right, honey. It's instinct." She attempted to soothe Margie's fears with her warm, milky voice.

"Ruby, aren't you scared?" Margie would never get over the shame of having a baby out of wedlock if she couldn't even look Ruby, a woman in the same situation she was, in the eye.

"Oh, honey, the last time I delivered a baby, it was easier than the time before, but you'll have help. Each time is different," Ruby said.

"You've already had a baby? More than one?" Margie asked.

She regretted disclosing that she had other children. Margie hadn't read the newspapers and wouldn't know her life history.

"This will be my fourth baby." She looked directly at Mrs. Washington, who didn't seem shocked by her admission.

They continued their dinner in silence, the conversation replaced with plate scraping. After a few minutes, Mrs. Washington reached over and put her hand on Ruby's. "Ruby, if you confess your sins, God will forgive you. He promised us that, don't forget. And if you want to talk, I'm available."

"Well, I might be beyond forgiveness, but I thank you for your kindness. Do you mind if I excuse myself? I'm feeling unwell. I think I'll rest on the porch and read the paper."

"Certainly. I understand."

For the three weeks she had been in Mrs. Washington's home, Ruby had enjoyed her free time—an unknown concept to her. At first, she floundered over how to fill it. Mrs. Washington expected her to be at meals on time, but the rest of the day belonged to Ruby. Her favorite activity was reading on the porch, where a shade tree nearby allowed a cool breeze, even in the heat. Mrs. Washington had provided a copy of the St. James Bible and some high school readers that Ruby had used with her students. The weekly newspaper, delivered on Sunday, became her lifeline. Ruby read every word about her arrest, attempting to glean news about Leon. She found that twenty people had been arrested, including both of the Pennington boys and all the employees. Several of their customers in other parts of the state —and country—had been taken in for questioning.

The news articles focused on Ruby. The arrest photo of her handcuffed took up one-quarter of the news page below the headline. They made her out to be the ringleader—the brains behind the outfit—and sensationalized the story using an exaggerated style. They somehow found a photograph of Baby Mary and displayed it on the front page next to Ruby's high school picture. NOTORIOUS CRIMINAL MOTHER ARRESTED AND TAKEN

TO HOME FOR UNWANTED WOMEN, the headline read, followed by HER BABY TAKEN TO CHILDREN'S HOME. The article contained gross untruths—that she owned a handgun, for instance—but Ruby admitted their angle likely sold newspapers. Reading about herself helped it sink in that she had lost another child, and in God's eyes—or anyone's eyes—her behavior had created a scandal and couldn't be excused.

Truth be told, Ruby ached to hold Mary, and she lay awake most nights imagining how her daughter coped at the children's home. Mary should be here with her, especially if Mrs. Washington had tried to arrange it. At times, though, she did enjoy the break from motherhood. Mrs. Washington treated her with respect, showed empathy, and fed her three tasty meals a day. Before bedtime, she luxuriated in the bath, using expensive scented soaps while enjoying indoor plumbing. She lived in a clean house without being responsible for the housework. But her thoughts always returned to Mary. Perhaps the preacher's wife visited her and took toys to her. Three weeks away from her mother would be an eternity for her little girl. Did she cry at night to be held?

She would get Mary back in a few weeks when this was all over. She vowed to be a better mother to Mary and Leon's baby as well.

Every time her attorney visited, Mrs. Washington sat in the next room out of earshot but on guard, in case Ruby might need something from her. Ruby wasn't convinced Mr. Peck had her best interests in mind. He disregarded her questions about Leon and her baby and focused on telling her the federal agents had built a good case against her, and he didn't have much hope of getting her off. Mrs. Washington accompanied her to the courthouse for her arraignment and sat off to the side as she stood before the judge. Her attorney wanted her to plead guilty and ask for leniency, but Ruby refused and proclaimed innocence. Mrs. Washington wrinkled her eyebrows and held a finger over her mouth but gave Ruby a nod of support. The woman didn't seem to judge. If she knew the whole story of what Ruby had done, she never let on.

Ruby folded the newspaper and returned it to the reading basket before going to her room for an afternoon nap.

~

A SOFT KNOCK on her door woke Ruby from her sleep.

Mrs. Washington cracked open the door and whispered, "Ruby, Agent Marconi is here to talk to you. He's in the parlor."

Ruby rose, combed her hair, and descended the stairs to enter the front room. Agent Marconi held his hat in his hands, and his balding head shone next to the lamp where he sat. She didn't sit directly across from him; instead, she picked up a pillow and sat on the far end of the sofa. Mrs. Washington disappeared from her sight. The agent had placed his notebook, its edges rumpled from being flipped through many times, on the sideboard. Ruby wondered if it contained his entire caseload or only notes about her.

Mrs. Washington had prepared him a cup of fresh coffee, and he sipped it, taking his time to get started. He took a couple of more sips and turned to her.

"Mrs. MacCallum, I have some confusion about how you didn't know that Mr. Pennington sold stolen goods. Look at this expense statement you prepared. There are no costs except salary. Didn't you ask him about where the products you sold came from?"

"I just worked there, Mr. Marconi. And did some paperwork Leon requested. Mostly, I arranged deliveries. That's all. I don't know what you want me to say."

"But where are the invoices from your suppliers?" He looked Ruby in the eye.

"That wasn't my department. I don't know what to tell you."

She couldn't meet his gaze and stared at his coffee cup. She would tell Mrs. Washington about the tiny chip in the handle later.

"I believe you know more than you're telling us. I'd like to explore that a bit. We'll get to your relationship with Mr. Pennington after that. To start, how did you know how many cases of cigarettes you could promise your customers if you never saw the paperwork on incoming goods? Where was the inventory sheet?"

Ruby rubbed her eyes and looked up at the ceiling.

"Let me try again, Mrs. MacCallum. You kept all the books and did the payroll. Didn't it seem strange to you that you never received invoices for the products you were selling? Your books are meticulous, but there's no mention of the cost to obtain them."

She felt at a disadvantage—Ruby didn't know what Leon and Ralph had told the investigators. She needed to talk to her attorney about whether or not she had to answer this man.

"Mrs. MacCallum, now damn it. Let me tell you what I know. Feel free to chime in. Leon's girlfriend, Lillian, said the items you sold were stolen from the Cincinnati, New Orleans, and Texas Pacific Railway warehouse. She said that you, Leon, and Ralph were equal partners and split the money. Does that sound about right?"

Ruby shook her head. Leon's girlfriend, Lillian? Leon had another girlfriend? He'd stayed with Ruby every night he came to town. They were only apart when he traveled. She wrinkled her eyebrows. Leon *had* been going out of town quite often before their arrest. She knew from watching his way with women at the dance halls that he was capable of having a sweetheart in every city.

"Leon has another girlfriend, does he?" She tried to contain her anger. "Well, Lillian doesn't know everything. And we weren't equal partners."

Agent Marconi opened his notebook and took out a newfangled fountain pen, fiddling with the cap to open it. "What was the partnership, then?"

The fury rolled out of Ruby's mouth. "Leon had been pilfering the goods from the railroad warehouse while his pa worked there. He started when he first got a job with them. He took over the management position when his pa quit. Best I could tell, Leon had been in the business of stealing for about two years before I came. I just joined him in January of last year. I had no idea what he was doing when I started."

Ruby answered every question Agent Marconi asked her as honestly as she could. She didn't care any longer what kind of trouble Leon would get in. He hadn't been honest with her, and she didn't need to protect him. Damn him!

She lay in bed that night and replayed the interview. She had taken Agent Marconi at his word about Leon's girlfriend. What kind of trap had she walked into?

# CHAPTER FIFTY

*J*oseph looked up from his school desk and saw Ruby's grandmother riding up in a wagon. Why in the world would she come to the schoolhouse, especially in the middle of the day? He instructed his students to read a chapter in their readers and stepped outside.

"Morning, Mrs. Turner. Is everything all right with you?"

"Well, no, Joseph. I just got back from visiting my sister in Knoxville. Look at this newspaper article I found on her coffee table. I thought you should know."

Joseph took the newspaper from her, folded to expose a bold headline, YOUNG MOTHER ARRESTED FOR RAILROAD THEFT. Joseph pulled his spectacles down his nose and held the paper farther away from his face so he could take it all in. He scanned the story for a bit before slapping the newspaper against his leg.

"What's the date of this paper, Mrs. Turner?"

"August 20, 1920. Three weeks ago. Ruby's been up to no good, joining Leon Pennington to run a ring selling stolen freight. I couldn't find any more recent copies of the newspaper there, but my sister Heloise said Ruby'd been featured on the front page for a while now. See right there?" Granny Turner pointed to the bottom of the page. "Baby Mary was taken to the Home for Friendless Babies in Knoxville. I talked to Robert, and he hadn't heard a thing from her in a while."

Joseph ran his hand through his thinning hair and went back inside to dismiss his students, asking the older kids to help the younger ones home. Class would have to be canceled for a couple of days while he traveled—there was no way around it. Mrs. Turner agreed to ride to Alice's house to let her know that Wilson would have to stay with her until he got back from Knoxville. He knew that Granny Turner would enjoy seeing Wilson and wouldn't hesitate to tell his family why he had left suddenly, even though Ruby was her own kin.

Ruby wouldn't give up Mary, would she? Wouldn't she telegraph him to come to get her if she did? Nothing about his former wife surprised him anymore.

Joseph hurried home to pack some clothes and came back into town in time to catch the five o'clock train to Knoxville. Even in his haste, he remembered to bring a photograph of Baby Mary so the orphanage would release her to him—if he could find her. Some pretty awful stories about the children's home had circulated in the mountains—that they housed twenty children to a room and gave them only minimal food and care, for example. He supposed they weren't called the Home for Friendless Babies without reason.

On the hour-and-a-half ride to Knoxville, he had the railcar to himself. He looked out the window and dreamed of holding Mary again. She would be with him now. He imagined the state he would find her in, both physically and emotionally. Would she even remember him? He pounded the seat, making his valise jump beside him. Ruby Sullivan had caused nothing but trouble and shame for him. She'd taken his surname and proceeded to associate his good name with a crime.

His stomach growled; he hadn't eaten since breakfast, had left his lunch in the classroom, and would arrive in Knoxville well after the boardinghouses served supper. However, he would be at the orphanage first thing in the morning before breakfast, no matter how hungry he became. Little Mary, now two, would be back in his arms before he concerned himself about eating. At her age, she might be terrified of strangers and ask for her mother. He shuddered to think of her state of mind.

Joseph checked into a house directly across the street from the children's home and crossed the muddy road to knock on the door. He examined the building; it probably hadn't been whitewashed in years, and a partially broken second-floor window allowed a view of several older children gazing outside. A dead tree stood outside like an omen. No one answered, so Joseph twisted the knob, and to his surprise, it opened. A dim light on the right radiated into the darkened hallway, and he followed the noise of several babies crying in the last room at the end of the hall. Six infants and toddlers in one crib screamed at the top of their lungs near the doorway. He spotted Mary in the back corner, sitting quietly with a couple of other children. She smiled at him—her large hazel eyes distinct like her mother's. Mary lifted her arms for him to pick her up, and he left with her as quickly as he had entered. As far as he could tell, no one would know she was gone.

Joseph and Mary spent the night together for the first time in months. Mary didn't complain about hunger, but he fed her pieces of a biscuit he found in the boardinghouse kitchen.

"Here you go, child. Are you hungry, little one?"

She ate the biscuit eagerly, never taking her eyes off him.

"Do you know who I am? I'm your Dada. Can you say 'Dada'? Daaa Daaa."

She remained silent and guarded. Joseph gave her his portion.

He used his undershirt as a diaper for her—the soiled one she wore had dried feces in it. Joseph tied the shoulder straps of his shirt at her sides to help it stay put for the night. He would find supplies the following day. She held on to him tightly, and he sang to her, smoothing her hair as he rocked her on the bed they shared. He covered them both and slid down to lie on the pillow. In no time, they both fell asleep.

When they woke up, he went back across the street to notify the home that he had picked up his daughter. A woman older than Granny Turner answered his knock and, with little ado, released her to him, not seeming to care whether or not he had a connection to the little girl. It would be one less mouth for them to feed.

Joseph bought some supplies and food in town and his ticket home. On the train in his lap, Mary silently took in the world as it went by. She stood up then turned to him to stare at his face. She traced his large nose and his lips tenderly. Touching each feature of her face, he recited the nursery rhyme his mother had taught him as a child. "Forehead Banner, Eye winker, Tommy Tinker, Nose dropper, Mouth Eater, Chin chopper. Gitty Gitty Goo." He tickled her under her neck and delighted in her little-girl giggle.

"More, Dada."

They played, and finally, she laid her head on his chest, her arms around his neck. He twiddled her hair between his fingers, making curls of the fine red strands as she napped on him. The sweet, sweaty smell of his daughter rose to fill his nose and his heart. When she awoke, he sang with her, not caring what the other passengers thought.

# CHAPTER FIFTY-ONE

*October 1923*

*A*fter Ruby had lived ten weeks with Mrs. Washington, her trial finally arrived. Last Monday, she met one last time with her attorney, Mr. Peck, and rehearsed her behavior in court. Oh, she hated that man. He wore his hair parted deep on one side and combed over to hide his bald spot. His nose turned up at the end, exposing large nostrils, and his jowls hung like sacks on each side of his face, reminding her of a pig.

"Don't look the jurors in the eye," he said. "And don't dress like a divorced woman, pregnant with another man's child. Cover every inch of your neck and wear an old woman's scarf around your neck. Wear something tight-fitting but not scandalous. We want everyone to see you're heavy with child. Cry during every witness's testimony. Do not smile for any reason." Mr. Peck's every instruction came with a serving of contempt.

The night before the big day, she laid out all her clothes for the trial, keeping her attorney's instructions in mind. She reclined on her bed for the night, only to toss and turn and fret about her primary concern: that she had informed on Leon to

Marconi. Ruby hadn't even told her attorney about the information she had given to the federal agent in their last interview. She hoped it wouldn't come up during the trial, but she had to admit, Agent Marconi would most likely use it against her—and Leon. Around dawn, a couple of hours after she fell asleep, Mrs. Washington was rustling around in the kitchen and woke her.

Ruby dressed, skipped breakfast, and waited for Mrs. Washington to join her in the parlor. She held her breath as the automobile arrived to transport them to the courthouse.

She wanted to appreciate the ride into town in this fine motorized vehicle, but she was too preoccupied to take it all in. The driver wound his way through the city streets, going faster than she ever had with horse and wagon. Ruby held on to her seat with one hand and onto her protruding stomach with the other. Mrs. Washington sat stoically next to her and reached over to cover Ruby's hand with hers, apparently in support. Swarms of people lined the streets, craning their necks to get a view inside their car as it passed by. The vehicle's speed blended all of those faces into one—one that condemned her before any testimony had been given. As if sensing her tension, the child kicked away inside her. She rubbed her belly to settle the baby. This day in court would determine the rest of her days: whether or not she would ever see her babies again and her future with Leon. Ruby soothed her curly hair, tucking a wayward strand behind her ear, and straightened Mrs. Washington's borrowed hat as they neared the courthouse.

Several photographers stepped into the street in front of their auto, causing the driver to slow down. As if on cue, one of them took advantage of this to take her photo through the window. He used an explosive mix of chemicals to create light, and Ruby ducked below the glass, throwing herself onto the seat for protection.

"It's only a photographer, Mrs. MacCallum." Mrs. Washington pulled her upright when the driver opened their door.

Ruby had never seen anything like it. People ran toward their car, pointing their fingers at her, and crowded behind the driver, knocking him off his feet. The lawn had filled with men, women, and children at the back of the three-story stone building—busy like an anthill stirring with activity. Mrs. Washington positioned herself right behind Ruby, becoming her backbone as they stepped out of the vehicle. The throng of reporters made it hard for them to make their way into the federal courthouse, so Mrs. Washington stepped ahead and led her, using her girth to burrow the way to the back door. Ruby pulled her scarf from her neck, covered her face, and placed her hands on Mrs. Washington's shoulders, ducking behind her to shield herself from the photographers. Her last-minute decision to put on a heavy brown overcoat, even though the weather didn't call for it, hid her bulging belly from public scrutiny.

When they reached the back door, Ruby took a deep breath. A marshal accepted the papers from Mrs. Washington and escorted them to the third floor, where Ruby scoured the hallways for Leon. If she could only catch his eye, she would know the status of their relationship. It had been over two months with nary a word from him.

She passed several men in handcuffs on benches in the hallway, but she didn't recognize any of them. Law enforcement officers stood by them with guns in a ready position. She wasn't even sure the seated men were here for this trial, though she suspected they had been her customers. The men looked down at the floor and, as if rehearsed, raised their heads one by one as she walked by. She wished they would talk to each other so she could recognize a voice from one of her business calls. She looked up and down the halls again, hoping to spot Leon. She needed to talk to him before they entered the courtroom.

Ruby's attorney walked up, carrying a wooden crate of folders. He had dressed to the nines and, as a greeting, looked Ruby up and down, scrutinizing her appearance. She looked down, catching her plain reflection in his shiny oxfords. "Thanks, Mrs. Washington, for bringing her. I'll take it from here."

Mrs. Washington squeezed Ruby's arm and slipped into the courtroom.

Mr. Peck sat on an empty bench in the hallway and placed his crate at his feet, then indicated that Ruby should sit next to him. He slid his fedora off his head and fixed his hair before he readjusted the hat, tapping it down to cover his eyes. Mr. Peck alternated between studying his notes and examining the other people gathering in the corridor. He didn't acknowledge Ruby's presence.

He rose to shake hands with a couple of other fellows, and from their conversation, Ruby gathered that these men were the attorneys for Leon and Ralph. She craned her neck to find Leon, scanning faces in the hallway, but she didn't see him. She bit her lip as she waited on the bench.

A marshal opened the courtroom door and beckoned the men who'd been seated on the bench to enter. He pointed to Ruby and her attorney, and they lined up behind the men. The entrance parade took some time, as the marshal removed all the men's handcuffs at the door. They filed into the third row of benches facing the judge's chair on the right-hand side. Two men spilled into the second row at the far end because they couldn't all fit on one bench. Ruby sat in the second row toward the center aisle, next to her attorney. Mr. Peck removed his hat and placed it between them. The first row remained empty as Ruby settled in. On the other side of the courtroom, the attorneys stood and talked in a low murmur with each other. Agent Marconi stood at the center of their circle.

A bailiff led Leon and Ralph in from the side door, their feet in chains and hands in cuffs. They swam in the ill-fitting striped jumpsuits given to them in jail and hadn't shaved in days. Ruby had never seen Leon with stubble, as he had been meticulous about his appearance. Everyone stopped talking the instant the men crossed the threshold of the room. Ruby smiled as Leon looked her way, but he scowled in return. Her eyes moistened in disappointment as she continued to watch him as, behind his brother, he moved toward the first row.

Ruby rubbed her stomach as Leon walked by to take his place. His shackles clanged with a dull thud on the wood as he sat down. Sitting behind and just to the left of him, she studied the side of his face. He stared straight ahead, not giving her a clue to his thoughts. Ralph turned sideways to look at her, shaking his head in disgust. At that moment, she had no doubt that Ralph—and most certainly Leon—knew about her interview with the federal investigator.

Ruby felt the distance between her and Leon, which felt much greater than the two feet that separated them. Tears streamed down her face; she wouldn't have to fake anything for the jury. Ruby hugged herself, trying to hold in a sob. What she wouldn't give for a five-minute talk with Leon alone.

The bailiff removed the chains and handcuffs from Leon and Ralph and returned to the front door. Leon's and Ralph's attorneys walked through the doors and sat by their clients, kicking boxes of paperwork aside. Their dark double-breasted suits clashed with the stained prison attire of their clients. The noise behind her in the press box rose in intensity.

A different door opened at the front of the room, and twelve jurors took their places in the jury box. Not one of the men looked at her as they scanned the courtroom. A few dressed like farmers in bibbed overalls, and one held his field hat in his hands. One man waved to his wife in the crowd. She waved back at him and then turned to glare at Ruby. Most jurors wore formal church attire, complete with expressionless faces, making it hard to read their emotions.

"All rise," the marshal said. "This is the courtroom of Federal Judge Stern."

Ruby stood as the judge entered the room and sat at his dais. His demeanor seemed grim, much like his name.

The judge shuffled some papers around on his desk before he spoke. "I have allowed only ten reporters in the courtroom. And they'll be removed if there's any ruckus. We'll try to keep this from being a circus. We are trying the case of Leon Pennington and others accused of larceny and possession of interstate freight. The grand jury in Knox County heard the case and found to be substantial in its merits. If necessary, we shall allow five days for trial. Prosecutors, let's start with your opening statement, followed by the defense. And we'll immediately continue with first witnesses."

"Your Honor, the district attorney of the Eastern District of Tennessee does find, charge, and present the following: that Mr. Leon Pennington, Mr. Ralph Pennington, and Mrs. Ruby MacCallum, known from here on as the defendants, along with their accomplices presented before you, have for at least the last two years preceding this trial falsely, unlawfully, fraudulently, and feloniously conspired, confederated, and agreed to commit diverse offenses against the United States of America."

The district attorney believed her to be one of the ringleaders in the cohort of criminals. They had it all wrong! She should be seen as an accomplice and serve minimal time—if any at all. She reached out to grab the bench in front of her, to stand up and correct him. Mr. Peck took her hand and placed it back in her lap, pressing his heavy hand on hers for emphasis. He shook his head at her and put a finger to his lips.

"They stole, carried away, and possessed with the intent to convert to their own goods and chattels the property of the Cincinnati, New Orleans, and Texas Pacific Railway. The said goods and chattels were a part of interstate commerce. They carried out said unlawful conspiracy and executed the following overt acts:

"Number One. On or about the 2nd of February 1920, Mr.

Leon Pennington had in his possession ten scalloped 'Lady Jane' cotton bedspreads, knowing them to have been stolen. These items had been shipped in interstate commerce on January 6, 1920, on waybill No. 584 from Danville, Virginia, to St Louis, Missouri, in Southern car number 160641. These ten bedspreads constituted a part of one case of cotton bedspreads shipped by Dan River Cotton Mills, Danville, to Charlestown Dry Goods Company, St. Louis."

Ruby wanted to laugh that they were starting with the bedspreads. That was a tidbit, not how they had made most of their money.

"Number Two. That Mr. Leon Pennington, one of the defendants herein named, on or about the 2nd of February 1920, had in his possession a part of five cases of ten thousand cigarettes each. These cigarettes were a part of the original shipment shipped from Winston-Salem, North Carolina, to Peter Hartmann, 500 North Fourth Street, St. Louis, Missouri. Mr. Pennington knew at the time of possession of said cigarettes that they had been stolen from interstate commerce. Mr. A.P. Brown received from him and had in his possession, with intent to convert to his own use, a large crate of cigarettes. He placed these cigarettes in with the stock in his store at Lansing, Tennessee. Mr. Brown was well knowing at the time of receiving and possessing these cigarettes that they had been a part of and had constituted interstate commerce."

Ruby could tell which man was Mr. Brown from how he rounded his shoulders and hung his head. He didn't look anything like she imagined from his voice on the telephone. The district attorney didn't mention her in this opening statement. But almost everything he said had come from her confession. Her face turned red at the knowledge, and she breathed shallowly in panic.

The prosecutor proceeded. "Number three. On January 31, 1920, and within the jurisdiction of this court, Mr. Ralph

Pennington called from Wartburg, Tennessee, by long-distance telephone, his co-defendant Mrs. Ruby MacCallum and engaged in a conversation with her concerning some stolen property. We have details about several shipments and inventory. We have registered the evidence, which you will see later in this trial."

The charges droned on. When Ruby looked at the clock in the courtroom, she realized one and a half hours had passed, just for the prosecution's opening remarks.

"We shall prove how each of these men, and, er, lady, was involved. We ask that the jury deliver individual verdicts of guilt or innocence for each of the accused. The judge will determine the sentencing." The prosecutor turned to sit down.

The judge asked the attorneys for the accused if they had anything to say in opening remarks, and they all declined to make a statement. Ruby turned to look at Mr. Peck, astonished that he didn't refute the charges on her behalf.

"Prosecutor, call your first witness."

"I call Mrs. Washington. She would like to go first so she can attend to a guest in her home who might need medical attention."

"Very well. Do you promise to tell the truth, nothing but the truth, so help you, God?" asked the marshal.

"I do." Mrs. Washington took a moment to caress the top of the Bible, where she had placed her hand to take her oath.

Ruby took a quick inventory of all the conversations she'd had with Mrs. Washington. She considered her host to be on her side; she didn't think she would testify against her. Mrs. Washington couldn't seem to get situated in her chair, turning toward the judge first, then straightening herself to face the prosecutor before her. She finally settled in and crossed her arms over her ample bosom. If only that posture would help her hold in information she had about Ruby. Mrs. Washington's eyes danced. Ruby had never seen her without her composure and feared Mrs. Washington would lose it.

"Mrs. Washington, how is it you know Mrs. Ruby MacCallum?"

"She was a guest in my home for the last two and a half months."

"And is there anything special about your home, Mrs. Washington?"

"Yes, I offer a place for women who find themselves unmarried and pregnant. After her arrest, Mrs. MacCallum became a guest in my home as a condition of the court, the arrangement paid for by the state until this trial."

"And Mrs. MacCallum is expecting a baby?"

"Yes, she is. She is about seven or eight months along, I believe."

Ruby looked sideways at Leon. He did not react.

"Did she tell you who the father of this baby might be?"

"We never talked about it. I don't sit in judgment of the women who live in my house. The father is rarely discussed."

"Did you have any conversations with Mrs. MacCallum about her relationship with Mr. Leon Pennington?"

"We did not. Most dinner conversations were about how the women were feeling and, for some, how scared they were to have their babies and start their lives over."

"Did Mrs. MacCallum tell you about her other children?"

"She mentioned she had given birth several other times."

"Do you know anything about those other children or the relationships Mrs. MacCallum might have with them?"

Mr. Peck interrupted. "Relevance, Your Honor."

The prosecutor—Ruby still didn't know his name—responded, "I wish to investigate Mrs. MacCallum's background a little bit so I can speak to her character, Your Honor."

"I'll allow it," the judge responded.

"Do you know about Mrs. MacCallum's other children or the relationships she has with them, Mrs. Washington?"

"She said one evening at supper that she had given birth three other times. And when she came to live with me, she asked if her youngest child could also live in the house with her. I told her the baby had been taken to the Home for Friendless Babies in Knoxville until the trial was over."

"And her reaction to that?"

"She didn't have a strong reaction. Mrs. MacCallum isn't an emotional woman."

"Do you know how old that baby is, Mrs. Washington?"

"About two, I believe."

"Do you know who the father is?"

"I assume it's the man she was married to before she moved to Knoxville to work with Mr. Pennington."

"Mrs. Washington, in your opinion, do you think Mrs. MacCallum is capable of running a crime ring that would steal goods from a railroad warehouse to sell across the nation to people interested in receiving stolen goods at a good price?"

Mrs. Washington looked at the ceiling as if the answer had been written there.

"She certainly is smart enough, in my opinion. But I don't know enough about her character to know if she's capable of doing something illegal. She's a nice young lady, but she may have committed these crimes. I simply don't know."

"Thank you for your testimony, Mrs. Washington."

"Any cross-examination, Mr. Peck?" Judge Stern asked.

"Yes, Your Honor." Ruby's attorney stood up and fastened the bottom button on his double-breasted suit jacket. He smiled at the judge and then Mrs. Washington before he walked to the far side of the courtroom.

Mr. Peck could be pleasant when he wanted to be. He actually looked handsome when he smiled.

"Mrs. Washington, did Mrs. MacCallum ever talk about her work with Mr. Leon Pennington?"

"She did not."

"Did she ever break any rules of your house, such as try to leave?"

"She did not."

"And did Mrs. MacCallum ask you to inquire further so that her baby could live with her in your home?"

"She did. I tried to intervene on her behalf, but the courts wouldn't allow it."

"Did she have any correspondence with Mr. Pennington since she came to live with you?"

"None to my knowledge."

"Did you ever catch Mrs. MacCallum in a lie?"

"I did not."

"That is all, Your Honor."

"You may step down, Mrs. Washington. You are dismissed from these court proceedings," said the judge.

"Your Honor," the prosecutor said, "I'd like to call Agent Marconi to the stand."

Agent Marconi, who Ruby had talked to several times, walked to the front of the courtroom. He acted smugly as if he held information no one else had been privy to.

"Place your hand on the Bible, sir. Do you promise to tell the truth, nothing but the truth, so help you, God?" asked the marshal.

"I do."

"Be seated."

The prosecutor reached into the box below his table, pulled out several pieces of paperwork, and placed them on top of his desk. He flipped through his notes before he began. "Agent Marconi, did you have an interview with Mrs. MacCallum this past August at Mrs. Washington's home?"

"I did."

"And before we get into the details of that interview, can you give an overview of what you learned during it?"

"Yes. Mrs. MacCallum denied she was the ringleader of the crime operations and insisted that Leon and Ralph Pennington were the brains of the business. She said she was merely the bookkeeper and payroll clerk. Her words."

Ruby remembered her confession to Agent Marconi after he'd told her about Leon's girlfriend. The side of Leon's neck turned red, and his neck muscles tensed as he gritted his teeth.

"Did she tell you how the Pennington organization got started?"

"She said that Mr. Leon Pennington started pilfering the goods while his father worked at the railroad as an inventory clerk seven years ago, around October of 1916."

"And what did he do with those 'pilfered' goods?"

"Mrs. MacCallum said she didn't know, that she was only the bookkeeper and payroll clerk."

"Did she deny her part in any criminal activity?"

"She did."

"But she said that she knew Mr. Pennington was involved in it."

"She did."

"How long did she work with Mr. Pennington?"

"She said she joined him in January 1922 to start work in the front office. She was desperate for employment after her marriage dissolved. She needed money for herself and her baby."

"Do you know anything about how Mrs. MacCallum was reimbursed in her employment, Agent Marconi?"

"She started with a salary, but after a few months, she became a partner of the operation, getting twenty-five percent of the profits. This was according to her payroll records."

"Your Honor, I would like to submit the payroll records as Exhibit 1A. I also have a transcript of my interview with her,

Exhibit 1B." The prosecutor distributed copies to the judge and the defendants' attorneys.

"Do you know if Mrs. MacCallum knew Mr. Pennington before she came to work with him?"

"According to my investigation in their hometown, they grew up together. As a boy, he worked with her on her grandfather's farm."

"Do you have any clue why she would leave her family and join Mr. Pennington in Knoxville?"

"According to Mrs. MacCallum's husband's divorce petition, she had an adulterous relationship. I assume it was with Mr. Pennington, but I don't know that to be a fact."

"Objection," Mr. Peck shouted as he rose from his seat.

"Sustained," replied Judge Stern.

"Did she leave any children with Mr. MacCallum when she left her hometown?" the prosecutor asked.

"Yes, a son, age three. Another son died a few months before her move. She brought her infant daughter with her."

"Did you find any evidence of Mrs. MacCallum's involvement in Mr. Pennington's criminal activity?"

"We did. We set a wire in her office. We recorded her conversations with her customers. Some of those men are sitting here in the third row. Mrs. MacCallum initiated all of those calls and asked for a certain amount of money for the orders placed by those customers. The goods were priced well below the market rate of legally procured items. The conversations were in code— they were careful about that. On occasion, however, Mrs. MacCallum talked with each of the Pennington brothers, and we heard about the warehouse supplies running low and their plans to beef up inventory by taking more from the railroad warehouse."

"Your Honor, I would like to present Exhibit 2, the transcript of the conversations as heard by agents." As casually as if pouring tea, the prosecutor delivered a copy to the judge and then stopped by the defense attorneys' desk to present them with the document. Ruby expected him to ask if they would like sugar with it.

"Are there any other conversations we should be aware of?" the prosecutor asked.

Agent Marconi sat up straight in his wooden chair. "Last January, we recorded a call between Mrs. MacCallum and Mr. Ralph Pennington. He mentioned cartons of cigarettes he had stolen in Wartburg, and Mrs. MacCallum acknowledged she needed them to fulfill a shipment to some of her customers. We have detailed cataloged records of deliveries and money received by her for the operation. We have testimony from some of those customers in exchange for a plea agreement. We have detailed accounting by the Cincinnati, New Orleans, and Texas Pacific Railway of items missing over time from their Knoxville warehouse. These items were the same ones sold by the operation run by Mrs. MacCallum. We marked the items before the Penningtons sold them so we could trace them when they arrived at a customer address."

"Your Honor, I would like to present the catalog of items reported missing and a corresponding inventory of items seized during our investigation. Exhibit 3. The customers' statements are Exhibit 4." The prosecutor grunted when he dropped the files on the judge's desk. "We'll go through the details of the inventory and customer statements tomorrow when we present our findings in detail."

Ruby heard this testimony and hoped, for a moment, that they were talking about someone else. She'd started the day with her head held high but lowered it with every mention of her name. It would be an easy conviction if they had all the evidence they said they had. Ruby pressed her lower abdomen when an intermittent cramp hit her. She'd had twinges throughout the morning, and the baby stretched uncomfortably inside her. She held her stomach, breathing slowly, but cried out and stood up when a sharper cramp occurred.

"Your Honor, may I ask for a recess?" Mr. Peck asked. "My client needs a break for personal reasons."

"After questioning is over," the judge said.

"Your Honor, I intend to keep Agent Marconi on the stand for several hours to detail his investigation. We may need a break before this—maybe even a lunch break." The prosecutor turned and smiled at the row of attorneys on the right-hand side.

"Granted, then. A recess of one hour. Let's go ahead and take lunch."

WHEN RUBY RETURNED FROM THE LADIES' room—formerly a closet in the basement — her attorney approached her in the hallway outside the courtroom.

"Mrs. MacCallum, in just the short time you took a break, I negotiated an agreement that avoids jail time for you. Given the powerful testimony and affidavits already presented to the jury, I think it would be in your best interest to accept it."

"What are the details? Just for me or everyone? Do I have to say I'm guilty?" She smoothed her dress over her protruding stomach and switched her coat to her other hand.

"All of your customers have agreed to a thousand-dollar fine and full cooperation if this trial continues. The distributors will receive three months of incarceration for their crimes and are in the courtroom signing their agreement as we speak. You'll get two years of probation. The terms are that you will have to report to the court and be gainfully employed in an 'unquestionable occupation.' That's the best we can get for you. And yes, you must confess before the judge and offer remorse. It's your only option, in my opinion, considering your child in the children's home and your baby that's on the way. But it's your decision. As I said, the customers have already accepted their offer and are willing to testify if you decline to accept yours."

"It's my only choice? Can I just talk to the judge so he understands my side of things?" Ruby wasn't ready to confess.

"You will not be allowed to do that. I advise you to take this agreement. I never expected you to get probation."

"What about Leon and Ralph? Did they get a deal?

"If they accept, Leon and Ralph Pennington would serve two years, with no chance of early release, in a federal prison in Atlanta."

"I'll take the deal." Ruby cried in relief for Leon's short sentence.

After lunch, everyone reconvened in the court, except for the Pennington brothers. Slowly, as if to add to the drama, the marshal led Leon and Ralph, both shackled, back to the front row. Leon faced Ruby while the marshal removed his handcuffs. He mouthed, *This is all your fault* before he turned around to take his seat. Ruby restrained herself; it was all she could do to keep herself from reaching out to him. Just as she'd feared last night, he blamed her for this entire mess.

The jury came back in, and everyone stood as Judge Stern entered.

"Gentlemen of the jury, I want you to know I appreciate your time and willingness to serve in this capacity. I believe we have negotiated a deal in this case for all defendants, so you will be dismissed."

The men in the jury box seemed stunned and disappointed as they filed out of the courtroom. The farmer stopped to look at the rows of defendants and shook his head in disgust before he walked out.

The judge called Ruby to the front of the courtroom. Without her coat to cover her, she stood before the judge and—

with every eye upon her—absorbed the shame for her criminal behavior.

"Mrs. MacCallum, let me be sure that you understand what you have agreed to. In exchange for a confession on your part, and if you ask for mercy from the court, you will be placed on probation for two years. For six months, you will be required to stay with Mrs. Washington and follow the rules of her house while she supports you during the rest of your pregnancy and the first months of your baby's life. After six months, you can live wherever you desire, as long as you report your address to your probation officer. The court is convinced that your release on probation will not endanger society."

Ruby nodded.

Judge Stern continued, "You will serve probation for a minimum of two years, and it is at the complete discretion of the court to extend that probation should you not act as an honorable citizen. Mr. Gran Davis of Wartburg, Tennessee, will be your probation officer. He will report monthly to the court on your daily life and conduct. You will be required to engage in some gainful and unquestionable lawful employment six months from today. You will report to him on Monday of each week, describing your work of the previous week, the amount of money you earned, and how you disposed of that money. You will state who is watching your baby and its general health and well-being. You will be required to refrain from violating any laws of the United States and the state of Tennessee and to refrain from visiting any place where such violations occur. I will remind you that the Volstead Act is now in effect, and you will not be permitted to visit any place that serves alcohol."

Did he have to mention unquestionable employment? Ruby wanted him to finish. How dare he try to humiliate her!

Judge Stern lowered his eyeglasses to the end of his nose and looked at Ruby. "You will not visit the penitentiary at Atlanta, Georgia, where Leon Pennington will be confined. Nor will you be allowed to live within twenty miles of that penitentiary. If you violate any terms of this probation, the probation officer is authorized to report the violation to the court for further action. Do you understand this, Mrs. MacCallum? You will be given a copy of this decree and asked to sign it before you leave today."

"I do, Your Honor. Could I ask about my baby girl, who was taken when I was arrested? Will she be returned to me to live at Mrs. Washington's house?"

"I understand that your daughter is no longer at the Home for Friendless Babies, Mrs. MacCallum. Your former husband picked her up a few weeks after your arrest, and she's living with him. The divorce court gave him full custody of her. I recommend that you leave well enough alone. Any further questions?"

"No, Your Honor."

"Then please make your statement to the court for the record."

"I confess to all charges against me, Your Honor. I regret my part and am sorry for my actions."

"Anything further? I would like to see a little more remorse. You have hurt businesses with your criminal actions, but I have to tell you that my main concern is your children. Have you thought about how this has impacted their young lives?"

Her children had a better childhood than she ever did; they would be all right. "I have nothing further to say, Your Honor."

"All right, then, Mrs. MacCallum. You may be seated. Your attorney will assist you in signing the paperwork before you leave."

"Mr. Leon Pennington and Mr. Ralph Pennington, please stand. You will be committed immediately to the federal penitentiary in Atlanta, Georgia. Mr. Leon Pennington, you will serve two years for this crime, starting immediately after you finish your incarceration for arranging an abortion for your paramour. You violated the terms of that probation and will be required to serve the rest of that sentence before you begin this one. Mr. Ralph Pennington, you are to serve two years, with no conditions for early parole. Do you both accept this agreement?"

Leon nodded and answered, "I do."

Ralph said, "I do, Your Honor."

"Do you have anything to say to the court?"

Both brothers hung their heads in reply.

"Very well. Marshal, shackle these boys again and take them to the county cell until transportation can be arranged."

The judge left the courtroom, and Ruby placed her hand on Leon's shoulder to get him to turn her way before they escorted him out.

He faced her. "Ruby, you betrayed me. You and your baby can rot in hell."

The marshal turned Leon away from her and led him out of the courtroom. Ralph shook his head at Ruby as he walked behind his brother.

Ruby reeled at the knowledge that she couldn't visit Leon in prison. The court specifically said she was not to contact him. But even worse, he didn't want her. Rot in hell, he said. She remembered she wasn't the first one to become pregnant by him. He had committed another crime by trying to dispose of a baby. He didn't want a child—but surely he wanted her. Leon couldn't run away from the fact that they had something special. She understood he must be angry now, but he couldn't mean what he said.

She left the courthouse and rode back to Mrs. Washington's home in a government car. As if it was Sunday, the woman served a roast for dinner. After dinner, Margie played the piano in the parlor, and Ruby retired for an early bedtime. As she lay in bed, it registered that she may never see baby Mary again. Mary had reunited with Joseph, Wilson, and the entire

MacCallum family back in Rock Bluff. Indeed, Joseph's family would provide the support he needed to care for two young children. But did Baby Mary even ask for her?

She lay awake for a long time that night. With the trial behind her and Baby Mary gone for good, she examined how she had lived her life. To others, Ruby was a scarred woman, marked as immoral. But she had lived before on the fringes of society; she could do it again. For now, she would await the birth of Leon's baby and take one day at a time. Leon had a right to be mad at her. Perhaps he would change his mind when he thought of the good times they'd had over the years and the child they would share. She would bide her time until his release.

# CHAPTER FIFTY-TWO

*December 1923*

uby read the daily newspaper while her new baby
boy, Davey, slept beside her in bed. Even though it
had been two months since the trial, the local news still printed
stories about her. She read most of them, thanking her lucky
stars for how fortunate she had been. The only federal prison
for women had just closed down in Illinois, and a new one in
the District of Columbia wouldn't be finished for a few more
months. Ruby had been given probation only because they had
nowhere to put a woman, let alone a pregnant one. This little
cherub beside her had been her godsend.

She picked up Davey when he whimpered and patted his
back as she waited for Mrs. Washington to bring in her breakfast. He had slipped out without much effort at all after a short
labor, Mrs. Washington glued to her bedside. Ruby named him
David Leon after his papa. She gave him Leon's last name,
despite their difficulties right now. If only you could see your
baby, Leon. Davey turned to her to eat once again, and as he
suckled, she studied him. She finger-combed her little boy's

light brown hair to one side. He looked like Leon; the baby had his eyes and dimpled cheek.

She considered contacting his parents to let them know they had a grandson. They lived only a few miles from Granny's house. She should visit Granny, too. Ruby would be starting over in a few months and would need all of the support she could get.

She didn't know what Joseph knew about her trial but imagined he had followed it. From what she understood, it had made the headlines all over Tennessee. In a few days, she would write a letter to him to inform him of the new baby's arrival and ask to visit Wilson and Mary. While holding Davey, memories flooded back of her previous births in Joseph's home. The flashbacks of her firstborn son caused her to wail during Davey's delivery—not from the pain of childbirth but instead the ache of Timmy's death. Timmy had expanded her heart to know love, stirring up emotions she had always held under the surface. She had grieved him as she pushed out her new son.

Mrs. Washington brought in a tray and took the baby from her, and Ruby rearranged herself to eat in bed. She nibbled at the eggs and bacon and sipped her coffee while Mrs. Washington took Davey into the other room to change his diaper. Margie had left last week to return to her family after a couple from eastern Tennessee adopted her baby. Mrs. Washington was entirely focused on Ruby now; she had never known such care.

As she ate, she started to consider where to live and find work when she left Mrs. Washington's home. Maybe she could stay in Lansing, on the train line close to Knoxville. Her brother Robert said he would come to Knoxville to pay her a call this week, though he hadn't been present during her trial. But she suspected he didn't want to be linked to her so he could continue to run his bootleg alcohol without suspicion. If it came up, she had decided not to work with him—it might look bad if she did.

Maybe she could get Granny to move with her to Wartburg, where there were more shops where she might find employment. She needed to sort out how Granny felt about her these days; they hadn't communicated since she left Rock Bluff. Without Pa's judgment getting between them, it should be easier to talk to her grandmother now.

What Ruby truly wanted was to move to Atlanta and settle there to await Leon's release. Certainly, he would forgive her over time. But the agreement stipulated that she had to wait until her probation was complete. For now, she could send letters to him. By then, she would have a few more dollars in her account and little Davey would be walking to make it easier to cart him around.

Ruby finished her breakfast, and Mrs. Washington brought her son back to her. She slithered down onto her pillow, where she and the baby would take a rest.

Tomorrow she would start writing many letters, exploring her housing and employment possibilities.

One day at a time—that was best.

This would all work out.

# CHAPTER FIFTY-THREE

*April 1924*

*R*uby packed all the necessities for her and five-month-old Davey into two large carpetbags and a smaller day bag. She could manage with a baby at the train station if she engaged the help of a porter to carry it all on board. In the next room, Mrs. Washington gave Davey some cuddles. The other ladies who had recently moved into the house cooed over him as well. With his easygoing temperament, he had given the impression that it was easy to be a mother, making it harder for the unwed women who would be giving their babies up for adoption.

A carriage was waiting outside to take her to the station. Mrs. Washington brought Davey to her and tilted her head toward Ruby, tears welling in her eyes.

"Mrs. Washington, I appreciate the time in your home. I've never in my life been treated so nicely." Ruby hugged her with Davey between them.

"It's been my pleasure, Ruby. I wish you well."

The other women followed suit and hugged her before she

walked out the door with Davey. Ruby would miss the excellent care she had received.

Granny had told her to go to Lansing to get started. They needed a waitress in the café in town, and Ruby was to report to work in two days. Granny's grandniece lived there and would tend to Davey while Ruby worked. Even if the hours were part-time, the job would satisfy her parole requirement. She sublet a room above the restaurant, which would do until she saved some money. Before she left, Ruby changed her married name back to Sullivan to avoid recognition as a convicted criminal. It might take people a while to figure out who she was—if they ever did. Granny said she would visit Ruby after she had settled in.

After the carriage was loaded, it pulled away. Only then did Ruby feel trepidation about being on her own. It was nice having the safety net of Mrs. Washington's house, though tech-nically, she had been imprisoned there. Davey whimpered, and she opened her dress a few buttons to let him nurse. It would be harder to do this on the train. The porter met the carriage at the station and helped her load her bags into the second-class rail-car. She jumped on the train as soon as the other passengers got off to secure a bench facing forward so she could sit alone with the baby.

Ruby still hadn't heard back from Joseph about whether or not he would permit her to visit with Wilson and Mary. She intended to write to Alice about it if he didn't respond. She thought Alice would sympathize with her—a mother's heart had to know what it was like to be away from her babies. Rock Bluff was only an hour's train ride from Lansing. If she didn't get permission to visit her children, she would ask forgiveness after dropping in on them. She had a right to see her children. Ruby wondered if Joseph was seeing anyone or still on his own. Her life with him seemed like a long time ago.

She would tell people she met in Lansing that her husband

had died in a buggy accident before her baby was born. She knew enough details about her papa's death to tell that story convincingly. As if she might forget them, she repeated the names to herself as the train slowly moved out of the station. Ruby Sullivan. Davey Sullivan. She watched the big city turn into countryside as Davey slept in her arms.

When the train approached Lansing, Ruby rose, gathered her day bag, and walked to the door. She tapped a porter on the shoulder. "Could you place those two bags on the platform?"

He nodded to her when she gave him a coin.

She walked the two blocks from the train station to the café, juggling Davey with one arm while carrying one bag ahead of her and leaving it while retrieving the bag behind her to move it forward. She arrived at the outside stairs to her new apartment right after the lunch hour. The café owners, a man and his wife, greeted her and helped her up the stairs with her belongings. The woman opened the blanket to peer at the sleeping baby and offered Ruby sympathies for her husband's death.

Ruby laid Davey down on the bed to continue his nap and quietly unpacked a few belongings. She took out some stationery and wrote her first letter to her probation officer.

*Dear Mr. Davis,*

*I would like to report that I live above Gilbert's Café on 42 South Pryor Street in Lansing with my baby. I have been hired to work at the café, and my pay without tips will be between twelve to fifteen dollars weekly. Babysitting and rent should total ten dollars a week.*

*I have relatives who live in the area, and they will give me some support.*

*Respectfully yours,*

*Ruby*

# CHAPTER FIFTY-FOUR

*June 1925*

*R*uby hadn't slept the night before—the storm kept her up. Whenever she started to nod off, Davey would wake up to ask for some milk. He took over half of the bed now, stretching out the length of her leg. He'd grown tall for eighteen months, getting his lankiness from his papa. As the sun rose, Ruby tossed and turned, thoughts of her old life disturbing her. She intended to go to Rock Bluff today to find her older children. After more than a year's employment, it would be her first weekday off from the café. She needed to make the trip before school let out for the summer. It would be easier to sneak into town during the week with school in session. Joseph and the whole MacCallum clan hadn't answered any of her letters, not even Alice.

If she remembered correctly, Wilson would get out of school at half-past two today. And on Wednesday, Joseph would open the store for a few hours in the afternoon, tying him up after school. She could find Wilson on his way to the MacCallum house or wherever he stayed until Joseph came home.

Ruby walked to the train station after packing up Davey. Though broken in from waitressing, her leather shoe had rubbed a blister on her heel. She sat on a bench to wait for the locomotive, placing her day bag on top of Davey's lap to anchor him while she repositioned her shoe. It occurred to her that the same railroad company involved in her crime ran the trains between Lansing and Rock Bluff; the Cincinnati, New Orleans, and Texas Pacific Railway had survived the thefts. She wished she could say the same about herself more than a year and a half into her probation.

Ruby planned to arrive at Granny's by noon, and she would ask her to keep Davey while she ran some errands and found Wilson after school. Wilson would know who kept Baby Mary during the day. She suspected Alice watched her, or maybe Nan, a widowed woman across the creek from the MacCallum compound. Ruby had picked out candy and a small toy automobile to entice Wilson to walk with her. She remembered his sweet tooth and fondness for things with wheels. On the hour-long ride to Rock Bluff, she played with Davey while pushing guilt to the back of her mind. Would Wilson remember her? He would be six in the fall. She'd left him the Christmas after his third birthday.

Ruby struggled through the long walk up the mountain to Granny's house. How many times had she traveled to this place, which had only represented hardship to her? Ruby put Davey down before entering Granny's long drive so he could toddle and give her arms a break as well. She finger-combed her hair and straightened her dress.

Granny came out the back door, her hand shading her eyes from the sun. She seemed younger than the last time Ruby saw her. Her grandmother ran to her and hugged her hard, something she hadn't expected. Ruby didn't blame Granny for her ill feelings about her childhood; Pa had been hard on them both.

The longer they hugged, the more the coldness between them thawed.

"It is good to see you, Granny. You're looking well."

"And you've matured. You've grown up. Let me have a look at that boy, will you?" Granny always did like the babies. She took Davey from Ruby's arms and struggled to hold him up to get a good look at him. "This one's a big boy."

"He is. Like his papa." Ruby immediately wished she hadn't mentioned Davey's father. She needed to be more careful.

But if her comment bothered Granny, she didn't let on.

"Joseph lets me drop in to see the children sometimes, but only when he's around to observe us. Wilson is so tall. Mary has your big hazel eyes, and she's almost reading. Can you believe that—reading at four? And what a temper! If Wilson teases her, she screams to high heaven. It's a commotion like you've never heard." Granny beamed.

Ruby smiled to hear her account. "Granny, would you watch Davey for a couple of hours? I'd like to see my old friend Mabel while I'm here if it's all right with you."

"Sure, I'll take care of this one. But you aren't going to bother Joseph, are you? I'd leave well enough alone. He's written you off—no doubt about that. I'm afraid that if he thinks I'm in cahoots with you, he won't let me near the children."

Ruby didn't answer, as she wasn't going to see Joseph. In fact, she hoped to avoid him. While Granny and Davey played pat-a-cake on Granny's rocker, Ruby started the long walk back into town. She had plenty of time to get there before Joseph dismissed school. Ruby cut through the woods to avoid any of the townspeople—she had nothing to say to them. How many times had she made this walk? The woods were thick with blossoms already—another late spring in the mountains. She followed the well-worn path she used to walk to school as a child, her link to something other than the hard days with Pa.

She arrived at the outskirts of town early and waited for the school's final bell, hiding in a thicket where she could see the entrance but not be seen. After a bit, Joseph opened the front door and used his tall body to hold it open. He looked tired—his shoulders hunched over like a man twice his age. Joseph used to stand so straight and proud. He used to act as if he was holding in the punch line of a joke, and she looked for his smile. His face had turned sober.

Carrying his satchel, Wilson walked out of school with some older boys. He laid it down to mimic those boys and tried to throw a rock into the woods as far as they did. The older boys, faster than Wilson, ran ahead. He picked up his books and resumed his path to wherever he went after school. This was Ruby's chance.

She stepped out of the woods and restrained herself from running to him. He stood before her, raising his head a little bit to look into her eyes.

"Wilson, hello. I'm your mama. Do you remember me?"

Wilson tilted his head to the side, puzzled. He remained silent as if he had encountered a ghost. She suspected he'd been warned about her. He lifted his shoulders high near his ears but otherwise didn't move. Though he hesitated, she could tell he knew who she was. He had grown tall, like his papa—he nearly came to her chest. He had that dimple in the middle of his long chin like all the MacCallums did.

"Wilson, I have a present for you. It's all right. Don't be frightened. I remembered that you like candy. It's taffy. And here's a toy too. Come here, sweet boy. Let's walk together, and you can tell me about school. I've missed you."

Hesitantly, he walked alongside her, reaching out to receive the candy and the toy. Ruby took his satchel so he could open the candy wrapper. Some children from the school walked past them, curious about who walked with Wilson.

"Father said not to talk to you. I better go, or I'll get in trouble."

"It's all right to talk to me on your way home, Wilson. I won't keep you. You won't be in trouble. I wanted to visit you and see what a big boy you are now. Do you remember our times together?"

"I heard Father say you were in jail You left Baby Mary on the street, and he had to go on a train to get her."

"I didn't leave her on the street. By the way, who keeps Mary while you and your papa are at school?"

"Nan, across the creek, watches her. I go there on Wednesdays when Father opens his store. I'll walk with you if you don't tell him." His cheeks puffed out as he chewed a wad of taffy.

Ruby remembered Nan. Her grandchildren were in her classroom when Ruby taught with Joseph the year before they were married. Nan might let her see Mary, but she didn't know what instructions Joseph had given her. Still, it was worth a try.

As Ruby and Wilson crossed the dry creek to Nan's house, Joseph rode up in his wagon. She suspected someone near town had seen her and reported the sighting to Joseph. "Stop right there, Ruby. Get away from Wilson and stay away from Nan's house. I have a court order to keep you away from the children. Wilson, run into the house and tell Nan to lock the door."

Ruby gave Wilson his satchel and turned to Joseph. "I'm not staying. I just want to see them."

Joseph hopped down from his wagon and placed himself between Ruby and Wilson, his quick breaths used to pump himself up as a shield between them. He turned to usher Wilson toward the door. "You can't be trusted near the children. They've forgotten about you and seeing you will only upset them. They don't ask about you, and they're doing just fine. Now, go. Go back where you came from. If I ever see you around here again, I'll have you arrested. Your probation officer might like to report your appearance here to the court."

Ruby had rarely seen Joseph be this way with anyone. Even after all this time, he was still furious with her for her betrayal.

"Goodbye, Wilson. I love you, son. Hug Baby Mary for me. Tell her that her mama loves her."

"Go on, get out of here. I'll give you a ride to the train station, but don't you ever come back to town, you hear? Get in the back."

"I'll walk, Joseph. I'm leaving, though I'm seeing Granny before I leave town."

She watched Wilson enter Nan's house. Nan held Mary up, who waved and pointed at her through the window. Mary appeared to be in good hands. Ruby turned and walked away from Joseph, silent tears pouring down her cheeks. She made no move to wipe them away.

She returned to Granny's to collect Davey. Granny didn't ask about her afternoon, and Ruby didn't give details. Ruby, still distraught from her encounter with Joseph, made up her mind about what to do next. While Granny left to use the outhouse, Ruby went into the woman's room and opened the top bureau drawer, taking some cash she always hid under her underclothing. After all those years of working on this farm, she had no misgivings about taking some of Granny's egg money. It would give her enough to buy a train ticket to Atlanta, to be closer to Leon. She would mail her some cash when she got settled. She packed up Davey and hugged Granny goodbye at the door after returning from the privy. It might be some time before she returned.

On her way back to the railway station, Ruby took a short detour to her old home—the one she and Joseph had built together. Most likely, Joseph had taken the kids to his family after she left so he could return to his store. But just to be safe, she stood in the same woods where Leon used to lurk and checked to ensure that the house was unoccupied. Joseph had planted more flowers around the house and placed a wooden swing in the front yard for the children. The support from his family and friends had helped build this house. It had always belonged to him. Though risking being seen by Joseph if he returned soon, she walked past the back porch where he had caught her with Leon. He had removed the bed from the sleeping porch, and an old washtub stood there instead.

It was hard to believe, but she had once been happy living in this house, giving birth to three of her children here. Joseph had taken care of her every need. And she had walked away from it. Her life looked very different to her now.

Ruby walked through the woods, up the hill to where they had buried Timmy. Joseph had planted poppies, her favorite flower, around his grave. She knelt beside Timmy's marker and let the tears come, crying for the loss of her oldest son—her Timmy. Ruby mourned her little boy and who she used to be when she'd lived here with him. She couldn't say she missed Joseph, but he had given her beautiful children, and now they lived with him. Joseph took care of Timmy's grave; he did that because it was the right thing to do.

# CHAPTER FIFTY-FIVE

*Fall 1925*

*R*uby had finally gathered enough money to get herself and Davey to Atlanta, with some cash to spare to set up a household there. After a long day of travel, she immediately found an apartment close to the prison. By the end of the week, she had secured a job and a babysitter. Her probation had almost expired, and Leon had another six months to serve. Ruby would get situated before his release. Then she would wait for him. She would be there when he got out.

Leon would meet little Davey and fall in love with him. Maybe he would see the resemblance to himself as a little boy. She had written recently to Leon in prison, and he had written back. At the start of his sentence, he had been surly when she wrote. She had, after all, spilled the beans to the federal agents. But recently, Leon seemed more open to a relationship with her —the way it used to be before this whole mess. His last letter held the most promise. He planned to stay in Atlanta with her after his release.

. . .

*Ruby,*

*I count the days until I get out of here. You will be waiting for me, won't you? I'll let you know the day of my release if they tell me ahead of time.*

*Are you settled in your new place?*

*Start saving any extra money you can so we can get a house. I want a backyard for Davey, if possible. How much money are you making these days?*

*Could you do something for me? All of my money was taken when I was arrested, but not all of it came from our business. Can you inquire about money in my name at Knoxville Savings and Loan? There might also be some at the Wartburg bank. You can tell them you're my wife if they ask. Do you remember where we hid some of the extra cash in the warehouse? Is there any way you could go look for that?*

*Yours truly,*

*Leon*

# CHAPTER FIFTY-SIX

*D*ear Mr. Davis,
     *I have moved to Atlanta and my address is now 105 Luckie Street, c/o W.J. Hamilton, Atlanta. Can you tell me how much longer I will need to write letters to you?*

*I'm making twenty dollars a week now and spend fifteen dollars for rent and shows when I can get a sitter. I am feeling just fine and the weather here is lovely.*

*Respectfully,*
*Ruby*

# CHAPTER FIFTY-SEVEN

*A* loud, rapid bang at her door startled Ruby from her nap. She gathered herself, hoping the knock hadn't woken Davey.

"Who is it?"

"It's Ralph, Ruby. Let me in."

Ruby cracked the door open to make sure it was really him outside and tried to evaluate his mood. Ralph looked older and hardened. He gave Ruby a half smile, which gave her the confidence to open the door farther. The last time he had talked to her, he looked as if he could have killed her.

"Leon gave me your address. He wants me to see if you got the money he talked about."

"I didn't find any money, Ralph. I think it was all taken by the feds. I only have what I've saved for Leon and me to get started when he gets out. They didn't let him out too, did they?" She looked beyond him to see if Leon stood there too.

Davey cried from his pallet on the floor, and Ruby picked him up and returned to the door. She wouldn't let Ralph in until she had a better feeling about him.

"He looks just like Leon. No mistaking who that kid's father is. And no one's behind me—Leon's still inside. He had to serve more time than I did because of his other, uh, incident."

Ruby continued to stand at the door, not sure what else Ralph wanted from her. Davey wiggled to get down and ran off to lie back down on his blanket.

Ralph watched her little boy for a moment through the door, then shook his head. "Ruby, he's using you to get money, kid. He's planning on being with Lillian after he's released. She's living with Ma and Pa right now. I hate to break your heart, but Leon's intentions aren't good. You should know that. Get over him, Ruby. He'll only use you. He'll never get over you talking to the feds."

With that, Ralph turned around and left. She didn't know whether or not to believe him. But there was only one way to find out.

RUBY ASKED for a week off work the following day, telling her boss that her mother had taken ill and needed her. She packed all of hers and Davey's clothes in two bags and headed to the train station. A ticket to Rock Bluff wasn't cheap, and taking time off work wasn't either. But she had to know if Ralph's words had merit.

It was time Davey, almost two, met his grandparents. They couldn't deny who the father was—he was the spitting image of their son. It took all day to return to Tennessee, with a connection in Chattanooga.

Ruby hired a horse at the Rock Bluff livery and bound Davey to herself with a long piece of a bedsheet she had brought for this purpose. As she wrapped him facing out, he seemed delighted to be riding a horse.

She rode from the station to the Pennington place, stopping for a moment before she approached the house. Leon's younger brothers, just teens themselves, were working in the field, and a woman of about Ruby's age was helping Mrs. Pennington hang the laundry on the clothesline.

Ruby rode until she reached the two women. "Mrs. Pennington, I'm Ruby, Ruby Sullivan. Do you remember me?"

Leon's ma sat her laundry basket down on the ground and ran to the field to get her husband. A boy of about six ran behind her, taking his cue from his mother.

Ruby knew instantly who the other woman was. Ralph was right; she had been used. After all she'd done for Leon—helping his business, giving him information at his first trial, and leaving her family for his affection—he had sent another love back home to his mother. Her chest heaved at the realization. She had waited for Leon for two years, preparing to raise their son together. This was the last time she would allow him to show his true colors.

The younger woman came over to Ruby. "I'm Lillian. I don't believe I know you."

Ruby unbound her son from her chest and handed Davey to Leon's girlfriend. He squirmed and reached back for Ruby, but she had already turned away.

Before she galloped away from the farm, she said, "Could you tell Mrs. Pennington that this is Leon's baby? His name is David Leon Pennington, and I'm leaving him with her."

Let Leon remember her for the rest of his living days. She had no intention of being reminded of him by raising Davey.

# CHAPTER FIFTY-EIGHT

*November 1, 1925*

*D*ear Mr. Davis,
  I've given my baby to Mr. and Mrs. Pennington, Leon's parents, as I can't care for him any longer. They have a son who looks to be only four or five years older than Davey, and they'll take good care of him. They are good people. I'm moving back to Knoxville to be near my brother.

Can you tell me if there's any money for me in Wartburg? Leon wants me to have any money of his that wasn't seized by the federal agents. He owes me back wages. I thought some of my money would be returned to me too. Can you find out and let me know?

I've made twenty dollars this last week and only spent fifteen dollars for rent and food. This will be my last letter to you as required by the court.

Respectfully,
Ruby

# CHAPTER FIFTY-NINE

*Knox County, Tennessee*

*The Honorable Granville Davis*
*November 22, 1925*

*Judge Stern, US District Court of Eastern Tennessee, Knoxville,*
*Tennessee*

*Re: Ruby MacCallum*

*D**ear Judge Stern:*
*     In response to a request by Clerk of Courts Mr. Beeker*
*on November 1, 1925, for a report on the above-named person, Ruby*
*MacCallum, I will say that I have been receiving letters from her*
*fairly regularly. I take it from her letters that she has been in Atlanta,*
*Georgia, and nothing in her letters indicates she is doing well.*
*     She has reported that she has given her baby to Mr. Pennington's*

*family to be raised by them. She is moving to Knoxville again, where her brother lives.*

*Mrs. MacCallum asks about any money owed her from seized bank accounts. She says she has permission from Mr. Leon Pennington to receive any money owed to him as well. There is none that I know of. Please correct me if all the assets taken belong to the Federal Government of the United States, or if some of it was money belonging to her or Mr. Pennington.*

*She has satisfied all the requirements of the court for her probation period. If it pleases the court, this will be my last report to you.*

*Yours very truly,*

*Gran Davis*

*Probation Officer for Mrs. Ruby MacCallum*

# EPILOGUE

*1929*

*A*fter five years of waitressing jobs, Ruby eventually found an office manager position with Mr. Ross, a handsome, successful businessman from Canada. She oversaw shipping and customer accounts for his export business in Knoxville. Ruby also arranged the undercover transport of Tennessee moonshine to a warehouse in Kalamazoo, Michigan —a holding place until it could be covertly trucked into Canada and distributed through the provinces. Due to the Volstead Act, it remained an underground operation in the United States, but perfectly legal to sell once it crossed the border into Canada.

Ruby married Mr. Ross, and they moved to Windsor, Ontario. Agents at the border asked her for her name, and she told them her maiden name in case they had access to her criminal record.

Unbeknownst to Ruby, Mr. Ross had another family in London, Ontario, two hours away. He had married Ruby without the benefit of divorce and his wife and two teen daughters were kept in the dark about Ruby. Mr. Ross traveled on business often, something his family had become used to, but he made sure to visit them at least once a month. Ruby missed her husband when he left on business trips, but she couldn't remember being so happy. Her husband delighted in her, and she in him. She hadn't known how tired she was until she had a chance to rest in Mr. Ross's embrace.

Over time, Ruby had two children by Mr. Ross. Her oldest, Samuel, became her favorite. He reminded Ruby of Timmy, with that same sweet face and uncanny ability to know what she thought before she said anything out loud.

RUBY PLACED baby Susannah in her crib for a nap and took Samuel outside by the creek to play.

"Samuel, which hand is the toy boat in?"

"Silly Mama! That one." He was right, of course. He always guessed correctly.

"Come closer to me, young man."

"I'm all right, Mama. Don't worry, I won't fall."

"Silly boy. How did you know I was thinking that?"

"I just know. Can I be your boy forever, Mama? Please, with gumdrops?"

Ruby almost spoke to reassure him but stopped herself. Life had a way of slipping through her fingers—nothing was permanent.

She looked to the north and saw a storm brewing. The pea-green skies darkened from a shelf of heavy black clouds moving her way. The dandelions in the field bent over with the weight of the ionized air, and a gust swirled fallen leaves around her and Samuel. Ruby gathered up her son to take him inside and set him down inside the door. Through the window, the sun peeked through the clouds in a single shaft of pale light that bathed Ruby before it disappeared within the turmoil outside.

"Samuel, I can only promise you today, my son. You can be my boy today."

# ACKNOWLEDGMENTS

Without the love, help, encouragement and support of many, this book would still be bouncing around in my imagination. Big hugs to those who believed.

To my husband Paul, my best friend and rock. I can't imagine this journey without you. For the record, our story is the best one.

Thank you to my children who always support my crazy ideas. To daughter Erin, who read the book when it was a baby, providing encouragement and assessment every step of the way. And to Scott and Stephanie, who gave support even though this took five years to write.

To my sisters: Jane—who keeps me straight on what is truth and what is fiction; Kathi—the true writer in the family; and Judy—who is still smarter than I am. I hope you all enjoy my telling of this tale. And to my brother Rick, who taught me to love a good book.

I am grateful for all my friends who always asked "How is the book coming along?" Thanks for your support. You are the family I choose and I love you all.

Thank you to my very first reader. You know who you are. I knew you would like the skinny-dipping scene.

To my writer group, Amy, Tom and Mark, who gave me so many good ideas and direction. Thanks for all of the encouragement and attention to detail, making sure I crossed the t's and dotted the i's.

Thanks to my editor Caroline Kaiser, who is a miracle worker. Thanks for the feedback and being honest with me. Your attention to detail helped me make this much better than I ever could perfected on my own.

A special thanks to Kim Lozano, who mentored me in the Women's Fiction Writing Association mentor program and helped me cut the chaff and keep the focus.

Mama, I come from a long line of wild, determined women. I hit the jackpot when I was given to you. Your legacy is remarkable and you broke the cycle to give me everything I needed.

# BOOK CLUB QUESTIONS

1. Talk about setting in this novel. Did the writer portray mountain life as rugged and a force to be reckoned with? If so, how did the adverse setting become a character in the plot?

2. Ruby's mother leaves her as a child and she is raised by Granny, her step-grandmother. What role does Granny play in Ruby's life? What causes Granny to become bitter when Ruby gets older?

3. Ruby had issues with her church when the deacon talked about Job and when Hattie's mother prayed over her at the altar. Where did Ruby go to find comfort and solace? How did she find peace there?

4. Ruby is a gifted child. How does that serve her? And how does it hurt her? How does she use her giftedness as an adult? Or does she?

5. In a time when people got married young to people who were much younger or older, what is your take of Joseph and Ruby's

marriage? Did you squirm in your chair when her teacher began to be interested in Ruby? Was it different at the turn of the 20th century than it is now?

6. What is your overall impression of Joseph? Ruby said that the only flaw the man had was losing things. Would you agree with her?

7. Why did Ruby fall for Leon? What did she see in that relationship for herself, even though he treated her badly?

8. What is Ruby's fatal flaw? What lesson did she need to learn but never did? If you were Ruby's best friend, what would you tell her about herself?

9. Which character would you most like to meet? Is there anything in particular that you like to ask them? Which character could you most relate to?

10. Is there any one line or passage that stood out to you? What part of it resonated with you?

11. The main character in this novel is based on a story the author heard about her grandmother. Do you have any family stories that you would like to investigate or explore?

# ABOUT THE AUTHOR

Kimberly Nixon is an emerging author of biographical fiction. She was blessed with a plethora of family stories, featuring strong, determined—and sometimes wild —characters. She wrestles these personalities into main characters in her works of fiction. She is a member of the Women's Fiction Writing Association, Alliance of Independent Authors, and the Writer's League of Texas. Kimberly lives in Austin, Texas with her husband Paul most of the year and travels for adventure when she can. This is Kimberly's debut novel. Visit her website for news on her upcoming memoir where she traces her father's footsteps in WWII at www.kimberlynixon.com.

Photo credit: Carrin Lewis Photography